THEIR C[illegible] ROYAL WEDDING

NINA MILNE

THE RIGHT REASON TO MARRY

CHRISTINE RIMMER

MILLS & BOON

First Published in Great Britain 2019
by Mills & Boon, an imprint of HarperCollinsPublishers,
1 London Bridge Street, London, SE1 9GF

Special thanks and acknowledgement are given to Nina Milne for her contribution to the *A Crown by Christmas* series

ISBN: 978-0-263-27271-0

1219

MIX
Paper from responsible sources
FSC™ C007454

This book is produced from independently certified FSC™ paper to ensure responsible forest management.

For more information visit: www.harpercollins.co.uk/green

Printed and bound in Spain
by CPI, Barcelona

THEIR CHRISTMAS ROYAL WEDDING

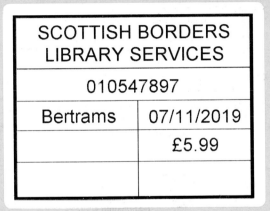

NINA MILNE

To the lovely community of romance writers
for being so kind and helpful!

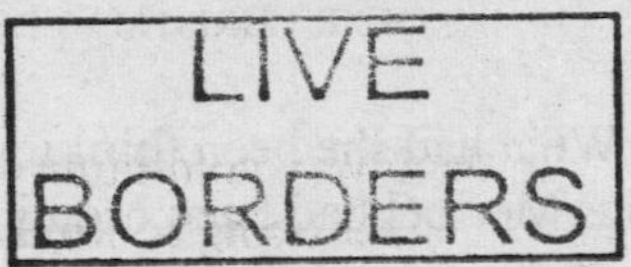

CHAPTER ONE

Royal Palace, Aguilarez, November

His Royal Highness Prince Cesar of Aguilarez looked down from the helicopter at the looming trees, the jut and crags of the mountainous terrain as the pilot began their descent to the helipad that topped the fortress-like palace he had grown up in. A palace he had visited only infrequently in the past three years. When need dictated.

The whir of the blades couldn't distract him from the grim tone of his thoughts. Now he'd been summoned back to a family summit—called, presumably, to figure out a strategy in the face of the scandal that had rocked the royal House of Asturias. And not just the house, but also the royal family of Valenti, rulers of the neighbouring country of Casavalle.

Two small countries that shared the same island—shared also a history of feuding and war. A relentless succession of invasion attempts had left both countries battle-scarred, until eventually a fragile peace had been negotiated. A peace that had endured for over two centuries as both countries had prospered.

A peace now under threat.

All because of his younger sister Meribel.

What had she been thinking? Like all five royal siblings Meribel had been brought up to know that Aguilarez came first, that duty was paramount, and emotions were an irrelevance.

So Meribel's actions defied belief. To date she'd jilted Crown Prince Luca Valenti days before their wedding. Whilst pregnant with another man's baby. The whole idea of the marriage had been to cement an alliance; now the alliance was in tatters.

Then they'd been hit by the next scandal, because it turned out that the Crown Prince of Casavalle wasn't the Crown Prince after all, because Luca had a long-lost, hitherto unknown older sister—Gabriella Ross.

To compound the situation Gabriella's existence had been discovered six months after the death of Casavalle's King, so just before Luca was due to ascend the throne of Casavalle. Now Gabriella Ross, a woman brought up in Canada, with no knowledge of her heritage or the royal blood that coursed through her veins, would take the throne.

The whole situation was a mess and little wonder the people of both Casavalle and Aguilarez were crying foul, with accusations of deceit and counter deceit on all sides.

Hence the summons to Cesar, requesting his presence at the Aguilarean palace. Though the request had been an order and, whilst he understood the need for a meeting, the manner of the summons tasted bitter in his throat: a curt demand with no hint of family affection. No surprise really—the Asturias family didn't do affection. Thus it had always been and thus it always would be.

No matter, he was here now, and as he alighted onto the helipad he braced himself as if for an ordeal, even as he inhaled the fresh snow-tanged mountain air with a sense of appreciation that he had come home to the country he loved.

Minutes later he entered the throne room, where his parents were already seated at the enormous circular wooden table, faces serious. Behind them up on a dais, the imposing stone throne embedded with jewels, the spoils of victories of the distant past, dominated the room. The surrounding walls were adorned with tapestries and paintings that depicted past battles and a pair of crossed swords topped the marble fireplace.

'You've cut it fine, Cesar,' King Jorge said. 'We are due in Casavalle for talks in a few hours and we have much to discuss.'

As he bowed first to his father and then his mother Cesar switched to ambassador mode, the role he'd been brought up to, destined for from the day of his birth. 'Apologies, Father.'

Present no reason as it will only be seen as an excuse.

His mother now. 'First we must talk about Lady Amelia.'

'We must?' Cesar could not imagine why this would be necessary—Lady Amelia Scott-Browne was his current girlfriend, though he was pretty sure a break-up was imminent. There had been signs of possessiveness, signs that Lady Amelia had forgotten the rules she'd signed up to. First and foremost being no long-term future. Because Cesar had no intention of getting married. Marriage equalled a bullet he fully intended to dodge. After all, he was the spare heir—there was no necessity for him to marry. Both his brothers had been marched to the altar, both had produced the requisite heirs. So there was no need for him to be entrapped in an unwanted union.

'Yes, Cesar, we must. You need to end the…association.' His mother made a small moue of distaste.

'Why?' It seemed a fair question; his parents had never interfered in his 'associations' before. Rather they tended to simply pretend they did not exist.

The King leant forward. 'Because we have a plan.'

'What plan?' Foreboding prickled his neck as he faced his parents.

'The best way to forge an alliance and show the world that Aguilarez and Casavalle are still friends is through marriage. So, Cesar. You will marry the new Crown Princess of Casavalle. Gabriella Ross will become your bride.'

Cesar felt the loom of the metaphorical wall at his back, could hear the hiss of the oncoming bullet.

Royal Palace of Casavalle, December

It was no good. Sleep was not going to happen. Gabi had counted two thousand seven hundred and five sheep, tried deep breathing, reminded herself that it was practically sinful not to be able to sleep on sheets this luxurious, surrounded by every comfort a queen-in-waiting could expect. But all to no avail; her brain buzzed and whirled with too many thoughts to allow sleep.

Queen-in-waiting. The words caromed around her brain, underlay every waking thought, every dream-filled night, and the bizarre surrealism made the whole situation seem nigh on impossible. How could she, Gabriella Ross, be royalty? For thirty-one and a half years of her life she had believed herself to be an ordinary person; she'd been brought up by her ordinary, elderly aunt and uncle in a small town in the Canadian mountains. She had inherited their bookshop, which she had adored, had built it into a thriving business—that had been her life.

Now…here she was in the palace of Casavalle. All because eight months ago she'd found two letters, written by her mother, who'd died when she was only three. One letter to King Vincenzo of Casavalle and one letter written to Gabriella herself.

Letters that revealed Gabi's true identity, the fact that her father had been King Vincenzo Valenti. A father she would never know, who had never known of her existence. The irony was obvious: in all her childhood reckonings, when she'd spent so many hours wondering who her father was, one of her fantasies had been that she was a secret princess. A fantasy she'd long since outgrown.

Giving up on the attempt to sleep, she sat up, propped up by sumptuous pillows on a mattress neither too hard nor too soft. As she looked round the shadowy splendour of the room, furnished in gold and red, a verdant Christmas tree in the corner, redolent with twinkling lights and beautiful painted baubles, a sudden burst of homesickness nipped her. Her tiny bedroom in Crystal Lake, the simple pine furniture, a poster of a hockey-player crush from her teen years still tacked up in her wardrobe…

Stop.

There was so much to be thankful for: she'd gone from having no family at all after the death of her aunt and uncle to gaining two brothers, both of whom she had bonded with instantly. As an added bonus Luca, a true prince, had fallen for Gabi's best friend, Imogen. And Antonio, her next brother, was soon to be married to Tia, who Gabi already loved. In addition, Queen Maria, the princes' mother, had welcomed her with dignity, grace and warmth. They all had.

Yet…guilt still haunted Gabi. Luca had been brought up believing himself to be the heir to Casavalle and now he had to stand aside for her. The impact on the whole family she had wanted so badly and already loved brought her disquiet. Along with an overwhelming fear that she couldn't do it; couldn't be the fair, just, wise ruler Casavalle deserved.

She didn't even know how to look the part. That was why sleep eluded her, held ransom by her nerves—because in mere hours that evening it was her Presentation Ball and the very idea caused her insides to curl in sheer horror. Because it was imperative she pull this off.

For the good of both Casavalle and Aguilarez, she had to win people over to her cause, try to stem the aftereffects of the scandals that rippled the country and caused unrest. But that meant she had to face all the dignitaries, her every movement scrutinised both at home and abroad. Had to face the Royal family of Asturias, including the formidable Prince Cesar, who, rumour had it, was less than pleased at being recalled home from his ambassadorial duties.

Sometimes it felt that simply by existing she was causing so very many problems. Life for both royal houses would have been easier if she hadn't found out the truth. The feeling horribly familiar—as a child she had known her aunt's and uncle's lives would have been easier, happier without having been burdened with Gabi. Peter and Bea had been an elderly childless couple, who had been unexpectedly landed with Gabi. And now Gabi had landed in Maria's… Luca's… Antonio's lives, had upended their lives just as much as she had Peter's and Bea's.

It was no use; she couldn't lie in all this splendour any more—the doubts, the weight of responsibility, the fear of making a fool of herself would crush her into the soft pillows and suffocate her.

She swung her legs over the sumptuous mattress and wriggled her toes into the soft plushness of the carpet. Pulled on jeans and an oversized sweater over her flannel pyjamas, tugged on a pair of running shoes. Maybe she'd tiptoe into the kitchens and make herself some camomile tea or even get a snack—she'd eaten nothing at dinner, too nervous at the idea of the ball.

Carefully she snuck down the vast passageway, told herself that there was no need to sneak—technically this was her palace. Only it didn't work like that—here she was hemmed in by rules and shibboleths, a hem woven by fear of bringing the Valenti name into further disrepute. As her mother had over thirty years before. Sophia Valenti had fled her royal marriage without explanation, deserted her husband and vanished in the dead of night. Once the scandal had died down she'd been written out of Casavallian history as the shortest of footnotes.

As she approached the kitchens Gabi's courage failed her. Despite the lateness of the hour she could hear activity, staff preparing for the next days and weeks. For the ball, for Christmas—it seemed as if the palace never slept. The idea of appearing unannounced seemed impossible; after all, she didn't even know where the teabags were…or if packets of cookies even existed in the royal lexicon.

It was then the idea came to her: she knew exactly where she wanted to be. The stables. There she knew she would find some calm and peace, with the magnificent beings that didn't care whether she was a princess or not. There would be no judgement. Plus, just that day a gift of two beautiful horses had arrived from Aguilarez—

and, ridiculous though it might sound, Gabi was worried they were homesick. She'd only been able to spend a few snatched minutes with them, posed for a photo and now suddenly it felt imperative to go check on them.

Before she could change her mind she tiptoed past the kitchens, along the vast corridor to a side door that led to the paved courtyard. Opening it quietly, she slipped out, braced herself against the cold bite of the winter wind, inhaled the tang of promised snow in the air. A scent so familiar and yet so different from the Canadian equivalent. She crossed the mosaic tiles, suddenly aware of the dead quiet of the night.

She entered the stables and instantly a sense of peace, of comfort, enveloped her and she headed straight for the stalls that housed the new arrivals. Gently she stroked the nose of the nearest, heard his whinny and moved closer to his warmth. If only these creatures could attend the ball tomorrow instead of the Asturias royal family.

A noise interrupted her fanciful thoughts, the sound of footsteps, the rustle of a coat… All sense of tranquillity disappeared, replaced by instant panic. Fear that she would be caught, a suspicion that royalty did not roam the stables in the wee hours of the morning with jeans pulled over their pyjamas. Instinct propelled her into the next-door stall and she dived down into the straw, lay still, her heart pounding her ribcage.

Cesar Asturias muttered under his breath as he crossed the courtyard of the Casavalle palace, having exited the palace after yet another meeting between the Asturiases and the Valentis. The whole situation had gone from bad to worse; the position seemed inescapable. He'd been called on to make the ultimate sacrifice: a political marriage. The diplomat in him applauded and accepted the necessity, saw that it would cement the alliance between Casavalle and Aguilarez, show the world that the Asturiases and the Valentis accepted Gabriella Ross as rightful Queen. The marriage would cancel out the insult of Meribel's defection. The irony was not lost on him. Meribel had baulked at the last hurdle, decided she couldn't go through with a loveless marriage for the sake of duty. So now it was Cesar's turn to step up. So here he was, ready to attend Gabriella Ross's Presentation Ball the following day.

The start of Campaign Marriage.

Because it was a campaign and he would plan it as carefully as any general had ever planned a military campaign. Obviously nowadays a royal bride and groom could not be forced into a marriage. And, as his father had pointed out, Gabriella Ross had not been brought up as royalty, might not understand or accept the convention of a marriage of political convenience. 'So you will have to approach this carefully, Cesar. Make the girl fall in love with you,' King Jorge had ordered.

'No.' Cesar's reaction had been unequivocal. 'I will not do that, Father, but I will convince Gabriella to marry me. But I ask you all—' he'd looked around the room, at his parents and Queen Maria '—to leave it to me. I do not want Gabriella to be instructed or coerced or "persuaded" by any of you. We have all seen how wrong that went with Meribel. I will do things my way.'

So it had been agreed that Queen Maria would not mention the proposed union to her sons or Gabriella. And thus began his first steps towards a ball and chain, the imprisonment of marriage.

Dark thoughts swirled as he headed towards his car,

and then he heard a whinny from the stables nearby. Another spurt of irritation huffed through him; he'd been horrified to learn that in a further 'gesture of goodwill' his family had gifted Gabriella two thoroughbred horses, one of whom Cesar himself was particularly fond.

His objections had been overruled.

No surprise there, then.

He remembered his father's cold, emotionless voice.

'The gift was necessary. If all goes well you will own those horses with Gabriella anyway.'

His mother, faintly exasperated.

'You are irrational, Cesar. You have hardly even been to Aguilarez these past years. To claim affection for these horses is nonsensical.'

There you had it: in the Asturias clan if something made no sense it was invalid. Emotions made no sense, hence his parents' marriage: a cold union, that had nonetheless produced five children. They had been faithful to each other yet not once had he ever seen either offer the other a sign of intimacy or simple affection. No wonder Cesar had vowed from an early age that marriage wasn't for him, had revelled in his bachelor lifestyle. Made sure he had enjoyed life, ensured every relationship included fun and passion in the short term. Now a similar fate to his parents' was before him; worst of all he understood that it was necessary.

A noise intruded on his thoughts, the soft whicker of a horse. Hell—it must be a sign. Perhaps he'd go and say hello to Ferron—nonsensical or not, he was fond of the beast. But as he entered the stables he halted, suddenly sure he wasn't alone. There had been movement, an indrawn breath, a rustle of fabric. Swiftly he moved forward towards Ferron's stall, saw the beautiful horse was fine. Noiselessly he moved towards the next-door stall, pushed the door open and stepped inside, all his senses on alert. Could be a saboteur, a horse thief…?

Surely that was a figure lying in the straw. Hoping to evade detection? Swiftly he pulled his phone from his pocket, turned on the torch, held the light up and blinked; there on the straw lay one of the most beautiful women he'd seen in his life. Long chestnut hair, straight classical nose, high cheekbones. And impossible, nay, criminal, to ignore the length of her slim curvy figure, clad in jeans and oversized jumper, over…he squinted at the cuffs of her wrist…checked flannel pyjamas.

OK, Cesar. Time to stop staring and time instead to figure out why Gabriella Ross, Crown Princess of Casavalle and his possible bride-to-be, was hiding in a bed of straw.

CHAPTER TWO

GABI LIFTED A hand to shield herself from the intrusive beam of light and instantly the man holding the torch redirected the rays to the floor. What to do, what to do? What on earth had possessed her to hide? Stupid, stupid, stupid. The urge to weep from sheer mortification was tempting but she refused to succumb.

Instead she had to embark on mission impossible to try and salvage even a semblance of dignity. As she looked up at the man, he stooped and held out a hand. 'May I help you up, Your Royal Highness?'

Fabulous; he'd recognised her. Any forlorn hope that she could somehow pretend to be a fainting groom faded.

'Thank you,' she murmured, figuring a hand up would be more dignified than a clumsy scramble to her feet.

His hand encircled hers, his grip cool and firm as he helped her up and then stood back. She darted a look at him, his face cast in shadows, the torch now by his side so she couldn't see him clearly. Yet even in the gloom she registered handsome features and the bemusement that etched them. Dark short hair, strong features, firm jaw, tall, muscled body dressed in clothes that discreetly indicated expense. His dark grey woollen coat moulded broad shoulders and to her irritation she felt a sudden surge of...interest.

Get a grip.

This man was a stranger in the Casavalle stables; belatedly she wondered if she should be scared. Yet he looked vaguely familiar. Oh, God. Was he perhaps someone she should know? She had been introduced to so many people over the past weeks it was nearly impossible to remember them all, though she was trying.

But surely she would remember who he was...if she'd met him before... She couldn't imagine forgetting a man with such a potent aura.

An aura that was messing with her head, making it whirl and think with her hormones rather than her common sense. Not the behaviour of a queen in waiting; she'd learnt that much. *Think, Gabi.* He was in the stables at midnight—good chance, then, that he had a reason to be here; something to do with the horses. Perhaps he'd been sent with the gift from the Asturias family, with Ferron and Arya. That would make sense. Perhaps she'd spotted him earlier in that whirlwind press photo and registered his presence. Maybe he'd come in to check on them.

Doubt flickered in her mind—to be brutally honest he didn't look like a groom, but she still didn't understand the hierarchy of how the royal entourage worked. Not that it mattered. The man was connected to the horses in some capacity—she didn't need to know any more than that. Right now what mattered was that she should stop gawping at him. Royalty did not gawp.

'Thank you,' she said. 'And...um...sorry about that.' She gestured to the straw with what she could only hope was a poised rueful smile. Knew it was more likely to be a grimace. 'I was checking the horses. Sounds stupid but I was worried they may be a little homesick.'

An arrested look came to his face, and his dark brown eyes flashed with empathy, surely a confirmation that this man must be connected somehow with the horses.

He smiled at her. 'That makes sense, or, if it does not, I do understand and appreciate it. But why the straw?' Reaching out, he pulled a bit out of her hair.

Gabi was pretty sure there was some royal protocol or other that made the gesture punishable by death. Yet this man made the move seem natural.

'I…you startled me and I just…dived for cover. I hadn't realised someone else would be coming to check the horses. I'm so sorry to interrupt your work here. Please proceed with your duties.'

For a fleeting second an expression she couldn't interpret crossed his face, and then he took the smallest of steps backwards, executed a bow.

'Ma'am. There is no need for you to apologise. These horses are now yours and are yours to visit any time of day and night. I know they will appreciate your care.'

'And I'm sure that they appreciated yours. Tell me, are you their…?' She allowed her voice to question and he took another small step backwards.

'I have been responsible for them. I stopped by tonight to ensure they have settled in, that they are not, as you say, "homesick". Soon I will return to Aguilarez.' He hesitated, studied her face. 'If you like, before I go, we could take a moonlit ride; you could get to know Ferron and Arya better.'

Her turn to hesitate now; were royal princesses supposed to go on moonlit rides with strangers? Possibly not…*but*…her brain scrambled into overdrive, wanting, seeking reasons to justify her instinctive desire to say yes. This man wasn't a stranger as such—he was part of the Aguilarez entourage. So this could be classed as a gesture of friendliness. Also he must love these horses and probably wanted a chance to have one last ride—it would be unkind to deny him that. And royalty often rode out accompanied by staff, and maybe she could use this as a fact-finding mission. Find out more about the Asturias family before the ball, especially Prince Cesar. And…dammit…she wanted to do this. Craved a ride on one of these magnificent animals in the company of this man.

'Thank you. I'd like that. As long as you don't have to be back…'

'No. I do not need to leave yet.' He gestured outside. 'It is beautiful outside but cold—if it is not too presumptuous, I could lend you my coat.'

'But then you'll be cold.'

'I am used to these temperatures, ma'am; I grew up here. My jumper will suffice.' With a smile that rocked her backwards he hitched off his coat and handed it to her.

'Thank you, though I suspect I'll look ridiculous.' Though perhaps no more ridiculous than she already did, with bits of her pyjamas protruding at wrist and ankle.

'I'll saddle them up,' he said.

'We'll saddle them up,' she corrected. 'Which one would you prefer to ride? Ferron?' After all, he'd gone to Ferron's stall first—perhaps that was his preferred mount.

'I would like that,' he said.

Gabi couldn't help but observe as he saddled the horse; his actions were deft and fluid as he tucked the stirrups under the saddle, manoeuvred the buckles of the girth—whatever his role he was familiar and comfortable around horses and Ferron seemed more than content. His murmured words and gentle touch demonstrated clearly that he was known to this horse and any minor doubts faded away.

Soon they had led the horses out and mounted.

'Where to?' he asked.

'Through the woodlands,' she suggested.

'Sure.' As he patted Ferron's neck and they set off curiosity beset her. Now out in the moonlight she could see him more clearly, saw that his hands were smooth, his clothes definitely expensive.

'So, have you worked for the royal family for long?'

'All my life. You could say it is a family tradition.' His voice was tinged with a low irony.

'Do you regret it?' she asked, and he frowned as if he wished he'd not given so much away.

'Not at all, but it is sometimes hard to have your life preordained.'

'I liked that about mine. My old life, I mean.'

'You worked in a book store in Canada.'

'I did more than that. My uncle and aunt owned the store and I inherited it on their death.' Peter and Bea had passed away within months of each other and Gabi had grieved them deeply. She had loved them and would always be grateful to them for taking her in, for sacrificing their own dream for her. Without them, the knowledge she was alone in the world had been difficult.

But after a while her natural drive had come into force and she had thrown herself into her work. Kept up with her teaching schedule, where she taught children and adults with reading difficulties, whilst working all other hours to make a success of the bookshop. 'It may seem like peanuts compared to ruling a kingdom but I loved my shop and it was thriving.' She could only hope it still was—she'd hired a manager to run it, still called as often as she could.

'And you had no idea of your heritage.'

'None.' She tried to keep bleakness from her tone, knew she hadn't when he guided Ferron closer to her, as if his presence could offer comfort.

'Then this must be hard,' he stated.

Gabi turned to him, met the directness of his gaze. 'You are one of the few people to have said that.' And he was. Many believed that she should be thrilled at her 'elevation' to a position of fame, fortune and power.

'Most people have a distorted view of royalty, that it is all about glamour and money and fame. That is part of it but there is a flip side to that coin.'

'Yes...the rules, the...' Gabi trailed off, suddenly aware that she mustn't sound as if she were complaining; that would not be within the Princesses' Behavioural Code either. 'Differences are hard sometimes. It is an enormous adjustment.' Change had come, huge, sweeping, terrifying change. Leaning down, she patted the horse's neck, knew she needed to direct the questions away from her. Because for some reason this man was disconcertingly easy to talk to.

'But what about you? You said you work for the royal family due to family tradition. Surely you're not bound to them.'

For a moment discomfort touched his aquiline features, dappled and shadowed in the moonlight that filtered the leafy glade. 'Tradition is important. My job pleases me…my life is a good one. I did not mean to sound as though I have regrets.'

Yet somehow she was sure he did and Gabi frowned, suddenly concerned. 'You know that I won't tell anyone about this conversation, or say that you have reservations about your work.'

Now he smiled, the smile warm and full of reassurance and it caused her tummy to flip as he reached out to touch her reins, careful, though, not to touch her and stupid regret coursed through her. 'I thank you, ma'am, and I assure you too that this conversation is confidential. But I do not fear the Asturias family.'

'Lucky you! I do…' The words fell from her lips without her intent, meant to be light but she suspected they had wobbled with fear.

'Why?' Curiosity and a sharpness touched his voice. 'What have they done?'

'No…they've done nothing. It's me. I am…worried. It's my presentation ball tomorrow…well, later today, this evening and, to be honest, I'm terrified.'

'Of the Asturias royals?'

'Not only of them. Of everything. If I'd been born to this, I would know what I'm doing. But I wasn't and I don't. There are so many things that could go wrong. I could say the wrong thing to the wrong person and spark a political row. I could fall on my bu— fall over, or use the wrong fork, or get spinach stuck between my teeth. I'll be on display to everyone and I'm dreading it.'

'You have nought to dread. You are royal and, if I may say, you are beautiful—you will dazzle the guests.'

Her skin heated at the man's words, because as he said them his gaze lingered on her and she felt a sudden shiver run through her. Of course, she knew he was just trying to make her feel better—she wasn't beautiful. Her hair was her best feature, long, glossy and chestnut, but she had no idea what to do with it. As for the rest of her, she was ordinary, veering at gawky at five feet eight.

'That's kind, but I don't want to dazzle anyone. All I want is to get through without making a fool of myself. I want people to believe I can do this role, can be a queen. And I doubt I'll be able to convince the Asturiases of that, especially Prince Cesar.'

Her companion stilled. 'Why do you say that?'

Gabi sighed, unsure why she was confiding in this man. Perhaps because she hoped, as a long-term staff member, he would reassure her. According to all she had learnt Prince Cesar had hardly been back home for years, his life a glittering ambassadorial whirl of diplomacy, travel and parties, usually with a beautiful woman on his arm. 'Apparently Prince Cesar is angered at being recalled home to attend this ball and be presented to me.'

The man hesitated. 'I would not trust gossip, ma'am. Prince Cesar is an ambassador. He will not be angered by the need to attend a ball for political reasons—that is his job.'

Gabi shook her head, suddenly realising she was gossiping. 'Perhaps he simply doesn't want to dance with me,' she said lightly. 'I have to dance the opening dance with him and he's probably heard I can't dance for toffee.' Another reason to panic.

'I am sure you underestimate yourself. I can see your natural grace from the way you ride.'

'That's different.' Yet the compliment warmed her. 'I've ridden since I was a teenager.' A hobby and a love that had also got her out from under her aunt and uncle's feet; aware that she had intruded into their life, Gabi had always done her best to give them space, wherever she could. 'Until I came to Casavalle I never danced, especially not a waltz. Now I have to waltz with a stranger with everyone watching me.' The idea made her shiver even in the warmth of his coat. Even worse that it was a stranger who was reputed to dislike her, whatever her companion said. 'And, believe me, I am the despair of my dance teacher.'

'I believe you will be fine, ma'am. You must have faith in yourself; imagine yourself as you are now. I promise you, if you have the grace and ability to ride a horse such as Arya you *can* waltz.'

His voice was full of conviction and she turned to him, felt her heart hop skip and jump at the strength of his words, wished she could siphon off some of that belief. 'It is not only about the waltz,' she admitted softly. 'It's the bigger picture too; I hope I'll be able to do my job and act the part of Crown Princess.'

'This is not a role, ma'am. You have no need to act a part; you are the Crown Princess, soon to be Queen.' His voice, low and vibrant, seemed to ripple off the evergreen branches of the trees and into the silvery moonlit air. 'This is not a part that can be abandoned at will, it is what you were born to be, albeit unwittingly.'

For a moment panic descended in a weighty thud and she could almost imagine her shoulders bowed. But she wouldn't let it show. As if in sympathy the moon scudded behind the clouds and she became aware of the time. 'We should turn back.'

'Ma'am?'

'Yes.'

He opened his mouth as if to speak and then gave a

small shake of his head. 'No matter. You're right. We should get back.'

They rode back in a silence broken only by the soft thud of the horses' hooves on the turf. But she couldn't help but study her companion, marvel at the tug of attraction she felt. He was not her type of man at all. The few men she'd dated in the past had all been average, pleasant…safe. This man was none of those. Though he'd been courteous, she sensed he would wield ruthlessness wherever necessary. As for safe—she could still feel the touch of his fingers in her hair as he'd brushed away the straw. Perhaps it was for the best that tonight he would return to his royal duties in Aguilarez; if she saw him again it would be a flash of a familiar face in a retinue.

They arrived at the stables; he dismounted with a lithe grace and headed towards her to help her alight. Hurriedly Gabi removed her foot from the stirrup and swung her leg over the horse's back. Too hurriedly as it turned out. The horse shook her head and pranced. Caught in the length of the borrowed coat, Gabi lost her usual balance and with a muttered curse slid in an ungainly fashion from the horse.

Was caught in a firm hold that steadied her whilst also sending her pulse rate into overdrive. She could smell his aftershave and the woodsy smell made her dizzy. She could feel the hard muscle of his body against her back, his arms around her waist.

For a heartbeat they remained standing there and then he released her, stepped back and she turned. Their eyes caught and he cleared his throat; dark brown eyes seemed to sear into her own. 'I should have remembered…to warn you… Arya always gets a bit spooked when you dismount.'

'It's OK. I should've known to take more care with a horse that doesn't know me.' Her voice too breathless as awareness swirled around them. He was so close she could reach out and touch him, so close that if she took a step forward and stood on tiptoe she could kiss him…

As if his mind travelled the same path his eyes darkened and desire sparked and ignited. 'Your coat,' she managed, through lips that seemed parched. Quickly she shrugged out of it, handed it over.

'Thank you.' Another stretch of silence and then, 'You had better get back in. I will tend to the horses.'

'Thank you for the escort and the midnight ride.' She wanted to say more, knew she couldn't. After all, she could hardly ask for a repeat date.

'You're very welcome, ma'am. And, truly, you have no need to worry about the ball tomorrow. You will dazzle everyone, including Prince Cesar. I know it.'

'Th…thank you.' Her brain seemed to be on auto repeat, because in truth their bodies were talking a whole different language. As if propelled by her hormones alone Gabi stepped forward, saw the man's eyes glance to her lips then back up to her face. For a second she thought he was going to kiss her, felt her lips part and her eyes close in sheer toe-tingling anticipation. Tried to grab onto common sense—princesses did not kiss strangers in the palace stables.

As if he recalled the same, he held out his hand, took hers and, lifting it to his lips, he kissed it. The old-fashioned gesture sent a shiver down her spine, and she wanted, yearned to take the initiative, step forward and cup his face, brush her lips against his.

But she couldn't. She mustn't. Because she was the

Crown Princess on the morning of her presentation ball. So she did nothing.

'Goodbye, ma'am.'

'Goodbye…' As he headed to the stables she watched him walk away, realised she didn't even know his name, wondered if she would ever see her mystery man again. Not, of course, that he was hers… That would be ridiculous.

CHAPTER THREE

CESAR ENTERED THE glittering ballroom, which was resplendent with Christmas glory. Two enormous, magnificently decorated trees shone and twinkled and filled the air with the scent of pine and festivity. Lit chandeliers hung in illuminated splendour from the vaulted ceilings. Wreaths adorned the walls, and the arches and pillars were festooned with trails of greenery. Cesar walked behind his parents, flanked by his older brothers and their wives and his younger sister Flavia. The united front of the Asturias family had scrubbed up well: his mother's ash-blonde hair sported the famous Asturian diamond tiara, her ice-blue gown was elegant and an echo of her eyes; his father and brothers looked supremely regal in their tuxes, their wives suitably designer-gowned and all gracious smiles. Flavia nudged him in the ribs. 'I feel sorry for poor Princess Gabriella. We look like an invading force for all our smiles.'

Now guilt pulsed as he remembered Gabriella's expressed fears, the dread she felt at the prospect of meeting the Aguilarez royals. Dammit—he should have told her who he was last night, offered reassurance. But once he'd realised she had no clue as to his identity, he had been unable to resist the opportunity to discover more about the real Gabriella Ross. He had little doubt she would have presented a very different side if she'd known the truth. Now at least he knew there was a spark of attraction, a base to build from. He'd sensed that from the moment he'd seen her sprawled in the straw; known with satisfaction, by the end of the moonlit ride, that the spark was mutual.

Anyway, there was no need for guilt; he had sent a letter of explanation so she wouldn't be taken by surprise. He suspected she'd be hopping mad but as a queen-to-be she would have to school herself to mask the emotion in public. Cesar did realise that a furious woman was not the best start to Campaign Marriage but his plan was to use the ball to advance a charm offensive.

'Cesar.' His sister's hiss pulled him back to the ballroom. Dignitaries and officials lined the walls, awaiting the all-important presentation that would indicate to the world that Meribel's actions and the arrival of a new ruler had not affected the alliance between Casavalle and Aguilarez.

His parents advanced slowly down the deep gold and blue carpet laid on the marbled floor towards where the House of Valenti awaited. Now Cesar's gaze was drawn unerringly to Gabriella and his breath hitched in his chest. The beauty that had poleaxed him the previous night was now on full display.

Her dress was an incredible concoction of elegance. Black and white, wide skirted, with an intricacy of lace and embroidered flowers over a white tulle. The straps were made of delicately shaped flowers that skimmed the creamy skin of her shoulders and Cesar's throat parched. Her chestnut hair fell in loose waves around a face of classic beauty, though he could see a shadow in her brown eyes, a tension in her smooth jawline. As she greeted his parents, he heard the murmur of her Canadian-twanged voice, the words a little breathless, a little rehearsed, the smile slightly strained, but overall she held up well and he found himself applauding inwardly. Next his brothers and now it was his turn.

Deep brown eyes raised to look at his face, the automatic greeting started, 'Welcome your…' then her voice trailed off, those brown eyes widened in shock and he realised in that instant that the letter had not reached her, decided that his hapless aide was toast. 'What are you doing h…?' Now her eyes narrowed as she put two and two together and he could see the anger dawn, heard the buzz of interest begin to hum round the room.

Cesar bowed. 'It is an honour to meet you, Your Royal Highness,' he said. It might be against protocol to interrupt but he knew it was better than allowing her to continue.

Gabriella looked down and then back up again and he could see the effort it took her to speak through no doubt gritted teeth. 'And you…it is a pleasure to see you here. I know your ambassadorial duties are heavy and I'm very happy that you were able to make it in honour of our countries' continued friendship.'

The words reeled off and only a slight flush on the angles of her cheekbones denoted her discomfiture as he moved on and she greeted Flavia. Cesar could only hope the damage had been limited, though he had little doubt the slip would be analysed, dissected and leaked to the gossip magazines worldwide.

Part of this was his fault, he knew, but Gabriella would need to learn to mask emotions and feelings if she was to survive the royal world.

'Cesar, what was that about?' His father's tone was cold, and with rueful grimaces his brothers melted from his side. 'The Princess looked less than happy to see you.'

'I believe she simply got confused, Father.'

'Please remember what was agreed.'

Ordered more like, Cesar reflected as he kept a filial smile on his face and accepted a glass of champagne from a passing waiter.

'You are to woo the Princess, not antagonise her. This marriage is important and we are trusting you to do the best for your country. As your mother and I did.'

And are you happy? The words withered on his lips—there was no universe where he could ask his parents that. They quite simply would not comprehend the question. To them it was an irrelevance—they had done what was right; it would have been unthinkable to do otherwise. Happiness didn't come into it. Oh, God—was this what he was doomed to? No. His marriage would be loveless but he would not let it be so cold and passionless and unfeeling. Couldn't live like that or ask anyone else to. *Easy words.* Once the knot was tied there could be no escape.

But there was no choice and his father was right. If he wanted to make this marriage possible *and*, more importantly, make it work, he did need to woo Gabriella; and he had to admit the courtship had not got off to the best start.

Time to regain lost ground and tread carefully on it; all eyes would be on them, watching every move. Gabriella was standing in a small group with Queen Maria and a couple of dignitaries, who she listened to with courteous interest.

He approached and, aided discreetly by Queen Maria, soon they were left alone, or as alone as it was possible to be at such a function. Her brown eyes glinted with anger but to her credit she managed a thin-lipped smile. 'Your Royal Highness. I hope you're enjoying yourself.' The words held more than a hint of bitterness. 'And my discomfiture.'

'Of course I am not enjoying your discomfiture, rather I would like to apologise for my part in this situation. I did send a letter of explanation but it appears you didn't receive it.'

'A letter?' Her voice was low, though her lips remained upturned. 'How thoughtful.' The sarcasm trembled her tone and as subtly as possible he manoeuvred them towards a garlanded pillar, hoping to shield her from view. 'It didn't occur to you to use something more…up to date? Like a phone. Or perhaps even turn up in person.'

'I was aiming at discretion.'

'Well, you missed your target.'

'Clearly. But here and now you have to do better than this. You need to look as if this conversation is enjoyable. People will have noticed that our greeting was strained.'

'I'm not an award-winning actress.'

'Then you need to learn. Fast. Part of being royal is an ability to wear a mask.'

'Well, clearly I am not royal enough. Why? Why didn't you tell me who you were?' She lifted a hand to her cheek. 'I am so angry and so mortified I could…'

'Could what?' His tone was low but harder now. 'Ruin everything you've worked so hard for? You told me this ball was important. For you and for your country. As it is for mine. If you don't want to blow this you need to pull it together. This is political now—if the public or the press believe we are fighting this will have ramifications on our two countries. Do you understand?'

Dear God, this was not going to plan but he needed her to get it and she did; he saw the understanding touch her eyes, watched her expression smooth to a semblance of serenity. She inhaled a deep breath and nodded. 'Fine. You're right. I understand.'

'Good. And, ma'am?'

'Yes.'

'I truly do apologise.'

She shook her head, but the smile on her face made the gesture appear casual. 'You let me make a fool of myself.' Now guilt touched him as he remembered again how worried she had already been about the evening.

'No! Gabriella. You didn't.' Without even meaning to he put a finger under her chin, tilted her face up so she looked directly into his eyes. And he saw the pain but also saw how hard she tried to conceal it. Remembered that until recently Gabriella Ross hadn't even set foot in Casavalle; she had not been brought up to mask emotions and play a role. And he had no right to expect her to.

He, Cesar Asturias, ambassador extraordinaire, had screwed up and now he needed to fix it. 'I swear it.' He would not have her undone for his own fault. So, 'Smile. Look at me as if you like me.'

'I'll try.' She sighed and the sheer weariness in that breath touched him, as he understood just how hard this was for her.

'You liked me yesterday. I am that same man.'

'No. You aren't. You are a prince, not an employee; you lied to me. Misled me, duped me, whatever term you wish to use.'

'I kept my identity from you and I truly apologise for that. It was a mistake. But everything else I said was true, was real. Think back to my words. None of them were lies. Not one.' He waited as she bit her lip, studied his expression.

'Not one?' she asked softly.

'No.' That he knew. 'I promise.'

Perhaps she heard the sincerity in his voice. In truth, for the past few minutes he had forgotten that they weren't alone, had wanted her to believe him with a fierceness that was out of proportion. Disquiet touched him and he dismissed it. It was vital he win her over, or the chances of her considering his suit were minimal. That explained the ridiculous swathe of relief when she gave a small nod and smiled a small but this time genuine smile.

'For the sake of this evening and for the man I met last night I will give you the benefit of the doubt. But I wish that letter of explanation had reached me.'

'Perhaps I could explain in person. Tomorrow. We could go for a ride.'

'I have engagements all day.'

'At the end of the day, then. We could have a picnic supper; leave the details to me. Meet me at the stables.'

As she hesitated, he suspected he knew the cause, knew he was right as he saw her lips twist half in rue, half in exasperation. 'I understand you need to check before you accept—that is part of royalty. Sometimes simple decisions have ramifications.' He also knew there would not be a problem. If she asked Queen Maria, consent would be granted—after all, Queen Maria had agreed this marriage would be a good one, though had stipulated she would not force Gabriella into it.

'If it is the genuine wish of both, and they both believe they can have a happy life together, then and only then will I believe that this will work.'

Gabriella nodded. 'I'll confirm with you later. And now I must mingle. I mustn't neglect my guests.'

'You are right. But remember the first dance is mine.'

Worry-laced panic now skimmed her expression and without thought he took one of her hands in his, gave a quick clasp of reassurance. 'I promise it will be a dance to remember,' he said. 'And, Gabriella?'

'Yes.'

'I told you I didn't lie and I did not. When I told you that Prince Cesar would be dazzled I was telling the truth. You look beautiful and I am truly dazzled.'

Now she looked adorably confused, her nose crinkled and her blush deepened. 'As if…' she muttered.

'I swear it. If there were not so many people watching I would prove it to you.'

'How?' Her voice was wary.

'I'd kiss you.' He smiled. 'Or I would ask permission to.'

'I… I… I…'

'What would you say?'

Suddenly she returned his smile; an impish dimple appeared in her cheek. 'Why don't you try me and see?' Clearly seeing that she'd wrong-footed him, she allowed her smile to morph into a small triumphant chuckle and he found himself laughing too. 'Now I really must mingle.' And with a look over her shoulder she glided away.

Had she really said that? Had she lost the plot along with the royal rule book? Gabi resisted the urge to go and hide behind a Christmas tree, to give herself a chance to regroup and figure out what had just happened. But she couldn't; the royal ship needed to continue its regal sail. So she had to overcome the fluster and somehow rein in her thoughts, hide the tumult going on in her brain and her body.

Her mystery man was Prince Cesar Asturias and by rights she should be furious at his deception. Especially when he'd had the temerity to tell her *she* needed to pull *herself* together. Problem was he'd been right. She had been livid, hurt, angry, confused…and she'd been showing it. Royal rule number one: show no emotion.

And then somehow Cesar had got past her fury, because the apology in his brown eyes had been sincere and so too had been the glint of admiration. Dazzled, that was what he'd said. And that was all it had taken; she'd metaphorically melted into a puddle and flirted… practically promised to kiss him. Cue mental eye roll. Was she that much of a pushover?

Enough; she would banish Prince Cesar from her mind and focus on what she should be doing. Creating the right impression, making all these people believe she had it in her to rule.

And just like that the crushing weight of responsibility, the fear she'd mess this up, returned. The strangeness of wearing a ball gown, the unaccustomed shoes, the splendour of the room itself threatened to overwhelm her. But somehow she summoned the royal smile, the one practised in front of the mirror until her cheeks ached, as Queen Maria approached her, with yet another person by her side to introduce.

An hour later and, 'You OK?' She turned to see Luca at her side and she smiled, relieved to see her eldest brother, a man who understood all this.

'I'm fine, maybe a bit overwhelmed.'

'You're doing great.'

'At looking the part.'

He shook her head. 'This isn't about looking the part, or playing a part. You are a princess, Gabi, and you will be Casavalle's Queen.'

'That's what Cesar said.' Gabi regretted the words as she saw Luca study her expression.

'Sounds like you got to know each other fast.'

'Yes.' Gabi pushed away the urge to confide; the relationship between the Valentis and the Asturiases was complicated enough. She didn't need Luca to get involved or fire up on his sister's behalf.

'Well, he's right, Gabi. You can do this. You've got this.'

'Thank you. To you and Imogen. For having my back.'

'That's what family is for, Gabi. And now you have a family. To support you.' Luca smiled at her. 'So let's show some Valenti-Ross solidarity and build on what you have started with Prince Cesar. I have spoken with his older brothers and his younger sister already. Now let's go get some more publicity.'

Gabi nodded, understood the importance of this public meeting of the families. Luca had told her that a few months earlier he and Cesar had gone to see Meribel, and they had all made their peace. But that had been a private meeting; this was a public showing of togetherness, an assertion that neither family bore a grudge, that both families were friends.

He looked round. 'But let's bring Imogen into the mix too.' He smiled as his fiancée headed towards him, clearly alerted by some mysterious couple radar, and for a mad moment envy tinged with wistfulness touched

Gabi. She was happy for her best friend, for her brother, but she couldn't help but wonder if she could ever find what they had. Could she ever find love, trust that someone would love her for herself?

'Let's do this,' Luca said. With smiles and murmurs to other guests they made their way through the glittering, designer-clad throngs together and now Gabi felt lighter, revelled in the feel of being part of a family unit. Reminded herself that she did have support and backup and she was thankful for it.

They approached Cesar, who was speaking with Queen Maria, and Gabi gulped. Standing beneath one of the magnificent chandeliers, dressed in a tux that moulded his body, showed off those powerful shoulders and that lean, mean, fighting-machine body, he took her breath away. Again.

As if he sensed it, his dark brown eyes flicked to meet hers and she saw an answering flare there and her insides knotted in sudden desire. And she'd asked him to ask permission to kiss her. Madness—Cesar was not a man to flirt with; she might as well flirt with fire, dance and weave through the flames.

'Cesar. Good to see you.' Luca's deep tone was pitched to carry without shouting and Gabi was aware that around them conversations slowed as the two men shook hands. 'Much has changed since we last met,' he continued, with a disarming smile. 'I wish to assure you and your family that I for one have no complaint at all as to how things have played out. I am a very happy man. I have gained a sister and a fiancée I love. Gabriella you have met, but now allow me to introduce Imogen, my fiancée.'

'It is a pleasure to meet you, Imogen.' Now Cesar

grasped Imogen's hand, seemingly oblivious to the buzz around them. 'May I offer my sincere congratulations and wish you both happiness from myself and my family.'

'Thank you.' Imogen's voice was clear. 'I appreciate that very much. And please tell Meribel we wish her as much happiness as we have found.'

'I will do that.' Cesar's smile was courteous; he was clearly appreciative of Imogen's diplomatic answer. 'And may I say you will make a wonderful diplomat if ever the urge takes you.'

At that moment the band struck up and Cesar's smile changed, as if he'd upped the brightness meter, and he turned to Gabi. 'My dance, I believe.'

She would swear she could feel the colour leech from her face; she, Gabriella Ross, was about to lead a royal ball, a ball in her honour. Crazy didn't cover it.

'You'll wow them, Gabi,' Imogen said. 'And we'll be right behind you.'

'You'd better be.' Gabi turned to Cesar, oddly reassured—he would know what he was doing so with any luck she wouldn't make a complete fool of herself.

'There is no need to be nervous,' Cesar said softly as he took her hand and they approached the dance floor, where the orchestra had started the introduction, the melody touching and humming the air with motes of beauty.

'There is every need to be nervous. I told you last night, this is not my forte.'

'And I told you last night that you can do this. Plus what I didn't tell you last night is that I have all the moves!' As she glanced up at him, he did a disco move reminiscent of the seventies, the move so unexpected that she halted and looked up at him in surprise.

His face creased into a grin and he chuckled and she grinned right back. Suddenly the whole idea of the dance seemed less of an ordeal and as the orchestra began to play, she inhaled deeply. 'OK. I can do this.'

'We can do this,' he said and then they were off.

Gabi focused on his left shoulder, murmured the instructions under her breath, tried to focus on the movements, but it was hard when Cesar was this close. So close his aftershave tantalised her, so close she now knew the muscles were real, hard under her fingers; she could see one errant black curl on the nape of his neck and she bit back a small moan. The feel of his arm around her waist was ridiculously intimate as he guided her with a deft gentleness that made her shiver. And all she wanted was to be even closer; somehow it felt as though the rest of the room, the guests, the noise, had all faded away to leave only them…no one else.

Until the music came to its haunting close and she blinked as if emerging from a dream, became aware of all the other couples on the floor around them, suddenly conscious of the attention they had attracted. Oh, hell! She hadn't done anything stupid, had she? Drooled all over that beautiful tux, ripped open the jacket…

With as much dignity as she could muster, she managed a smile that she hoped looked cool but friendly. 'Thank you. Your moves helped a lot.'

This pulled a return smile, but his was way more than friendly and his gaze felt like a caress.

'Let me get you a drink,' he suggested. 'Before you take up your duties. There are many people who you must dance with tonight. But if we don't get a chance to speak properly again, I hope to see you tomorrow evening. We have much to discuss.'

They did? Gabi watched the breadth of his retreating back, turned to smile dutifully at the elderly gentleman, an English lord, who now approached her. But as she spoke with him her mind and her body dwelled on Cesar and anticipation twisted her tummy at the thought of their next meeting.

CHAPTER FOUR

COUNTLESS HOURS LATER and Gabi looked round the now empty reception room with a sigh of relief and eased her high heels off. 'That feels better.'

'Perhaps.' Queen Maria's voice held no censure, but it did hold a certain gentle implacability. 'But you need to keep the shoes on, Gabriella. It is possible that a guest will return, or a staff member enter—it would not look good for you to be seen barefoot, unprepared.'

Human... The thought entered Gabi's head as she slipped her aching feet back into the pointed, strappy, beautiful torture chambers. It would make her look human. Yet it didn't surprise her that there was a royal protocol that dictated a sight of the royal feet was taboo.

Maria reached out and placed a gentle hand on her arm. 'Thank you and you did well tonight.'

Gabi wasn't so sure; she knew she'd made mistakes, had knocked a glass of water over at the table and she was pretty sure she hadn't used the correct cutlery. All the while she'd been, oh, so aware of Cesar's presence; half of her had wished he'd been next to her, half of her relieved he wasn't. Instead she had spoken with his parents, wondered if she'd imagined the assessment in their eyes, the coldness behind the smiles. It was as if they saw the princess but not the person. But that was true of everyone. Except Cesar. Last night, this evening, he had treated her as a human being.

Now she glanced at her stepmother. 'Cesar asked me to meet him tomorrow evening.' A glance at the ornate grandfather clock in the corner of the room showed her the time. 'This evening,' she amended. 'I wasn't sure if I should or not?'

'Do you want to?' Maria's eyes met hers and to her annoyance Gabi felt a blush creep over her face.

'I'm not sure,' she settled for, which was no more than the truth. Part of her wanted to go, to satisfy her curiosity as to why he hadn't revealed his identity the night before. Part of her wanted to go because…

You want him to kiss you...that insidious voice whispered at the back of her mind.

No! No! No!

That was nuts. Because Cesar Asturias was not her type of man and no doubt he had simply been flirting with her out of…habit. The man had certainly dated his share of women, all far more beautiful than Gabi.

Maria surveyed her. 'There can be no harm in meeting him,' she said. 'It would show that the two royal families are friends; would demonstrate the Asturias family's acceptance of your position.' The Queen's expression held its usual serene inscrutability but there was something in her eyes, something elusive that Gabi couldn't read. 'But that can be done in public. I would not expect you to meet privately if you dislike him.'

'I didn't dislike him…' Now the flush deepened and clambered over her cheekbones. 'I… I think I'll meet him.' After all, she wasn't going to kiss him and she did deserve an explanation. And she would get to ride Arya again.

The Queen nodded. 'Now you should get some rest; it is a busy day tomorrow. You did truly well tonight.'

'Thank you.' Gabi knew praise did not always come easy to the other woman, that she expected a certain standard from her own sons and now from Gabi. But she knew too that she owed Maria so much. The Queen had shown no resentment towards Gabi, the woman who had usurped her own children's line to the throne. Instead she had gone out of her way to help her, guide her and advise her. On impulse Gabi moved over and gave the older woman a hug. 'And thank you for everything and the way you have welcomed me to Casavalle.'

For a second Maria froze, then she relaxed into the embrace, patted Gabi on the back before stepping back.

'It has been my pleasure. I see how Luca and Antonio have taken you to their hearts. And I know your father would have been proud of you.'

The words caused a lump in Gabi's throat: the familiar conflict of emotion. If only she'd found her mom's letters sooner, then she would have met her father. For a moment she brooded on the second letter, the one she had told no one about. The one where Sophia explained that she had wanted to return to Casavalle. Once Gabriella was born she'd realised she had been wrong to flee, that she loved her husband and wanted to work it out, that she wanted to take back her request for a divorce. But then she had discovered that Vincenzo had started seeing someone else, a suitable woman, someone who 'would be the wife I could never be', 'the wife Vincenzo needs' and so she had decided it would be better for everyone if she remained in Canada.

Now, as she looked at Maria, Gabriella vowed again never to reveal that letter, knowing it would hurt Maria, impact her memories of a successful marriage, make her play the game of if and but. Gabi knew now too that if the papers got hold of the information they would splash it around with glee, uncaring of who they hurt in the doing.

'Thank you,' she said. 'I so wish I could have met him, but I am so very grateful to you for everything.'

Knowing Maria would be super uncomfortable if she saw the tears that prickled the backs of Gabi's eyes, she smiled, blew the older woman a kiss and left the reception room. Hoped sheer exhaustion would allow her to fall into a dreamless sleep that did not feature Prince Cesar of Aguilarez.

And when they next met she would not be beguiled into flirting, would not be befuddled by the feel of his arms around her and there would be no observers so she would have no need of diplomacy. She would get an explanation for his behaviour.

As the sun set over the courtyard, Cesar crossed the mosaic paving to the Casavallian stables and nodded to the stable hand who was already at work saddling up Arya. He stroked the horse's nose and then opened Ferron's stall. 'I'll saddle up Ferron.'

Twenty minutes later the horses were ready and he led Ferron into the courtyard and saw Gabi approaching, in jeans and a short navy-blue padded jacket with a furred hood from which he could glimpse a glint of chestnut hair. And she looked as beautiful as she had in full ball regalia. But today her eyes held a combatant gleam, though her expression softened as she walked up to Arya and patted her neck.

'Good evening.'

'Hi.'

'I've arranged for a picnic to be brought to the maze.'

'The maze? Is that allowed? I thought it was about to be opened to the public.'

She mounted Arya with an easy grace, leant forward to pat the horse and murmur words in her ear.

'I've cleared it all with the palace gardeners, the Queen and anyone else I could think of. I thought it would be nice for you to see it in its festive beauty.'

As the horses trotted side by side he glanced across at her, tried to read her expression, but she seemed lost in thought and for a while he let the silence envelop them. Sensed that she was revelling in the evening sounds, the cold, crisp, dusky air, the puffs of breath from the horses, the orange red of the setting sun. In the silence after the hustle and bustle of the ball yesterday and her round of engagements today.

It gave him a chance to run over his strategy, the tactics necessary to win Gabriella. Again, today, his father had made his views clear.

'Make her fall in love with you, Cesar. Turn on the charm for which you are so famed.'

The idea had been endorsed by Queen Adriana.

'It is the best way. Gabriella is not like us; she will expect the more vulgar emotions.'

Anger had sizzled through him; Cesar did not believe emotions were a good thing but he wouldn't condemn them as vulgar. Neither would he lie to Gabriella; to trick her into falling in love with him with promises of an emotion he could not feel was dishonourable. And unlike his parents he did not believe that in this case the end justified the means. It would make for a disastrous marriage and also be an illusion that would be impossible to sustain.

Cesar hoped and fully intended to achieve his goal in a different way. Yes, he would use charm. Because charm worked. He'd figured that out as a child; it had been a survival strategy. The best way to win over the stream of royal nannies had been charm, cuteness with a soupçon of cheekiness. An acceptance that to them he was a job, not an object of love or affection. Acceptance that they moved on. Cesar could still feel the wrench in his gut he'd experienced when his first nanny had left. *Never again.* Oh, she'd been nice enough, had been sad to leave him, but she'd still gone. To have a family of her own. Lesson learnt. Charm the nannies to maximise their care of him; smile and the world smiled with you. A cliché that worked, even if sometimes the smiles were fake.

Perhaps now it was indeed time for a smile, time to start the charm offensive. He shot a quick glance at her, straight backed and poised on Arya's back. 'So, did you enjoy last night?' he asked.

'It had its moments.' A memory of their dance, how she had felt in his arms, shimmered in the air. 'But on the whole? Honestly?' Gabriella shook her head. 'I felt out of my depth and utterly exhausted. The things that come effortlessly to you, to Luca, are a struggle for me. I'm not used to being the centre of attention and I hate it. The idea that everyone is watching me makes me nervous.'

'You will need to get used to it.'

'I know.' The idea clearly was not one that filled her with joy and she gave her head a small shake as if to try and dispel the gloom. 'And I'm sure it gets easier. But it's not just the spotlight, it's the public interest; most mornings I read stuff about myself that is either malicious, or untrue, or taken out of context or is surely not of any interest. I mean, how can how I like my eggs be interesting?'

'The press is something you have to accept and in time you will learn to ignore the hurtful and preposterous. You will make connections with positive journalists and learn to use them to your advantage.' Another example of the way charm and making the best of a situation could be useful.

'I hope you're right.' As if hearing her own doubt, she shook her head again and then she frowned. 'But that's not what we're here to talk about. You're going to explain why on earth you didn't tell me who you were.'

'It's complicated.'

'I'd still like to know.'

'And I will tell you.' Deep breath here. 'When I walked into the stable I was annoyed, upset…'

'Why?'

Well, partly because he had felt the imminence of the metaphorical ball and chain, but that was not something he would share with Gabi. To tell her marriage was anathema to him would hardly prosper his suit and anyway that anathema was now irrelevant. Because he had accepted the necessity and he would make the best of it. 'Because I had not been consulted about the gift of Ferron and Arya,' he admitted, and was rewarded by a sympathetic smile. For a moment he felt a pang of guilt, which was foolish, as his words were truthful. 'Ferron was a particular favourite of mine.'

'I understand that and if you want I will gift him back. Happily.'

'That isn't necessary.'

'Then please know that whenever you wish to ride

him you can. But I still don't get why you didn't tell me who you were.'

'Well, my annoyance disappeared as soon as I saw a beautiful woman sprawled on the straw.'

Again true, and he derived a pleasure from seeing the flush on her cheeks, felt an immense gratitude that they were indeed true, that there was a genuine spark between himself and Gabi, a spark that he believed and hoped would make all the difference to their marriage.

'Fine words,' she said, 'but they don't answer the question. Unless you're going to try to spin me that my beauty gave you temporary amnesia?' The words were tart but with an undertone of honey and her lips curved upwards as she spoke, calling an answering smile from him.

'Would you believe me if I said that?'

'Nope. So, come on, no more sugared words.'

He raised a hand in acknowledgement. 'To begin with I assumed you would recognise me. Arrogant? Perhaps. But I thought that you would have been studying the Asturias family.'

Her sigh was deep. 'I did. I have. But…'

'I didn't stick in your mind?' He allowed mock chagrin to crease his face, put one hand on his heart as if wounded, and she grinned.

'Obviously not… But to be fair to me it was dark, secondly, I felt like a fool having been caught hiding in straw, third, I thought that there was no way Prince Cesar of Aguilarez would ever come into the stables.'

'Why not?'

'Because I didn't think the suave, sophisticated playboy ambassador would get his hands dirty.' Her eyes narrowed. 'Plus, I made the not unreasonable assumption that Prince Cesar would introduce himself. Not mislead me into believing he was a member of staff.' She pulled lightly on the reins, murmured to Arya and came to a stop. 'And you *still* haven't told me why.'

He too halted.

Deep breath. Choose your words carefully.

'I wanted to see what you were like. Really like. The real you.' The real her. The woman who had admitted to doubts and fears, the woman who had told him she would keep his words confidential, the woman he'd caught in his arms, the woman he'd desperately wanted to kiss. 'If I had told you who I was you would have been much more formal.'

'I'd also have been a whole lot more discreet.'

'Exactly. The whole political stance, the Asturias-Valenti relationship would have been a priority. I didn't want that. I wanted a chance to get to know you, without that layer.'

'Why?'

The million-dollar question. Looking round, he saw they were very nearly at their destination. 'Why don't we get some food…? And I will answer. I promise. First I want to show you this.'

Gabi realised she had been so absorbed in their conversation she had lost track of time and their surroundings. Now she realised that they would soon approach the maze, a truly incredible complex creation, the boxwood hedges dating back centuries.

But nothing had prepared her for how it looked this evening, in its Christmas splendour, and she gave a gasp of wonder. 'It's magical.' Gabi stared in utter delight. The twinkling lights had been woven and twisted into the verdant greenery to form an iridescent beautiful pattern of stars. Beautiful coloured lanterns lit the path leading to the maze, hung from the trees, each lantern a bauble of Christmas glittering beauty highlighted by the moon's beams.

'It's beautiful. Like a winter wonderland.' She frowned. 'We can't take the horses in, though.'

'No need. I've arranged for someone to meet us here and take them back to the stables. We will be picked up later.'

'You've thought of everything.' And it made her heart flutter. Because she knew he would have had to speak to a lot of people to get this set up just for them.

'I have tried. I want to show you that I am sorry for the unfortunate outcome of my deception. And I wanted you to see this.'

'Do you have anything similar in Aguilarez?'

'My country is more mountainous, craggier, less gentle; perhaps that reflects on our culture. But it is a magnificent country, a place that takes your breath away.'

'I would like to explore it.' Gabi could hear his love for his country in his voice, wondered then that he visited so infrequently. Of course his work kept him abroad but even so…

'Perhaps you will allow me to be your guide.'

Before she could reply, the sound of a car intruded and within minutes the large four-by-four had parked and a group of people climbed out. A few unloaded the boot and set off into the maze, whilst two youths headed towards Gabi and Cesar. As they approached both Ferron and Arya whinnied in recognition. Gabi dismounted, chatted to the newcomers and then watched as they mounted the horses and trotted off.

Cesar gestured towards the illuminated maze. 'Shall we? I do know the way but I am happy to wander round getting lost if you would prefer?'

Gabi sighed. 'I know the way too. There was a photo shoot; a publicity thing with Luca and I bonding by finding our way through the maze together.'

But, even with their knowing the way, the maze with its twisty wending turns and alleys was still both fascinating and breathtaking. Tucked into corners were wooden sculptures to depict a Christmas theme, elves, reindeer, robins all elaborately carved and placed for maximum effect. The lights twinkled and shone and glinted off the greenery and Gabi loved it.

'I love how Christmassy it all is. It sounds mad but I was so caught up with my presentation ball I'd almost forgotten how close Christmas is. Plus although the Casavalle palace is beautiful all the decorating is done by staff. I'm not complaining,' she said, quickly, 'but I'm used to decorating the book store myself.'

'I suppose this is very different from your usual Christmases.'

'Yes.' Gabi was silent for a moment. 'When I was a child Christmas was pretty quiet, but that was OK. Uncle Peter would get the tree and Aunt Bea and I always decorated it.' The memory was precious—it had been something the two of them could do together, a time where she'd felt a tenuous but real bond. 'We'd exchange a few gifts.' Always necessary items for Gabi, a new pair of shoes for school, a pair of gloves because her old ones had worn out, because that was always what she had asked for, not wanting to impose, always aware of what the elderly couple had given up for her both financially and emotionally. Their savings and their dream. 'After

Christmas dinner, we'd go for a walk.' There hadn't been much conversation but the silences had been companionable; it had been a time when she'd felt closest to them both. Gabi had always sensed she was accepted rather than wanted; when she was eight she'd understood why. An overheard conversation between Bea and a friend.

'She's a pretty little thing,' the friend had said and Gabi had beamed to herself. 'Sweet as well, polite.'

Then her Aunt Bea: 'I know she is and thank goodness for it. It was all a bit of a shock, really. Peter and I never wanted children and we had a plan for our retirement years. We were going to travel round Europe and end up in sunny Spain. Of course, we could never have done that once Sophia died. Gabriella is family and we would always do right by family. But sometimes I can't help but imagine how different life would be.'

Though her aunt and uncle had never told her of their thwarted plans, the words had haunted her for years, still caused a guilt that would tug at her for ever. She'd done her best to make it up to them, vowed to herself that somehow she would save enough so that one day they would still be able to travel. But it wasn't to be. Bea and Peter had passed away before that had been a possibility.

Gabi blinked herself back to the present, aware that Cesar was studying her expression, also aware of his words of the previous day—that royals should mask their feelings. And here she was, standing in a reverie of regret and guilt and haunted memories.

'Sorry. I got a little lost in the past. I bet your Christmases must have been a lot noisier than mine, with five siblings.'

'Noise wasn't encouraged in the royal household. Aguilarez does not embrace Christmas with the same verve as Casavalle. Or at least my parents do not. Our palace has one huge tree in the gardens for the public to see but we did not decorate inside like you do. Nor do we have anything like this maze.'

'So tell me about your Christmas Day.'

'We went to church, then we would visit the estate and we would open state gifts. The family didn't exchange gifts as we got so many from the public. We would send individual thank-you letters, of course—my parents believed it should be done by hand and done on Christmas Day.'

'At least you got loads of gifts.'

'We weren't allowed to keep them.'

'Why not?'

'There were too many and so my parents decreed none could be kept. So we donated them to charity.'

'That must have been really tough.' She frowned. 'But why didn't you exchange gifts, in that case?'

'Yes, we spotted that flaw.' Cesar shrugged. 'The general feeling was we were so lucky and privileged to be royal we didn't need gifts, I suppose. Christmas was more seen as an opportunity to give to the people than to celebrate in private.'

Gabi glanced at him. His voice was matter-of-fact. No anger or frustration, simple acceptance. And, she supposed, why should he complain? He was a prince, and he did have a fantastically privileged lifestyle. Yet he had missed out on the magical Christmases that were so important to childhood. Not because of the lack of gifts but because of the lack of Christmas spirit and family cheer.

'What about now?' he asked. 'How do you usually spend Christmas?'

'I kept the book store open so that people could come

and have some festive fare and some company. I realised there are a lot of lonely people out there. People on their own at Christmas. So I'd make some turkey sandwiches, *tourtière*, a Yule log, Christmas cookies and mulled cider and people could just drop in as they liked. I loved it.' Homesickness threatened and she blinked quickly, reminded herself again that royals didn't show emotions. 'What about you?'

'I tend to holiday at Christmas, sometimes skiing, sometimes tropical, always fun.'

No doubt the fun included a gorgeous girlfriend, but that was none of her business and before she could reply they arrived at the centre of the maze where Gabi halted. 'Oh, my goodness.'

The space had been transformed into a magical grotto. A wooden carved nativity scene made her catch her breath as she went over and examined the lovingly exquisite detail, marvelled at the talent that had created the small figures, the people and the animals, the cradle, the Virgin Mary, all somehow imbued with a sense of simplicity, grace and awe.

A table had been set up, covered in an embroidered damask tablecloth, laid with gleaming cutlery and starched napkins. The centrepiece was a magical burst of Christmas colours. Heaters had been set up to combat the wintry night air, and additional lights cast a golden illumination. The air was rich with the scent of food laid out on the table in a display that made her mouth water.

Three staff members were putting the finishing touches to the table. One approached them with a smile. 'Welcome. All is ready, Your Highness. The champagne is chilled, the picnic is laid out. I hope you both enjoy the food.'

With that, all the staff melted discreetly away and Gabi stared in delight at the tableau. 'This is what you call a picnic?'

'Yup. Picnic Cesar Asturias style.'

'Impressive. It's beautiful.' And her heart gave a hop, skip and jump. *Whoa.* Keep this real, Gabi. You may be nearly Queen, but you're still Gabi Ross, gawky book nerd. Not Cesar's type of woman at all. This was a political gesture, nothing more.

Cesar pulled a chair out and Gabi sat down, waited for him to seat himself opposite her. He looked impossibly handsome and for a moment her head whirled. *Focus.* Instinct told her that perhaps this was more than a gesture. This was a man schooled in diplomacy, a man whose every word and action were no doubt dictated by policy.

'Thank you,' she said as she accepted a crystal flute brimming with champagne, lifted it in toast. 'To answers,' she said. 'Speaking of which, I'd like some. What is all this about? What was the night we met about? Why was it so important to get an impression about the "real" me?'

He helped himself from a bowl of pasta salad, the shapes gleaming with oil, dotted with olives, capers and cubes of a tart, local cheese, and studied her across the table, his dark eyes thoughtful, his expression neutral, the only sign of tension the tautness of his jaw.

'I'm Canadian as well as Casavallian,' Gabi reminded him. 'We favour the direct approach. There is no need to be diplomatic here. I'd rather you cut to the chase and told me.'

A shrug and, 'OK.' He nodded. 'I wanted to see if there was a compatibility between us. Because I believe we should consider a marriage.'

'Whose marriage?' The stupidity of the question was apparent to her even as she spoke the words. Yet surely he couldn't possibly mean…

'Our marriage.'

'You and me? You think *we* should get *married*?' Panic threatened and she shoved her chair back; her fork fell with a clatter onto the china plate. 'One waltz and a sip of fizz and you are proposing?'

Cesar rose to his feet. 'Hold on. It is not a proposal. It is an idea for us to discuss. To consider as a possible future option.'

'I think you'll find that is the *definition* of a proposal. I don't need to consider it. I need to leave. Now.' She stood up. Was she overreacting? Gabi gave it a couple of seconds' consideration and decided not.

He inhaled deeply. 'Please stay. Tell me why you won't consider it?'

Gabi opened her mouth and then closed it again. There were so many reasons, all so incredibly obvious to her. 'Why *would* I consider it?'

'For Casavalle. For Aguilarez. For our countries.'

The words, in their simplicity, echoed round the glade, caromed off the dark evergreen leaves, magnified and filled the air. Gabriella fought the urge to turn and run from the weighted knowledge that her life was no longer her own to live. Instead it belonged to her country.

'You know our countries' histories,' he continued.

'I do, and I know that in the past the enmity was deep and bloody. But there has been peace for over two centuries.' Which surely meant the whole need for a marriage was ludicrous.

'Yet right now the situation is precarious. There are still many who feel it is foolish for one small island to have two countries, two royal families. Others think royalty should be replaced by democracy. Right now even royalists are unhappy. Many in Casavalle feel that Meribel has insulted the House of Valenti, many in my country feel Luca should have backed out, that he would have married Meribel under false pretences.'

'And there are also those who believe that I am a usurper and that Luca is the rightful King.' Gabriella sighed. 'Perhaps I made a mistake. Perhaps I should just stand aside, allow Luca to fulfil the destiny he was brought up to, take the throne.'

Cesar shook his head. 'You cannot put the genie back in the bottle, Gabriella. You are the rightful heir; you are King Vincenzo's oldest child.'

'I know. I have been through it all in my head so many times. Luca, Antonio and Maria all believe I should take the throne.'

'I too agree with this. Both countries must unite behind a position: the honourable one, the right one. Our marriage would represent that union.'

'I am sure our countries would survive without our marriage,' she said, her fingers tight round the back of her chair.

'Of course, they would.' The deep voice was full of reassurance. 'Please, sit down. Let me explain. I am not trying to force you into a course of action you do not want. I cannot do that even if I wished it. But I believe this is an idea that would benefit both our countries.'

An insidious tendril of disappointment snuck through her; she'd thought…thought what? That Cesar liked her, was attracted to her, was interested in her. Well, the last at least was true, though not for the reasons she'd naively, foolishly hoped. She was royalty now, soon to be

Queen, and she needed to get real. Cesar Asturias had been linked to numerous beautiful, sophisticated women in his time…he wouldn't have given Gabi a second look if it weren't for her crown.

But at least he had had the courtesy to be honest and in return royal manners dictated that she listen to him. *Then* she could tell him to shove it.

So she sat down, right on the edge of her seat. 'OK. Explain.'

CHAPTER FIVE

WITH AN ABILITY born of years of top-level diplomacy Cesar didn't let the relief show on his face, tried not to show the fact that he was rattled. This was not going according to plan at all. Perhaps his insistence that Queen Maria not interfere, not lay the groundwork had been a mistake, but he'd been convinced that this agreement had to be between himself and Gabriella. Her decision not tainted or influenced by either his family or hers.

'First, I'm sorry—I thought that maybe given the fact that Luca was meant to marry Meribel, you would perhaps have considered an alliance through marriage between our countries.'

'Given how that worked out it is hardly surprising I didn't,' she pointed out and he had to admit the point was valid. 'If that marriage had never been considered it would have been way easier for everyone.'

'Easier isn't always right.'

'Do you believe they should have gone through with it?'

'No. I don't. Foisting a fake heir onto Casavalle would have been a disaster. That scandal would have been even worse than the scandal of leaving Luca at the altar. I believe that Meribel should not have allowed herself to get into the situation she did.'

'I don't know exactly what happened. But perhaps Meribel fell in love—how could she have prevented herself from doing that?'

'She could have closed it down as soon as she felt anything for Dana. People don't just fall in love in an instant.' And yet…he remembered the look on his sister's face when she had spoken to Luca. Tears had slid down her cheeks as she'd admitted the guilt she felt over how she had treated him, brought shame to her house. But when Meribel had declared her love for the father of her baby, for Dana, her face had glowed with a belief and a certainty and he'd known that his sister had changed. Would go to the wall for this love. *Stupidity.* Though Luca seemed to have understood.

'Yes, they do,' Gabriella said. 'Look at Luca and Imogen; they certainly didn't mean to fall in love. Neither did Antonio and Tia. But they did. Antonio and Tia are getting married in a few days; their baby is due in a couple of months.'

'And I wish them every happiness.'

'But…?' There was a challenge in her voice.

But their pursuit of happiness had resulted in Cesar having to take a forced march to the altar. As far as he was concerned Meribel… Luca… Antonio had all lost the royal plot, leaving him and Gabriella to put events back on track. *It is as it is, Cesar. Make the best of it.* The Cesar Asturias motto.

'But I don't believe that is the only way to find happiness, especially for royalty, especially for rulers.' In truth he didn't buy the whole love gig, the whole head over heels, giddy, goofy idiocy. 'Royals don't live normal lives and I don't think love does conquer all. And I don't think it can necessarily survive exposure to royal protocols and pressures.'

A shadow crossed her eyes again and he knew the words would have reminded her of her mother. 'I am sorry to cause you pain but…'

'But my parents' love didn't survive.' Her voice was flat, her expression guarded. 'My mother fled those protocols and pressures.'

'Yes,' he said simply. 'I do not blame her or accuse her. I understand how hard it must have been for her at a court full of unfamiliarity, where emotions had to be hidden and stifled and masked. I do not judge her, but I think it sensible to learn from her, from your parents. That perhaps sometimes the way to happiness is not through love.'

'But you don't want to marry me for the sake of happiness,' she said softly. 'You want to marry me to forge an alliance between our countries.'

'Yes. Yet I believe it could still be a happy alliance.'

'Why? How?'

Now he smiled, wanting to make her frown disappear, wanting to chase away the memories that shadowed her brown eyes. 'Well, for a start I'm part of the package and I am well known for my charm and wit and brilliance.' Her gaze met his with a startled expression and his smile broadened as he nodded. 'I am what is known as a catch.'

'You forgot an attribute,' she said.

'What's that?'

'Your endearing sense of modesty.'

That pulled a chuckle from him. 'Hey, if you don't believe in yourself, who will?' He reached out, covered her hands in his own, felt a thrill at the softness of her skin. 'But in all seriousness, I do believe we could make a go of it; I think we have something to build on.'

'What's that?' She looked down at their clasped hands and he knew his touch affected her as much as it did him.

'This,' he said softly. 'This spark; I felt it from the moment I saw you.' He gave a small shrug. 'And I know you feel the same way.' He grinned. 'I realise how arrogant that sounds but we've established I have no sense of modesty.'

'I…' Gabi shook her head. 'You can't decide to get married just because there is a spark. Sparks can go out.'

'Sparks can also be ignited into flames that can be stoked and nurtured, a fire that can continue to burn. I believe our spark is that kind of spark—and I promise I will do all I can to make that happen.'

Her eyes widened now and he saw desire and doubt in them. 'Let me show you. You said to me yesterday that I should ask your permission to kiss you. I ask that now.'

There was a slight quiver to her low laugh. 'You're offering me a taster, a sample?'

'I'm offering you proof this spark has life to it, that it will not fizzle out.'

She took a deep breath. 'Then… I grant my permission.'

Gently, his breath catching in his throat, he lifted one hand, gently stroked the crease that lined her forehead, ran his thumb over the fullness of her lower lip and heard her small intake of breath with deep satisfaction, a visceral reaction that stoked his need, a need becoming more primal, more necessary by the second.

He leant forward, his heartbeat accelerated, then his lips met hers, and he tasted the linger of spices, the tang of champagne and all that mattered was the surge of sensation, the drumbeat of desire. All he'd intended was a simple brush of the lips but her small groan undid him and he deepened the kiss, felt desire twist his gut as her fingers tangled in his hair and she matched him passion for passion.

The sound of a bird's long drawn-out call pulled him back to reality and gently he broke the kiss and they stared at each other. As their ragged breath mingled, a sense of panic assailed him.

Because suddenly the momentum hit him with a whoosh. If all went to plan that would be the first kiss of a lifetime of kisses; he would never kiss another woman again. The idea was huge. Not because he questioned his ability to be faithful, but because this made it real. Not an idea, not a political or diplomatic exercise, but a proper flesh and blood union.

A sudden image of his parents forced its way to his brain, soured the moment. Their relationship had been a political alliance and whilst they had had five children their union had yet been devoid of any sense of passion or joy. It had been founded on duty and evolved no further. And so Cesar had promised himself to eschew marriage and opt for the fun and passion of light hearted affaires.

Now here he was headed towards the altar. But this marriage would not be like his parents'—that kiss had shown him that. And for that he was suddenly immensely grateful—his emotions see-sawing by the second.

Wait a minute. Emotions? See-sawing?

He needed to relax. Gabi was looking at him, her eyes wide with a mixture of shell shock and vulnerability and muted desire.

Think, Cesar.

Before the silence stretched too long, before he succumbed to the overriding urge to kiss her again. The idea of losing control was not congenial—after all, this was a marriage campaign and that meant he had to be *in* control. Digging deep into his reserves of charm, he managed a smile, one of his best, used when it behoved him to epitomise Prince Charming.

'So did the sample pass muster?'

Now her expression changed, cooled, and she looked down, almost absent-mindedly dabbed her finger onto the crumbs on her plate. Then raised her head and her gaze met his, almost amused as she nodded.

'Yes, you passed. Well done,' she said. 'The spark box is now ticked. However, obviously there are still a lot more boxes to go. You can't build a marriage on one kiss.' Now she was arranging the crumbs in a line. 'What about us?'

Now it was his turn to frown. 'Us?'

'Yes. Us. Two human beings. You are proposing we get married, live together, have children, commit to each other.' The words in their enormity caused a small shudder of panic to ripple his body, one he quelled instantly. 'Yet I don't know you. You don't know me. And that doesn't seem to matter to you.'

'I know this must be hard for you to understand as a concept. But it is what we were brought up to accept as the norm. Marriages made for reasons other than love.'

'But it's so impersonal. You want to marry the Casavallian Queen—not me, Gabriella Ross.'

He drummed his fingers on his thigh. 'But Gabriella Ross is the Queen of Casavalle.'

'That's semantics and you know it. If I were still Gabi Ross, book-store owner, you wouldn't be proposing marriage.'

'No, I wouldn't.' There was no point dressing this up. 'But you aren't.'

Her forehead creased in another frown and she narrowed her eyes at him. 'I get that. My point is you would be proposing to whoever was sitting this side of the table.' Abandoning the crumbs, she pushed her plate away, picked up her glass and sipped the champagne. 'You would have set this up for any woman, kissed any woman, regardless of who she was as long as she was the next ruler of Casavalle.'

'No.' Now Cesar shook his head. 'That is not true. I set this up for you. I wanted you to see the maze in all its Christmas magic, I wanted to ride here at sunset with you. And I definitely wanted to kiss you.'

'But you would have tailor-made a different evening for a different woman.'

'Perhaps. But at the end of the day this is about you and me.'

She shook her head. 'This is about the Prince of Aguilarez and the nearly Queen of Casavalle. Not about Cesar and Gabi. As I said, you would never have proposed to Gabi Ross, book-store owner.'

'No.' Again there was no point in muffling the reality of their situation. He kept his gaze on hers. 'But I would have been attracted to you. I would have wanted to kiss you. The spark between us—that is real, that is between you and me. Gabi and Cesar. And that is important.'

'There are other things that are more important,' she said.

'I agree. And I realise I have sprung this idea on you, that you need time to process it. All I ask is that you consider what I have said today.'

'I promise I will think about it.'

'I can't ask more than that.' Indeed he couldn't. He topped up their glasses and raised his. 'To good thoughts,' he said. 'Now let us finish our meal—the selection of desserts is amazing. We can eat them in the moonlight and simply talk about other things. And then I will escort you home.'

The next morning, seated in the splendour of the palace library, her favourite room in the whole palace, the one where she felt most at home, Gabi prepared herself for her usual morning routine. A cup of tea by her side, curled up in an ornate overstuffed armchair, newspapers and netbook on the table in front of her, she fervently hoped that an imposition of normality could somehow balance out the surrealism of the previous evening. Cesar Asturias wanted to marry her. Cesar Asturias had kissed her. Gabi closed her eyes as her entire body tingled at the memory.

Enough. That kiss had meant nothing to Cesar—it had been a sampler, a proof that their marriage would contain a spark. He would have kissed any woman like that—he was an expert after all. Though just after, for an instant she would have sworn his eyes held a look of shock that no doubt mirrored her own. But then he'd blinked and she'd decided she must have imagined it.

Especially when he'd smiled the slow, satisfied smile of a man who knew he'd scored a winner. Which was when reality had doused her like a downspout of freezing water—the kiss might have been completely outside Gabi's experience…but not out of his.

Cesar Asturias was a man with a whole lot of experience in the kissing department, and she would not let herself be manipulated into marriage based on one expert lip lock.

In which case perhaps she should stop thinking about the damn kiss, and brace herself for her morning dose of the headlines.

Two minutes later she gave a muffled shriek as she absorbed the words, stared at the newspapers' headlines, at the netbook screen open to the celebrity pages. Shock rippled through her.

Royal Romance in the Air?
Could This Be Love?
A Private Picnic?
Diplomacy or Dalliance?

The accompanying photographs were even worse. Pictures from her presentation ball. Her and Cesar in conversation, her expression fierce. Then that waltz, her face tipped up with an intent look, as if her life depended on him. Then the actual article, nauseating paragraph after paragraph of speculation as to how a rocky start had led to a dance of dreaminess.

Then there were pictures of the picnic hampers being driven to the 'rendezvous'.

Sources confirm a romantic supper 'à deux' was requested by the clearly besotted Prince.

Besotted. Ha! When she got her hands on the 'sources' she would—

At that moment there was a knock on the door, it swung open and one of the palace staff entered. 'His Royal Highness Prince Cesar of Aguilarez,' he intoned.

Ah…the besotted Prince himself, looking anything but.

'Thank you, Leo.' She waited until the staff member had gone and then, 'Have you seen these?' she demanded.

'Yes. I came straight over so we can discuss a publicity strategy.'

Gabi looked at him open-mouthed. 'A strategy? How about complete outright denial?'

'That is one option,' he agreed.

'I sense that you have other preferred ones.'

'That depends.' He came further into the room, sat opposite her and despite her horror at the headlines she couldn't help her body's awareness of his proximity, that strange ripple in her tummy his presence caused. 'On what you have decided after our discussion last night.'

It was a question she had tussled with for most of a sleepless night, thoughts whirling in a restless vortex around her brain, interspersed with vivid images of their kiss. Because whilst Cesar was the epitome of the handsome prince and he had her hormones in a twirl… she had to remember that this was not a book, not a classic romance or a fairy tale. This was real life. Her life, his life, and scarily the decisions they made now would impact on the politics and well-being of their two countries as well as themselves. Eventually as she'd dropped into a doze as the dawn light had crept through the windows, she had come to a decision. 'I *had* decided that there would be no harm in discussing the matter further, rather than dismissing it out of hand.'

'Good. Then there is another viable strategy to deal with these articles. Apart from denial.'

'Such as?'

'We go along with it.'

Gabi blinked, tried to modulate her voice, tried to

keep herself from grabbing him by his broad shoulders and shaking him. 'And why would we do that?'

'Because these articles are feel good; they are positive—there is a tacit acceptance that you are royal, there is no mention of scandal, usurpers, pregnancies, jilted at the altar. All that is positive.'

Gabi stared at him and her eyes narrowed. 'Anyone would think you'd planned it yourself. Did you "leak" any of this; are you the "source" quoted?'

'I didn't plan it, but I didn't stop it either.'

Fabulous. 'So you have tacitly encouraged these fluffy, sickly, completely incorrect stories?' Unable to help it, she started to pace—perhaps she should be being suitably royal and poker-faced, but tough.

'Yes. I could have shut it down. I chose not to. Because I prefer to have a certain level of control of the stories, otherwise the press can pretty much make it up.'

'So instead you have made it up?'

'Yes. And I think we should continue to do so.'

'But it is insane. Surely they can't believe what they are writing. They must know that we barely know each other.'

'They are writing to sell their publications and people like romance. They want to believe the fairy tales. Think how they work out. The prince fits a glass slipper onto a mystery girl's foot and they live happily ever after. The prince fights through brambles, kisses a sleeping princess he has never even met because she has been asleep for a hundred years and they live happily ever after. People like stories like that. They almost see us royals as fictional characters, so why not provide a feel-good story?'

'Because we aren't fictional. We're real. And newsflash…we may *not* get married. In fact the chances of us getting married are marginally marginal. And even if we do there won't be any fluffy romance, any glass slippers. No fairy-tale ending.'

'But we can give an illusion of romance whilst we decide what we want to do. This kind of press is good publicity. Good for both our countries. It will distract attention away from all the scandals. We are planning to spend some time together getting to know each other; we can manage the publicity. Use it to our advantage.'

'So you think we should encourage the press to speculate that there is "romance in the air" whilst we spend time together figuring out if we want to make a cold-blooded alliance.'

'Not cold-blooded, no,' he said softly.

And there was that ripple of attraction. Again. To her relief a timid knock at the door was followed by the entrance of another of the palace staff, pushing a laden trolley in. 'Leo asked me to bring refreshments, ma'am.'

'Thank you, Donna,' Gabi said, waited as the young woman busied herself arranging the tea things on the table, caught the quick speculative glance she threw at Cesar before she left.

Cesar waited for the door to click shut and then, 'For example, we could have used that opportunity to give the impression of romance, let the spark show a little—then Donna would take that story back to the kitchen staff and that's how rumours grow.'

'Let the spark show.' Gabi closed her eyes in disbelief. 'Right now I'm not sure whether to be pleased or horrified that a spark exists at all, so the idea of deliberately flaunting it in public doesn't fill me with joy.'

'Flaunting is too strong a word,' he said blithely. 'The occasional look, the brush of our hands, a hand on the arm…no more than that, nothing that detracts from royal dignity. But to create an illusion, you have to live the illusion.'

Gabriella stared at him. 'You make it sound so easy.'

'It will be easy. The attraction exists—there will be no need to act. Do not look so worried. It will be like the waltz—we will pull it off.'

Like the waltz. The memory of his arms around her, the feel of his body next to hers…the attraction existed all right.

As he poured her a cup of tea, he raised his eyebrows as his hand hovered over the milk jug and he glanced at her in question.

'Just black, please. It's rooibos, one of my favourites.' Gabi gave a small laugh. 'For heaven's sake, you don't even know how I take my tea, but you want to marry me.'

'But after today I will know. We will learn about each other. And if we decide we will not suit then so be it. But in the meantime, I believe the romance strategy works. What do you think?'

Gabi tried to focus, to consider her options. She and Cesar were going to spend time together regardless; they couldn't tell the press the truth as to why and there would be speculation whatever they did. So… 'Fine. I'll do it.'

'Excellent. I will coordinate the publicity with your palace secretary.'

'Sure.' All of it was suddenly overwhelming and as she sipped her tea the taste was so very evocative of her book store, of her former life, that she felt a sudden threat of tears, closed her eyes to try and blink them away.

'Hey. Are you OK?' She heard the clink of a cup being placed down, felt his approach and opened her eyes as he squatted down in front of her chair.

'I'm sorry. I just had a wave of homesickness; a yearning to be sitting in my book store with a book and a cup of tea, chatting to customers, or students.' Back to her safe, ordered world. She kept talking, as much to distract herself as anything else. 'The book store was more than a job—it was like my home. My aunt and uncle bought it when I was young.' The all too familiar guilt hit her again. They had used the savings they had planned to spend on their adventurous retirement and they had run the store competently, but without passion. But it had been different for Gabi. For her the shop had been magical. 'I grew up in it and I always loved it. Loved the books, the smell of them, the feel of them and the sheer magic of them. I could literally escape into them. Live a different life, befriend the fictional characters.' She broke off. 'Sorry. I get a bit carried away.'

'That's fine. It's nice to see. Even if I don't get it.'

Gabi frowned. 'You must get it a bit. Think of your favourite book.'

This was greeted by silence.

'I do not read.'

'Excuse me?' Gabi put her cup of tea down and leant forward.

'Well, obviously I read reports and official documents and I read the news. Religiously. But if you mean books, fiction, poetry, then, no, I do not.'

'OK. But what about a childhood book? Once you learnt to read didn't you sit under the bedcovers with a torch, reading? You must have read something? Books about wizards? Books about princes? You must have read, or surely your parents read you bedtime stories.'

That was something she knew Sophia had done, one of the few snippets her aunt had let fall. And if she tried really hard Gabi was sure she remembered, had a faint elusive memory of a soft, modulated voice, reading, making farm-animal sounds, singing softly at bedtime. Her mother, barely remembered except as an almost dream, hard to distinguish between what she had imagined in her grief and sadness and how much had been real.

'No.' His brown eyes shadowed. 'None of the above. I did read the history of our countries, and there were some local authors that I was told to read from time to time. But fiction was seen as unessential.'

Gabi stared at him and he gave a sudden chuckle. 'You look absolutely horrified.'

'I am utterly horrified. How can you exist without reading? It doesn't have to be classic literature—it can be anything at all. But reading…it's a means of escape.' And you could do it anywhere. Reading had saved her as a child; allowed her to escape the knowledge that she was a burden. 'And it's enjoyable and…to me it's necessary.'

'So you think I should read?'

'I think everyone should read.'

'That's a little dictatorial.'

'Nope. It would be dictatorial if I chose their reading material. Everyone likes different things, different genres, different authors. Some people really can't take to fiction, others may only like short stories. Then there are biographies and information books and history books and I guess for some people a technical book will float their boat or…' She paused, waved her hand expansively. 'You get the picture. What I mean is everyone should be encouraged to read. Especially in this world of technology, it's important. For kids and for…' She stopped—what was she doing? Waffling on about books to a man who had made it clear that nothing was more important than duty to one's country, a man willing to pull the strings of the press, marry in the name of duty. Did Gabi spending time reading help her people, further her country's purpose? No, it didn't.

'Anyway,' she said. 'Sorry. I guess once a book-store owner, always a book-store owner.'

'I think I can see why you were so successful at it. You're clearly passionate about books.' He smiled. 'Your whole face lights up and your enthusiasm—it is infectious.'

'I *am* enthusiastic. I ran a store, ran literacy classes, and a book club. But now my life has changed.'

'That doesn't take away from everything you achieved.' As if he could hear the sadness in her voice he stepped towards her. 'I would have loved to see it, your book store, your former realm. To have met you whilst you were that person, but that person is still a part of you. The past doesn't just vanish…it makes us who we are today. Your reading, everything you got from books, everything you learnt from building up a business you love, you'll use all that. You really will.'

'Thank you.' The words made her feel better, made her feel as if her past life was important, rather than being swallowed up by this whole new world. 'I hope so.' She glanced at him a little shyly. 'I did think that maybe I could open this library up. Redesign it to make it more accessible to staff—not force anyone to come and read, but maybe simply offer access? I could get lots of tables, comfy chairs, drinks machines and obviously catalogue the books. Put the valuable ones up high, get a better mix of authors in…' She shrugged, clocked the intensity of his dark brown eyes. 'Or is that a stupid idea?'

'I think that's a great idea.'

'You do? Really?'

'Really. I don't say things I don't mean, Gabriella.' She could see his sincerity and it warmed her, as did his toe-curling smile.

'And now why don't you start with me?' he said.

For a minute she had no idea what he meant. Start with him how? Perhaps she could move forward, lift her hand, touch his cheek, move her hand down and cover the beat of his heart, stand on tiptoe, brush her lips against his…

Bad idea. That box was ticked; kissing him again would mess with her head, fuzz her brain, to say nothing of pandering to his ego. And that wasn't what he meant anyway, she realised as she saw him turn to scan the bookshelves.

'I would like you to choose me a book,' he continued.

Gathering herself together, she looked round at the shelves. 'A book?' she echoed.

'Yes. You have shown me how important books are to you—I would like to try and understand that.'

The idea touched her; perhaps all he could offer was an alliance, but at least he was trying and she appreciated that. 'OK. That sounds good.' A few moments' thought and she headed over to a corner of the room. 'This is where I've put my keeper shelf. Here, try this and this.' The first a book she was sure he'd love, an incredibly clever account of the life of a centenarian, and second, 'This is a book I've read and reread all my life. A Canadian classic—the story of a red-haired girl.' An orphan like herself.

Reaching out, he accepted the books and she forced herself not to react as his hand brushed hers; told herself it was scientifically impossible to have such heightened sensitivity that the fleeting contact triggered a shiver over her skin.

'Thank you,' he said.

'I hope you enjoy them, but if you don't that's fine too. There are plenty of others I can suggest.' Resisting the urge to reach out and grab his hand, to put scientific theory to test, she reminded herself of why Cesar was here. 'We seem to have got distracted—what happens next? With us?'

'I suggest we go on a date.'

'A date? So, like a fake date?' Visions of being paraded in front of the press filled her brain. 'How would it work?'

'Leave it to me. What is your schedule today?'

Gabi checked her netbook diary, showed the screen to Cesar, who scanned the timetable and grimaced. 'Is this a sample of a typical day?'

Gabi nodded. 'There is so much to learn.'

'There are different ways to learn,' he said. 'I will pick you up at twelve; you are supposed to be studying.'

It was time she set aside to studying Casavallian history, wanting to learn as much as she could about her country, the country she would soon rule over.

'Leave it all to me,' he declared. 'Just dress up warm.' Now his smile would melt the polar ice caps and she felt her toes curl. 'And don't look so worried. A date with me is not an ordeal. I promise.' Now his voice was a low, deep melted-chocolate rumble that slid over her skin. 'The idea is to have fun.'

Fun. Surely that was a good thing, right? As long as she kept her head, remembered the date part was a show for the press. Yet unwanted anticipation sizzled her veins. Giving up, she smiled back. 'I'll wear my favourite toque.'

CHAPTER SIX

GABRIELLA WAS TRUE to her word. At twelve exactly she entered the reception room with a red and white striped woollen hat sitting jauntily atop her head; she wore a red fleece-lined coat over jeans. And worry in her eyes.

'I take it the press are waiting outside.'

'Yes, but it'll be fine,' Cesar said. 'Trust me. We only have to face them for a few minutes tops until we get to the car. And your hat…"toque", was it?…it will bring you luck. Come.' Without thinking, he held out a hand and when she put her hand in his, he felt a sudden warmth. Hand-holding was not something he did—too cosy, too intimate… Belatedly he reminded himself it would look good for the cameras, felt a jangle of discomfort that that hadn't been his motivation. Enough. 'Ready?'

She nodded and he pushed the door open and they walked hand in hand towards the car, a security detail between them and the pack of reporters.

'Where are you going, Princess?'

'Is it a date, Cesar?'

He smiled easily, but said nothing as the door to the car was held open for them and Gabriella slid in.

Once in the car, he directed the driver to, 'Go, Roberto.'

Gabi turned. 'Won't they follow?'

'I'm counting on it.' He met her gaze. 'Relax, Gabriella—as I said, this will be fun. I promise.'

'OK. I'll try. Maybe you should tell me where we are going.'

'But that would ruin the surprise.' Anticipation curved his lips at the prospect of seeing Gabriella's face when she saw the venue of their date. He wanted to see her smile; knew that the headlines had worried her, knew that the prospect of marriage must be preying on her mind. 'I will give you a hint. I am taking you to Aguilarez.' He gestured to the window. 'Perhaps you can consider this to be a geography lesson. If you watch you will see how the landscape changes; the countryside becomes craggier, more mountainous. Harder. In terms of history sometimes I believe it shows the differences in our cultures, as I told you at the maze.' Gabriella turned to look, continued to study the countryside, the towns and villages as their journey progressed. Cesar took the opportunity to study her, the classical beauty of her features, the regal straight back, the gloss and shine of her hair.

After a while she turned to face him. 'I see what you mean. It is very different from Casavalle.'

'And I believe the difference in geography has impacted on our countries' histories,' he said. 'On Aguilarez crops were harder to grow, conditions were harsher, tougher and that meant my people either resented or looked down on your people who enjoyed better harvests and an easier lifestyle. So unrest began and grew into full-scale war. At other times it was Casavalle who was the aggressor—wanting to rule the entire island, to get rid of the constant need for defence, the constant threat.'

'And now?'

'Now modern technology, worldwide trade, imports

and exports, tourism, the treaties and agreements made by our ancestors have meant we are both prosperous countries and allies. Yet…'

'You still believe that alliance to be fragile.'

'It is difficult. As children my brothers used to play with toy soldiers and the opposing armies were from Aguilarez and Casavalle. One day my oldest brother will be King and my next brother is rising the ranks in the army, as was ordained from birth.'

'And you? What did you do as a child?'

'I tried to broker a truce—after all, even then I knew diplomacy was my future.'

'What would have happened if you hadn't wanted to be a diplomat? What if you'd decided you wanted to be a surgeon or a banker or a teacher or…?' She broke off. 'You get the picture.'

Cesar shook his head. 'It didn't work like that in our families. Some options, most options weren't on the table. It was accepted each of us would take on one of the designated royal roles. So it was best not to consider anything else.' He looked at her. 'But do not feel sorry for me. I love my job; it gave me an opportunity to meet many people and I hope to do good, for Aguilarez and other countries too.' The trips abroad, to ravaged, war-torn countries, the children who had literally nothing, invaded his mind, the images stark and vivid. In truth, those were the people he wanted to help the most.

But when he had asked his parents if his role could change, become more humanitarian, if perhaps he could set up a foundation, take up a more hands-on role with charities close to his heart, they had vetoed the suggestion. Now when he could he made anonymous trips, made anonymous donations and wherever possible he used his diplomatic influence to increase foreign aid.

Seeing the way she scrutinised his expression, he pulled himself to the present. 'And as a diplomat I believe that it would be good for Aguilarez and Casavalle for us to marry.'

As the car started the steep, almost vertical climb up the mountain roads, she clutched her arm rest. 'Where does this lead?'

'To the palace of Aguilarez.'

'Oh.'

Her face scrunched with worry and he understood immediately. 'We aren't meeting my family or anything like that.' As the car slowed he nodded at her. 'Ready.'

'Hold on. I'll just put my toque on.' She smiled. 'It's a bit like a security blanket.'

He opened the door and climbed out at the gates that led to the Aguilarean royal palace. The gates were ornamental and spiky; set in the vast stone wall that surrounded the estate, they imposed their presence, made it clear that only those welcome could enter. Even now the temptation was there to look up and to check for defenders on the parapets.

Behind them a few hardy reporters had followed and cameras clicked and whirred. Reporters shouted questions. 'Are you taking the Princess to meet your family?'

This time Cesar stopped for a moment. 'Keep calm, guys. My family are not here. I am taking the Princess for a toboggan ride—on private royal property. No doubt we will see you again on our way out.'

A few photos later and they got back into the car and headed towards the palace.

'I hope tobogganing is acceptable?'

'Try and stop me. I love tobogganing. In fact, I, Princess of Casavalle, challenge you, the Prince of Aguilarez, to a race. Instead of fighting it out on the battlefield we'll take to the slopes.'

Her smile lit her face and he could almost feel it warm him. 'I accept the challenge, Princess. But, tell me, what is the winner's prize?' His gaze lingered on her expression, snagged on her lips. 'A kiss?'

A silence and then she tossed her head in a regal acceptance; he'd known she wouldn't back away from a challenge. 'Agreed.'

Gabi hadn't felt like this since she'd arrived in Casavalle—in truth she wasn't sure she'd felt like this ever. Her whole being felt alive as they stepped out of the car into the crisp sunlit air. 'It's beautiful,' she breathed. All around them was the brilliant white of the snow; the air tasted different at this altitude, tanged with cold and snow and dappled with sunlight. As she looked out at the peaks and crags and the loom of the palace in the distance she could feel exhilaration swell through her.

Turning, she faced him and now her heart pitter-pattered, leapt and bounded as she recalled their bet. Waited as he opened the boot of the car and tugged out two toboggans. Simple, sturdy and wooden, they looked brand new and Gabi had to admire Cesar's ability to make things happen.

'Right. This way,' he said, and they started to tramp across the snow to the start point at the top of a hill. 'A practice run and then we race?' he suggested and she nodded agreement and lowered herself on the toboggan.

And with that she was off, an adrenalin-fuelled cry left her lips and carried on the cold air as she zoomed over the compact white snow, manoeuvred the toboggan skilfully, oh, so aware of Cesar running parallel to her. The journey to the bottom of the hill was one of unalloyed joy and she climbed off and beamed at him. 'That was amazing. Now I'm ready to race.'

'Then let's do this.'

Once they were back at the top her breath caught and it was nothing to do with the uphill climb and everything to do with Cesar and his sheer masculine beauty, enhanced by the slight flush to his cheeks, the light in his brown eyes as they rested on her. 'May the best person win,' he stated.

This time the descent was different; oblivious to the scenery and driven by a desire to win, Gabi focused on the end goal. Balanced her weight, used her instincts and willed her toboggan to fly straight and true to the finish line ahead of Cesar. And in the final seconds she edged it, skimmed over the finish line by a whisker, climbed off the toboggan with a whoop of triumph. 'I did it.'

'You did.'

And as they stood there it was the most natural thing in the world for her to say, 'In which case, I claim the winner's prize.'

Stunned by her own daring…stupidity…madness, she stepped towards him; her hormones punched the air and did a happy dance. Her brain tried to intervene and Gabi shut it down. What better time, what better place than this? No fear of hidden cameras, of having this moment recorded and splashed across the media. And it wasn't as though she were committing to anything—it was just a kiss. The result of a challenge, no more.

Enough justification. She *wanted* to kiss him, wanted it with an intensity she had never experienced before.

Desire pulsed through her, seemed to make her veins fizz, propelled her forward so she was standing flush against him, so close she could smell his unique scent, and slowly she lifted a hand and placed it on his chest, on the thick cable-knit wool of his sweater.

Slowly, as if they had all the time in the world, his dark brown eyes fixed on hers, as if she were the only woman in the universe, and she wondered if it was possible to drown in anticipation. Her skin heated, her nerves end tingled and, wow, he hadn't even kissed her yet.

Then his lips touched hers, his fingers tangled in her hair and she was lost. The kiss was gentle, his lips firm against hers. She pressed against his body, his muscles hard, and he deepened the kiss, gave a small groan and her head whirled as she lost herself in the moment.

Time stood still and Gabi had no idea if the kiss lasted a minute or hours…but then a cold breeze gusted and penetrated the fog of desire and he broke the kiss. Gabi opened eyes she hadn't realised she'd closed and stared at him.

So much for just a kiss, nothing more. But she mustn't show how affected she was; she had to remember that for Cesar this was 'normal', that he'd shared millions of similar kisses with other women, more beautiful and sophisticated than Gabi could ever hope to be.

Play it cool.

'Thank you,' she said. 'That was a prize worth winning. Now how about a rematch but this time no prizes?'

'Sure.' There was something elusive in his voice but his expression maintained his usual easy charm. 'Let's get back to the top and when you're ready I've arranged for lunch in my quarters in the palace.'

* * *

An hour later Gabi followed Cesar through a side entrance and into the Aguilarean palace, caught a glimpse of her reflection in an enormous black gilded mirror and gave a small gasp of horror.

'You're sure no one will see me?'

'I'm sure. This is my private entrance.'

'Thank goodness. If Maria saw me now she'd…well, I'm not sure what she'd do but she wouldn't be happy.'

'Well, Maria isn't here and personally I think you look beautiful. I like the windswept look.'

'Wind-battered more like.' As they entered his apartment she glanced round. 'Is this where you lived before you left on diplomatic duties?'

'Yes.' His glance around was perfunctory. The room was comfortable without being ostentatious, the furniture sleek but comfortable. The flat-screen TV mounted on the wall was state of the art. Gabi liked it, she realised.

'Lunch should be here any minute.'

'In which case I will hide in the bathroom until it is,' Gabi stated firmly, suiting action to word.

Five minutes later she heard Cesar's, 'All clear,' and she exited. 'That looks delicious.' The table had been set beautifully with a centrepiece of flowers, silver cutlery and starched napkins.

'I think the kitchen staff want to impress you,' Cesar said.

'Consider me impressed.' Gabi grimaced. 'I should have come out and thanked whoever brought it. I didn't think.'

'It's OK. Daniella didn't realise you were hiding.'

'She just thought I was in the washroom—Maria

would say that's worse. I'm not sure royalty are supposed to use washrooms.'

She sat down opposite him. 'This is incredible.' A tantalising aroma of tangy lemon and thyme wafted up from her plate, where a portion of risotto was perfectly presented. In the centre of the table was a simple green salad. Gabi served herself and took a mouthful and closed her eyes in astonishment. 'The dressing is sublime.'

'I'm glad you like it.'

'I love it. I wish I could cook like this.' She took another mouthful and looked at him. 'Can you cook like this? I mean, does royalty get taught how to cook?'

'It is not part of the royal curriculum, no. There are royal chefs who prepare every meal.' He shrugged. 'I do remember wanting to learn how to bake but I couldn't convince anyone to show me how.'

'Your parents?'

Cesar gave a small laugh. 'My parents don't work like that. You met them, albeit briefly. Can you imagine either of them baking cookies? I very much doubt either of them has even entered the royal kitchens, unless it was for some sort of publicity shot.' He nodded. 'I think once my mother did pose with Flavia and me with a bowl and a wooden spoon. In fact, I think that's what triggered my desire to bake. The hope she'd actually make good.'

The words were matter-of-fact, said with a suggestion of lightness, but Gabi sensed an undercurrent of sadness, and an image of a young Cesar flashed across her brain. A small dark-haired boy who had *truly* hoped his mother would make good, make the publicity illusion into truth.

'Wasn't there anyone else? I mean, how does a royal childhood work?'

'There were many nannies.' Again there was a shadow in his eyes. 'And a royal agenda devised by our parents. An agenda that did not include baking. The idea being we had more important things to do, and achieve. That it was our privilege and our duty to act for Aguilarez and the ability to bake a cake would hardly advance our country in any way.'

'But that doesn't sound like much…fun.'

'Fun wasn't a priority in our childhood.'

Gabi wondered if that was how her father had thought, understood more now why her mother had panicked, hadn't wanted to bring her child up in the royal household, bound by royal rules.

'Is that what you believe? How you would want to bring up your children? Because that isn't my plan. I am going to be a hands-on parent and if my child wants to bake then my child will bake. And I don't care if it advances Casavalle or not.'

'I take it you know how to bake?'

'I do. My Aunt Bea taught me, though she didn't let me lick the spoon and it was what she called "functional baking". So that I would be able to make the meals, make useful things.' After Bea's death Gabi had discovered a well-thumbed book on how to raise a child, including a section on functional baking. The find had touched her, made her realise anew that Bea and Peter had been thrown into a guardianship they had been truly bewildered by. 'I always used to imagine, though, that my mother would have baked gooey chocolate creations with me, with sprinkles and icing and…' Sometimes the image had been so clear she had almost been able to hear Sophia's laughter. 'Not that I am complaining. Functional baking is important too.'

'It would be OK to complain.' Cesar hesitated. 'It must have been hard to lose your mother so young, however good your aunt and uncle were.'

'I don't really remember her, just a few elusive memories that I'm not even sure are true. And there are no photographs. I understand why now—she must have been worried about being recognised.'

'And you had no idea who your father was.'

'None. I know now that my aunt and uncle must have known—they can hardly have missed the fact that my mom married a king—but they maintained complete silence. All they told me was that my mother had never told them the identity of my father.' They had rarely spoken of Sophia and, soon realising they didn't like to discuss her mother, Gabi had stopped asking. Now she understood their reticence—the letter from her mother had explained that she had asked for the promise of secrecy, and Bea and Peter had maintained that promise to the end.

'That must have been hard.'

Gabi nodded. 'It was. In the end I made up a story; well, actually, I made up lots of stories. My father figured as a doctor, a soldier, a firefighter… Every hero in every book. Then every villain—I had him down as a criminal, a married man, et cetera, et cetera. Eventually I settled on a guy who couldn't deal with the idea of parenthood.' She lifted a hand to her face. 'The worst thing was wondering if I'd passed him on the street, or if he was a customer in the shop. The realisation I wouldn't have known him from Adam.'

Cesar studied her. 'I think you would have. If Vincenzo had met you—there is a definite family resemblance.'

'Did you know him well?'

'No, not really. I met him on formal occasions—he was a formal man. I am not sure if anyone knew him well. Perhaps your mother did, perhaps Maria did, but he wasn't a man who welcomed or wished for closeness. But he was a good ruler—he and Maria were respected and liked throughout Casavalle.'

The words were a reminder of why they were sitting here, to consider the idea of a marriage. One that would be like Vincenzo and Maria's—an alliance made in the hope of winning their people's respect and liking. A marriage that offered respect and liking but not love. Though she believed that Maria and Vincenzo had achieved a closeness and a mutually supportive marriage.

But she must be careful not to forget the boundaries, not get lost in the illusion.

Putting her cutlery down, she gestured to the table. 'That was delicious. Thank you, and thank you for the replacement history lesson. I truly enjoyed it.'

He glanced at his watch. 'But now you need to return to Casavalle. Of course. But you are happy to arrange another date? I believe we should attend Antonio and Tia's wedding together in three days' time, but if we can fit another date in before that we should.'

'Yes. But if it is OK with you, I'll arrange it.' It was time she took some sort of control; before he dazzled her into seeing this proposed marriage in a soft rose-tinted light. 'I'll contact you with the details.'

CHAPTER SEVEN

CESAR APPROACHED THE Casavallian palace, aware of a sense of well-being, a swell of happy expectation. He frowned, suddenly uneasy though he wasn't sure why. Campaign Marriage was going better than he could have hoped; the more he got to know Gabriella, the more he liked her, the more he believed that they could make a go of it. So there was no need for unease.

Instead he needed to continue the good work. He entered the palace, where a staff member greeted him and led him up the ornate winding stairs.

'Princess Gabriella is through here.' Cesar followed through a state guest apartment, through the richly furnished living area to a spacious kitchen, where Gabriella stood by the marble-topped counter.

She smiled at the retainer and thanked him and once the grey-haired man had left she turned to Cesar, who surveyed the preparations for their date. Two aprons, a recipe book and an array of ingredients, including a big mixing bowl and two wooden spoons.

'We're going to bake,' she explained. 'It's what you wanted to do when you were little and I thought it would be fun.'

Hell, there was that warmth again; the odd sensation of…of what? Being cared for?

'Don't worry,' she added. 'I have also alerted the press, who will be allowed to come in and take photos of us in our aprons and take a picture of the fruit of our labours.'

'What are we making?'

'Decadent chocolate cake.'

'Sounds good.'

'Yes. I haven't made it before. Imogen gave me the recipe book, said she'd heard it's good. I've got the ingredients, now I need to read the instruct…' Her voice trailed off and as he looked at her, he saw a small flush mount her cheeks.

'What's wrong?'

'Nothing,' she said quickly but she shielded the book with an arm as she spoke.

'Come on, Gabi. Tell me.'

'There's nothing to tell… It's…well…the instructions… they are a little…um…racy.'

He raised his eyebrows. 'Racy?'

'Look. It really doesn't matter. It just implies the cake has some…well…aphrodisiac properties.'

'I think I'd like to see this.'

'No…really.' Quickly she shut the book and moved it out of his reach as he headed closer to her. Grabbed it as he reached for it and turned to face him with a shake of her head, her back against the counter, holding it above her head, with a half-laugh.

'Nowhere to go,' he said teasingly.

And then he realised how close she was, so very tantalisingly close; he could smell the scent of pine from the tree mixed with her clean vanilla-spiced scent, and desire spun his head. As if she felt the exact same thing, her hand dropped to her side, still holding the damned book.

'I don't think we need any help from the cake,' he murmured. And then he was kissing her, kissing her as if his life depended on it and it felt…incredible. Magnificent.

He heard the thud as the book fell to the kitchen floor and she moved against him, and he entangled his hands in her hair, the soft silken tresses against his fingers, deepened the kiss and tasted her gasp of pleasure. Then all that existed was the scale of his desire; he wanted this woman with an unparalleled fierceness and it was only the recognition of the depth of that yearning that penetrated the fog of desire. Reminded him who this woman was. Gabriella Ross Valenti, soon to be Queen of Casavalle. This had to stop here, before he was no longer able to stop.

He gently disengaged, his breathing laboured. Each jagged breath seemed to accelerate his heartbeat further—just looking at her flushed face, the desire-dazed look in her eyes—and he wanted to kiss her again and hang the consequences.

OK. Stop right there.

For once he couldn't think of what to say.

'I…' She stopped, reached out a hand to the counter as if to steady herself and tried again. 'I…we can't keep doing this—kissing on every date.' Her voice still hitched. 'It's… I'm worried it will mess with my head, fuzz my judgement and I…we can't afford that. The decision we have to make is too important for that.'

'Agreed. If you decide to marry me I need to know it is for the right reasons; I need to know we entered this agreement on the same page.'

She smoothed her hair, ran a wondering hand over her lips and nodded.

Forcing positivity into his voice, he gestured to the ingredients. 'Now let's bake this cake.'

A nod and she leant down, picked the book up off the floor with a rueful look, and found the page with the recipe.

The first ten minutes were spent in sharing the tasks, whilst fighting off the memory of that kiss. No easy task in itself, as they were of necessity still so close that he could catch a waft of her shampoo. As he read the instructions over her shoulder he had to fight the urge to lean over and nuzzle kisses along the nape of her neck. Knew the smell of cocoa powder as it dusted the air would always bring him back to this moment.

'It's good practice for children, isn't it?' she said and he blinked.

'I think I may have missed a bit of the conversation.'

'I meant that one day I can imagine showing my child how to do this and it got me wondering.' She turned her face from him, stirred the mixture in the bowl harder and then paused, turned to look at him. 'Tell me what sort of father you want to be.'

'Why do I get the feeling this is an interview question?'

'Because in a way it is.' Her voice was serious now. 'If we get married it's not like a fairy tale where we waltz off the page into the horizon of happy ever after. We have to think about the reality of what comes after we say we do. This is real.'

'I understand that,' he said.

'Good.' She stirred with a little less gusto and then handed it over to him to continue. Almost as if it were some sort of symbol. 'So what sort of father *do* you want to be? You must have thought about this, thought about the idea of having children?'

'Um…' He stared down at the mixture in the bowl, searched for inspiration. In truth the furthest he'd got to thinking about children was the general idea of not having them.

Because the whole idea of parenthood terrified him. When he remembered how much he'd craved affection, love, attention, he knew that that was what he needed to give a child. Problem was he wasn't sure he could, because he'd never been shown how, and the thought of letting a child down was unacceptable. If there was any chance of that he wouldn't take the risk. An easy choice as he'd had no intention of marriage anyway.

But now… That had all changed and panic clawed his chest. How on earth could he be a father? The idea threatened to choke him with its enormity. What if he really couldn't be the father he knew every child deserved, couldn't offer love? What if he was simply conditioned to repeat his parents' mistakes?

Gabriella was studying him. 'Sorry. I know it's a big question. But it is an important one. If we are to get married then hopefully we will end up responsible for another human being and that is an awesome and a huge responsibility. And here and now I am willing to put my credentials on the line. I have always wanted children, but only if it would be right for them. I wanted it to be the right time in my life so that I would be able to give them security, a home, as well as love. I wanted them to have a family life with two loving parents and siblings and huge Christmas meals and family holidays and…' She shook her head. 'I know I am painting a rose-coloured picture. I know there will be difficulties and arguments and tiredness along the way. I do know it will be real. But I want all that too.'

A family. Kids in the plural. Christmas lunches. Family holidays. Events completely unlike the ones he'd experienced. Himself and Gabriella with a brood of dark-haired children, children with Gabriella's wide smile and dimple. With her serious brown eyes, that could light up with laughter. The wave of panic threatened again and he forced himself to stem it as he faced the seriousness of her expression now.

As she continued. 'I didn't have a father and I wanted one so very badly. I vowed that when I had children I would make sure I gave them a good dad, a good man who would care for them, protect them, carry them round on his shoulders, help them with their homework…be there for them. I can't marry a man who won't be a good father.'

'I…' Dammit—she deserved better than the platitudes he knew he could reel out, the diplomatic assurances he could craft. 'I'll do my best,' he said, the lameness apparent to his own ears, and he knew she deserved more than that as well. He watched as she carefully spooned the mixture into a cake tin. 'I realise that sounds meh at best. But it's hard for me to imagine being a good father, because I don't have a role model. And I don't have the sort of imagination you have to be able to picture one.'

'What about your own father?'

Cesar hesitated and then shrugged, knew she deserved a real explanation. 'My parents…they did everything for duty, for Aguilarez. Including having children; sometimes I felt as though we were their gift to the country, a duty done. Then after we were born it was their duty to mould us into the sons and daughters of Aguilarez. But by so doing it was as if that absolved them of any duty to make us feel wanted on a personal level. So I saw very little of him and when I did it was more of an audience, an update report, a tick-the-box exercise.' He could still remember the discomfort of the starched clothes, the perfectly combed hair, the exhortations from the nanny of the day not to fidget, to enunciate, to be polite. 'A time where I had to be on best behaviour.'

'And did you always behave?'

'Yes. Especially once I'd figured out that it wasn't only us who bore the consequences if I didn't, but it was the nannies too.' He flushed now, slightly uncomfortable. 'It sounds horrible now but I did realise that gave me a level of power. It was always easier to persuade them to give us a treat just before a parental meeting.'

Gabriella looked at him. 'So your childhood was really a string of negotiations.'

'Life is a string of negotiations,' he said.

'Maybe, but it shouldn't be and childhood certainly shouldn't be that. And I don't want it to be that way for my children.'

'Neither do I.' And that was the honest truth. 'I would do my best, Gabi. To be there for them, to kick a ball around, teach them how to ride a bike or bake a cake. I'll try to be there for them.' Somehow he'd conquer the terror that twisted his guts with the fear he'd get it wrong. After all, Cesar Asturias feared nothing.

'Thank you,' she said softly. 'Sometimes all we can do is our best.'

And he was man who had always made sure his best was good enough.

Picking up the cake tin, he went over and popped it

into the oven. 'As this has become a kind of interview, I too have a question I need to ask. Perhaps we could have coffee whilst the cake bakes and we can talk.'

Gabi's head whirled as it tried to process the information he had given her about royal childhoods. Cold, damaging, miserable, sad…all those words chased each other around her head. Most of all though she wanted to offer comfort, but she knew that would not be welcomed.

'Fire away,' she said as the smell of the cake, the rich deep chocolate, started to pervade the kitchen.

He waited until he had made the coffee and she accepted the cup with appreciation.

'There is something we have not spoken of,' he said. 'My relationships have been in the public domain, but we have never discussed your past relationships.' He raised a hand. 'I am not trying to pry but from a publicity angle I do need to know if any ex-suitors will come out of the woodwork.'

Gabriella shook her head. 'I had two relationships. Both serious at the time.' Though now, somehow the memories had faded, seemed blurred and sepia.

'Tell me.' The words were a touch on the curt side and for one dizzying, stupid moment Gabriella wondered if it bothered him. Then her brain told her not to be stupid. As if. Cesar didn't care. Any more than she cared about all his exes.

Only that wasn't true, was it? She did care, not because she was jealous, but because they made her feel inadequate. For an instant an image of his most recent girlfriend, Lady Amelia Scott-Browne, popped into her head even though she knew that Lady Amelia and Cesar had broken up some time ago. Yet Lady Amelia had been so poised, beautiful, always immaculate, elegant, versed in which knife and fork to use.

Realising that he was still waiting, she regrouped. 'Steve and Paul.' Resolutely she pulled them to mind. Steve—blond, blue-eyed, medium build, kind features, slightly receding hairline, sweet, average. Paul, brown-haired, hazel-eyed, craggy features, long hair, sweet, average. 'They were both really nice guys. But somehow it didn't pan out either time. I met Steve very soon after my aunt and uncle passed away and I was in the throes of grief and I dealt with that by throwing myself into work. I got so caught up in the book store that in the end he got frustrated. Wanted a girlfriend who had more time for him. I was sad. But I understood.'

Cesar frowned. 'Surely he could have been supportive, understood how important it was to you.'

'Perhaps,' Gabriella said. 'But I was…well, I was quite obsessed really and I should have been more willing to spend more time with him. It was the same with Paul. He wanted me to slow down. We both wanted the same things; we just had different ideas about how it would work. He assumed when we got married, I'd sell up or delegate more and I didn't want to do that. Or at least it never quite seemed the right time. In the end they both moved on.'

'But you loved them both.'

Gabriella looked back into the past. Had she loved them? 'I genuinely believed we matched; were on the same page, could bring up children together and have a normal, happy family life.' The thing she'd craved all her life. 'But in the end I wasn't enough for them.'

So how on earth could she ever be enough for this man? Doubts swirled. She'd been with Steve and Paul for eighteen months and two years respectively. That was the length of time she could keep an average man—what hope did she have with Cesar?

It was a relief when the ping of the oven indicated the cake was ready.

CHAPTER EIGHT

TWO DAYS LATER Cesar gave his reflection a perfunctory check, made sure there was no spot on his tie, no dust on his suit because, despite the fact that Antonio and Tia's wedding was to be private, there would still be photographers covering the arrival and departure of guests—a fact he had every intention of using to his advantage.

His and Gabriella's.

He rolled his eyes as he caught the small goofy smile on his lips, brought about by the thought of Casavalle's Queen-in-waiting.

Enough. There was no need for goofiness, rather the smile should be one of satisfaction, that his courtship was going well, that there was a certainty of a union less cold than that of his parents. The kisses they had shared had shown him that—his body still tied in knots.

Turning away from his reflection, he headed for the door and the chauffeur-driven car that would take him to Casavalle, where he'd arranged to meet Gabriella prior to the ceremony, so they could make the walk to the chapel together.

Forty-five minutes later he alighted in the courtyard, raised a hand in acknowledgement as the photographers clicked, made sure that the small package was just visible in the pocket of his suit as he entered the palace and made his way to the reception room.

He pushed open the door, and felt his lungs constrict slightly. The dress she wore was perfect for the occasion, navy blue, simple in its structural cut and demure neckline, but made that little bit different by the statement flared sleeves. Her chestnut hair fell free to her shoulders. 'You look stunning,' he said simply.

Gabriella looked down at herself. 'I have to admit I am having doubts. Fashion was never my thing.'

'It's beautiful,' he assured her.

'You've scrubbed up pretty well yourself.'

'Apart from the shadows under my eyes,' he said, with a smile. 'I stayed up late reading.'

'You did?'

'I did.' In truth it had started as a homework exercise—he wanted to be able to show Gabriella that he had tried. Had decided to read a chapter. But to his astonishment the book had gripped him, and it had only been the chime of the clock at an advanced hour that had forced him to turn the light out. 'It was a good choice.'

'I'm glad.'

'Now *I* have brought you this.' He handed her a slim box, watched as she opened it to reveal a posy of flowers designed so that they could be pinned to her dress. 'From the Aguilarean palace gardens.'

Her brown eyes surveyed him. 'So if I wear it, it will send out a subtle romantic message for the press to pick up on. And it could also be seen as a symbol of our countries' friendship.'

'Yes.'

'An excellent prop,' she said coolly. 'For our double act.'

'That is what I thought. I also hoped you would like

them; I did pick them myself.' He hesitated. 'Is something wrong?'

Her expression relaxed. 'Yes…no… It's just hard for me to get my head round a political alliance and fake romance. Our last two "dates" were different, more private—the press were hardly there. Today they will be watching and I don't want them to focus on us rather than on Antonio and Tia's wedding and—'

'Hey. Slow down. There would be public interest in you regardless of our supposed romance. And from what I know of Antonio he will be more than happy for the attention to be diverted from him.'

She inhaled a deep breath and he watched her straighten up. 'You're right.'

'I am. Now let me pin it on,' he said, seeing her small grimace of frustration as she made the attempt.

He headed towards her, aware that he was holding his breath as he carefully pinned the arrangement to her dress, closed his eyes briefly at her proximity, at the sheen of her chestnut hair, the scent of jasmine that tantalised his senses. Felt the tiny shudder that rippled her body and knew she felt it too.

'Shall we go?' Her voice was breathless as she stepped back. 'I said we would meet everyone else in the reception hall, then we can all walk to the chapel together. Antonio is already at the church with Luca. But the rest of the party is here.'

He nodded. 'Tia, her mother Grace, Miles.' The palace secretary who, rumour had it, had fallen hard for Tia's mother, Grace Phillips.

'Yes. Antonio has also invited Gina and Enrico, who are valued staff members, and Tia has asked her bosses from the UK—Lucia and Giovanni. They are lovely.' She glanced at him. 'No doubt you've done your research.'

'Of course. I am here, after all, to represent Aguilarez.' He smiled at her. 'But after the wedding I have our next "date" planned.' And again there was the sense of anticipation. 'We are going on a plane journey so I can show you an aerial view of our countries.'

'Another geographical history lesson?'

'Perhaps. But it is also a venue where the press cannot follow us—where we can be private. So if you are worried about the press now just think about later, when we will escape them.'

'Thank you.' Her smile was genuine and he felt a satisfaction at being responsible for the lightening of tension in her face.

They walked down the marbled hall, then entered the reception room. He smiled at Tia, whom he had briefly met at the presentation ball. She was pretty and right now she glowed with a radiance it was impossible to ignore. She was dressed in a simple floaty, flowered dress, her happiness evident, as was her pride in her pregnancy, shown by the protective hand over the curve of her belly. They were doing the right thing, but again the timing of this could not be worse. More scandal, more rumour and speculation.

But now wasn't the time for this. Now was the time to focus on the small talk, circulate the group, chat to each and every one. Then the walk across the courtyard to the chapel; this was all important as he knew there would be eagle-eyed reporters who would spot the flowers pinned to Gabriella's dress, would also note how close they stood together. Zoom in on the light touch to her arm as he pointed something out. Satisfaction at a job well done inexplicably battled with a frisson of unease, the knowledge that he took way more than a clinical pleasure in her closeness. A strange desire to protect her, mixed with more primeval desire.

It was with relief that he entered the chapel, heard Gabi's intake of breath, and as he looked round he understood why.

'It's spectacular,' she breathed as Tia turned to her mum.

'Mum. It's gorgeous, perfect. Thank you.'

The older woman beamed and suddenly Cesar felt a small wrench—his own mother had never once looked at him like that; no one had. Next to him he felt Gabi tense, knew she was missing her own mother.

'You're welcome, sweetheart. It wasn't just me, though. I couldn't have done it without Miles.'

Next to her the palace secretary smiled self-deprecatingly, but his expression as he stepped closer to Grace Phillips was full of warmth and affection.

'I know that and I truly appreciate all your help, Miles. With everything.'

Tia's mum suffered from chronic fatigue and therefore her words were not mere gloss, they were valid. And that made Miles' love even more worthy. In sickness and in health. Words Cesar planned to say soon enough to the woman standing next to him now. And again the thought made the whole plan more real, more intimate, made moisture sheen his neck.

As he followed Gabriella to the front pew to join Imogen and Queen Maria he glanced to the front where Antonio stood, upright and proud, his entire being focused on his bride. It was not Antonio Valenti's way to show emotion, but the look in his eyes said it all for him. And again Cesar wanted to shift from foot to foot, felt inexplicably small and uncomfortable as the ceremony progressed.

Grace walked her daughter down the aisle and it was impossible now to believe this marriage was one simply of honour, when he saw the way Antonio and Tia looked at each other, the way they exchanged their vows as if each and every word mattered, love abounded in every syllable. He glanced over at Luca and Imogen and saw how they looked at each other, the way they held hands. Then of course there was Tia's mother and the palace secretary. Everywhere he looked there was an aura of love and it was making him distinctly uncomfortable, especially when he thought he detected a hint of wistfulness in Gabriella's smile.

For a moment he wondered if he should have swallowed his scruples and pretended to offer her love, pretended to emulate the sap and pap and sighs and giddiness. But how could that work? How could he build this union on illusion and deceit? How would he be able to sustain the illusion for decades? And he had no wish for or ability to feel real love. After all, if you'd never been shown love how could you feel it? And why give anyone that sort of power over you anyway? So better for them both to go into marriage with the same goals. That was the way to build a working relationship, a lasting partnership.

He returned his focus to the couple at the front. 'You may kiss the bride.'

Antonio leaned forward and, oh, so gently…oh, so filled with awe, as if Tia was the most precious person on this earth, he kissed her.

Around him Cesar could hear the intake of breath,

had no doubt there was a tear in the corner of every eye except his as the swell of classical music touched the air.

The now wed couple walked back down the aisle, their faces lit up, hand in hand, and soon the small congregation followed. 'That was beautiful,' Gabriella said and now he could hear the wistfulness in her voice, knew she didn't mean the actual quality of the dress or the flowers. She meant the love that permeated the occasion. And that he couldn't offer her.

Gabi admired the beautifully decorated room, one of the numerous reception rooms in Casavalle's palace. Once again she marvelled at the décor, given how busy everyone had also been with Christmas preparations.

But it was more than that; Grace Phillips had wanted to make this beautiful and personal for her daughter. And she had definitely succeeded. She must have spent a long time considering how to make this room different from the others and she'd done so through simplicity. The whole room was themed with green and white, the use of delicate white flowers and green foliage almost ethereally pretty. Delicate, fresh, new and somehow joyous.

Gabi looked round at the small gathering of people and swallowed the lump in her throat. Just months ago she hadn't known these people, even that this place existed. Now she had a family. Two brothers, now a sister-in-law and soon she would be an aunt.

Her gaze skimmed to Cesar, who was chatting to Antonio, looking relaxed and smiling. This was a man who wanted her to be a wife, a mother to their children. The idea was so surreal she closed her eyes. Images hit her—of a small dark-haired boy with Cesar's brown eyes.

'You OK?'

She turned to see Imogen, her best friend, now also her brother's fiancée, at her side. 'I'm fine. Are you OK?' She saw Imogen's eyes rest on Tia, one hand on her belly.

'Yes. I am happy for Tia. Truly I am. As for us, Luca says we will figure out a way to have a family if that's what we want. But if it doesn't work out I am more than enough for him.' Imogen's lips curved up into a smile. 'And the wonderful thing is I know he is telling the truth, because I feel the same way.'

There was a twinge of envy again, but alongside it was the knowledge that it would be easier, less pressured for Luca and Imogen now that he wouldn't be ruler. Did Cesar have a point—maybe love was more 'affordable', more likely to thrive if you weren't a ruler.

Imogen's gaze turned to Cesar and then turned back to Gabi. 'Tell me, what is going on there? I saw the speculations in the press, but I've learnt to take them with a hefty pinch of salt.'

'It's complicated.' Gabi could feel her skin heat and her gaze skittered away from Imogen's blue eyes. 'We're just spending some time together.'

Imogen raised her eyebrows. 'So there is some truth to the press reports.'

'No…yes… It's…complicated.'

'Isn't it always with these royal princes?' Imogen grinned and somehow Gabi felt more grounded. After all, Imogen's life had completely changed as well and she had never seen her friend happier. Ah. But Imogen was in love, had a fiancé who adored her. Love was not on the table here and this marriage was a negotiation, each date the equivalent of a meeting shrouded in the illusion of romance.

Before she could say any more Luca and Cesar headed

over to them as Antonio tapped a spoon against his glass and once the hum of conversation subsided, he began to speak.

'As you all know, we decided to keep this ceremony private as both Tia and I wanted something simple with just friends and family. We also decided to forgo the usual formal speeches, but I would like to briefly say how very, very happy I am. Tia means the world to me and I cannot wait to welcome our baby into the world. My only regret is that my father is not here and neither is Tia's brother, Nathan, my best friend, who died in the line of duty. I would have been honoured to have him as my best man.' He raised a glass. 'To those we've lost.'

Gabi lifted her glass, felt the ache of grief for the father she'd never known, the mother she barely remembered except as an elusive voice, a scent, a feeling of arms around her. For her aunt and uncle who had taken her in for duty but had at least not abandoned her, had provided her with a roof, with food and a muted love. For Tia's brother, Nathan, taken at the prime of life. Like Sophia, a life cut tragically short.

Next to her she felt Cesar move closer to her, took comfort from his warmth.

Now Tia stepped forward.

'I miss Nathan more than I can say. But I know exactly what he'd say now. He'd want us to get on and celebrate—appreciate what we have and enjoy the moment. He would be thrilled his best friend was marrying his little sister—and I hope and believe that somehow, somewhere he does know and is giving us his blessing. I would also like to raise my glass now to my mother, who is the most loving, wonderful mother a daughter could ever hope for.'

Once more glasses were raised and soon after that waiters circulated with more canapés; soft music played in the background until it came time for the newly-weds to leave.

Gabi moved forward to hug them. 'I am so happy for you both,' she said.

'Thank you, big sister.'

'It still feels strange to hear you say that.'

'But it is true.' Antonio spoke softly now. 'Gabi. Follow your heart—and do not let anyone pressure you into anything simply to win approval. Things have changed in the Valenti family—duty is important but not at the cost of your happiness.'

Gabi looked at him, wondered if he knew of or suspected Cesar's plans. Perhaps to a royal they were obvious.

'Thank you, and have a wonderful honeymoon.'

Once the happy couple had been waved off Cesar turned to Gabi. 'Shall we go?'

Gabi glanced at him, sure that the man next to her, despite the smile on his lips and all the suave sophistication on show, wanted to shake the dust off his feet and flee the wedding and the company.

'I'll change into something more comfortable and then, yes, I'm ready.'

An hour later Cesar felt a loosening of tension as the Cessna levelled out flying over the verdant ever green beauty of Casavalle. It felt good to be flying high above the cloying confetti-strewn scenes of everlasting love, good to watch Gabriella's expression as she gazed out at the panoramic vista. He wanted to see her smile; knew that the wedding of her brother had brought mixed emotions for her as well as for him. The clusters of deep green trees that dotted the sweep and roll of the snow-dusted hills, the misty, mystical crags and peaks of Aguilarez's mountainous terrain in the distance were more than enough to bring a sense of joy.

For a while they gazed out in a silence only broken by the thrum of the plane's engines. Then she turned to him. 'It's awe-inspiring. It gives you are a real perspective—up here I feel free. Up here if I wanted to I could take off my boots and wriggle my bare toes and no one would tell me I was breaching royal protocol. I could paint my nails bright scarlet.'

'If you'd told me I'd have brought some nail polish.'

Her smile was rueful. 'It's mad, really. I never wanted to paint them scarlet before—it's only now I know I can't.'

Her honesty made him smile in return. 'It will become easier; once your position is more settled, once you get used to all the rules. Then you'll be able to figure out which ones you can break. And you'll learn the all-important royal requirement—how to wear a mask. That helps.'

'Is that what you were doing today?'

The question caught him off guard. 'Meaning?'

'At the wedding I got the impression you were…not uncomfortable, exactly, but that there were other places you'd rather be.' Surprise creased his forehead; how on earth had Gabriella noticed that? Hell, he must be losing his royal diplomatic touch.

'I did find the whole event…a little disconcerting,' he admitted. 'It was hard to believe the evidence of my eyes—to see the Valenti princes behaving in a way that seems so out of character. I knew the court had changed since the King's death but I had not expected to see Antonio, usually so reserved, so outwardly happy. And Luca—he is like a different person with Imogen.'

'And you disapprove.'

'It is not my place to approve or disapprove. It just felt surreal.'

There was a silence. 'I think it took both my brothers by surprise as well. Neither of them intended to fall in love.' She inhaled an audible breath. 'So maybe it could happen to you.'

'No.' The word unequivocal, no quarter or doubt, because he needed her to know that if she married him, she must not harbour delusions of or hope for love. 'That will not happen to me.'

'I don't understand how you can be so sure. As you said yourself, both Luca and Antonio have changed their stance towards love.'

Cesar suspected that Luca and Antonio had been able to show love, feel love because their upbringing, though similarly rooted in duty, had also contained love. True, King Vincenzo had been distant, formal, but he had once known the headiness of love with Gabriella's mother, and had had a good relationship with Queen Maria, even though it had not been a love match. And Queen Maria was a little softer than his own mother, had managed to temper the dictates of duty with some show of feeling towards her children. Perhaps made them believe in the possibility of love, made them foolish enough to open up to the risks. 'But I'm not made that way.'

'So what if *you* too change your mind?' she asked. Then, as if reading his expression, she raised her hand, her face flushing, sheer horror in her eyes. 'Oh, God. I don't mean do you think you will fall in love with me! I meant what if you fall in love with someone else?' Cesar frowned; why would she assume it would be possible for him to fall in love but not with her? 'Like Meribel did.'

'That will not happen.' How to convince her of something he knew with bone-deep certainty? 'Love is not in my vocabulary, not in my dictionary, not in my lexicon. Look at the mess and misery Meribel caused. I know Luca says that she did no wrong, that there is nothing to forgive.' He had been there when Luca had met with his sister, had admired the Valenti prince's eloquence and generosity. 'I know he now believes love trumps duty, that love is a driving force, but, whilst I respect that belief, I am not made that way.'

And so whilst he would not have chosen marriage he had accepted the necessity, and now as he looked at Gabriella it no longer felt like a life sentence—instead it felt like something that could work.

'I truly believe a marriage will work better without love. If Meribel had not met Dana, not fallen pregnant, if the marriage had gone through as planned, then Luca and she could have, would have been happy together.'

'But not as happy as they are now?'

Cesar shrugged, looked out of the window over the vast vista, where green and grey and brown swathed the landscape, the people not even tiny dots. 'Who knows? Love brings its own risks, of loss and grief. It complicates life. If we marry you do not need to fear I will fall in love with anyone.' He could hear the twist of disdain in his voice, hastened to sweeten it. 'I will be a one-woman man. Your man.'

Now awareness shimmered on the air, in echo of the mist outside, and the words felt like a vow. 'I would not be unfaithful—in truth I cannot imagine why I would want to be.'

As he looked at her, saw her gaze out over a country

she had been called upon to rule, he was struck anew by her beauty, and by a visceral desire. Her brown eyes held vulnerability and doubt. 'How can you know that? You are a man who is used to variety—you've been with so many beautiful women. How can you possibly swap from a playboy lifestyle to that of a married man?'

It was a fair question. 'It will not be a problem.'

'They are easy words to say.' She turned to him. 'After all, just a couple of months ago you were involved, had a girlfriend. Amelia. Amelia Scott-Browne.' A ghost of a smile. 'That is common knowledge. She is blonde and beautiful and titled. Yet you've got over her remarkably quickly.'

'I was involved with Amelia but not in any deep sense. We had an agreeable interlude but it was never serious. There was nothing to get over.'

On his part, anyway; yet he had for once completely miscalculated with Amelia and annoyance tugged his gut as their break-up scene flashed into his mind.

'Amelia, we have had a good time, have we not? A lot of fun. But this is a good time for an ending. I must go back to my country and help sort out the problems there.'

'I can wait.'

It was then he'd realised it was going to be difficult.

'Perhaps now is a good time to talk about beginnings, not endings. I want to marry you, Cesar. I love you and I believe you love me.'

Yet her green eyes had held assessment rather than love, or was that wishful thought on his part?

'I would make an excellent ambassadorial wife. No scandal, always the right conversation, and I'm good with people. We could make it work.'

As he'd listened, his brain had whirred. There would

be time for anger at himself later; now he had to figure out damage limitation.

'I am sorry, Amelia, but I will not marry you. There is no question of love. You always knew that.'

'But I thought that when you saw how well I understood your needs you would change your mind. Think of all I can offer you, Cesar.'

'I have no doubt you would make an excellent ambassadorial wife, Amelia. But you know full well that I never had any intention or desire to get married. And if I do it will only be for my country's benefit. That is as it is. But I would like us to part amicably.'

Her green eyes had narrowed in what now seemed obvious calculation. *'It wouldn't be a good time for another scandal to hit your country.'*

So much for love, he thought.

'It wouldn't,' he'd agreed easily. *'But in the long term it would hurt you more than it would me. I still won't marry you, and neither will anyone else in diplomatic circles.'*

Her eyes had widened and her lips had tipped up into a smile that hadn't reached them.

'I understand that, and of course I wouldn't cause a scandal.' Her voice had emerged through gritted teeth. *'I hope that we can remain friends.'*

Thus they had parted, and in truth he had given Amelia very little thought since, his focus on the events here and his impending marriage. And in the past days on Gabriella, who was looking at him with a troubled expression.

'So you could walk away without a regret, just move on?'

'Yes.' There was little point in pretence. 'I have always

been upfront with any woman I have been involved with that I could not offer permanence or anything serious.'

'But what if it had become deeper? What if you had started to have feelings for each other?'

'I don't know,' he said simply. 'But that never did happen.' He'd made sure it couldn't, kept it all light and on a superficial level. 'I always made sure that I kept the relationships short term. Prevention is better than cure, after all.'

'You make it sound like an illness, a disease that you have had to avoid.'

'Not an illness but a foolishness that I have been happy to avoid.' Why risk hurt or being hurt?

'All these women, Lady Amelia, the others, they meant nothing to you?' Now Gabriella looked horrified. 'They were *meaningless*. Yet you think you can sustain a marriage.'

Now irritation sparked in him. 'Those women weren't meaningless. They were all individuals who I liked, who liked me. We spent time together, enjoyable time, had fun. But a future together was never an end game; I made that clear at the outset and they were in complete agreement. With you the rules are different. A future together is the start point.'

'So you're offering me the long-term, marriage-included package deal.'

'Exactly. And I fully intend it to be a sustainable working partnership.' Cesar gave an inward wince. Could he make this any less appealing? Time to lighten it up. 'I also propose that we have some fun and, of course, there is also great sex on offer.'

The change of tactic caused a small gasp to fall from

her lips. 'You can't really expect me to marry you for great sex?'

'Not *just* for great sex. But it would be a bonus.' He wiggled his eyebrows. 'A big bonus.'

Gabriella gave a half-choke of laughter and shook her head. 'I cannot believe you said that.'

Cesar grinned and shrugged. 'Why not? In a negotiation it is important to stress the benefits on offer.' He met her gaze and now his tone was serious. 'I think it does matter. The attraction between us. It is a good thing.' This he knew—he'd seen how lack of passion led to a coldness, an aura of apathy and indifference. A stifled joyless atmosphere.

Gabi looked at him closely, studied his expression and he continued.

'I can offer you liking, respect, support, fidelity, fun, great sex.' He took a deep breath. 'But I can't offer you love. So our marriage won't work if love is what you want.' Cesar felt his jaw tense as he awaited her answer, knew it would essentially be the make or break in the negotiations. Hoped she could see that his offer was a better proposition than the uncertainties and vagaries of love. Watched as she turned away and looked out of the window. Realised he was holding his breath as he waited for her answer.

Gabi looked out over the jagged mountainous magnificence of Aguilarez. To her left the sweeping green of the Casavallian hills. Their countries were separated by a border and so much more, yet shared the same island, both surrounded by deep blue ocean. Sharing a history and two cultures, friendship and enmity that spanned centuries. There would have been alliances through marriage in the past; no doubt she wasn't the first ruler of Casavalle to weigh the necessity of love.

She'd always assumed she'd marry for love but now… the assumption blurred and faded. Liking, support, respect, fidelity, fun and, of course, the great sex. There was so much to be said for that. The idea of someone to help bear the weight and responsibility of ruling, a prince at her side who understood how it all worked. The fact that simply by saying I do she would help unite their two countries—surely the enormity of that outweighed the need for love.

A love she might never find anyway. Especially now. How would she ever know whether someone loved her for herself or for her position? Even if someone did fall for her how could she expect them to give up their life, their privacy and end up in the spotlight with her? If she fell in love with an 'ordinary' person what chance would that love have?

Imogen would say that love conquered all, that it would be possible to work it out. Whilst Cesar would say that that was a risk not worth the taking.

What would her parents have said? Gabi wondered. They had fallen in love, must have married with so much hope and happiness for the future.

Just eighteen months later her mother had fled, convinced that she was the wrong wife for a king, not wanting to bring her child up as a royal. Then, when she'd decided to give love a chance, it was too late. The King had met Maria and Sophia had decided not to complicate his life.

Had she been right or wrong? Gabi didn't know.

She remembered the words of Sophia's letter, every syllable etched on her brain.

Gabriella,
I want you to know that I did love your father, but I do believe he was better without me.

Love complicated his life. I complicated his life—I won't risk that again. Not now he has found a suitable wife who will, I hope, make him happy in a way I never could.

And Vincenzo had been happy; however much he had loved Sophia he hadn't tried to track her down, had granted the divorce without any attempt to persuade her to change her mind. Why? Luca believed it had been pride. But perhaps Vincenzo had known that love and ruling could not go hand in hand. Perhaps he had believed Sophia would be happier without him. She'd never know and that brought sadness with it; this decision was hers alone to make. But perhaps she could learn from the past. Maria and Vincenzo had been happy; they had done right by each other and Casavalle. Perhaps she needed to do the same.

Here above their two countries, where she could almost see the dividing line that separated them, she knew she had to do all in her power to serve her country, to keep the beautiful island below them united and at peace. But doubts still crowded in…this was still her life. Hers and his. And she wouldn't, couldn't rush into a decision here and now.

She turned to face Cesar. 'Love isn't a necessary component in any arrangement we may come to. I am not yet ready to make a final decision, so this isn't anywhere near a done deal, but I'm willing to go on to the next stage of negotiations.'

Relief touched his face as his shoulders relaxed and

then he smiled. 'That sounds good to me. I believe we can build a happy marriage, based on attraction, trust, shared beliefs and a desire to do the right thing for our countries. It is now my job to persuade you of that.'

His job. Negotiations. It was now his remit to bring negotiations to a close and suddenly a sheen of sadness touched her thoughts, an idea that this wasn't how it was supposed to be. But it was as it was. She wasn't Gabi Ross book-store owner any more—she was a princess, soon to be Queen, and she had to think differently.

'So we will continue to date,' Cesar continued, 'and I will continue to liaise with Miles over the publicity angles.'

Cesar and Miles did their job all too well, as it turned out. Because over the next few days, to Gabi's astonishment and discomfort, the media, expertly encouraged by Cesar and Miles, went nuts for the romance angle. A number of dates and occasions were agreed, and through necessity, given the number of royal engagements in her diary, Cesar simply came with her.

And… Gabi no longer knew how she felt. About anything. Could no longer distinguish between reality and illusion. All she did know was his proximity messed with her head and made the public engagements paradoxically both harder and easier.

Harder because she was on edge, her body preternaturally aware of him at all times, ever conscious that she had to act like a woman falling in love. Easier because with Cesar at her side she felt less alone; less daunted by the fear of making a mistake.

Thank goodness she and Imogen had decided to sneak

a little girl time this evening; as if on cue there was a knock on the door. 'Come in.'

Imogen entered and as always Gabi felt a rush of gratitude that she hadn't lost her friend, that Imogen had come with her on this royal journey.

Imogen smiled widely at her. 'Now, let's not waste time.' She sat down on the armchair in front of the fire, tucked her legs under her and accepted the glass of red wine Gabi handed her with a smile and a murmur of thanks. 'Tell me what is happening with Cesar.'

'I don't know,' seemed the safest way forward. Especially as it also had the benefit of being truthful.

'Do you like him?'

'Yes…' Hearing the doubt in her own voice, she shrugged. 'I do like him, but I still don't feel as if I know him. We see each other in public, we're on show. Sometimes I wonder if Cesar is always on show. Always diplomatic, a smile and the right word always to hand.'

'I think that is how the princes here are, be they Casavallian or Aguilarean. They mask their emotions; Cesar perhaps even more so than Luca and Antonio. According to Luca, Cesar's parents were even more distant than Vincenzo and Maria. But I think the real Cesar is worth knowing. Luca likes him.'

'He's easy to like,' Gabi said, heard the slight undertone of bitterness. 'He has that natural royal charm that I lack. I'm so…rough around the edges. And the press, the publicity—I find it so hard to deal with. It feels like everyone is waiting for me to do something wrong and sometimes whatever I do is wrong. So, I can't win.'

Imogen leant forward, her blue eyes full of both sympathy and empathy. 'It is such early days. The princes have had their whole lifetime in the spotlight; they've learnt how to handle it. As will you. And if anyone can help with that, Cesar can.'

'Sometimes I wonder whether I should simply have stayed home, in Crystal Lake.'

Her friend's forehead creased in a frown of concern. 'You don't really mean that, do you?'

'No. I guess not. Sometimes, though, it all feels a bit much.'

'Perhaps you should think about making the final cut and sell the book store.'

'Sell it?' Panic flared. Her book store was her safety net; her back-up plan. The safe haven she still fantasised about a return to.

'Yes. Give someone else the opportunity you thrived on. To make it theirs. Because, in truth, are you really going to go back?'

Gabi shook her head. 'I don't know, Imogen. It could be that in the end I do stand aside, if the people truly revolt. Then Luca will end up on the throne.'

Imogen shook her head. 'That won't happen. Luca believes it is yours by right and he will do all he can to ensure you become Queen. In fact, there is an idea I would like to talk to you about.'

'What idea?'

'Luca feels that his presence here is harming you—it is a reminder to people that he was once heir. But he still wants to show his support to you and Casavalle. He wondered if you would consider him taking on an ambassadorial role abroad for a while.'

'When?' Gabi struggled to keep her voice steady; the idea of losing her brother and her best friend caused tears to threaten but she knew she had to consider this as a ruler.

'Soon. The plan is to go away for a while now, perhaps get it all set up, and then return for your coronation.'

'You don't need my permission; I want you and Luca to be happy so, of course, if this is what he wants, I agree.' And it was the right path—after all, Imogen had always wanted to travel and this would give Luca a chance to experience a whole new life. But the sadness persisted and for some reason an image of Cesar came to mind. A realisation that if she didn't marry him, he too would leave. Return to his ambassadorial duties. And she wasn't sure she wanted him to go. She raised her wine glass. 'To new beginnings,' she stated.

'And old friendships,' Imogen said.

And the two best friends clinked glasses.

Cesar tried to focus on the report; try as he might he kept seeing Gabi's face instead of the diplomatic words on the paper. A face that looked a little pinched and a little shadowed under the expert make-up. She was playing her part but he could sense her tension, how much it cost her to do so.

Being royal was tough, and she would have to learn how to carry the mantle but, dear Lord, her vulnerability didn't sit well with him; he didn't like to see the doubts in those beautiful brown eyes and didn't like the knowledge he was responsible for some of them.

He looked up at the knock on the door and blinked as Luca Valenti walked in, his face dark. 'What exactly are you playing at, Cesar? With my sister?'

Cesar raised his eyebrows. 'Hello to you too, Luca.' He and Luca got on, but right now Luca was clearly in protective brother mode and Cesar didn't blame him.

Perhaps if he, Cesar, had been a better brother to Meribel, much scandal could have been averted.

'Spare the diplomatic words, Cesar. You will not charm your way out of this one.'

'I do not wish to charm my way out of anything. Sit down. Tell me the problem.'

'What are your plans for Gabi?'

'That is private between Gabi and myself.'

'I do not want to see my sister hurt.'

'I would never hurt Gabriella. For that you have my word. But I will not discuss our relationship with you.'

'I understand that and I believe that you do not intend to hurt Gabi. But please remember that I did not intend to hurt Meribel.' Luca's voice was fierce with truth. 'I would have sworn the same to you.'

'Point taken and understood and I repeat: I will not hurt Gabriella.'

'Then why does she look so tired? She will not talk to either myself or Imogen about it and my mother simply tells me to leave be. That Gabriella is a grown woman.'

'Your mother is a wise woman.' Though Luca was right, Gabriella did look tired and Cesar needed to do something about it. He sat back and for a moment the two men regarded each other. Then Cesar repeated. 'I will not hurt her.' After all, he couldn't; that was the beauty of not bringing love into the mix. Because where there was no love, there could be no hurt.

Cesar watched as Luca considered and then he nodded. 'You will answer to me if you do.'

'Understood. Now relax, have a beer. Tell me your plans.'

And so the two men settled down to talk.

CHAPTER NINE

THE NEXT MORNING Cesar entered the Casavallian palace—at Gabriella and Queen Maria's behest he now had the run of the grounds and was an accepted presence. But today was the first time he had entered the royal kitchens and there was a buzz of interest at his appearance.

The head chef approached and Cesar smiled at the man known only as Marcello, a chef famed throughout the land, rivalled only by the royal chef Davina of Aguilarez.

'Good morning, Marcello.'

'Your Royal Highness. How may I be of help?'

'First can I congratulate you on your *pasta con le sarde* at the ambassadorial lunch? It was perfect.'

The chef beamed at him.

'Next I was wondering if I could take Princess Gabriella's trolley to her this morning.'

'Of course. It is nearly ready. The papers have been delivered.'

'But first I would like to make a small adjustment. I know she usually has tea but today I would like to make her something different. But I need your help.'

Ten minutes later, Cesar reached the library, knocked and entered.

‘Thank you, Bened—’ Gabi broke off as she saw who had entered, and a smile lit her face, a smile she quickly suppressed.

‘Oh. I wasn’t expecting you.’

‘But you are pleased to see me.’ His smile held satisfaction and her eyes narrowed, though whether in annoyance with herself or him he wasn’t sure. ‘I am pleased to see you too,’ he offered as he pushed the trolley closer to where she was curled up in an armchair. ‘And I have brought you this.’

‘What is it?’

She eyed the tall mug and turned to him with a question in her eyes.

‘It is a double-double,’ he explained. He had done some research and, according to Luca, both Imogen and Gabriella loved this type of coffee, made with cream and sugar at a well-known Canadian outlet. ‘As near to authentic as possible, though Marcello has given it the Marcello touch.’

Gabi blinked, raised a hand to her eye and then picked up the mug. ‘Thank you. That is really thoughtful.’ Another blink. ‘Enough to make me cry.’ But then a look of weariness touched her eyes and she glanced at the door. ‘Will I need to pose for the press over this romantic gesture?’

‘No.’ In truth that hadn’t even occurred to him; the realisation pinged a small message of worry before he dismissed it. A cup of coffee was hardly newsworthy. ‘I just wanted to cheer you up.’

But he realised that she was no longer listening. Instead her eyes were riveted to the pile of newspapers on the trolley.

Reaching out, she picked up the topmost one. 'What the…?'

Cesar watched as she read, saw the colour leech from her face, and then she looked up and he saw anger sparkle in her brown eyes.

'Show me.' He held out a hand and she put the paper in it, keeping her eyes on him as he scanned the article.

Wake up and smell the roses! And I don't mean a romantic bouquet!

In the past week speculation and rumour has been rife about the 'budding' romance—see what I did there?—between Princess Gabriella of Casavalle and Prince Cesar of Aguilarez. And romance does seem to be blooming—which has made everyone forget that in mere weeks Princess Gabriella plans to take the throne of Casavalle.

Now, some may claim she is an impostor—but this is technically untrue. DNA and legal proof show that she is indeed the late King Vincenzo's rightful heir. Morally speaking, though...it is a different matter.

Let's look at the facts.

Fact: Princess Gabriella's mother, Sophia Ross, left King Vincenzo whilst she was pregnant, without telling him of the pregnancy—if we're speaking of morality here, this is not moral.

Fact: The divorce was apparently requested very soon after her flight—King Vincenzo still didn't know of the pregnancy.

Fact: King Vincenzo granted the divorce just weeks after the birth of Gabriella, a child he didn't know about.

Fact: If he had known he would have granted the divorce as soon as it was requested and Gabriella would not be his heir.

Even putting aside these facts as easily as Prince Luca seems to have put aside his duties and the throne, we have to question whether Gabriella Ross is fit to be Queen.

This is a woman with zero training in royal duties, who is the daughter of a woman who had no respect for or understanding of royalty.

How can Gabriella be Queen? What if she follows in her mother's footsteps and does a runner when it all becomes too much...? As, of course, it will. Especially if this romance withers and dies.

So, wake up, Gabriella. Smell the Casavallian roses and then go home.

To Canada.

Cesar read to the end and then looked across to where Gabi now paced the library floor, coffee in hand. 'I wouldn't take it too personally.'

'How can I not take that personally? She is saying I'm not up to the job and she has twisted the facts to make my mother sound like a terrible irresponsible person and she wasn't. I can't let her get away with it.'

'There is nothing you can do. Responding to these articles simply makes it worse. You must read and move on.'

'I can't.' There was a crack in her voice and he rose to his feet, headed towards her, took her hands in his and for the first time ever, he felt an urge to call out a journalist, to make her think about the effect of her words.

'I hate that they are speaking about my mother with so little sympathy. I hate that they are judging me.'

'This article is one woman's interpretation. She did not know your mother. She does not know you.' His eyes searched hers for clues. 'The past months there have been so many articles, so many stupid assertions, ill-conceived, ill-informed opinions in the press. You have ignored them all.' But perhaps each one had taken its toll, seeped its insidious poison into a woman who was not used to the horrific glare or the ravenous insatiability of public interest.

She inhaled a deep audible breath and straightened her shoulders. 'You're right. Of course, I need to ignore it.'

But he could still see the hurt in her eyes, sense the effort it had taken to say the words. There was nothing he could do about that; it simply came with the territory and Gabriella would learn to deflect the negativity with time. So he should let it be now…but he couldn't. Because he suspected there was more to it than she was admitting, because he wanted to see the defeated look in her eyes vanish. 'Or you can tell me why this article has hit such a nerve.'

'I…'

He tightened his hands round hers. 'Maybe I can help.'

'I don't think you can. Have you ever felt that you can't do something? Felt helpless, unsure?'

He recalled the helplessness that bombarded his senses when he saw first-hand the tragedies and the poverty, the senseless violence and the unrest in the world. The frustration he felt when he realised that his parents could only see what was good for Aguilarez, didn't particularly care about the 'bigger picture' he'd tried to explain. When they had vetoed many of his ideas for their country to be more of a force for good.

'Yes,' he said, now. 'I have. Truly I have.'

For a long moment she studied his face, perhaps read the sincerity there.

'Is that how you feel now?' he asked.

'Yes. It is. What if she is right?' Her voice was small now, tired, almost defeated. 'Everything she says is true. I have no training, no innate understanding of how royalty works. At my presentation ball I know I shocked at least four important personages; every day there is an article that snips or snipes at me. For being too direct. Too Canadian. For not grasping protocol. For usurping my brother's throne. For being my mother's daughter. So what if that article is right? Maybe morally I should stand aside.'

'We discussed this—you seemed sure that you had made the right decision, that your brothers and the Queen wished for you to rule.'

'They do, because they believe that it is technically and morally the right choice, the honourable choice. But that doesn't mean I can do it. And I know that if I stood aside Luca would be an incredible ruler. Perhaps I made the wrong choice, for the wrong reasons. I was so happy to have a family. Perhaps it clouded my judgement.'

Still holding her hands, he tugged gently and led her to an opulent sofa, urged her to sit and sat next to her, twisted his body so he could see her face. Momentarily distracted by the closeness of her, that vanilla scent, the amber flecks in her brown eyes, he blinked to focus himself. 'If Luca thought you could not rule, if he thought you would be bad for Casavalle, he would not have relinquished his claim.'

'But what if he is wrong? What if he is seeing what he wants to see?' The anguish in her voice tore at his chest and for the first time he truly began to understand the enormity of what had happened to her. The extent of the upheaval, the impact on her life.

'I absolutely believe you can do this. In fact I believe you are exactly what Casavalle needs. A breath of fresh air, someone who has not been brought up with all our stuffy rules and traditions. Perhaps you can instil some new traditions of your own.'

'Really?' Her eyes lit up slightly with a sparkle of hope.

'Really. But it has to be what you want to do. This is a job for life, a role that requires wholehearted commitment to your country and its people.'

'I know.' She closed her eyes, then opened them again. 'I'm sorry, Cesar. I didn't mean to fly into such a fuss.' She hesitated. 'I am just a bit emotional. Imogen told me yesterday that she and Luca are leaving Casavalle.'

Cesar nodded. 'I have spoken with Luca and believe he would make an excellent advocate for you and your country.'

'I know. But…'

'But you will lose your brother and your best friend.' Cesar could see the pain in her eyes, knew too that she wouldn't have shown it to either Luca or Imogen.

'Yes.' Now she smiled, a smile that tugged at his heart strings with its bravery. 'I am pleased for them but it has made me feel very alone.'

'You don't have to be alone,' he said, the words falling from his lips instinctively, imbued with an emotional depth and a meaning that caused caution to rear its head. This was not about emotions; this was about practicality.

She didn't need to be alone; they could work together. He could offer the practical support that she needed. 'You could marry me.' Seeing her brown eyes meet his in question, he hurried on. 'I am not trying to take advantage of a moment of weakness.'

'Is that what you think this is? A moment of weakness?' Now anger sparked her eyes and voice; she pulled her hands away and rose to her feet.

The question stopped him in his tracks. Did he believe that—that to show emotion was weakness? It was a question he wasn't sure he wanted to analyse. 'That came out wrong. I simply wanted to say that as your husband I would be able to offer you support, make the task of ruling less lonely.' The words stilted and he saw her expression change, close down to cool neutrality.

'I'll bear it in mind.' Her tone was even. 'And I'm sorry for letting emotion get the better of me. It's foolish. I know it is better for Luca and Imogen to go. Just as I know whatever I do the press will find some angle to pillory me for. I guess I need to grow up and figure out how to be royal.'

Again Cesar knew he should applaud the words, laud the mask he could see her layer on. Yet instead he felt like a first-class horse's backside. Felt he'd lost something that he wanted back.

Stupid.

He needed to think practically—Gabriella was a woman on the edge and that was not good when right now her every action would be under scrutiny, when more articles were bound to spew forth the closer to her coronation it got. A plan began to form in the recesses of his mind.

CHAPTER TEN

GABI RESISTED THE urge to yawn, managed to swallow down the tiredness, focused on keeping her eyes wide open and an expression of interest on her face. In normal circumstances she would be interested; the official was explaining the tax system in Casavalle and how it impacted on the people. Whilst tax wasn't exactly her hobby horse, she did want to get her head around the economics of normal people's normal lives in this country, versus what she had known back home. Wanted a good standard of living for everyone.

But today it all felt too much. She was surrounded by officials and courtiers and staff and even family and yet she felt more alone than ever. A loneliness she must conceal. No more moments of weakness. Instead she forced her tired brain to focus. Smiled at the official. 'I truly appreciate your time and your patience. I will read all these documents and I am sure I will come back to you with further questions.'

The grey-haired man positively beamed at her. 'Thank you, ma'am, for listening so attentively and I look forward to further discussions.'

Once the man had left, Gabi yawned discreetly, stretched and tried to recall what the next official engagement was. She turned to face the door at the sound of the turn of the handle, royal smile back in place.

'Cesar?' Her heart gave a little hop, skip and jump—it clearly hadn't caught up with the fact that this man would deem such a reaction a *physical* weakness, no doubt. She frowned. Surely she wasn't supposed to see him until an official dinner the following evening.

'Surprise,' he said.

Gabi had no idea where he was going with this so contented herself with silence.

'I'm whisking you away,' he announced.

Huh? 'I don't understand.'

He entered the room and stood in front of her. 'I have cleared your schedule and I am taking you away from it all,' he announced with a theatrical flourish. 'On a Christmas break. It is a week until Christmas. I would like you to visit my country and see some of the Christmas traditions of Aguilarez. You need a break. Some time out.'

'But…'

'No buts. I have cleared it all with the Queen.'

'But… I haven't even packed.'

'All sorted. We are leaving now.' Gabi tried to get her brain to assess the situation but it was simply too tiring. The idea of a break made her whole body tingle with relief. The idea of a break with Cesar made her whole body tingle. Full stop.

'Where are we going?'

'To a royal residence in Aguilarez. The car's waiting outside.'

Gabi felt a giddy sense of anticipation as she rose to her feet; this was really happening. 'There are also photographers waiting outside,' Cesar said and a tiny dart of disappointment quivered. Of course this was a publicity stunt, part of the romance illusion. No doubt Cesar had upped his game in response to the article of the previous day and she should be grateful for that. Or perhaps her moment of weakness had made him think it was expedient to whisk her away before she actually ran away. As her mother had.

As if he read her mind his lips twisted in a grimace. 'I have done a deal with them. In return for a few smiles now and the promise of a future story they will leave us be for a few days. I can't guarantee utter press blackout but it will be easier.'

'Thank you.' God, how she wished she could read his mind, see underneath the diplomacy. Figure out if all of this was a cool, calculated attempt to persuade her to marry him or whether he cared. *Whoa. Careful, Gabi.* It was a pointless question and she shouldn't care about the answer. Caring didn't come into it, other than the basic respect and liking that Cesar had offered her.

She followed him to the car, held his hand and smiled with what she hoped was a regal yet love-dazed expression on her face.

Once the vehicle had set off at a smooth glide, Cesar glanced at her and said, 'Why don't you take the opportunity to sleep?'

The idea was tempting but she knew she wouldn't be able to do it—would be too worried she might snore or drool or say something mad in her sleep. Especially if Cesar Asturias should venture into her dreams. She glanced at his handsome face, the cool features, and decided instead to take this opportunity to try and find out something about him. Maybe even get some insight into who this man was. She'd caught glimpses but it was as if he guarded himself so well he had forgotten who he was.

'I'm fine but I'd like to use this break to get to know each other better, so maybe we should start now. Perhaps you could tell me a bit about your job, about your life these past years.'

His stance was relaxed but she sensed a hint of wariness. 'I'm an ambassador. I promote Aguilarez. I make sure we play our part on the world stage. We may be small but we are still significant. Both our countries are. Our tourist trade is booming. We also export wines and olives and, of course, people are always interested in our royal family.'

'Do you enjoy it? That first night you said that sometime it chafes to be what you have been preordained to be.'

'I should not have said that. My job is one that I enjoy and am good at. It also brings all the perks of an enjoyable lifestyle.'

Gabi frowned, sensed that what he said was true but that there was another stratum beneath the words. 'There's something you aren't telling me.'

Cesar looked as though he sincerely wished she had opted to take a nap. 'Not at all,' he said lightly. 'It's a great job, hard work but fun as well. Of course, there are some frustrations.'

'Such as.'

'Being royal has its disadvantages. People are always more interested in my latest relationship or which star-studded party I may attend next, or what my family is up to. There is also the fact that I have to always remember I am a mouthpiece for the Asturias clan. But these are simply minor inconveniences.'

No. It was more than that—she wasn't sure how she knew, but she did. Could detect a bitter tinge to the flavour of the words. She regarded him thoughtfully. 'More interested in your relationships than in what? And does that mean that sometimes you have different views from your family?'

'I didn't say that. I think you may be overanalysing here.'

'That's a polite way to tell me to mind my own beeswax.' But suddenly she didn't want to as frustration and a dollop of anger hit her. 'Fine, but over these past days I have talked to you. About topics I care about. You have given me nothing but facts; I have no idea what you care about. Except your duty to your country.'

'Maybe there is nothing else.'

'I don't believe that and I need to know something more...personal about you. How can I contemplate marriage to someone who sees life through a filter of detachment?'

There was a silence.

Then he shrugged. 'OK. You were right. There are times when I would like to speak out about things I do care about, that aren't connected to Aguilarez. About humanitarian aid, about trying to make the world a better place, not just privileged countries like mine. I have travelled in my ambassadorial duties to places where I have cried at the plight of children and families. Seen sights I would not have believed possible in war-torn countries... And, yes, I would like my country to do more, give more humanitarian aid. I would like to be deployed more to those countries, perhaps in a different capacity. But my father decided I would serve Aguilarez better in my current role.'

He said the words with almost clinical dispassion and she sensed he hadn't wanted to say them at all. Yet it didn't take away from the undercurrent of sincere, palpable feeling underneath the layer of civility and she wondered exactly how bitter his disappointment had been.

'That must have been hard—it sounds as though it meant a lot to you.'

'It did. But I see my father's viewpoint and I see little point in defiance—that would not help my cause. Instead I did persuade him to agree to some increased foreign aid, and I do what I can in a different way. I influence decisions and sometimes I go on anonymous trips funded by myself in an unofficial capacity.'

Gabi felt a warmth swell over her, and her mind whirled with the information. It hadn't occurred to her that Cesar would have a charitable side, such a serious side, and there was no doubt that he was serious. There was a set to his lips she hadn't seen before and it gave her a sudden thrill to know that he had such a depth to his character.

But she could also tell he regretted the confidence, had given more than he'd meant.

'Not many people are aware of what I have told you and I would appreciate it if it goes no further.'

'Of course. Thank you for telling me.'

'Also—' he frowned now '—please do not get this out of perspective. I have no complaints. My role is Aguilarez ambassador, not a humanitarian. I do what I can but it is not a life mission for me.'

Gabriella frowned, could almost hear the sound of the diplomatic back-pedalling. Wondered if in truth he preferred to keep that caring side of himself locked down and hidden away even from himself. Whatever it was she smiled now, reached across and brushed a kiss on his cheek. 'I think the fact that you care is incredible, something to be proud of.'

Big mistake. Not the words but the action. The feel of his skin against her lips, the closeness of him, the desire to 'miss' her aim and target his lips nigh on impossible to resist. But somehow resist it she did. Scooted across the seat and looked out of the window, realised the car had started a steep ascent up a rocky, mountainous path.

'Nearly there,' Cesar stated with a slightly over-the-top breeziness and she figured he would be as relieved as she was to arrive. 'Keep looking. That way you get the full effect.'

The car continued to climb, curved round a bend in the narrow road and Gabi gave a gasp as their destination appeared. The mini castle was incredible; it loomed into view with a magnificent beauty. It looked as though it had been carved into the mountain, a fortress-like creation that called to mind the force of nature combined with the power of man.

'It's like a smaller version of the main palace,' Cesar said.

As the car drew up Gabi's eyes widened at the sight of the gardens. Exotic green shrubs, immense trees weighted with a layer of snow and ornate gilded water fountains that rocketed streams of water into the air where they glistened in the late morning sun. Made the whole into a magical winter's spectacle.

The driver opened the door and she climbed out with a murmur of, 'Thank You, Lorenzo.' Then followed Cesar through the arched splendour of the door and into a cavernous hallway, the stone walls hung with tapestries that glowed with a lustre that made the scenes seem to come alive as she studied them. Battles, everyday life, people and actions from centuries before.

Next he led her into a huge oak-panelled room. A roaring fire sent out swathes of welcome heat; the flames flickered and danced in a glow of red and orange and yellow. The whole scene was so welcoming and cosy her whole being basked in the warmth of it all.

There was a huge sofa scattered with cushions; a fluffy rug of enormous proportions covered the hearth. The whole room was redolent of polished woods and varnished history to be seen in the portraits and landscapes on the walls, and she loved it. Then she saw a basket of books by the sofa, some from her keeper shelf, others brand new.

She turned to Cesar in question.

'I brought them from the place and some new ones Imogen said you may like. I thought maybe what you'd like is some time to curl up by a fire and read.'

Gabi turned to him, felt a sudden glisten of tears.

'How did you know that?'

'Lucky guess.' Only it wasn't. It was because he'd listened to her over the past days, really listened. And now her gaze went to the tree in the corner—a Christmas tree, huge, luxuriant, and as yet undecorated.

Cesar looked a little embarrassed. 'This is just an idea. You said that you missed decorating a tree this year so I thought, well, maybe we could decorate this one. Obviously you don't have to.'

'I'd love to.' Gabi eyed the tree. 'But we'll need a lot of decorations.'

'I thought we could go and buy some. The nearest town has a Christmas market. If we go this afternoon and we wrap up so we look inconspicuous I doubt anyone will recognise us. Because no one will have figured out where we are yet. We have the place to ourselves. My housekeeper will pop in with supplies but otherwise we are going to fend for ourselves.'

Without the trappings of royalty, not even a skeleton staff. Just them. Her heart skipped a little. 'Then let's go. Show me to my room and I will get myself disguised in the twinkle of an eye.'

'Hold on. To complete the disguise.'

She grinned as she saw what he held out. A pot of bright red nail polish. 'Perfect. I'll see if I can think of any more royal protocols to break.'

To her own surprise her tiredness had melted away, replaced by an anticipatory buzz of…happiness. *Careful, Gabi.* No, for this break she didn't want to be careful. It was OK to be happy—for a few days she would be free of royal rules and duties. She wanted, needed, to make the most of it.

Cesar glanced down at Gabi as they walked through the medieval town, over the ancient cobbled streets, thronged now with Christmas crowds. Chatter and laughter hummed on the air, redolent with the scent of spiced wine and Christmas delicacies.

'This is magical,' Gabi breathed, gesturing upwards at the glittering, sparkling illumination of the Christmas lights that looped and twinkled overhead in an array of stars. A reflection of the sky itself.

'Yes,' he agreed, and realised he didn't mean the setting, beautiful though it was. He meant her—she looked relaxed and happy, her lips curved up in a generous smile, her eyes sparkling as she enjoyed the atmosphere and bit into the enormous pretzel he'd bought for her.

The fluffy red hood completely hid her chestnut hair and also shielded her face from passers-by, and, dressed simply, she blended into the crowds. Cesar wore a woollen hat and had also wrapped a scarf round the lower half of his face. They looked, in fact, like any other couple out to do some Christmas shopping and the security detail were discreet enough to be virtually indistinguishable from the crowds.

They approached the cluster of stalls that made up the market, each one displaying goods and wares that caught the senses. Bright woollen garments, delicacies and pastries, *glühwein* and marshmallows and hot chocolate. And Christmas decorations.

Gabi lingered over the choice and Cesar took the chance to watch her, the care with which she examined each trinket, the concentration on her face as she debated colour schemes. 'We could go for a blaze of colour or we could keep it simple. What do you think?'

'I really don't mind. What do you normally do?'

'Normally I try to do a theme around a book. Christmas books mostly, though I did do a wizard theme one year.'

'That sounds hard.'

'It was a bit. But I enjoyed it—I really did. It was worth it to see the kids' faces when they came in. And I'd always hang little wrapped chocolates on there as well. Because kids deserve to have a magical Christmas.' Her eyes fell on a young couple with a family nearby, absorbed in the study of a nativity scene. 'Like them. You can see the love there and the magic of Christmas.' The dark-haired woman leant down to listen to what her daughter said, dropped a kiss on her head, and the father lifted his son up to show the toddler something and beamed as the little boy pointed in excitement..

Seeing the sadness in her eyes, Cesar knew that she was thinking of the loss of her mother. 'And adults deserve the same. So this next two days will be devoted to Christmas magic.'

The sadness vanished and there was her beautiful smile again. 'Then let's make the tree a magical one. We'll go for white and gold and make it the kind of tree that you'd find in a fairy tale. Let's go and decorate.'

CHAPTER ELEVEN

'RIGHT,' SAID GABRIELLA. 'We need a plan. The lights have to go on first, then the tinsel.'

'I am completely in your hands,' Cesar said, and revelled in the blush that touched her cheeks. A satisfaction that morphed into a desire to kiss her, an urge that was hard to deny. If she married him, of course, then they would be able to kiss whenever they wanted, the idea both scary and wonderful. Scary enough to cause him to focus on winding the lights around the tree.

The next hour was…fun, he realised when, breathlessly, they surveyed the end result of their efforts. The tree swirled with magic, illuminated by the white lights that twinkled and glinted, the gold ornaments lit by the flames of the fire. The whole creation was topped by a star of multi-faceted crystalline beauty.

'One last thing,' he said.

Gabi turned to him in question and then her face broke into a smile as he pulled a box out of one of the shopping bags.

'Chocolates,' he explained. 'To hang on the tree. For us.' He glanced at the tree slightly guiltily. 'As long as it doesn't spoil the overall pattern.'

'Chocolate can never spoil anything. Thank you. This

was really thoughtful.' For a second he held his breath. Half hoping, half terrified that she would kiss him again. His cheek still tingled from the butterfly kiss she'd given him in the car.

She stepped forward and then back again as if common sense had overcome desire; perhaps she too had the same breathless, heady sense of nerves.

'You're welcome.' He gestured to the sofa. 'Come and sit down and survey the splendour of our creation and I'll go get us some hot chocolate.'

Gabi stared into the flames, watched as they leapt and danced to the crackle of the logs. For the first time in such a long time she felt relaxed…normal, and it was wonderful. And all thanks to Cesar. She looked up as he re-entered the lounge, bearing two large steaming mugs.

'That smells divine.'

'I've put in a secret ingredient—a shot of rum.'

He sat next to her and the reassuring bulk of his body felt warm and cosy and intimate as they both watched the twinkle of the Christmas lights on the tree.

'Thank you. It was lovely to decorate a tree with someone again.'

'You said you used to decorate with your aunt?'

'Yes. The first Christmas after my mom died Aunt Bea took me to buy tree decorations. I was only four but the memory is really clear. I think it was the first time Aunt Bea had bought so many decorations. To be honest I don't think they bothered with a tree before they took me in. After that we used the same decorations every year—even when they got tatty, I insisted. In my head they were somehow traditional, connected with my mother and family.' Gabi swallowed a sudden lump in her throat; decorating the tree had been a time when she had felt truly close to her aunt. She could still remember the way the elderly woman had followed the ritual every year, pushing her glasses up her nose every time she stood back to check on their progress. 'After they died, I couldn't bring myself to do it any more. I decorated the tree in the book store instead.'

'You must have missed them very much.'

'I did—I still do. Right after they died I felt so… alone in the world. Orphaned all over again. I don't really remember much of my mother, but I do remember a warmth, a sense of safety and love that I associate with her. And I also remember the utter confusion, the bewilderment I felt when she died. I was too little to comprehend what it meant. But Aunt Bea and Uncle Peter were there for me.' At such a personal cost. 'And I will always be grateful for that. It's good to talk about them.' Something she seldom had the opportunity to do.

'Tell me about them.'

Gabi hesitated—wondered if the crackle of the flames, the absolute marvel of being alone with no staff, no schedule, no expectations, no publicity had gone to her head. Or was it the genuine interest in Cesar's eyes. Who knew? But she wanted to share some of her life with him.

'Uncle Peter was my mother's older brother. Half-brother, in fact, and he was much older than her. Nearly thirty years; they weren't close at all. He was already in his late fifties when my mother left Casavalle, and he was in his sixties when she died. He and my Aunt Bea had no children through choice. I think I…bewildered them.' She was tempted to confide it all—that overheard conversation, the fact that they had given up their dreams for her, but she didn't. Knew her aunt and uncle had never wanted her to know, wary too that Cesar might see the revelation and its impact on her as an emotional moment of weakness. 'But they did their best.' Just as Cesar had promised to do as a father. 'They bought the book store, started a whole new career, made sure I got a good education, taught me so much. And I will always be grateful for that.'

'They sound like good people,' he said softly. 'The times you have described with them are good memories. They spent time with you, you cooked together, walked together, gave each other gifts, decorated a tree together...they encouraged your love of books.'

Now she could see the shadowed pain in his eyes, knew he was remembering his own childhood where his own parents had spent minimal personal time with him.

Her heart bled for the young Cesar, bred through duty not love, and then treated as a royal pawn rather than a little boy, and she shifted towards him. Said nothing because she sensed sympathy or pity would be anathema to him, hoped that somehow her closeness would convey understanding.

They sat like that for a timeless moment, and then he turned and smiled at her. 'I wish I could have met your aunt and uncle. Thank you for sharing your memories.' He rose to his feet. 'Now I think it's time for dinner. Wait here and I will get it.'

'We're going to eat here?'

'Yes.' His expression looked unsure. 'Unless you'd prefer to sit at a table. I thought you'd appreciate as much informality as possible.'

Again a funny warmth touched her. Again she wished she knew if this was a ploy or real. Or whether it actually mattered.

* * *

Ten minutes later Cesar re-entered the lounge, pushing a trolley forward. Two plates covered with silver-domed cloches. 'Here we are,' he announced as he approached the sofa and removed the covers with a flourish.

Gabi broke into a delighted peal of laughter. 'Pizza!' she exclaimed.

'But not any old pizza. This is Aguilarean pizza. The base is sourdough and the olives are home grown and the tomato sauce is a state secret. Truly, you will never have eaten pizza like this.' He handed her her plate, picked up his own and sat down next to her.

Gabi gave a small exhalation of pure satisfaction. 'No cutlery in sight,' she murmured. 'Perfect. Finger food I can manage.' She took her first bite, closed her eyes in appreciation and Cesar felt his own lips curve into a smile even as desire tugged inside him. 'This is incredible. Why haven't I tried this before?'

'I don't know. You could go and request pizza from the Casavallian kitchens, but it wouldn't be as good. Or better yet go in person and ask.'

'I wouldn't dare!' Gabi looked horrified. 'They are so busy and they terrify me. Plus I'm not sure Maria would like it.'

'Maria is a wonderful woman and an excellent queen, but she is a different person from you. You need to do things your way.'

Gabi bit her lip. 'It's not that easy. I have so much to learn; and everyone else knows more than I do about everything.' She picked up another slice of pizza. 'I know that's a bit sweeping but it's true.'

'No. It isn't. I can think of something you know more about.'

'You can?'

'Yes. Books.'

'Right… But I'm not sure that's a great help to ruling.'

'Actually I disagree. You don't just care about books. You told me that you believe everyone should read. That sounds more like a policy in the making than a hobby.'

There was a short pause and her eyes lit up in sudden understanding, sparked into enthusiasm as she stared at him. 'I could promote literacy in Casavalle. I ran classes myself in Crystal Lake, taught people of all ages. Did you know, according to some reports, it is possible that two in five Canadians have low literacy? Sometimes it's because they have undiagnosed dyslexia or they have low attendance due to their home life. And it holds them back all their life—makes it harder to get a job, makes so much of everyday tasks more difficult and deprives them of the sheer pleasure of reading. I am sure that there are people here who have the same difficulties.'

He nodded, touched by the sheer passion and vibe to her voice, the belief in the cause. Lord knew, he understood that.

'You could also speak with my father about the idea of rolling out a similar programme in Aguilarez.'

'Speak with your father?' Her face dropped. 'I… I…'

'He is not a tyrant,' Cesar said. 'He is driven by duty and I believe he will see that this is a worthy cause that will benefit his people. It is just not something that has occurred to him.'

He watched as she tackled another piece of pizza, could almost see her brain whir and process ideas. 'I'll need to talk to my Education minister.'

Cesar hid the small smile as he heard her describe the

minister as 'hers' but, as was her wont, she caught it and smiled right back at him.

'Don't I sound all grand and regal?' she said. 'But, truly, I'm excited about this. I'll need to review the education statistics, look into any charitable foundations that already exist. Call in the people who run them.'

He nodded, sensed her energy and verve. 'Speak with some teachers, find out how much provision is made for children with reading difficulties.'

'And why stop there? I need to think about all children, all people with learning difficulties, mental-health issues.' She waved her pizza. 'Would you mind brainstorming with me?'

'I'd love to,' he said, almost surprised to know he completely meant it.

As they spoke and swapped ideas over the rest of the pizza, followed by chocolate ice-cream, the atmosphere seemed to crackle and buzz in time with the sizzle of the logs on the fire, the pop of the flames in the air. And gradually, as the words began to run dry, awareness grew as he observed the animation on her face, the gesture of her hands, the brightness of her eyes, her sheer vitality.

Until the words seemed to slow down and finally trickled to a stop and he realised just how close Gabriella was—so very, very close… And as if she realised the same she stilled, and her brown eyes widened as their gazes caught.

He knew he had to say something and the words came naturally. 'The more I get to know you, the more I believe you are the exact ruler Casavalle needs. You bring a change of attitude, because you have experienced life as a non-royal and you bring a different perspective. You will be a great queen.'

'Do you really think so?' Her voice held shyness, doubt, but a growing confidence as well.

'Yes.' He kept his voice steady, willing her to believe the words. 'I really do.'

Now there was a silence, but this silence echoed and reverberated with unsaid words, unnecessary words as mutual yearning hovered and meshed the very air and drew them towards each other until now the gap between them was infinitesimal. Then Gabriella closed that gap, and brushed her lips against his. Cesar released the breath he hadn't even known he held, and he lifted his hands, threaded them through the silken mass of her hair. The tang of dark chocolate, the scent of her vanilla shampoo, assailed his senses and he was lost.

She deepened the kiss, pressed against him with a small moan; her fingers fumbled with the buttons of his shirt, slid over his chest and he groaned her name and then they somehow tumbled off the sofa onto the fleecy softness of the rug, warmed by the flames whilst outside moonlight dappled the stone turrets and the ornate fountains.

A sudden pop of a log penetrated the intense fugue of desire and Gabriella pulled abruptly away, scrambled up to a sitting position and looked down at him, dismay breaking through the dazed look of desire as they stared at each other.

She looked so damned beautiful and guilt fought its way to the surface—he should not have let this happen. 'I'm sorry,' he said. 'I didn't mean to get so carried away.' And he hadn't. That had not been part of his marriage campaign; in truth the campaign hadn't so much as crossed his mind.

She caught her lower lip between her teeth. 'Neither did I. I'm sorry too.'

All he wanted now was to take the stricken look from her face. 'Then we are both sorry, but look at me, Gabi. Please.'

She did so, her gaze half shy, half vulnerable, and he continued, 'I find it hard to regret, because I wanted to kiss you, you wanted to kiss me. What happened here—it wasn't wrong and we were at least saved by the fire from going any further. It is done—let us simply remember it as a beautiful memory, rather than something we regret. Deal?'

A pause and then she nodded. 'You're right. It's a deal,' she said.

CHAPTER TWELVE

GABI OPENED HER EYES, blinked at the unfamiliar canopy above her, turned her head to see the vast bedroom, filled with heavy dark furniture, the loom of a mahogany wardrobe in the corner, the sharp edges of the ornate desk by the barred window. Another blink and memories tumbled into her still-sleep-drowsed brain. Had it all been a dream?

Nope…the feel of Cesar's body pressed against her, the soft fleece of the rug, the warmth of the fire, his lips on hers… That had all happened. Lifting her fingers to touch her swollen lips, she closed her eyes, tried to tell herself that at least they had come to their senses before they had actually slept together. That would have been stupid. Yet, stupid or not, a part of her cursed that falling log, wished that they had continued that magical journey, her whole body still alive and alight and wanting more.

Gabi exhaled a sigh——what had happened to not letting physical attraction fuzz her brain?

Well, it was time to face the music, endure the sheer awkwardness of the morning after.

And yet when, twenty minutes later, she entered the cavernous kitchen Cesar turned from the counter and smiled at her with such an easy, natural smile that the tension left her shoulders and she even managed a return smile.

'Good morning,' he said. 'I thought we could have breakfast in the morning room and then laze the day away reading in front of the fire.'

The mention of the fire caused a flush to heat her cheeks but she welcomed the plan, was grateful for his aplomb and for the offer of escape into a fictional world. And once she was actually curled up on the rug, close to the warmth of the fire, a cup of tea by her side, she did indeed lose herself in the pages and watched with satisfaction as Cesar did the same. His absorption was genuine—she could see that from the way his dark eyes focused, the steady pace at which he turned the pages, the fact his tea was left untouched as he read the classic fantasy adventure that she'd hoped he loved as much as she did.

The only disturbance was a break for lunch—ciabatta bread with cold meats and regional cheeses—and not long after that his phone rang. He left the room, then popped his head round the door. 'I've got to go out for a bit to pick up some supplies. Keep reading and I'll try not to be gone long.'

But it was a while before he reappeared, and as she looked up at him she saw an expression she couldn't interpret on his face. Excitement? Nerves? It was hard to tell.

'Actually—we're going out,' he said.

'OK.' Gabi slipped her bookmark into the book and closed it. 'Where to? Do I need to change?'

'Just wrap up warm,' he said. 'And meet me outside.'

Fifteen minutes later Gabi ran lightly down the stairs and across the stone floor to the imposing arched front door. Stepping outside, she gave a small gasp of wonder; outside on the snow-covered ground was a sleigh, at the front of which were two of the most beautiful horses she had ever seen. A man in a top hat and tails was seated behind the horses.

Cesar stood to one side. 'Enter,' he said with a bow and she approached the sleigh, and let him help her in, waited as he climbed in after her and pulled the wonderfully fluffy white blanket over them.

'I didn't even realise it had been snowing.'

'Me neither.' He grinned. 'Flavia rang to tell me and it occurred to me that you may like this.'

'I love this.' She gestured to the landscape: the pristine white of the freshly laid snow stark against the green glimpses of the trees, the sky above a dazzling blue, the late afternoon sun glinting down in wintry splendour. The sound of the runners over the snow, the snuffle of the horses—all of it added to the magical feel of the day.

'Thank you. For today and yesterday as well. I needed this break. It's given me new energy, a fresh perspective. Made me feel stronger.' But she knew it wasn't only the break—it was this man sitting next to her, the man who had made her laugh, had helped decorate a tree, had been compassionate and caring and kind.

'I am glad.' He paused. 'In a few minutes we will be at our destination—a place important to Aguilarean history. A woodland glade where legend has it just over two centuries ago the King of Casavalle and the King of Aguilarez met, after a series of bloody and awful battles. They met and decided enough was enough, that the wars were tearing both countries apart and somehow a peace must be brokered. And so it ended, because two rulers trusted each other, against all odds, and put their people's futures above the feuds and wars and greed. And made a truce.'

'A truce that has held to this day.' Gabi felt a shiver of history, a realisation that those two men of long ago were linked to Cesar and herself.

And she sensed, knew, that Cesar had a purpose other than mere sightseeing in taking her here. And now as the sun dipped down over the horizon in a magnificent blaze of red and orange glory and the day slipped into dusk her tummy tightened with nerves, tension, panic, *all* the emotions. Her senses heightened, the pine-scented breeze intensified in scent, the crunch of the horses' hooves echoed in her ears, the feel of the blanket over her legs heavier as the sleigh pulled to a halt.

'Come,' Cesar said. Somehow, she forced her legs to move, alighted from the sleigh and felt a small thrill as he helped her down, his hand round hers. Then he led her across the crisp crunch of snow into a small woodland glade where she stopped as surprise halted her feet.

The trees were festooned with lights and baubles that glittered in the canopied glade to create a magical tableau. Starlight seeped through the branches and dappled the ground, the snow-covered trees with their contrast of dark green and white adding an almost magical sylvan beauty.

Cesar took her hands in his, his grasp firm and sure.

'Gabriella.' Cesar's voice sounded tight, the word came out with an effort, and he cleared his throat, shook his head and smiled at her. 'Sorry. I'm nervous,' he admitted and the admission touched her. 'I want this to be right. Gabriella Ross Valenti, will you marry me? I pledge you my support, my loyalty, my respect and my fidelity. I will stand by you and I will do my very best to be a good father to our children.'

Gabi tried to think, knew that she had to think. This was a huge decision that encompassed the rest of her life, and also impacted on her country. Her mind went to those two kings of long ago. Had they stood right here, weighing each other up, trying to broker a peace and a trust? Could she marry a man without love? The answer was suddenly simple.

Of course, she could. Love would make this too complicated; love had caused a huge amount of difficulty for her mother, had caused her anxiety, despair and, in the end, heartbreak. Maria and Vincenzo's marriage had stood the test of time from start to finish and brought respect, fidelity, loyalty—what more really could she ask for?

Than this prince, whose brown eyes were locked on her face, a man who would give her what he had pledged; she took in his strength, his aura, his sheer certainty.

'Yes,' she said clearly. 'I will marry you, Cesar Asturias.'

He released her hands and now he delved a hand into his pocket. Pulled out a small jeweller's box. He flicked the box open and took the ring out. Gabi held out her hand and he gently slid the ring onto her finger.

She looked down at it, could feel the thud-thud-thud of her heart against her ribcage as she stared down at the ring that represented a commitment so huge. The colours of the stones were a combination of the Casavalle and Aguilarez flags. The ring a reminder that their marriage was an alliance, a proud alliance, and it would be a happy one.

'It's beautiful. Truly beautiful.' And then he kissed

her. This kiss was different; she knew it from the moment his lips touched hers. It was a kiss of affirmation, a statement kiss, and it called up a deep desire, one that tugged and demanded and yearned for more. This was the first of a lifetime of kisses and she shivered as she pressed against him, felt the pull of possession, the realisation that from now on they belonged to each other.

'I think we should get married very soon,' he said. 'What do you think of a Christmas wedding, on the eve of Christmas?'

'Are you serious?'

'Yes. I think it makes sense to marry before your coronation in the new year. And for entirely personal reasons I would like to marry you sooner rather than later.'

She had no problem with that—her insides still positively squirmed with desire. 'Works for me. On both points. But do you think we can organise it in time?'

'As long as you are happy with a smaller, more private ceremony. It will be too late for foreign dignitaries to rearrange their Christmas schedules.'

'But most of them will come to the coronation anyway and I would much prefer a smaller wedding. And we could honeymoon here. Back in the castle.' Spend Christmas Day in front of the tree they had decorated together, lie in front of the fire as husband and wife.

'Then let's make this happen.'

The days that followed were a whirlwind, of publicity, organisation, planning, there was so much to do: a dress to choose, a reception to organise, a guest list to negotiate.

At least, though, the wedding was to be small. The two royal families would of course attend, with the exception of Meribel, who had decided that she didn't want any adverse publicity to spoil her brother's marriage. And not even Cesar's words would budge her. Other than family there were diplomatic friends and colleagues of Cesar, and Gabi had invited Jonas, who managed the book store, and Rachel, an old friend from Crystal Lake, along with her husband, Tom, and baby Ben.

Then finally her wedding day dawned.

Gabi spent the morning almost in a daze as she got ready. There was little point in pretending she had any input. Imogen, Luca, Tia and Antonio had arrived back in Casavalle the previous day and now Imogen and Tia had taken charge. Gabi had attempted to point out she was a grown woman, not a doll, had also suggested that at seven months pregnant maybe Tia should be resting. But this last had been met with a most unladylike snort from Tia herself.

'Compared to waitressing, pregnancy is a doddle. Plus, Antonio spent the whole honeymoon fussing over me.'

'The *whole* honeymoon?' Imogen asked, her eyebrows raised in a suggestive wiggle.

All three women fell into gales of laughter as Tia admitted, 'Well, maybe not quite all. But my point is that I have plenty of energy and I wouldn't miss helping you get ready for the world. I'll just keep the tea coming and I'll be fine.'

Tia's love of a good cup of tea was known by all and so they took turns boiling the kettle as they set to work.

Gabi sat back and let them get on, watched her reflection as she morphed into a bride. Her hair was expertly coaxed into gentle waves that seemed to gloss down to her shoulders in a chestnut waterfall. The make-up was subtle but effective, brought out the depth of brown in her eyes, accentuated the height of her cheekbones.

And then the dress. Gabi had known from the instant she saw it that it was The One. The one that she hoped would stop Cesar in his tracks. It was deceptively simple, long sleeved with an eye-catching wide neckline that cleverly twisted around her shoulders to fall into a low back. The gown was made of a dense weave fabric with a subtle yet distinctive flower motif. The fitted bodice topped a full pleated skirt at the front and a long flowing train at the back.

Now she was ready and there was a tsunami of panic in her tummy; nerves fluttered and curled in waves as the royal party made the short journey across to the Casavallian chapel.

'You ready?' Luca asked as they stood at the doors to the ancient stone church.

'I'm ready.'

They stepped forward and now all she could see was Cesar—he filled her vision as each step took her closer to him, each step matched the breadth and thrum of the swell of music, that seemed to roll and wave in the air in recognition of the moment. Each step so significant, each pound of her heart stronger. He was so goddamn beautiful, this soon-to-be husband of hers, who waited at the altar, a smile lurking on his lips and in his eyes. A smile that encouraged her to keep moving forward. His gaze encompassed her, made her feel as if she were the only woman in the world for him.

For a fraction of an insidious second, she realised that she was—the only Queen of Casavalle in the vicinity. He would be marrying any woman who wore the crown. For a second, she almost faltered, sensed Luca's grip on her arm tighten, oh, so slightly, as if in question. Then she looked at Cesar again, and he gave the smallest, quickest of winks and suddenly it was all OK again. Now she had reached the altar and he smiled down at her; his gaze unfaltering; no hint of doubt flecked the dark chocolate-brown depths.

Next came the vows, made in this historic beautiful church that had seen so many other royal marriages take place. These walls had witnessed so much, joy and pain, life, death, christenings… So many rulers of Casavalle would have been wed here, indeed her own mother must have wed her father here. The idea sent a shiver down her spine.

Cesar spoke each word clearly and she followed his lead, focused on each syllable, until it got to the vow to love and honour and then there was a beat of hesitation, so fleeting she was sure no one but the two of them would have noted it.

Then it was done.

They were husband and wife, wedlocked.

He pushed her veil back and, oh, so gently he kissed her, his lips feather-light and yet so sensuous. Joy and a tremor of desire coursed her veins and she lifted her hand to gently cup his cheek.

The walk back down the aisle was dreamlike—she even thought she saw Maria wipe a tear from the corner of her eye, which surely must be an illusion. As they emerged into the cold, snow-tanged air she looked round at the blue-grey of the sky, the ancient beauty of the churchyard, and all she could think was the word married. She'd got married. Married. *Married.*

Then it was time for the photographs but today she sailed through the usually hated pastime. Because Cesar was next to her, oh, so close, arm around her waist, her hand lightly resting on his chest, and a new awareness dawned, a thrill of anticipation at the night ahead.

An awareness that simmered as they arrived at the reception, held in one of the Casavallian ballrooms, resplendent in Christmas beauty. The flags of Aguilarez and Casavalle fluttered at the doors. The columns and pillars were draped with beautiful white flowers that trailed and garlanded down with fairy-tale beauty and added a tinge of scent to the air.

An enormous table displayed an array of canapés. Gabi had decided against the formality of a sit-down dinner, preferred the idea of allowing people to mingle. Instead she'd asked for tables to be dotted round the room so that people could sit or stand as they pleased.

'I think it's working,' she said to Cesar as they stood together watching their guests as they laughed and talked. Imogen and Luca circulated, making introductions. Antonio and Tia sat with Miles and Grace, all laughing.

'Even my parents look happy,' he agreed, watching King Jorge smile and nod as Imogen spoke to him. 'Clearly Meribel's faults have been forgotten.'

Now that a different Asturias had married a different soon to be ruler of Casavalle.

'Then hopefully Meribel will feel able to attend my coronation and bring Dana with her.'

'Perhaps. But enough of my family. What about you, Gabi? Are you happy? Are you enjoying yourself?'

'I am. I spoke with Jonas as well and I have told him he can have the book store.'

'Are you sure? I know how much it means to you.'

'It does but it would be selfish of me to hang onto it now. I know it was the right choice. My life is here now.'

With you.

She bit the words back, reluctant to show even a hint of sappiness. Instead, 'Now we should mingle.'

Cesar nodded and with a small wave she moved away. As she did so she spotted a tall, willowy blonde woman who was standing watching her, partly shielded by a fluted, flowered pillar. Gabi smiled and then the smile froze into a rictus as she realised the identity of the guest. Lady Amelia Scott-Browne.

How? Why? No way would she have missed the inclusion of Lady Amelia on the guest list. Equally no way could anyone have gatecrashed this venue. Had Cesar asked Lady Amelia? The thought sent an icy jag through her veins. No, of course he wouldn't, or at least not without telling her. Would he? Perhaps in a loveless marriage he assumed it wouldn't matter to her. It shouldn't matter to her. That Lady Amelia was so beautiful, so elegant, so poised, so…

Stop, Gabi.

Right now, it was imperative that she maintain her poise; no hint of scandal could touch this wedding.

Plus, there was no need for the stabs of jealousy she could feel pinprick her whole body. Cesar and Amelia had been history before Gabi came on the scene and she would not allow herself the indulgence of petty jealousy.

It was the future that was important.

It was simply unfortunate that her immediate future obviously involved a conversation with Lady Amelia. But as she approached the other woman, Gabi was careful to keep a friendly smile on her face.

'Your Highness.' Amelia's voice was low, well-modulated and completely cordial. 'I know you must be wondering why I am here. I assure you that Cesar has no idea I am here.'

'I must admit that I'm a little curious, yes.'

'I have come as the guest of Ferdinand Bastillo, one of Cesar's diplomatic colleagues. And *I* must admit I was guilty of a little subterfuge; Ferdinand believes I have Cesar's permission to be here and it is he who convinced your palace secretary to add me to the guest list at the last minute. But I only came because I wished to talk with you.'

'Oh?'

'I do not know how much Cesar told you about "us" but I believe you are entitled to the truth and I couldn't think of another way to speak with you. I know that letters and emails get censored.'

It was true. Gabriella knew how much trouble Miles had got into for passing her original letter on to Maria, knew too how hard it had been for Tia to get in touch with Antonio. She had been forced to simply turn up as Lady Amelia had now.

'Go ahead,' she said, though every instinct told her to cover her ears with her hands and run away.

Lady Amelia nodded. 'I'm not sure if Cesar has been honest with you, and everything I have seen and heard indicates to me that you have fallen in love with him.'

Gabi hesitated—she could hardly tell Lady Amelia that it was all for the camera.

'I…'

The blonde woman gave a trill of laughter. 'I do understand that obviously you had to ham it up for the press but I believe you have really fallen.'

The realisation hit her like a rock dropping from

the chandelier-adorned ceiling. She did love Cesar. Of course she did—now the thought had entered her mind she knew with absolute blinding certainty that it was true. Oh, she'd told herself she understood the rules but her heart, her body, her very soul had been unable to comply with the orders of her brain.

Because love wasn't like that.

It couldn't be forced or coerced to arrive or leave.

Amelia watched her closely, her green eyes full of sympathy. 'And I can't let him play you like that,' she stated. 'Cesar only broke up with me because his parents told him to, so that he would be free to marry you.'

The words and their import slammed into her. It couldn't be true. It couldn't. Could it? Only it could—her brain was in control now, thinking events through with icy logic.

'Did he tell you that?'

'Not in so many words. Cesar is too wily a diplomat for that. He went to Aguilarez for a meeting with his parents and Queen Maria and on his return he broke up with me. Out of the blue.' Lady Amelia's voice held sadness now. 'Next thing I knew I saw the press speculation about you and him. I know I shouldn't have been surprised; Cesar has always been a man to do his duty, so I understood his decision to sacrifice love.'

'Love?' Despite her best intent her voice raised in pitch.

Amelia shrugged. 'Yes. I think it took him by surprise—at the start of our relationship he was very sure about his short-term plans but as time went on… we fell in love.' The words twisted in Gabi's heart, each one a vicious turn of the knife. 'We were so compatible, had so much fun and he knew I would make an excellent diplomat's wife, so he would have been able to marry me with his parents' approval. But then he was called on to marry you.'

Every word rang with the possibility of truth, gelled with everything Cesar had told her, bar the reason for his break-up with Lady Amelia. And Cesar could not have told her that truth; to do so would have scuppered all his chances of making an alliance with Gabi. And also Cesar was a good man—he wouldn't have wanted to hurt her either. But it all made a horrible poisonous sense.

His words echoed in her brain: *'Love brings its own risks, of loss and grief. It complicates life. If we marry you do not need to fear I will fall in love with anyone.'*

Because he already loved Lady Amelia. And who could blame him? She was beautiful, sophisticated and part of his world.

Lady Amelia continued. 'I just wanted you to know; I also wanted to assure you that I will not pursue Cesar. I will not cause scandal. I intend to get on with my life and I wish him well. I wish you both well. But I couldn't bear to see you expose yourself to hurt.'

Too late. Pain gripped her, a deep ache, and she wondered if the whole room could hear the crack of her heart. Perhaps, but that was all the evidence they would get. She would wear the royal mask, as Cesar had advised, as he had taught her. She would be a Queen.

Even as her soul shrivelled with the realisation that history was repeating. Her past echoed into her present and her future. She was a duty and a burden again, as she had been to her aunt and uncle.

But right now she had to put her country and her pride first. As for her love, she had to squeeze that, compact it and hide the knowledge away. No one must ever, ever suspect that she truly loved Cesar.

She smiled at Lady Amelia, a smile as friendly and regal as she could manage. 'I truly appreciate the effort you have gone to, to tell me this, and I am happy to be able to set your mind at rest. Cesar and I understand each other; he has been honest with me and we look forward to a happy and long-lasting union.'

She had no idea whether or not the words even made sense but she was fairly sure they gave nothing away, would hold up to being quoted to the press if it came to it.

The rest of the reception passed in a daze; her head ached as she chattered and laughed and stood with Cesar in a desperate attempt to appear normal. But now her body no longer yearned for the night to come; instead dread and anticipation weighted her tummy. Because come what may she knew she couldn't sleep with Cesar that night. In truth she didn't even know what to do for the best.

CHAPTER THIRTEEN

CESAR HAD WATCHED the conversation between Amelia and Gabi, had known instinctively that something bad had gone down. But there was no way to discover what it was, no way he could risk any speculation or notice by marching over to join the conversation.

Instead he waited until they had finished, then moved towards Gabi.

'Hey,' he said softly. 'All OK?'

'Fine. Why shouldn't it be?' Her voice was calm, a smile tipped her lips—she seemed every millimetre the happy bride. Dammit, she'd learn how to don a mask all too well, almost well enough to fool him.

Almost.

Because as the reception progressed through the speeches, through the laughter and banter and cacophony of good wishes that accompanied them, he knew she was faking, sensed she was more brittle, more edgy, more…elusive.

Yet he was sure no one else would have the least suspicion and her composure, the way she was acting the part of loved-up, happy regal bride, made him feel edgy himself. This was too reminiscent of his own parents' marriage, every public show of affection an act. The idea that his touch now made her uncomfortable was one that caused a cold hand to grip his insides.

Then finally it was time for the bride and groom to leave. Gabi was whisked away by Imogen and Tia to change into her going-away outfit, a simple off-white trouser suit cinched at the waist with a glittering belt, her shoulders covered with a faux-fur shrug. Cesar received a clap on the shoulder from Antonio, a hug from Luca.

'Look after her,' his new brother-in-law murmured.

More hugs from Imogen and Tia; his parents wished them well with cool hauteur, but at least accompanied by smiles.

The car journey back to Aguilarez, achieved in stilted silence, was laden with a sense of foreboding. Sadness touched Cesar along with trepidation—this was not how it was supposed to be. The day had started with such beauty and happiness—he would never forget the sight of Gabriella headed towards him down the aisle, stunning in her radiance.

Now he could see pain and tiredness etched on her face and all he wanted to do was make it go away. He reassured himself that it was all a misunderstanding that could be sorted out with a few words. After all, what could Amelia have said to cause this utter change in Gabi?

Once Roberto drove up to the palace door, they alighted. Cesar had planned to carry his bride across the threshold, could see now that such a move would be rebuffed.

Instead he led her into the lounge.

'I'll get a fire going.'

Gabi shrugged and went and sat down, chose a single armchair, perched on the end, her hands clasped together.

'We need to talk,' he said.

'Yes,' she agreed, her voice colourless, cold, so unlike her usual tones fear gripped him again.

'I am assuming Amelia said something.' He frowned. 'What I don't understand is why you seem to have already condemned me. Without giving me a chance to explain.'

Gabi's laugh contained no mirth. 'So you can try to cast an illusory word web, spin a diplomatic codicil to our marriage agreement, a waiver, a...'

'That isn't fair.'

A shrug of her slim shoulders and then, 'OK. You're right. I suppose I should have fact-checked. Why did you split up with Lady Amelia when you did?'

The question froze him in his tracks; his brain jumping ahead, he saw the train headed down the tracks. 'It was time to end the relationship.'

'Don't play word games with me, please.' Now her voice cracked slightly, but her eyes met his, the challenge clear. 'Did you split up with her so you would be free to marry me?'

Think. But his brain refused; he knew he couldn't lie to her, knew he didn't want to. 'Yes.'

'Did you love her? Did she love you?'

'I can't answer for Amelia but I don't believe she really did love me, regardless of what she might have said. I didn't love her.' Surely she could hear the truth in his voice. But she couldn't—he could see the doubts converge in her expressive eyes, in the clench of the nails into her palms. 'Did Amelia tell you I loved her?' Dammit—he should have closed Amelia down better during the break-up conversation, had been too worried about further scandal and hadn't foreseen this.

'But you would say that, wouldn't you?' she said softly. 'You could hardly tell me, the woman you wanted to marry for political reasons, that you are in love with someone else. And you wouldn't admit it now. Because you wouldn't want to hurt me and you want to make the best of the situation.'

Somehow he had to make her see that this was not how she thought it was, but for once words wouldn't come, his brain fuzzed by panic, by the sear of guilt that he had hurt her, by the idea his marriage was already falling apart. 'I did not love Amelia.' She had to believe him. 'I had no wish to marry her. I had no wish to marry anyone.' Oh, God. That had come out wrong as well. 'Except you.'

'For duty. Because your parents told you to. For the sake of our countries.' Her voice was dull.

Try again.

'You knew this marriage was not about love, but about forging an alliance.'

She nodded. 'I did know that our marriage was based around duty but I also believed you were truly free, that your break-up with Amelia was nothing to do with me. If I had known the truth, I wouldn't have married you.'

And now he could taste the ash of bitterness in his mouth and still he couldn't find the right words to protest, to reassure, to tell her she had this all wrong. Because words had deserted him as emotions roiled.

Now he saw a tear glisten in the corner of her eye, saw her impatient swipe to get rid of it. 'I'm not sure I can be second choice. Again. For the rest of my life.'

'That's not how it is.'

'That's exactly how it is. My aunt and uncle—they were amazing people and they did do their best. But they didn't really want a child; they had their life exactly how they wanted it and they had plans. They had saved for years in order to go travelling and then retire to sunny climes. Instead they took me in, gave up their dream. For duty. To do the right thing. You are doing the same.'

Every word slammed into him as he tried to figure out the flaw in her argument, tried to work it out. 'It isn't like that.'

'To me it is exactly like that. You sec…' She gave a tired smile. 'I am not trying to be difficult. But now it feels to me as though I am second best. Again. A catalyst to sending someone's life down an unwanted path. Again. I don't think I can live the rest of my life like that.'

Still no words would come. He looked at her and his heart tore. 'It wouldn't be like that.'

Another shake of her head and then she rose, the weariness evident in her movement. 'We'll talk tomorrow. I'm too tired now to find a way out of this mess. I will sleep where I slept before. Goodnight, Cesar.'

All he wanted was to move over and take her in his arms, hold her and tell her it would be all right. But he couldn't, knew it wasn't all right. Knew he had to figure out a way to make it all right, if he could just subdue the emotions that crashed and tore through him, made thought impossible, were filling him with unfamiliar panic and loss of control.

So he watched her leave, before slamming his fist into the wall.

Gabriella changed out of her going-away outfit, chosen with such care and excitement and now a garment she wished never to see again. Her movements were jerky, almost uncoordinated, as she dropped the jacket to the floor, a horrid, torrid reminder of what had started out the happiest day of her life and then degenerated into this. It would have been bad enough but what made the whole mess even worse was the fact that she loved Cesar.

Still loved him. What was she going to do? How could she spend the rest of her life with a man who loved someone else? A man who had given up his life for duty and relegated Gabi to the role of burden once again.

Her glance fell on her suitcase and the pain, the mortification intensified as she recalled the sleepwear she had brought with her. All designed for a honeymoon, for nights of decadence, for the great sex that had been on offer. Instead she pulled on jeans and a T-shirt, followed by more layers as she realised sleep would be impossible. Knew she couldn't stay here, not tonight, not on her wedding night. The urge to run was overwhelming. Necessary. She glanced out of the window. The sky looked cloudless; she knew that snow was on the way.

She and Cesar had laughed, joked about a white Christmas, about being snowed in together with nothing to do.

But the snow was not due yet and even if it came she wouldn't go far. Cesar had arranged for Ferron and Arya to be brought here so they could spend time riding on their honeymoon. She would ride just a little way, remain on royal grounds.

She added more layers, woollen ones to keep her warm, her waterproof fleece parka, woollen hat, scarf, gloves, warm riding boots, slipped out of her room and hesitated, knew that Cesar would veto this night-ride idea. But she didn't care; she had to leave. Carefully she slipped down the back stairs.

Not letting herself have time to think, she carefully

opened the front door a crack and slipped out and headed for the stables, entered and stood close by Arya, taking comfort from her uncomplicated nudge of greeting. Soon after she set off, her breath white in the dark cold air, the moonlight bright and cold on the path ahead.

Her brain hurt as she tried to see a way forward. She imagined the scandal if she ended the marriage now. Impossible. The headlines, the fallout would be too much. The only way possible would be to continue forward, trapped in a marriage she could no longer tolerate. Yet the idea of leaving Cesar wrenched her with hurt too, but better the pain now than a constant mind-numbing, soul-destroying ache of a one-sided love, in the knowledge he would have preferred a different life with a different woman but was stuck with her, putting a brave face on it. The mortification in itself stabbed her with a new pain.

The thoughts jostled and scrambled, hurled themselves round her brain. Was this how her mother had felt? All those years ago when she'd fled Casavalle, trying to decide if her marriage had been a mistake, if she could live with being a burden to the man she loved. As the thought added itself to the mix Gabi suddenly became aware of the swirl of snowflakes.

Dammit. She'd lost track of the time—come to that she'd lost track of her surroundings. A rookie mistake. Yet the snowflakes were welcome, a sudden dose of reality. What the hell was she doing? She was running away—as her mother had done. Fleeing from the problem, rather than trying to find a way to sort it out. Her mother had regretted her flight, had left it too late before she'd decided to go back. If Sophia had stayed, spoken with Vincenzo, everything could have been so different.

Gabi knew that her situation was different from her

mother's; Vincenzo and Sophia had been in love whereas Cesar didn't love her. But why was she so sure that Cesar did love Amelia? His denial had been steadfast, but it had also been clear he was racked with emotion. Her thoughts fought for clarity but could find none, yet she knew with a bone-deep certainty that Sophia would tell her to turn, go back, that running solved nothing. If Cesar did love Amelia then they still had to work out the best way forward. Together. She tugged on the reins and Arya obeyed but the snow was falling thick and fast now and Gabi felt a sudden sensation of panic. Told herself to stay calm.

It was then that the horse gave a whinny of fright. Gabi saw the glow of eyes looking at her from behind a bush and then Arya reared.

Cesar paced the spare bedroom, up and down, driven by sheer anger with himself. For messing up so spectacularly, for hurting Gabi, for not being able to make it right. Dammit, that was what he did—he made things right. And instead he'd stood there like a fool, an idiot, a gibbering, incoherent ass.

He couldn't leave it like this; he had to see her, talk to her. He pulled open his door and strode down the corridor, knocked on her door.

'Gabriella. Let me in. It's me.' He knocked again, louder this time. 'Please, Gabi. We need to talk.'

More silence. Cesar frowned. Gabriella was not the sort of woman to cower in her bedroom in silence. He tried the door, realised it wasn't locked, hesitated and pushed it open. The room was empty. The bathroom door was open and she clearly wasn't in there.

Turning, he made his way down to the lounge, the kitchen, and it was then that it struck him. She'd be in the stables. Sure he was correct, he left the castle and ran across the flagged courtyard, registered the swirl of snowfall; the cold flakes sizzled as he entered the familiar hay-scented warmth and looked round.

His heart skipped a beat as he realised Gabi wasn't there. And neither was Arya. Panic impaled him—a swirl of snowflakes could transform into a storm up here on the Aguilarean mountains and Gabriella was out there somewhere.

Fear clutched his heart, squeezed it, pulled the strings until breathing became difficult. And it was in that moment that the truth dawned on him. He loved her; he loved his wife.

Then he moved. Raced around for provisions, wrapped himself up warm and then mounted Ferron. Set off on the route he assumed she would have taken. It was impossible to see any tracks, the snow coming down too hard now, the sheer cold combated by the adrenalin that propelled him forward, calling her name. *Gabriella. Gabriella. Gabriella.* The echo seemed to get lost in the increasing deluge of snowflakes that poured relentlessly from the sky, obliterating any signs of the path Gabriella might have taken.

Bent low over Ferron's neck, he scanned the small area he could see in front of him, terrified that if she had fallen, he would miss her or, worse, trample her. Then he heard the soft thud of hooves and felt a surge of short-lived relief. It was Arya but the horse was riderless and panicked, lathered in sweat, eyes rolling, and he cursed as he managed to grab the bridle and secured her reins to Ferron's saddle. Soothed and calmed whilst inside terror raged.

Where was she? Lying somewhere injured, hurt or…

No! He would find her. Had to find her. Tell her that he loved her. Fear churned deep and cold—the idea that he wouldn't be given a chance to tell her he loved her, say the words, that he might lose Gabi, his love, his wife, his life, brought a chill sheen of moisture to his skin.

He rode on, tried to quell the rise of fear. And then out of the corner of his eye he saw something, a flicker of colour through the dense snowfall. He squinted, rode towards where he thought he'd seen it, recognised it as a scarf, a bright red woollen scarf tied around the branch of a tree. It was one of Gabi's and hope surged, along with thankfulness for her resourcefulness.

On and on they trudged, until eventually he made it to the tree, looked around, and there she was. She was scrunched in a ball; he could see that she had tried to dig out a snow cave for warmth, an action that could undoubtedly have saved her. He dismounted, tethered the horses to a tree and dropped down next to her.

'Gabriella.' His heart stopped; she lay so still, her eyes closed, her face frosted and pale and so, so cold. Worse, there was a trickle of blood on her forehead. 'Gabriella.'

Then her eyes fluttered open and she breathed his name.

'Yes, it's me. It is going to be all right. I love you, Gabi. I love you.' As he uttered the words over and over again, he lifted her up, assessed her situation quickly. Thankfully her clothing was warm, but it looked as though she'd tumbled off Arya. The forehead wound was superficial but he wasn't sure if anything else had been broken.

'Here.' He pulled out the thermos he had brought with him and held the drink to her lips. As if the smell of the hot tea woke her, she opened her eyes, looked up at him.

'Did you say you loved me?' Her smile was so sweet, so happy, she took his breath away.

'Yes, I did.'

'Good.' She sipped the tea. 'I love you too. Now I think I'll go to sleep.'

'No, Gabi. Not yet. You need to come home. With me.' She loved him. The words soared through him and he dampened the joy. *Not now.* The words could simply be born of delirium and either way his priority now was to get her home.

Somehow, by dint of coaxing and lifting, he managed to get them both up onto Ferron. Gabi, half-awake now, tried to help, but she was hampered by a twisted ankle and the fact that the cold had seeped through to her very bones.

'I love you,' he murmured again, the words so tender and so true and so blindingly obvious. He needed her to hear them, hoped she would remember them, but knew, if she didn't, he'd have the rest of his life to tell her.

But right now, as they set off on their journey back, Arya in tow, he wanted to say it all.

'I love your smile, your courage, your bravery. Love how much you care about books and literacy and your family. I love the way you frown. I love the way you have taken on your new role, your new family. I love that you have shown me that it is OK to risk my heart; I will do everything I can not to hurt you, or lose you. But if you can't love me, I'll accept that and, yes, it will hurt, but I still wouldn't change loving you. You've made me look inside myself. Made me realise that I can be more than a superficial person. It's good to make the best of things but sometimes you have to do more than that. You have to put yourself out there. And from now on I will. I want to do more for the causes I believe in. I also love your courage, the way you laugh, your inner beauty and your outer beauty, the way you lose yourself in a book. You make me happy, Gabi, and I love you with all my heart.'

Finally, they approached the castle, and he helped Gabriella off Ferron next to the stables, calling for the stable hands to take care of the horses, then gathered her into his arms, carried her across the courtyard and over the threshold. And as he did so she looked up at him and there was that beautiful smile again. 'I was hoping to be carried over the threshold,' she murmured.

Once inside he laid her gently on the sofa; soon he had a roaring fire going and then he ran upstairs and brought her down a change of clothes. On his return she was sitting up and she smiled at him, a small shy smile.

'Will you be OK if I go and make us some cocoa?'

She nodded. 'I'm feeling much better, now I've warmed up.'

'Then I'll be back in five.'

Gabi changed swiftly. The warmth had begun to permeate to her freezing limbs and extremities and her mind now buzzed. Had he meant all those beautiful words? Could he love her? Could he? What if he had just said it to get her through, keep her alert, awake. Surely not, and she allowed a tendril of joy to spread. Until another doubt raised its head. What if she'd imagined it all? Hallucinated the entire event?

She settled on the sofa, waited for Cesar to come back, stared into the leap and swirl of the red orange flames. Tried to read the future, hoped and hoped and hoped that his words had been real and true. Shyness, anticipation and hope vied with each other and her heart hop-skip-jumped and flipped as he came in.

'Is it true?' she blurted out. 'Everything you said?'

'Every word.'

'And Amelia?'

'I swear to you, Gabi, I give you my word I did not love Amelia. I have never loved any woman until you. Please believe me.'

'I do.' It was impossible not to. This man would not lie to her; sincerity blazed from his eyes and in that instant the memory of Amelia Scott-Browne was cast into oblivion.

'And… Gabi?' His unusual hesitation made her look at him closely. 'And you? Did you mean what you said? That you love me?' There was a wonder and a vulnerability in his voice that brought tears to the backs of her eyes.

'Yes. Of course I did. I love you, Cesar. I know it was not supposed to happen but it did and I couldn't have stopped it. Couldn't have stopped you from making your way into my heart.' She sipped the cocoa, savoured the warmth as he came and knelt in front of her.

'I did not know it was possible to feel this happy. This grateful that you are here. Safe. I have never been so terrified as when I thought I may have lost you. Wouldn't have the chance to tell you I love you.'

'I felt the same way. I had already decided to come back when I realised how bad the storm had become. Then Arya saw a wolf or some wild animal in the gloom and she panicked. It took me by surprise and she bolted and I came off. It took me a while to get myself together and then I realised I couldn't walk; I'd twisted my ankle too badly. I was so scared that I wouldn't be able to come back, that you'd never know I wanted to sort it out, give us a chance. It would be like my parents all over again.'

'Your parents?'

Gabi nodded. 'My mother left my father, left Casavalle because she thought it was the right thing to do. That she could never be the Queen he needed, couldn't bring her child up the royal way. But she changed her mind. She was going to come back, give it another chance. But by then my father had met Maria and she decided the best thing she could do for him was to stay away. I didn't want that to happen to us.'

'It won't.' He came and sat next to her, swung his legs up so they were side by side, snuggled under the blanket. 'It can't. Because we love each other and nothing will come in the way of that. I won't let it.' His confidence and assurance were things she loved so much about him. 'I only wish I'd realised it sooner, but, you see, I didn't think I was capable of love. The very idea terrified me—I didn't think you could feel what you haven't experienced. I couldn't see the point of risking hurt—I learnt young there was little point in getting attached to people because they leave and move on so I learnt to suppress, quell, bury any such feelings before they had a chance.'

Her heart smote her and she laid her head on his shoulder. 'I won't leave,' she promised. 'You told me all the reasons you love me. Now it's my turn. Right from that first night when I met you, you were easy to talk to. I felt comfortable around you. I trusted you. That's why I was so upset at my presentation ball, but after that you were…well, you were so much fun. I don't think I've always been very good at fun, but you've made me see how important it is. You've given me confidence, a belief that I am worthwhile, that I can do this. Can be Queen, a good ruler.'

'I know that you will be a great queen. Your sense of right, of justice, will shine through and you will make a difference to your people.'

'And you too will make a difference? Did you mean what you said earlier? About wanting to do more for the causes you believe in.' She shifted to face him. 'Because I want you to know I will support you in doing that. This marriage won't be all about you supporting me. It will be two ways. I want to help you to help others. Build a foundation, support overseas charities.'

He nodded. 'I would like to do that and I have plenty of ideas to brainstorm with you.'

'That sounds wonderful.' And it did. 'You are a caring person, Cesar. That is yet another thing I love about you. Everything you've done has been caring: the chocolates for the tree, the sleigh ride, whisking me away…'

'That's because I have loved you from the start. I have cared from the moment I saw you sprawled in the straw. I kept telling myself that I was doing all these things as part of a marriage campaign but I wasn't. I wish I had realised earlier that I loved you.' Gently he stroked her hair. 'I am so very sorry for the hurt I have caused you, for my idiocy and my clumsiness. I love you, Gabi, with all my heart.'

'It really doesn't matter—nothing matters now but this. Us. I love you so very much and I truly couldn't be happier than I am right now.' Gabi turned and brushed her lips against his, felt joy, a sense of rightness as he kissed her just as the clock chimed midnight and Christmas Day arrived.

EPILOGUE

Casavalle, January 2nd

CESAR LOOKED AROUND the table at his parents, his brothers and their families, Meribel with Dana… Flavia. His gaze travelled to take in Antonio, Tia, Luca and Imogen. Grace and Miles were also present. Meribel and Tia were deep in conversation, no doubt comparing pregnancy notes. Imogen was hand in hand with Luca. Even his parents looked more relaxed than he'd ever seen them.

The Asturiases and the Valentis…all sitting down for an informal meal following the pomp and splendour and formalities of the previous day—the day of Gabi's coronation.

And now Cesar's gaze rested on his wife and his chest swelled with pride. She had been incredible—had accepted the crown with regal grace and utter sincerity and a humble understanding of the position and duties she had sworn to uphold.

The occasion had been weighted with history. But so too was today—a meal organised by Casavalle's newly crowned Queen. No additional guests, no publicity. Just family. All eating pizza together.

Cesar wondered if his mother had ever eaten pizza

before, watching her gamely and elegantly approaching it, wielding her cutlery with grace, unfazed by the toppings falling off.

Gabi, on the other hand, picked hers up with her fingers, and to his astonishment Queen Maria followed suit.

Cesar knew that indeed times were changing.

Gabi rose to her feet and raised her glass. 'I want to thank you all; I am so incredibly happy to have you all here. My family. The Valentis and the Asturiases. United. As a small token of our appreciation Cesar and I have bought you all a gift, something small and frivolous after the ceremony and importance of yesterday.'

Cesar and Gabi had come up with the idea, wanting to introduce the concept of gift-giving to his parents, to show everyone that royalty and frivolity could go together.

Reaching under the banqueting table, Cesar picked up the bag of gifts and walked around distributing them. Amongst them was an expensive lipstick in a brighter than usual colour for his mother, an expensive set of bubble bath and shaving brushes for his dad, a beautiful friendship bracelet for Imogen, a teapot for Tia. A set of brightly coloured, vivid socks for Luca, a snow globe depicting a scene in Picco Innevato for Antonio, and a set of a slightly brighter than usual nail polishes for Maria. Every present given lots of thought.

He returned to his place next to Gabi and took out the final gift in the bag. 'For you,' he said.

'And that is for you.' She pointed to a small gift-wrapped box by his glass.

He opened it and grinned. Cufflinks in the shape of toboggans—a reminder of their first date.

Next he watched as she opened hers. A delicate charm

bracelet. The charms included a crown, a book, a horse, a plane, a toboggan, a sleigh, and of course a heart.

Gabi smiled at him, the smile that never failed to catch his breath and swell his heart with joy, and he knew he was the happiest man in the world.

* * * * *

THE RIGHT REASON TO MARRY

CHRISTINE RIMMER

For MSR, always.

Chapter One

It was a cloudy Friday afternoon in mid-October when Karin Killigan finally had to face the unsuspecting father of her unborn child.

It happened at Safeway, of all places. He was going in as she went out.

She had her hands full of plastic shopping bags. Her mind was on dinner and the thousand and one things she needed to whip into shape at the office before the baby came. She was staring straight ahead and didn't even see him.

But Liam Bravo saw *her*.

He grabbed her arm. "Karin. My God."

His touch, coupled with the low, rich sound of his voice, set off a chain reaction of emotional explosions inside her. Shock. Guilt. Total embarrassment. A flare of thoroughly inappropriate desire. She let out a ridiculous squeak of surprise and almost dropped a bag full of dairy products as she blinked down at his hand on her arm. Even through the barrier of her coat and the sweater beneath it, she could feel his heat and his strength.

Slowly, she forced her gaze upward to his gorgeous face. The cool autumn wind stirred his dark blond hair and his sun-kissed brows had drawn together over those summer-sky eyes of his.

Somehow, she made herself speak. “Hello, Liam.”

“Excuse me.” The impatient voice from directly behind her reminded her sharply that they were blocking both doors.

“Come on.” Liam tugged her away from the doors and along a short concrete walkway.

She followed numbly, despising herself for never quite working up the nerve to break the big news to him, thus forcing them both to face it now—at Safeway, of all the impossible places.

“Here.” He pulled her in close to the brick wall of the building, between a bin full of pumpkins and stacks of bundled kindling. “Let me help you with those.” He made a grab for the shopping bags dangling from both of her hands.

“No.” She shook her head at him. “I’ve got them. I’m fine.” Total lie. She was very far from fine.

“You sure?”

“Positive,” she said way too brightly. “Thanks. I’m, um, really surprised to see you here.” Understatement of the decade. He lived in nearby Astoria and somehow, since the last time she’d seen him the previous March, she’d never once run into him in Valentine Bay. Until now. It wasn’t that she’d been avoiding him, exactly. But she certainly hadn’t sought him out. “I mean, there’s a Safeway in Astoria, right?”

"I stopped in to see Percy and Daffy and this store was on my way home." Percy and Daffodil Valentine were brother and sister. Neither had ever married. In their eighties now, Liam's great-uncle and -aunt lived in an ancient Victorian mansion on the edge of Valentine City Park.

"Oh, I see," she said, because he'd fallen silent and it seemed that she ought to say something.

His gaze had wandered downward to her giant belly, only to quickly jerk back up to her face again. "This is awkward." *Oh, no kidding.* "Please don't be offended..."

"No. Of course not." How could she be? She should have told him months ago, on the night she broke it off with him. But she was a big, fat coward. She hadn't told him then, nor had she managed to work up the courage to call him and ask for a meeting. And now the poor guy had to find out like this. Her cheeks and neck were too hot. They must be flaming red. And her heart? It pounded so hard she couldn't hear herself think.

"You're pregnant," he said.

"How did you guess?" It was a weak joke and neither of them laughed.

Beneath his golden tan, his face seemed to be growing progressively paler. "I'm sorry, but I couldn't help thinking that..." He faltered, which broke her heart a little. Liam Bravo never faltered. He was always so smooth. Even way back in high school, he could make a girl's clothes fall off with just his smile. He wasn't smiling now, though. He drew in a shaky breath. "I have to know. Is it...?"

There really was no putting this off any longer, so she answered the question he couldn't seem to ask. "Yes, Liam. It's your baby."

He flinched and his eyes widened. He started to

reach for her again, caught himself and let his arm drop to his side. After that, he just stood there staring at her, his sexy mouth hanging open.

God. What a horrible way to tell him. But at least she'd finally done it.

People bustled by them, going in and out of the store. "We can't do this here," she said. When he only continued to gape at her, she went on, "Tell you what. I'm going straight home..."

A low sound escaped him, kind of a cross between a grunt and sigh, but no actual words came out.

"Home," she repeated. "The house on Sweetheart Cove? I'll be there the rest of the day. Feel free to drop by when you're ready to talk." Carefully, so as not to bump him with her bags of groceries, she turned and made for her car.

He didn't say anything or try to stop her. But she knew that wouldn't last. He was bound to have questions—a million of them. Starting with *why the hell didn't you tell me*? She figured she had an hour, tops, before he appeared at her door.

Probably breaking the land speed record for a hugely pregnant woman on foot, she waddled toward the relative safety of her Chevy Traverse.

Karin lived with her dad, Otto Larson, and her two children, Ben and Coco, on the first floor of a large beach house owned by her brother, Sten. As she pulled the Traverse into the garage beneath the house, her dad came down the inside stairs, seven-year-old Coco close on his heels.

Otto went straight to the hatch in back to get the groceries.

Coco, in blue tights, red shorts, a blue T-shirt and

shiny red rain boots, had stopped at the foot of the stairs to spin in a circle. The kid-size red blanket tied around her neck for a cape fluttered as she twirled. "Mommy, I'm Supergirl!" she shouted as Karin carefully lowered herself from behind the wheel. "Don't worry, I will save you! I have *vast* superhuman strength, speed and *stanima*, X-ray vision, super breath and also, I can fly." Arms out, she "flew" at Karin, who laughed in spite of what had just gone down at Safeway.

Coco halted at Karin's big belly. Reaching out her small arms and tipping her head back, she gave both Karin and the unborn baby inside her a hug. "I love you, Mommy, and I love our baby, too!" Coco beamed a smile so big it showed the gap where she'd recently lost two lower baby teeth.

Karin bent to plant a kiss on the top of her curly head. "And I love you. Lots."

Otto shut the hatch. He had all the grocery bags, two in each hand.

"I'll help, Grandpa!" Supergirl proclaimed. She planted her rain boots wide, stuck out her little chest and propped her fists on her hips. Otto set two of the bags on the garage floor, fished out a block of Swiss cheese from one and passed it to her. The cheese in one hand, both arms spread wide, cape rippling, Coco ran back up the stairs and into the house, slamming the door behind her.

"You gotta love that enthusiasm," said Otto as he bent to pick up the bags again. Karin just stood there staring down at his bent head. His hair was all white now and thinning, his pink scalp showing through at the crown. He met her eyes as he stood again. "What happened?" he asked quietly.

She replied in a small voice. "I saw Liam at Safeway."

"You tell him?" Her dad and her brother, Sten, and Sten's wife, Madison, knew that Liam was the baby's father. Sten and Otto had been after Karin for months to tell the man that he was going to be a dad. Madison mostly stayed out of it, though Liam was actually one of her long-lost brothers.

Karin stared into the middle distance, thinking of Madison for no particular reason. Sten's new bride had been switched at birth, of all impossible things. She'd met Sten when she came to Valentine Bay last March to find the family she'd just learned she had.

"Karin. You tell Liam?" her dad asked for the second time.

She blinked and made herself answer the question. "Uh. I did. Yes. I told him."

"And?"

"And I said I was going straight home, that if he wanted to talk about it, I'll be here."

"You're thinking he'll be coming by, then?"

She nodded. "And soon, would be my guess. If you could maybe keep the kids downstairs…?" The house was really two complete houses in one. Karin, her dad and the kids lived on the first floor just above the garage. Sten and Madison had the upper floor when they were in town, which they weren't right now. Madison was a bona fide movie star. Currently, she and Sten spent most of their time in LA or on location wherever she was filming.

"No problem," said Otto. "I'll keep an eye on the kids and send Liam up when he gets here."

On the top floor of the house, in Sten's quiet kitchen, Karin brewed a cup of raspberry leaf tea. As she waited for it to steep, she stood at the slider that opened onto the wide upper deck and watched the layers of clouds over the water. The waves slid into shore and retreated, leaving the wet sand smooth as glass in their wake.

"Karin." Liam spoke from directly behind her.

She stiffened in surprise and turned to face him. His hair was kind of standing on end and his eyes had a haunted look. "Hey. I, um, didn't hear you come in."

He stared at her for several seconds with a numbly disbelieving expression on his face before he finally said, "Your dad. He told me to just go up."

"That's fine. Great. Let's sit down, why don't we?" She gestured toward the sitting area.

"No, thanks." He blinked at her. "I'd rather stand."

"Maybe some tea or something?"

"No. Nothing." He turned on his heel and strode away from her. When he reached the hallway that led to the bedrooms, he turned again and came back, halting in the same place he'd been before he stalked off. "You're pregnant."

Hadn't they already covered that? "Yes, I am."

"I can't… I don't…" It was just like at Safeway. The poor man seemed incapable of completing a sentence. "I mean, uh, you said it was…"

"Yours, Liam," she gently confirmed again. "Yes. The baby is yours."

"And you're due…?"

"In a week."

"A week." The wild state of his hair made more sense as he put both hands to his head, got two fistfuls of hair and pulled. "Mine. Wow. Mine." And off he went again, his long legs carrying him swiftly past the table, on through the sitting area to the hallway that led to the bedrooms. Next to the hallway, stairs led down to the lower floor. For a moment, he just stood there, his head going back and forth, as though he couldn't decide whether to run down the stairs or set off along the hallway.

Karin didn't know what to do, either, so she just waited by the slider. Eventually, he turned and came toward her again.

"A week," he repeated when he stopped a foot away from her. "I'll be a dad in a week is what you just said."

Excuses weren't going to cut it. She offered them anyway. "I'm so sorry, Liam. I was going to tell you earlier, but I didn't really even know where to start. And there's not much you could do at this point, anyway. So I thought I would just wait until after the birth."

"You thought you would just wait..."

"Yes. Liam, I promise you, there's no pressure. You can think it over, decide how much involvement you want to have." Okay, yeah. No matter what he decided, eventually, she would be after him to spend a little time with his child. And he would have to cough up some child support, too. But it felt beyond rude to hit the poor guy with all that today when he seemed so completely torn up to learn there was a baby on the way.

"No pressure," he echoed blankly.

"That's right. There's no big rush to make decisions. Truly, you can just take your time, figure out what works for you."

He raked his hair back with both hands. "But... married, maybe? We should get—"

"What? Wait." Now she was the one frantically blinking. "Married? Us?"

"Well, uh, yeah."

She needed to nip that terrible idea right in the bud. "No, Liam. Don't be silly. Of course not." No way was she getting married just because there was a baby coming. Been there, done that. Bought the T-shirt, saw the movie. Lived through the heartbreak. Never. Again.

And dear God in heaven, could she have made a bigger mess of this?

"Listen," she said. "After the birth we'll do DNA. You'll have plenty of time to deal with this. You really will—and you know, you look awful. Liam, come on. You need to sit down." She reached for his arm.

He jerked away before she could make contact. "I'll stand." They just stared at each other.

She cast desperately about for something meaningful to say. "Liam, I really am so sorry to—"

"Stop." He actually showed her the hand.

And then he spun on his heel again and paced off toward the stairs, shaking his head as he went, turning right back around and coming toward her once more, halting stock-still a few feet from where she waited. He looked wrecked, ruined, but he held his broad shoulders straight and proud. "Last March, when you broke it off with me, did you know you were pregnant then?"

She wanted to lie to him, make herself look a fraction less like a complete jerk for the way she'd handled the situation. But she didn't lie. "Yeah. I knew then."

His forehead crinkled in a frown. "You broke it off, but you didn't bother to tell me you were having my kid?"

"I felt awful. I couldn't make myself admit to you that we were having a baby. I mean, why me? How many women have you been with?"

He fell back a step. "What's that got to do with anything?"

"Liam. I know you. I grew up with you. We were in the same grade at school. We even went on two dates in high school, remember?"

"Of course, I remember."

"My, um, point is, you're hot and easy to be with. The women have always loved you and you have loved them right back. How many of those women did you get pregnant?"

"Karin." He was pulling his hair again. So strange to see him like this, at a loss. Undone. "Come on, now. Where is this going?"

"The answer is none of them, right—not until me?"

Now he looked worried. "Why do I feel like anything I say right now is going to be wrong?"

"Oh, please. No. You are not wrong. This is not your fault—it's not my fault, either, though. Or at least, that's what I keep telling myself. But I also can't help asking myself, why does the condom fail only for *me*? Why couldn't *I* have sense enough to get back on the pill—or better yet, get a contraceptive implant? But every time you and I got together, I really thought it would be the last time. What was the point, I asked myself? I wouldn't be having sex with anyone again anytime soon. But then I would get a free evening and I would remember how you said to give you a call anytime—I mean, think about it. Four times, we got together."

That first time had been last December, at Christmastime. Then there'd been once in January, once in February and that last time in March. The first time, she'd promised herself it would be the only time. The second time, too. And that was the one where the condom must have failed.

After that, it hadn't mattered anyway, whether she got herself an implant or not.

"Four times together," she muttered, "and *this* happens." She looked down and shook her head at her protruding belly. "What is the matter with me, to do that to you?"

"Uh, Karin, I—"

"No, really. You don't have to answer that. It's not a question that even needs an answer. And I swear I was going to tell you about the baby that last time, in March. I saw that last night as my chance to let you know what was happening…" She ran out of breath. But he only kept on staring.

So she sucked in another breath and babbled on. "When I called you that night in March, I swear it was my plan to tell you. But then, well, you kissed me and I kissed you back and I thought how much I wanted you and how long it was likely to be before I ever had sex with a man again. I thought, *one more time*, you know? I thought, *what can it hurt*?"

Still, he said nothing.

She couldn't bear the awful silence, so she kept right on talking. "I promised myself I would tell you afterward, but then afterward came, and the words? They *wouldn't* come and then I started thinking that you didn't need to know for months. Liam, I messed up, okay? I messed up and then I didn't reach out and the longer I didn't, the harder it got. And now, well…" She lifted her arms out the sides. "Here we are."

He just continued to look at her through disbelieving eyes. For a really long time. She longed to open her mouth again and fill the silence with the desperate sound of her own voice. But she'd already jabbered out that endless and completely unhelpful explanation of essentially nothing. Really, what more was there to add to all the ways she'd screwed up?

He broke the silence. "I have to leave now."

She felt equal parts relieved—and desolate. "Okay."

"But I will be back."

"Of course."

"We'll talk more."

What was she supposed to say to that? "Sure. Whenever you're ready."

"Okay. Soon." And then he was striding away from her for the fourth time.

She watched as he vanished into the stairwell and didn't move so much as a muscle until she heard his car start up outside and drive away. After that, for several grim seconds, she thought she might cry, just bawl her eyes out because she felt so terrible about everything and she'd done such a crap job of telling poor Liam he had a baby on the way.

The tears never came, though. Eventually, she turned around and stared blindly out at the ocean for a while.

By the time she remembered her raspberry leaf tea, it was cold.

Chapter Two

Liam got halfway to the gorgeous house he'd built for himself in nearby Astoria before he realized that he needed to talk to his oldest brother Daniel.

Years ago, when their parents died, Daniel, eighteen at the time, essentially took over as the head of the Bravo family. He became a second father to all of them. Daniel was only four years older than Liam. Didn't matter. When Liam needed fatherly advice, he usually sought out his oldest brother.

He called Daniel's cell from the car.

"Where are you?" Liam demanded when Daniel picked up.

"Hi to you, too. I'm at the office." Daniel ran the family business, Valentine Logging. "What do you need?"

"Long story. I'll be there in ten."

"Good enough."

Valentine Logging had its headquarters on the Warrenton docks between Valentine Bay and Astoria. Liam parked in front of the hangar-like building that housed the offices.

Daniel was waiting. He ushered Liam into his private office, shut the door and gestured toward the sitting area on one side of the room. "You look like hell. What's going on?"

"I need to talk." Liam sank to the leather sofa. "You know Karin Killigan?"

"Of course." Daniel dropped into the club chair.

"Karin and me, we had a thing last winter."

Daniel frowned. "Wait a minute—Karin's pregnant, right?"

"Yeah. How did you know?" Did everyone know but him?

"Keely told me." Keely was Daniel's wife.

"How did Keely know?"

"She hung out a little with Karin at Madison and Sten's wedding. According to Keely, Karin was noticeably pregnant then—but you missed the wedding, right?"

"Right." He'd felt bad to miss it, but he'd had a work conflict in Portland, one he couldn't put off or get out of.

Liam owned Bravo Trucking, which he'd built up from a few rigs that hauled strictly for Valentine Logging into a fleet with over two hundred trucks and two hundred fifty employees. His original terminal was nearby, right there in Warrenton. Last year, he'd opened one in Portland, too.

Daniel was leaning forward again. "Are you saying the baby is yours?"

"Yeah." The word scraped his throat as he said it. "Karin says she's been trying for months to work up the nerve to tell me. I probably still wouldn't know if I hadn't seen her coming out of Safeway a couple of hours ago." And he had that feeling again, like if he sat still, he might just lose his mind. So he jumped up, paced to the door and then paced back again.

Daniel said, "You never mentioned you were dating Karin."

"Dating?" He stopped by Daniel's chair. "I wouldn't call it dating. It was only a few times, whenever she could get away. She wanted it kept just between the two of us. I agreed it would be the way she wanted it and I never told anyone else that we were hooking up."

"Liam," Daniel said quietly. "Sit back down. Come on, man. It's all going to work out."

He dropped to the couch again. "I guess I'm kind of in shock."

Daniel got up. "Scotch or water?"

Liam braced his elbows on his spread knees and put his head in his hands. "Neither. Both." Dropping his hands from his facc, hc flopped back against the cushions and stared up at the ceiling.

Daniel asked, "Didn't you and Karin date in high school?"

"Briefly." Liam shut his eyes. "I always thought Karin was cute, you know? Senior year, she asked me to a Sadie Hawkins dance. We had a great time. I took her out to a show a couple of weeks later. But when she started hinting that she wanted to be exclusive with me, I told her what I told all the girls, that I didn't do virgins and I wasn't getting serious with anyone. Ever."

"Classy," remarked Daniel wryly. "And I'm guessing that was it for you and Karin in high school."

Liam let out a grunt in the affirmative. "When we met up last December, it was so great to reconnect with her. She's smart. She takes zero crap, you know? A guy can't get ahead of her. Better-looking than ever, too, with those gorgeous eyes that look blue at first glance but are actually swirled with green and gray. Plus, she has all that wild, dark hair. And her attitude is seriously snarky. She's fun." He couldn't help recalling the shock and guilt on her face when he'd stopped her at Safeway. "Not so snarky today, though. She really felt bad, that she'd waited so long to tell me…"

"Here you go."

Liam opened his eyes. Daniel stood over him, a bottle of water in one hand, a glass with two fingers of amber liquid in the other. "Thanks." Liam set down the glass on the side table and took a long drink from the water bottle. "I should go." He drank the rest of the water and set the empty bottle by the untouched glass of Scotch.

"Hold on," said Daniel. "I thought you said you needed to talk."

"I did talk." He rose and clapped his brother on the shoulder. "Thanks for listening."

Liam's new house in Astoria was four thousand square feet and overlooked the Columbia River. He'd had a decorator in to furnish it in a sleek, modern style, lots of geometric patterns and oxidized oak, pops of deep color here and there.

As a rule, coming home made him feel pretty good about everything. He had a thriving business, a fat bank account and a gorgeous house. By just about any standards, he'd made a success of his life so far.

Today, though, a big house and money in the bank didn't feel all that satisfying. He was going to be a dad.

Just like that. Out of the blue—at least, that was how it felt to him.

Karin had kept saying that he didn't have to do anything right now.

Wrong.

He needed to do *something*. He just didn't really know what.

Maybe he should call Deke Pasternak. Deke was in family law. A little legal advice couldn't hurt about now, could it?

The lawyer answered on the second ring. "Hey. Liam. Good to hear from you. How've you been?"

"I just found out I'm going to be a father. Baby's due in a week."

Usually a fast talker, Deke took several seconds to reply. "Well. Congratulations?" He said it with a definite question mark at the end.

Two could play that game. "Thanks?"

"So… You want to meet for a drink or something?"

"How about a phone consultation?"

Five slow beats of complete silence, after which Deke asked, "You okay, man?"

"I'm working on it. Just bill me for this call and tell me what you think."

Deke did some throat-clearing. "What I think?"

"Yeah."

"About your being a dad?"

"That's right."

"Are you asking as a friend or do you want my legal opinion?"

"You're billing me, aren't you?"

"Uh, sure. So this isn't anyone you were dating seriously, then?"

Liam thought of Karin again, standing there by the

sliding glass door in her brother's empty kitchen, looking miserable. "Why does that matter?"

"Let me put it this way, how did you find out that the baby's yours?"

"She told me."

"Ah. Right there. That could be a problem."

"Well, she should have told me sooner, yeah. She admitted that."

"No, Liam. What I mean is, what she told you proves nothing."

"She's seriously pregnant, man. I saw her with my own eyes."

"Not what I'm getting at. I'm trying to say that before you take *her* word for it, you need to let me arrange for DNA testing. It's best to clear up any doubts right out of the gate. I hate to say it, but it's a possibility that this baby isn't even yours."

Liam had always been an easygoing sort of guy. He never got worked up about anything. But hearing Deke Pasternak imply that Karin Killigan had lied to him about her baby being his? That just pissed him the hell off. "You're way off base there, Deke. She already mentioned a DNA test, as a matter fact. She's a straight-ahead woman and she's not trying to trap me."

"I'm just trying to help you."

"No. Uh-uh. You don't know this woman."

"Well, I—"

"She would never try to trap a man—she's so independent, she called off our relationship before I could figure out a way to convince her that we should even have a relationship. She wasn't even going to *tell* me about the baby until after the birth. I think she would have put off sharing the big news with me forever if that had been an option for her. But she's a good woman and that wouldn't be right. So, no. If she says the baby's mine, it's mine, damn it."

"Liam. Come on. Don't get me wrong. I'm not disrespecting the, her, mother of your child."

"Yeah? Coulda fooled me."

"I only meant that it's important to prove paternity once and for all. You need to get irrefutable proof and proceed from there. You do that, you know where you stand. And when you know where you stand, you can decide what to do next."

Why was he even talking to Deke? The guy had always irritated him. "You just don't get it, do you, Deke? I'm going to be a *father*. Like in a week! I have no clue how to be someone's dad." True, in the past year or so, he *had* been thinking that it was time for him to start considering having a family of his own.

But not in a week, for crying out loud!

"I'm sorry, Liam. But I don't really think it's legal advice you're looking for here."

Liam had to agree with that. "You're right. Gotta go. Have a good one, Deke."

"You, too. Ping me anytime you—" Deke was still talking as Liam hung up.

He dropped his phone on the sofa table, took off his boots and stretched out on the couch. That lasted maybe thirty seconds, at which point he realized that no way could he keep still.

Sitting up again, he put his Timberlands back on.

He needed to…know stuff. A lot was expected of a guy as a dad. Witness Daniel, for example. Married at nineteen with three brothers and four sisters to raise. And now he had twins from his first wife, Lillie, who'd died shortly after the twins' birth. Twins, and a daughter with his second wife, Keely.

The responsibilities never ended for a guy like Daniel. He worked all day and then went home to a wife, a couple of three-year-olds, a nine-month-old baby girl and their youngest sister Grace, who hadn't moved out on her own yet. Daniel made it all look pretty effortless, mostly—or at least, he had since he and Keely got together. He was a happy man now.

Liam could learn a lot from Daniel. He really shouldn't have just jumped up and run out of his brother's office like that. He had a million questions and Daniel would be the one to answer them.

However, to get advice from Daniel, he would be required to sit still and listen. That wasn't happening. Not now, not today.

Grabbing his phone and the jacket he'd shucked off when he entered the house, he headed out again—back to Valentine Bay and Valentine Bay Books down in the historic district, where the fortyish blonde clerk greeted him with a big smile. "How can I help you?"

"I'm having a baby. It's my first and I need to know everything."

"Well, of course you do." She led the way to the baby and childcare section and recommended a few books on first-time fatherhood.

He grabbed those. "I'm just going to look around for a while."

She left him to it. An hour later, he'd chosen more than twenty new-dad and baby books. After all, he had a lot to learn. And that could take a lot of books.

Back at home, he stuck a frozen pizza in the oven and sat down to begin his education in fatherhood.

At two on Saturday morning, he was still reading. Not long after that, he must have dropped off to sleep. He woke to daylight at his breakfast nook table with his head resting on *The Expectant Father: The Ultimate Guide for Dads-to-Be.*

He made coffee, had a shower and called both of his offices, where for once everything seemed to be rolling along right on schedule.

At a little after nine, he was knocking on the door of the house on Sweetheart Cove, a bag of baby books in one hand—just the ones he thought had the most to offer, in case he needed to refer to the experts while discussing his upcoming fatherhood with Karin.

Karin's daughter answered the door. She was a cute little thing with big blue eyes and curly hair in pigtails.

"You came yesterday, didn't you?" the child demanded at the sight of him.

"That's right, I did."

"Grandpa told us to stay in the great room when you came, but I peeked." Her little mouth drew down at the corners in a puzzled frown. "Who *are* you?"

Otto Larson appeared from the living area. He wore a patient smile. "Coco, this is Liam Bravo. Invite him in."

"Come *in*, Liam Bravo." She swept out an arm in the general direction of the arch that led to the downstairs living area.

"Thank you, Coco." He stepped into the foyer.

"You're welcome."

Liam shut the door as Coco darted to her grandfather and tugged on his hand. Otto bent close and she whispered in his ear.

He gave Liam a wink. "Yep. Liam is one of *those* Bravos. Your Aunt Madison is his sister."

"I knew it!" crowed Coco. She aimed a giant smile at Liam, one that showed a gap where she'd lost a couple of lower teeth. "Aunt Madison is my *friend* and we have to be careful and not talk about her to most people because she is a movie star and she needs her *privacy*. But since you're her brother, I can say what I want about Madison to you."

Liam made a noise in the affirmative.

Coco Killigan chattered on. "I'm seven and I go to second grade. I have two best friends in my class and for Halloween, I will be Jewel from *101 Dalmatians*." Coco pointed at the bag of books dangling from his left hand. "You brought books. I like books."

"Coco," said Otto fondly. "I think Liam's here to talk to your mom."

Coco giggled. "Okay!" and skipped away through the arch into the other room.

"Come on," said Otto. "I'll get Karin." He turned and led the way into the first-floor living area, where a boy a couple of years older than Coco sat at the table with a laptop, a paper notepad and a stack of schoolbooks. Otto introduced the boy as Ben, Karin's son.

"Nice to meet you," said Ben, sounding much older than his nine or ten years. He had straight brown hair and serious brown eyes.

As Liam tried to think of what to say to him, Karin spoke from behind him.

"Liam."

He turned to her. She wore jeans and a long, ribbed sweater that clung to the front of her, accentuating her enormous belly. Her wild hair was pinned up in a sloppy little bun. She wore no makeup and the shadows under her eyes made her look tired—tired and soft and huggable, somehow. He wanted to wrap his arms around her and bury his nose in the curve of her neck, find out if she still smelled as good as he remembered.

"I wasn't expecting you." She didn't seem all that happy to see him.

Too bad. He was going to be around. A lot. She would need to get used to that. "I said I'd be back."

She glanced past him, at Otto. "Dad, I'll just take Liam on upstairs?"

"Fine with me," the older man replied.

She focused on Liam again and pasted on a tight smile. "This way…"

Liam followed her back into the foyer and up to the empty top floor, where she offered him a seat in the living area.

He took the sofa and set the bag of books at his feet.

"So, how are you doing?" Karin lowered herself into one of the chairs.

He had so many things to say and no idea where to start. "Uh. Good. Fine. Really. I talked to my lawyer."

"Well, that's good." She gave an uncomfortable little laugh. "I think…"

Now she looked worried—and he didn't blame her.

Seriously? Deke? He had to go and mention Deke? Nothing good was going to come of telling her what Deke had said. "He, um, wasn't helpful, but the point is I'm realizing that everything is workable. You need to know that I will provide child support—and I've read a little about parenting plans. We'll get one of those."

"That's great." She sat with her knees pressed tightly together, like someone waiting for an appointment she wasn't looking forward to.

He leaned in. "I also want you to know I'm here for you, Karin. Whatever you need, I'll make sure that you get it."

She nodded at him, an indulgent sort of nod, like he was her seven-year-old daughter, or something. He felt a flare of annoyance, that she so easily categorized him as someone she didn't have to take too seriously.

The annoyance quickly faded as he realized he missed her—missed the *real* Karin, the woman who kissed him like she couldn't get enough of the taste of him, the one who was always ready with some wiseass remark.

He wanted the real Karin back.

He also wanted her to learn to count on him, to trust him, though he'd never been the sort of guy who was willing to work to gain a woman's trust.

But he'd never been almost a father before, either.

Somehow, impending fatherhood changed everything. She was the mother of his child and he wanted her, wanted to be with her, to take care of her.

One way or another, he would get what he wanted.

Karin wasn't sure she liked the way Liam was looking at her. It was a thoughtful kind of look, a measuring look. It was also intimate, somehow.

He was a beautiful man, all golden and deep-chested, with hard arms and proud shoulders. It would be so good, to have those arms around her, to rest against that strong chest. Looking at him now, in the gray light of this chilly fall morning, she couldn't help wishing…

No.

Never mind.

Bad idea.

She and Liam weren't a couple and they never would be.

"So," she said to break the lengthening silence between them, "What's with the bag of books?"

"Research." He granted her a proud smile. "You know, first-time fatherhood, pregnancy, labor and delivery. All that. I've got a lot to catch up on and I've been doing my homework. I stayed up late trying to get a handle on all the stuff I need to know."

He was too sweet. He really was.

She'd been awake half the night, too, feeling bad about everything. And now she sat across from him waiting for him to get thoroughly pissed off at her—that she'd gotten pregnant in the first place when he used a condom every time. That she didn't bust to the baby when she broke it off with him and then, for all those months and months, that she'd never once reached out to let him know he was going to be a dad. He probably wondered if she ever *would* have told him.

And frankly, if he hadn't spotted her at the supermarket yesterday, she had no idea when she would have pulled up her big-girl panties and gotten in touch with the guy.

They stared at each other across the endless expanse of Sten's coffee table. Liam looked like he had a million things to tell her—tender things. Kind things. Helpful things.

The man truly wasn't angry. Not yet, anyway. He was sweet and sincere and he just seemed to want to be there for her and for the baby, to do the right thing.

His kindness reminded her sharply of how much she'd liked him when they met up again last year. In addition to his general charm and hotness, Liam Bravo, high school heartbreaker, had grown up to be a good man.

And right now, that just made her want to cry.

He said, "I was thinking…"

"Yeah?"

"Looking back on that night in March when you broke it off, I knew there was something weighing on your mind. I should have tried harder to get you to open to me."

She couldn't believe he'd just said that. "Liam. You were great. Don't you dare blame yourself."

"Look, I just need to know what *you* need."

"I'm good, I promise. Everything's pretty much ready. We're just waiting for the baby to come."

He frowned in a thoughtful sort of way. "Have you been going to childbirth classes?"

"I took the classes, yes. Like I said, I'm ready."

"A labor coach?" he asked and then clarified, "Do you have one?"

"I have two, as a matter of fact—Naomi and Prim." Naomi Khan Smith and Primrose Hart Danvers had been her best friends since kindergarten. Both women were married now. Naomi had two boys.

"Prim and Naomi. Makes sense." He'd grown up with her BFFs, same as she had. "And even though I get that you're all set and Prim and Naomi will take good care of you, I want to be there, when the baby comes."

She tried not to picture him standing beside her while she sweated and groaned with her legs spread apart. If he wanted to be there, he had the right. "Yes. That's fine. Great."

"So you'll call me, when you go into labor?"

"I will, absolutely."

Liam had a million more things to discuss with the soon-to-be mother of his child. But sitting here across from her in Sten Larson's too-quiet great room, he couldn't seem to remember a single one of them.

She just looked so brave and uncomfortable—and alone. Beyond being smart and good-looking and self-reliant, there was something that hurt his heart about Karin Killigan, something walled-off and sad.

"What else?" she asked. He knew she was trying not to sound impatient, but it was obvious to him that she couldn't wait for him to leave.

And why stay? She didn't really want him here, there was nothing he could do for her at the moment—and he hated the feeling that he contributed to her sadness.

"Nothing else—not right now, anyway," he heard himself say.

She stood, a surprisingly agile move given the size of her belly. "Well, all right then. Come by anytime. I mean that. Or call. Whatever."

"Thanks." He grabbed his bag of books and followed her down to the lower floor.

Her little girl stuck her curly head into the foyer as Karin was showing him out the door. "Bye, Liam Bravo."

"Bye, Coco."

"Can I call you just Liam?"

When he glanced at the silent woman beside him, she shrugged. "Up to you."

He gave Coco a smile. "Just Liam works for me."

"Okay! Bye, Liam. You can come and see me anytime." Coco waved as Karin ushered him out the door.

Liam went back to Astoria and had breakfast at a homey little diner he liked. From there, he went on to his office at the Warrenton terminal and put in a half day of work.

That evening, he drove the few miles to Valentine Bay and stopped at the Sea Breeze on Beach Street for a beer. His baby sister Grace was behind the bar. She served him his favorite IPA and asked him if something was bothering him.

"It's all good," he lied and Gracie left him alone except to give him a refill when he signaled for it. He sat there sipping his beer, feeling kind of gloomy, going back and forth over whether or not to just tell his youngest sister that he was about to be a dad. At some point, he would have to break the big news to the whole family.

Soon, actually. The baby would be here in no time at all.

It all felt so strange. Completely unreal. He still had no clue how he was going to do it—be a dad.

But he wasn't giving up. Uh-uh. Karin and her sad eyes weren't keeping him away. He would be there for her and for his kid whether she wanted him around or not.

"Is Liam your boyfriend, Mommy?" Coco took a big sip of her milk and then set the glass carefully down. She picked up her fork and speared a clump of mac and cheese with ham.

Karin and her dad shared a glance across the dinner table. Otto lifted one bushy eyebrow. Karin read that look: *it's as good a time as any.*

She cast a sideways glance at Ben. He was watching her, wearing what she always thought of as his Little Professor look. Serious. Thoughtful. Ben never just burst out with things the way Coco did. He watched. He waited. He made carefully considered, responsible decisions.

"As a matter of fact," Karin said to her daughter, "I've been meaning to talk to both you and Ben about Liam."

"I like Liam!" Coco speared a green bean and stuck it in her mouth.

Dear God. Where to even start? "I like Liam, too," Karin said, trying to sound relaxed and natural and feeling anything but. "And several months ago, I…went out with him."

Ben's forehead scrunched up the way it always did when some complex math problem didn't compute. "You were dating Liam?"

Not dating, exactly. "Uh, yes. I was. We're not, um, dating anymore, though. But we are friends. And that's a good thing. Because, as it turns out…" Was she blowing this? Most likely. She forged on anyway. "We will all probably be seeing a lot more of Liam because he is the new baby's father."

Ben said nothing.

Coco was incredulous. She set down her fork. "*Our* baby's father?"

"Yes." It was official. She was a terrible mother who needed lessons in how to share awkward, confusing information with her own children. "Liam is our baby's dad."

Coco frowned. "Is he going to come and live in our house?"

"No, honey."

"But doesn't he want to be with the baby?"

"Yes. Yes, he does. And he will be here often to see the baby. And when the baby gets older, the baby will probably stay with Liam some of the time."

"Oh," said Coco, and picked up her fork again. "Okay." She stabbed herself another big bite of mac and cheese.

Karin glanced across at her dad again. He gave her a shrug and a reassuring smile.

Ben, who understood the mechanics of reproduction, asked the question she'd been dreading. "How come you didn't say who the baby's dad was when I asked you before?" He'd asked several months ago, not long after she'd made the announcement that he and Coco would have a new brother or sister.

Because I'm a lily-livered scaredy-cat, she thought. She said, "Well, sweetheart, as I said then, I wanted to talk to the baby's dad first."

"You took a long time to talk to him."

Ouch. "Yes, I did. I'm sorry about that, I really am."

Ben tipped his head to the side, pondering. "Why? Were you nervous, to tell him?"

Understatement of the decade. "I was, yes."

"But now he knows and he's happy that he'll be a dad?"

"I haven't asked him that question. But he seems very determined to be a *good* dad."

Ben was still looking kind of troubled over the whole situation.

But Coco wasn't. "Our baby will like having Liam for a dad," she declared. "Liam's nice—and I finished my dinner. What's for dessert?"

Otto chuckled. "I think there might be a full carton of chocolate ice cream in the freezer."

Karin brushed Ben's arm. "Want to go talk about this in the other room, just the two of us?"

Ben shook his head. "Thanks, Mom. I'd rather just have some dessert."

On Sunday, Karin went in to work at Larson Boatworks, the boat-building and refitting company her dad had started thirty-five years before. Karin ran the office.

That day, her dad kept an eye on the kids at home

so she could spend several hours tying up loose ends on the job before the baby came. When she got back to the Cove late that afternoon, her dad reported that Liam had dropped by.

"Should I call him?" she asked.

"He didn't say to ask you to."

"Did he mention what he needed to talk to me about?"

Her dad gave her a look, indulgent and full of wry humor. "I'm not sure he *knows* what he needs to talk to you about."

For the rest of that day and into the evening, she kept thinking that she probably ought to call Liam, check in, ask him if he had any questions or anything. Somehow, though, she never quite got around to picking up the phone.

Monday, her leave from work began. Her dad dropped the kids at the bus stop and then went on to work.

It was nice, having the house to herself. She took a half hour just deciding what to wear and ended up settling on a giant purple T-shirt dress with an asymmetrical hem.

Really, she didn't want jeans or leggings wrapped around her balloon of a belly today, so she settled on thigh-high socks in royal blue with her oldest, comfiest pair of Doc Martens boots on her feet.

Once she was dressed, she felt suddenly energized, so she vacuumed and dusted and rechecked the baby's room for the umpteenth time, making sure everything was ready. Around eleven, just as she finished assembling two large baking dishes of lasagna and sticking them in the freezer to reheat when needed, she heard the doorbell ring.

It was Liam. He had a pink teddy bear in one hand and a blue bear in the other.

"I forgot to ask. What are we having?" He smiled that killer smile of his, and she felt way too glad to see him.

She laughed. "It's a boy."

And just like that, he threw the pink bear over his shoulder and handed her the blue one.

The man was too charming by half. "Thank you—and I think we should save the pink one, too."

"Is there something you aren't telling me?" He pretended to look alarmed. "We're having twins, aren't we?"

"Oh, God, no. I just meant it seems wrong to leave it lying there on the front step."

He went and got the pink bear. "Fine. The baby gets two bears."

It seemed only right to offer, "Would you like to see his ultrasound pictures?"

"I thought you'd never ask."

She ushered him in. As he brushed past her, she got a hint of his cologne, a scent of leather and sandalwood that caused a sudden, stunning remembrance of the two of them all those months ago, naked on tangled sheets.

He paused in the arch to the living area and glanced back at her. "Something wrong?"

"Not a thing." She shut the door and followed him into the first-floor living area.

In the kitchen, she put the blue bear down on the counter. He set the pink one beside it as she went to the double-doored fridge, which was covered with family pictures and artwork created by both Ben and Coco. "Here we are." She took the two ultrasound shots from under a strawberry magnet and handed them over. "These were at eighteen weeks."

He studied them. "Wait. Is that…?" He slanted her a grin.

"What sharp eyes you have, Liam Bravo. Yep. A bona fide penis—and I have a video of that same procedure. Want to see it?"

"Oh, yeah."

She stuck the pictures back on the fridge and led him to the table where she'd left her laptop. He laughed in a sort of startled wonder as he watched his son wave his tiny arms and feet, yawn and suck his thumb.

After he'd seen the whole thing through twice, he glanced up at her. "You said you were all ready for him. Does that mean he has a room and everything?"

She grabbed the two teddy bears and gestured toward the hallway to the bedrooms. "Right this way." He followed her as she explained, "We're lucky this house has so many rooms, including five bedrooms on this level. I had a sort of craft room/home office in one." She led him to the end of the hall where the door stood open. "Ta-da!" She put the bears on the dresser by the door.

"Wow." Liam seemed really pleased.

And out of nowhere, she was recalling one of the depressing fights she'd had with Ben, Sr., before Ben was born.

Bud, as everyone always called him, had kept promising to help her paint the tiny closet of a spare room at the apartment they'd shared back then.

Somehow, though, he never found the time to keep his promise. Bud had loved the life of a commercial fisherman and he was always out on a boat, working the fisheries up and down the Pacific coast, from Southern California to Alaska. He just kept saying "later," every time she tried to pin him down as to when, exactly, he would put in some time on the baby's room.

In the end, she fixed up the room herself, though not until after they'd had a doozy of an argument over it—one in which they both said a lot of things they shouldn't have. It was always like that with her and Bud. They would argue bitterly.

And then Bud would go off to work and be gone for weeks.

In the end, she'd tackled the nursery nook alone. When Bud came home, she showed him the finished product. He'd waved a dismissing hand and said it looked "fine" in a dead voice that communicated way too clearly how trapped he felt.

Liam's voice drew her back to the present. "The mural is amazing."

Covering the whole wall behind the crib, the mural included a snowcapped mountain, a starry night sky, an airplane sailing by the moon and tall evergreens standing sentinel off to one side, everything in grays, greens and silvers.

"Northwest outdoorsy," Liam said. "I like it a lot."

She rubbed her belly. The baby was riding really low and she'd had some contractions.

He was watching her. "You okay?"

"I'm fine. This baby is coming *soon*."

His eyes got bigger and he straightened from his easy slouch in the doorway. "As in now?"

She waved a hand and chuckled, thinking that this visit was going pretty well and she was glad about that. "Relax. Probably not today."

"Whew." He gazed at the mural again. "You paint that wall yourself?"

"More or less. Stencils. You can't beat 'em."

He shifted his gaze to her. He had a way of studying her, like he was memorizing the lines of her face.

He used to do that months ago, sitting across from her at whatever bar they met up in, or later, naked in bed. One night, she'd teased that he should take a picture. He'd promptly grabbed his phone off the table by the bed and aimed it at her, snapping off two shots.

She'd demanded he delete them, because who needs naked pictures of herself on a guy's phone?

He'd handed her the phone. She'd seen then that he'd only taken close-ups of her face. And when she glanced up at him, he gazed back at her so hopefully, like it would just be the greatest thing in the world, to have a couple of shots of her grinning, with total bed-head. She'd agreed he could keep the pictures—and then grabbed him close for a long, smoking-hot kiss.

Liam was still watching her. "Have you chosen a name for this baby boy of ours?"

"No, I have not. I kind of thought you might want input on his name."

Apparently, that was the right answer because he granted her a beautiful smile. "Thanks. I'll be thinking about names. I'll make up a list of ones I like. We can talk it over." Solemnly, he added, "I read all about baby daddies. I don't want to be that guy."

Her heart felt like someone was squeezing it. She hardly knew what to say. "You have *other* children?"

"Huh?" He seemed horrified. "No! Wait. I get it. You mean 'baby daddy' as in a flaky guy who has kids by different women, but I wasn't so much referring to the multiple baby mamas aspect. I meant a flaky guy, yeah. But in this case, a guy with only one baby, a guy who's basically a sperm donor with minimal involvement—that's what I *don't* want to be. I want to be on board with this baby, available, helping out. I want to be *there*, you know? Tell me you know that." He seemed so intense suddenly, as though it really bothered him that she might not understand his sincerity about pitching in.

"Hey, really. It's going to be okay, Liam."

"I hope so."

"It really is. I know I dropped the ball in a big way by not telling you what was going on sooner. I should've pushed past all the crap going on in my head and gotten in touch."

He watched her way too closely. "What crap, exactly?"

Uh-uh. Not going there. "My point is, I promise you that we *will* work together. You don't have to freak out."

"I'm not freaking out," he said vehemently—and a bit freakily.

Was this all going south suddenly?

And just when they'd both seemed to be feeling more at ease around each other.

She kind of wanted to cry, which was probably just hormones. But still. She really did want to get along with him. "Okay. You're right. You're not freaking out and I shouldn't have even hinted that you were and I'm really, um…" Her already weak train of thought went right off the rails as she felt something shift inside her—a gentle shift, yet also a sudden one, a tiny *pop* of sensation deep within.

And then something was dripping along the inside of her thighs.

Frowning, she looked down, which was pointless. Her giant belly blocked her view and whatever was dripping down there, it was only a trickle. So far, her thigh-highs seemed to be absorbing it.

"Okay," said Liam. "Something's happened. What?"

She made herself look straight into his startled blue

eyes and she put real effort into speaking calmly. “My water just broke. Would you mind driving me to Memorial Hospital?”

Chapter Three

Even more stunned than he'd been for most of the past few days, Liam croaked out, "Drive you to the hospital? Yes! Yes, I can do that."

"Great." With a low groan, Karin gripped the crib rail and lowered her head.

"Karin, are you…?"

She put up her free hand. "Just a contraction. Hold on…"

He stood there in the doorway waiting, feeling completely useless, as she panted and groaned some more.

Finally, she let go of the crib rail and looked straight at him. "Where's my phone?"

"I think I spotted it on the kitchen counter?"

"Right." One hand under her enormous stomach, she lumbered toward him. He fell back from the doorway so she could get by and then trailed after her as she made for the main room.

In the kitchen, she snatched up the phone. “This'll only take a minute. I've got a group text all set up—to Naomi, Prim and my dad. All I need to do is hit Send.” The woman amazed him. Was there anything she wasn't ready for? She poked at the phone. “There. I'll call my doctor on the way—now get me a bath towel. Try the hall bathroom, first door on the left. I'll meet you at the front door.”

“A towel?” He just stood there gaping at her because somehow his feet had forgotten how to walk.

“You want me to leak amniotic fluid all over the seats of that fancy blue Supercrew pickup out in front?”

“Uh. No?”

“Then go.”

That got him moving. He raced off and returned with the towel. She had a suitcase ready, just waiting in the hallway. He took the suitcase and helped her into her coat. She grabbed her purse from the table by the door and off down the outside stairs they went, pausing midway for her to weather another contraction.

At the truck, he threw the suitcase in back, spread the towel on the seat and helped her in. She was already on the phone with her doctor as he turned the pickup around and headed up the hill behind the house.

At Memorial, he learned that the doctor was on the way and they were ready for Karin. They whisked her into a labor and delivery suite and let Liam tag along.

Luckily, he'd studied up on what the father should do during the birth. He'd learned that his sole mission in the delivery room was to be a source of strength and support, to be as patient and attentive to his baby's mother as he possibly could.

He really tried to be that, even though when her girlfriends showed up, he was mostly relegated to staying out of the way as they stepped up on either side of her to comfort her and coach her through her contractions. They fed her ice chips and helped her to the bathroom when she needed it. The whole thing took hours, with the doctor in and out, the delivery nurses, too.

Once he asked if he could take pictures.

Naomi turned to him and spoke gently, "It's so great that you're here, Liam, but Karin doesn't want you taking pictures of her lady bits."

"I would never do that," he answered fervently. "Just…maybe of the baby and then maybe of Karin with the baby and then maybe I could hold him, too—I mean, after he gets here, of course?"

On the far side of Karin, Prim was stifling a giggle.

Naomi grabbed him in a hug. "Isn't he adorable?" she asked Karin and Prim as she let him go.

He was trying to decide whether or not his manly dignity had just been impugned when Karin said, "Of course you can take a few pictures with your son." She met his eyes directly and he knew she was remembering that night in February, when he'd snapped a shot of her in his bed and she'd assumed he'd gotten more than just her face.

"Terrific," he replied, suddenly just crazy happy, right there in the delivery room, crazy happy and sure that everything was going to work out fine, though exactly what "fine" entailed he had no clear idea.

Things got messy soon after that. There were fluids and a little blood and Karin's groans started to sound more like screams and angry shouts.

But then the baby's head was crowning and everything sped up. As soon as the little guy's shoulders emerged, it was all over. The rest of him slipped out quick and easy. He was so tiny and wrinkled and red, covered with sticky whitish goo, wailing as the doctor caught him and laid him in Karin's waiting arms. Naomi grabbed Liam and pulled him around to stand in front of her, right next to Karin and the naked infant on her chest.

On Karin's other side, Prim stepped back so the nurse could wipe some of the goo off the baby and the doctor could deal with the umbilical cord. All Liam could do was stand there and stare.

He'd never realized how much he wanted children.

Not until this moment, when he actually had one—yeah, he'd had vague yearnings in the past year, to get more serious about his life, to get married, start a family.

But only in a generalized sort of way.

Until today.

Today, he knew exactly what he wanted—to be a father to this perfect little miracle he and Karin had made.

"Take a picture, Liam," Karin teased softly as she stroked the baby's shoulder, her hand gliding down the fat little arm to the tiny fist. Instantly, the baby wrapped his itty-bitty fingers around her thumb and held on.

Liam got out his phone and snapped a few shots.

The nurse gave him a towel to put on his shoulder. She let him hold his son for the first time. That was amazing, though it didn't last long.

He passed Naomi his phone and she got a few pictures of him with the baby. Too soon, the nurse took the little guy back and gave him to Karin again and she nursed him for the first time. Liam thought maybe he should turn away, give her some privacy. But she didn't seem concerned and nobody else cared. He watched as his son latched right on and went to work, the fingers of his right hand resting on the upper slope of Karin's breast, opening and closing as he sucked.

Liam watched not only his newborn son, but his son's mother, too. He stared and marveled and thought how, from that first night they'd had together last Christmas, she'd been constantly keeping him at arm's distance, giving in to the attraction between them, yeah. But then, once the hot times were over, pushing him away.

And what about the last few days since he'd found out about the baby? She'd continually reminded him to take his time, think it over, figure out just how *involved* he wanted to be.

As though a man could choose his level of involvement when he became a father.

There was no choosing with something like this. When it came to fatherhood, a man needed to be all in.

And he was. *In* this. Going for it. All the way.

Okay, he got it. He knew he had no idea, really, what the hell he was doing. But he could learn. And he *would* learn. One way or another, he was making it work with Karin. He damn well would create a family with the mother of his child.

Last Friday, that first day he found out she was pregnant, he'd stuttered out a half-assed proposal of marriage. She'd said no before he even really got the words out.

No wasn't going to cut it.

She glanced up from the baby and into his eyes. "Liam?" She seemed alarmed. "What's wrong?"

"Not a thing." He felt so calm, so absolutely determined. He held her gaze, steady on. "Marry me, Karin," he said.

Karin was wasted, completely exhausted.

She'd done this twice before, yes. But experience

didn't make having a baby feel any less like pushing out a watermelon. She just wanted to lie there and nurse her newborn and be grateful that labor was over, thank you very much.

But no.

Liam had to go to the marriage place. Hadn't they already agreed that marriage was no solution to anything?

And did he have to be so sweet about it? Sweet and determined and handsome and even-tempered and so damn helpful.

Liam Bravo was a dream.

Someday, he would make some lucky woman very happy.

But that day was not today and that woman was not her. No way was she going to be the one that Liam Bravo married because he felt he had to.

After the ongoing disaster with poor Bud, she'd had this fantasy that someday, maybe, she would actually get it right. In that lovely, impossible illusion, she'd imagined finding a man who would love her just for her, and then fall in love with Ben and Coco, too. That man would marry her for love and love alone. Duty and obligation and doing the right thing wouldn't even enter into it.

Later, they would have a baby or two, maybe. Like normal people do.

As of now, she was reasonably certain her fantasy was never actually going to come true. But that didn't mean she would settle for less.

Liam was still standing right beside the bed, staring down at her and the baby as though he could *will* her to agree to his well-meaning but totally unacceptable proposal.

The doctor had left the room and the nurse and

Naomi and Prim had fallen dead silent the moment Liam said the *M* word.

"Would you all give Liam and me a moment alone?" Karin asked her suddenly speechless friends and the too-quiet nurse.

"Of course." The nurse gave her shoulder a pat.

And the three women filed out the door so fast you'd think there was a fire. Or maybe a gas leak.

"Liam…" Karin kissed her baby's head and shifted a fraction so he was settled more firmly at her breast.

The man beside her bent closer. He was so good-looking, with those fine blue eyes and that mouth that made her think of deep, wet kisses. He also just happened to be kind and thoughtful and determined. Everything a woman could ask for in a man.

"Just say yes," he commanded. "It will work out. We'll be happy, you'll see."

Was she even a tiny bit tempted?

Of course. She was a heterosexual single mom. What was *not* to adore about Liam Bravo? The guy was practically perfect—at least right now, as he stared down at his newborn son after the excitement and drama of birth. Blinded by the wonder of new life and eager to do right by his child and his child's mother, marriage would naturally seem like the only choice to him.

The resentment, the growing certainty that she'd trapped him, the longing to be free of her—all that would come later.

Except it wouldn't. Because she wasn't going to marry him. No way. "Liam, we've been over this."

He shook his golden head. "We haven't. The other day, you said no before I even got the question out."

"I'm sorry I didn't hear you out, but my answer wouldn't have changed no matter what you said or how convincing you were or how patiently I waited for you to finish saying it. I'm not getting married just because we have a baby together. I need you to believe me when I tell you that."

"Listen." He straightened and stuck his hands in his pockets. "Don't give me an answer right now. Take your time. Think about it."

"Liam, I've already—"

"Think about it." A thread of steel had crept into his tone.

She had no need to think about it. Zero. Zip. Nada. She'd already given him her answer. Twice now. But he wasn't listening and an argument right now wasn't going to be good for her, for him or, most important, for their baby, who'd just been ejected from the warm, quiet safety of her womb. "All right. We'll talk about it later. If you need to. But my answer won't change."

"Just tell me you'll think about it."

She gave him a nod, though she really shouldn't have. He might construe any positive gesture as encouragement. But right now, she would do just about anything to stop this pointless marriage talk.

"Thank you." Liam bent close again. He brushed her forehead with his big, warm hand and placed a sweet, light kiss where his palm had been. "Thank you for my son and for promising to keep an open mind about marriage."

An open mind? Uh-uh. Her mind was locked down and dead bolted on that subject.

But for right now, he could go ahead and refuse to accept what she'd told him twice. Eventually he'd get the message. She even dared to hope the day would come when he would be grateful to her for not taking advantage of him at this emotional time.

As for the touch of his lips on her skin, she shouldn't have liked that so much, shouldn't have let herself sigh just a little when he bent near.

Really, she shouldn't even have allowed that kiss, should have turned her head away when his fine lips descended. He was a wonderful guy and she needed to begin developing a strong coparenting relationship with him—one that wouldn't include kisses, not even on the forehead.

Today, though, was a special circumstance. She'd just given birth to his baby. Surely, this once, a kiss on the forehead couldn't hurt…

Per hospital policy, Karin stayed the night at Memorial. Her girlfriends left after she was all settled in a regular room in the postpartum unit.

Liam stayed on. Karin suggested more than once that he ought to go home, get some dinner and a good night's rest. He said he wasn't tired.

A nurse came in with the birth certificate forms. They hadn't chosen a name yet, so the nurse helped them fill out everything else and told them where to send the form when the name had been decided. The space for the baby's last name didn't go empty. Liam wrote "Bravo" in there and Karin didn't object. No, she wasn't going to marry the guy, but she was determined to be respectful of his place in their baby's life.

The nurse left and finally, at a little before seven, Liam went off to get something to eat in the cafeteria.

Not five minutes after he went out the door, her dad and the kids arrived to meet the new baby. Apparently, Otto had spoken to them about how to behave in the hospital. Coco was as enthusiastic as ever, but she kept her voice down and sat with her little hands folded in her lap, a wild-haired, blue-eyed, second-grade angel. Ben was just Ben—curious and serious, even more polite than usual.

They each held the baby and seemed to enjoy that.

"He's kind of red," remarked Ben. He looked up. "But that's normal. I read that newborns have thin skin and the red blood vessels can show through."

When Coco's turn to hold her baby brother came, Ben leaned close and gently touched his head. "Soft spots," he declared with a solemn little nod. "They are called fontanels and there is one in front and one in back of the skull so that the baby's head can be flexible when he's coming through the birth canal and also so that the brain can grow quickly, now that he's born."

"He is so cute," Coco said in a carefully controlled whisper. "But his nose is kind of squished."

Ben loftily explained that a flattened nose also tended to happen during birth. "It's a tight squeeze," he said to his sister. "But his nose will assume its normal shape over time."

Coco looked up, frowning. "Mommy, what's our baby's name?"

"We haven't decided yet," Karin answered with a smile. *Note to self—ask Liam if he's made that list.*

Otto took the baby from Coco and declared him absolutely perfect. He'd just returned him to Karin's arms when there was a tap on the half-open door.

Liam had returned. "Hey. Should I come back?"

"Liam!" Coco exclaimed—and then realized she'd almost shouted. She clapped her hand over her mouth briefly and then stage-whispered, "Hi."

"Come on in," said Otto. "I've got to get these kids home, anyway. Homework to do, baths to take."

Liam glanced at her for permission.

What could she say? She waved him forward.

A few minutes later, after Karin's dad had assured her that he'd reached Sten in LA and reported that the newest member of the family had arrived safe and sound, Otto herded the kids out the door.

Liam said, "I'll bet you're tired."

"Oh, maybe just a little..."

"I'll leave you alone. But can I hold him—just for a minute?"

Her heart kind of melted at the longing in his eyes. "Of course."

He came close and she handed the baby over. Liam adjusted the swaddled blanket around his little face.

Karin leaned back against the pillow. "I keep meaning to ask if you've thought about a name yet."

He gently rocked the blanketed bundle from side to side. "I really can't decide."

She shut her weary eyes. "Well, think about it. We need to call him something other than 'the baby'."

"Will do." And he started whispering—to the baby, she assumed. She couldn't hear what he said, but the soft sound of his voice was soothing and she was so tired...

When Karin woke, Liam was gone and the baby was asleep in the plastic bassinet beside her. She didn't learn until breakfast time that he'd spent the night in the waiting room.

"I stayed just in case you might need me," he said when he came in with a sausage and egg sandwich in one hand and a paper cup of coffee in the other. He had bags under his eyes and his hair was slicked back as though he'd used the hospital restroom to splash water on his face. "When will they release you?" he asked.

"Later this morning or this afternoon, after my doctor comes by to check on us and sign us out of here."

"I'll drive you to the Cove."

She shook her head. "My dad's coming. He'll have the baby seat all hooked up in the car, ready to go."

He sipped his coffee. "Right. I need a baby seat."

She couldn't help chuckling. "Most conscientious single dad. Ever. Like in the history of dads."

That gorgeous smile lit up his face. "Thank you." He toasted her with his paper cup. "I do my best."

After he ate, he held the baby again. When he handed the little boy back, he said regretfully, "I suppose I need to check in at work, maybe even go to my place and take a shower. But I'll see you both later on today."

"Sure. As I said, I don't even know for certain what time they'll release us."

"No problem. I'll see you soon." He kissed the baby on the cheek and left.

As it turned out, the doctor didn't come to release her until the afternoon. Otto got one of the moms to bring Ben home from soccer practice. He picked up Coco from school and brought her to the hospital with him. She chattered away as they put the baby in his car seat and headed home.

At the Cove, the garage beneath the cottage next door was wide open. Karin spotted the back end of Liam's F-150 Raptor parked inside. Back when they were hooking up, he drove a black Audi Q8. The pickup suited him better, she thought, a true guy's guy sort of vehicle.

Not that what car he drove mattered to her in the least. What mattered was that the garage next door was wide open and his pickup was in it. The smaller house was a rental and vacation property. Sten kept it fully furnished, but he hadn't rented it to anyone since Madison had stayed there last spring.

Karin turned to her dad. "Do you have any idea why Liam's truck is parked in the garage next door?"

"I thought you knew," her dad replied. "Liam called Sten and Sten leased him the cottage."

Chapter Four

In the house, Coco ran to her room. The minute the little girl disappeared down the hall, Karin pitched her voice low and asked her dad, "Would you keep an eye on Coco? I'm just going over to talk to Liam for a minute."

"Kary." Otto spoke gently, like she was made of glass and about to shatter. "He's a great guy."

"Did I once say he wasn't?"

"Just give him a chance, that's all I'm suggesting."

"You're right. He's terrific and I intend to work with him and honor the importance of his place in our child's life. What more do you want from me, Dad?"

"Well, you could open your eyes. You're as bad as Sten was with Madison—pushing a good thing away for all you're worth."

"Not true." Yeah, Sten had been a thickheaded fool about Madison, ridiculously certain for way too long that it couldn't work out for them. But Sten and Madison were a completely different situation than Karin and Liam and her dad really ought to know that. "My eyes are wide open, I promise you."

"That man next door? He is not Bud."

As if she didn't know that—and she felt obligated, as always, to defend her dead husband. "Bud was a good man."

"Never said he wasn't."

The baby, whom she'd carried from the car in his baby seat, gave a questioning cry. "Shh, now. It's okay," she whispered to him. To her dad, she said, "I really can't have this conversation right now. I need to go next door. Will you keep an eye on Coco?"

Otto studied her face for several uncomfortable seconds before finally giving it up. "Sure."

"Thanks, Dad." She gave him a grateful smile and hustled to the baby's room as her newborn fussed in the seat. He quieted as soon as she wrapped him close in the baby sling Prim had given her for a shower gift.

At the cottage, she went in through the open garage door and was halfway up the interior stairs when Liam pulled open the door above that led into the laundry room.

"Hey." He beamed down at her like she was the one person in the whole world he'd been waiting to see. "Come on in." He stepped back and ushered her inside, leading the way to the kitchen that opened onto a deck with stairs down to the beach. The cottage had a similar footprint to the main house, with the entrance facing the hill behind it and the main living area looking out over the ocean.

Liam had all the kitchen cabinets open, with groceries piled on the counters. He gestured at the table by the slider. "Have a seat."

"No, thanks. I won't stay long." She stroked the curve of the baby's back. He wiggled a little, then settled against her.

"I like that sling thing. I need to get one." Liam stood too close, right there at the end of the counter with her—really, did he have to be so tall and broad and manly? "Keely has one," he said. "She uses it constantly. My niece Marie loves it."

"Liam. We need to talk about this." She tried to sound stern—but understanding, too.

He chuckled. "You sound like Mrs. Coolidge. Remember her, fourth grade? She'd get so disappointed if I didn't turn in my homework. *Liam*, she would say. *What am I going to do with you?*"

No way was she getting detoured down memory lane with him. That could be a very long trip. They'd known each other since the beginning of time, after all. "Moving in here, just out of the blue like this, is a little extreme, don't you think?"

"No, I don't think it's extreme in the least." He leaned back against the counter and folded his arms across that hard chest. He wore a lightweight blue sweater. The sleeves were pushed up, revealing forearms with just the right dusting of silky-looking hair and those sexy veins that only served to accentuate his gorgeous, hard muscles. "I'm really glad I thought of it. Lucky for me, it was empty. Sten says he took it off Airbnb and Vrbo because he's in LA most of the time. When he *is* here, well, Madison doesn't really want strangers right next door anyway. People can get intrusive, living next to a movie star—they're going to try to make it home during the holidays, did you know that?"

Karin rubbed the baby's back some more, soothing herself as much as her little boy. "Yeah, I knew that."

"The downstroke is that your brother said this cottage is mine for as long as I need it. He even gave me the go-ahead to fix it up any way I want, including a room for the baby. I'm thinking deep blue and a mural on the crib wall, like the one you did, except not. Maybe a dinosaur mural. Or stars and moons…"

She tried again to get through to him. "Liam, I just don't think it's a good idea, you living here. There are, well, boundaries, you know? We need to observe them."

"And I am observing them."

"No. You're moving in next door."

"Karin, come on. I'm in this house and you're in the other house. We definitely each have our own defined space. It's not like I'm suddenly asking to share a place with you."

"But I would rather that you—"

He cut her off. "Look, I know what our baby needs most now is you. But if I'm living here, he's going to know me as part of his life from the start. That matters to a kid and it matters to me. I can play backup parent from the beginning. Anytime you need help, I'm right next door." He pushed away from the counter and stepped in too close again. She steeled herself against all that charm and hotness. "This is a good thing, me being close by. You have to know that."

She backed away a step and tried another tack. "What about that beautiful house you built in Astoria?"

He gave an easy shrug. "It's too far away from my son. When I get around to it, I'll put it on the market."

"Just like that? But you *love* that house."

"My priorities have changed. But don't worry about it. I'm not selling it right away. If I suddenly decide I can't live without that house, it'll still be there. Right now, though, I need to live *here*, near you and the baby."

Oh, this man. Her heart could melt into a hot puddle of goo just listening to some of the things he said.

And that was the whole point, now wasn't it? *Not* to get a melted mush-ball of a heart just because a good man was trying to do the right thing by his child. She needed to stand strong on her own, be supportive of Liam as a coparent to their son, but remain mindful that he had his life and she had hers and having a baby together did not mean they *were* together.

"You're just going to do this, aren't you?" she demanded. "You're living in this house next door to *my* house no matter how I feel about it."

He took her by the shoulders, his big, warm hands so strong and steady, and he captured her gaze and held it. "You'll see. It's going to be great."

Back at the other house, her daughter greeted her at the front door. Coco had changed clothes. Now, her shorts were blue and her T-shirt was red. Yellow knit arm warmers covered her wrists to her elbows. She had a swatch of gold mesh fabric tied around her head and a red construction-paper star pinned to it in the exact center of her forehead.

"Wonder Woman, how's it going?"

Coco crossed her arms in front of her face. "Just tell me you need help, Mommy, and I will save you." Coco wiggled her eyebrows over the barrier of her arms.

"Whew." Karin made a show of wiping imaginary sweat from her forehead. "That is really good to know."

"I have lots of powers, Mommy." Oh, yes, she did. Coco had an iPad and she knew how to use it. She always did her research, superheroine-wise.

"What powers, exactly?"

"I have superhuman strength and I never get tired. I glide through the air on the wind. I have super speed and *agitally.* I can smell everything and see everything and hear the most smallest sounds."

"I feel safer already."

Coco stood tall. "You're *welcome*, Mommy." And off she flew toward the kitchen.

As for Karin, she went straight to her bedroom, pulled out her phone and called Sten.

He answered on the first ring. "How's my new nephew?"

"He's sweet and beautiful," she said loftily. "You're going to love him."

"I can't wait to meet him. Liam tells me you haven't settled on a name yet."

"No, we haven't—and about Liam…"

"Yeah?" The single word was freighted with challenge. She could just picture Sten drawing his shoulders back, standing a little taller. "What about him?"

Reminding herself that she would stay calm and not yell at her brother—for the sake of the innocent child sleeping next to her heart if for no other reason—Karin paced back and forth at the foot of the bed. "I am really upset with you," she said in a purposely soft, calm voice. "You could have at least discussed it with me before you leased him the cottage."

Sten snort-laughed. "And have you make up a thousand meaningless reasons why I shouldn't rent to him? No, thanks. He's family, Karin, in case you've forgotten. He's my brother-in-law and he wants to be near his kid. There's nothing wrong with that."

"I am actively resisting the powerful need to start shouting mean things at you."

"Go right ahead and shout. I can take it. Because I'm pissed at you, too. You have to give that man a chance, Karin. He wants to be there for your baby and it's part of your job to help him do that."

It was essentially the same thing their dad had said. It had aggravated her the first time she heard it. This time, it made her want to throw back her head and scream. She took a slow, deep breath before replying. "I *am* helping him, Sten. I support him totally as the baby's father."

"And yet you took forever to get around to telling him he was even going to be a dad. Karin, I really was starting to think you never would."

"Sten, okay." She stroked the baby's nearly bald head with one hand and pinched the bridge of her nose with the other because sometimes Sten gave her a headache—and because, yeah, he was right. "I messed that up, I admit it. But at least he knows now. He was there for his son's birth. And now, thanks to you, he's even living in the house next door."

"You're welcome."

She heard the humor in her brother's voice and couldn't help but smile. "I think Liam plans to be the most *involved* dad that has ever existed in the whole of time. And I think it's great, I really do. I am not getting in his way, I promise you. Liam will have every chance to be there for his kid."

"Good," said her brother. "That's how it should be. And now he's got the cottage, it will be so much easier for him to help you out whenever you need him."

"By that you mean you won't tell him that you've changed your mind and the cottage isn't available after all?"

"Way to go, little sister. I think you're finally getting the picture."

* * *

Karin did take her brother's words to heart.

She invited Liam over for dinner that night. He showed up right on time. When the baby cried, she let him do the comforting. A little later, for the first time, Liam changed his son's diaper—a loaded one, too.

Really, her baby's dad was one of the good guys.

And that was the problem. He was a good man and he wanted to do right and it would be oh, so easy to let herself believe that they could share more than a son.

She would just have to keep holding the line against any suggestion that the two of them should get married. Eventually, he'd come to see that her saying no had been the best thing for everyone involved.

Thursday after dinner, she asked her dad to watch the sleeping baby so that she could go over to the cottage and discuss DNA testing with Liam.

He answered the door looking way too handsome in black jeans and a dark sweater with the sleeves pushed up those amazing forearms. Really, it wasn't fair that he looked so good. She, on the other hand, wore the outfit she'd thrown on that morning—a stretched-out gray Henley-style tunic and yoga pants. She'd also run out of the house without bothering to check her hair or freshen her lip gloss.

Had she actually been naked with this gorgeous specimen of a man on four separate and glorious occasions? It seemed so very long ago…

And yet, it really had happened and she had the baby to prove it.

"Hey."

"Hey."

"Where's the baby?"

"Sleeping. My dad'll call if he needs me."

"Come on in." He gave her that smile of his, the magic one that could make a girl's panties combust, and led her to the sitting area.

She took a chair and got down to it. "I came to talk DNA. There's a lab right here in town. We can all three go together, you, me and the baby. Just name a date and time—or I can meet you there, if that works better for you."

"DNA?" He dropped to the sofa. "It's not necessary. I know the baby's mine. I don't need a DNA test and I don't care if we have one."

"*I* care, Liam."

His burnished brows drew together. "Don't do that."

"What?"

"Don't give me that look, Karin. Like you disapprove of me."

Now, she felt awful. "I didn't. I *don't*." She stuck her hands between her knees and leaned toward him across the coffee table. "Not at all. What I meant was, well, proof is so easy to get now. There's no reason *not* to get it. All it takes is a cheek swab and you'll never doubt that our little boy is yours."

He shook his head her. "I already have no doubts. I know you, Karin. You have absolute integrity. If there was a doubt, you would have told me so that day at Safeway." He spoke with total conviction.

Now, her cheeks felt too warm and her tummy all fluttery. "Thank you." Her throat had clutched. She gulped to loosen it up. "That was a beautiful thing to say to me."

He leaned forward, too, so earnest and determined. "I don't need a test, Karin."

"I hear you. But *I* do—and not because I have any doubt you're the baby's dad. It's just, I want that, for you to have objective proof. Even though I accept your word that you don't need it."

He dropped back against the cushions with a hard breath. "Sorry. I don't get it. But if it's what you want—"

"It is. Please."

The following Monday afternoon, together, they took the baby to a lab right there in town to have their cheeks swabbed. Liam, eager to use the new car seat he'd bought, did the driving.

Later, back at the Cove, mindful of her resolution to treat Liam with kindness and consideration, Karin invited him to dinner again. "About six, if you can make it."

He accepted with a wide grin and showed up an hour early. She refused to let herself get annoyed about that. Instead, she reminded herself that the guy planned to stay at the cottage indefinitely and she'd better get used to having him around.

Really, what was not to like about Liam? He was easygoing and also easy on the eyes. He even offered to help in the kitchen.

"I've got this. But you can help the kids with cleanup after if you insist."

He had a beer with her dad and jumped to his feet when the baby cried. "I'll get him." He headed for the bedrooms and she didn't stop him.

When it was time to eat, he carried the blue bundle with him to the dinner table, where Coco fawned all over him and the baby in his big arms.

Coco did have one complaint, though. "Liam. Mommy. Our baby needs a name. Nobody likes to be called just 'the baby.'" Coco wrinkled up her little nose in disapproval.

"He's a newborn," said Ben. "He doesn't know how to talk and he doesn't understand words. That means he has no idea what we're calling him."

Coco tossed her curly head. "Well, *I* care what we call him and I'm his big sister." She smiled sweetly and actually fluttered her eyelashes. "I will be happy to choose a name for him. How about Brecken? There's a boy named Brecken in my class. He talks without raising his hand and chews with his mouth open, but I still like his name. Or how about Kael or Ridge?"

Karin met Liam's gaze across the dinner table as he glanced up from the baby in his arms. His eyes gleamed with humor. The moment tugged at her heartstrings, somehow. She was reminded of the past, of their long history together.

When Karin and Liam were Coco's age, he'd had a big crush on their second-grade teacher, Miss Wu. One morning, he brought Miss Wu a handful of wilted wildflowers he must have picked on the way to school. At recess, a couple of the other boys had razzed him. They'd called him a kiss-ass. Liam had just laughed and walked away.

Karin, flanked by Prim and Naomi, had watched the exchange. She and her friends waited, wide-eyed, for the two bullies to follow him, taunt him some more, maybe even throw a punch or two.

Didn't happen. The boys just stared after him, looking baffled. Liam simply had that way about him, always had. A born charmer, so easy and comfortable in his own skin. Bullies never knew what to make of him.

Really, the only time Karin had seen the man at a loss was recently, in the first few days after he found out about the baby.

Across the table, Liam tipped his head to the side,

watching her. He offered, "My dad's name was George. Maybe George for a middle name?"

Coco piped up with, "I like Brecken better."

Otto stepped in. "Excellent suggestion, sweetheart. But I think your mom and Liam will be making this decision."

Coco released a gusty sigh. "Well, o-*kay.* I don't need to be the decider, I guess. Just as long as my baby brother gets a name."

Otto reached over and patted her shoulder as Karin asked Liam, "What do you think of Riley? Riley George Bravo?"

He bent to the baby and whispered something. Then, still leaning close, he turned his head as though listening for a reply. He straightened in his chair with a nod. "He likes it. Riley George, it is."

Tuesday around nine, after everyone had left the Cove but Karin and Riley, two of Liam's sisters knocked on her door. Harper and Hailey had come to fix up the baby's room over at the cottage.

Hailey said, "But we wanted to stop by, say hi to you and meet Riley first."

Karin invited them in and made them coffee. They took turns holding the baby and filling Karin in on their mutual dream, which involved hosting children's parties and producing community events at an old theater downtown. Both blue-eyed blondes, the sisters were less than a year apart in age. They'd gone off to OU together, majored in theater arts together and graduated together the year before. Now, they both lived in town.

"My new nephew is the cutest guy ever," declared Hailey when it was her turn to hold Riley.

Harper agreed. "He is adorable—and Liam is so happy. All he talks about is the baby."

Hailey asked, "Can you blame him? I mean, look at this little guy." She grinned at Karin. "Liam likes *you* a lot, too."

Karin wasn't sure how to respond to that—mostly because she was constantly reminding herself *not* to like Liam too much. "He's a really good guy." She tried not to wince at how lame that sounded.

Harper said, "Okay, maybe this is out of bounds…"

"But we're just gonna ask," Hailey picked up where her sister left off. "If you don't like the question, tell us to mind our own damn business."

"We won't be offended."

"Fair enough." Karin sipped her tea. She had a pretty good idea where this was going.

Harper scooted closer to the table and wrapped her hands around her coffee mug. "So…what's the story with you and Liam? We didn't even know you guys were a thing."

"Well, we weren't a thing, not really." Karin turned her teacup in a slow circle as she tried to decide how much to say.

"Riley here would beg to differ." Hailey bent close and nuzzled his fat cheek. "There must have been *something*."

Karin confessed, "You're right. There was." It really had been terrific, her long-held secret fantasy come true—a few hot, stolen nights with the guy she'd crushed on so hard back in high school.

Harper reached over and gave her arm a reassuring squeeze. "Don't be sad."

Hailey looked concerned. "We didn't mean to upset you."

"You haven't. No way. It just, um, happened, between Liam and me. It started last December, on a girls' night out…"

She'd almost canceled on Naomi and Prim that night. Ben had come down with something and was running a low fever. She'd decided to stay home. But her dad and Sten had ganged up on her. She deserved a break, they said. Ben would be fine, they promised her. And she would only be a phone call away.

So she'd gone. "Believe me, with two kids and the Boatworks to run, I hadn't been getting a lot of nights out. My girls and I met up at Beach Street Brews. Liam just happened to be there that night, too, with some of his trucker buddies. He and I started talking. It was so easy between us. I couldn't get over that—then again, we've known each other all our lives, so why wouldn't we be comfortable with each other, right?" She met Harper's eyes and they shared a smile. "It was a great night. And so were the other nights we got together. But he wasn't looking for a relationship and neither was I. It was just for now and just for fun. And then, well, surprise, surprise. Riley came along."

Harper nodded. "It happens."

"Wedding bells, maybe?" Hailey asked, looking hopeful.

"No," Karin said gently. "He's an amazing guy and I like him a lot, always have." Maybe too much, but his sisters didn't need to know that. "We're not in love, though." It caused an ache in her heart to say it. But sometimes the truth hurt. She finished softly, "We just want the same thing and that's to do the best we can for Riley."

They left it at that. The sisters stayed for another half hour or so. Before they left for the cottage, Karin gave Hailey the blue teddy bear Liam had brought over that day Riley was born. "I want him to have it for the new room."

That Friday, the DNA results came through.

It was official. Liam was Riley's biological father.

That evening, Karin took Riley over to the cottage to talk to Liam about a parenting plan.

"Hey." He gave her his killer smile. "Come on in."

In the kitchen, he offered her something to drink. "I'm guessing no alcohol, with the nursing and all, but I've got juice and I picked up some of that raspberry tea you like."

"I'm good, thanks."

He let his gaze trail down to the baby, who was attached to the front of her as usual, lately. Karin kind of loved watching his face when he saw his son. His mouth got so soft and his eyes a little dreamy. It was too damn cute by half. "Mind if I hold him?"

She eased Riley out of the sling and handed him over. The baby blinked up at his father and then yawned.

Liam bent his head close and nuzzled Riley's button nose. "Lookin' good, RG." He glanced up and caught her watching him. "What?" But then, before she could answer, he gestured her forward. "First things first. Let me show you his room."

She followed him down the hall to the bedroom next to the master suite. It was all ready for Riley. "Wow. That was fast."

He looked up from whispering to the baby. "Yeah. I got right on it. Lots of online shopping with overnight shipping. I gave Keely a credit card and she ordered most of the blankets and baby clothes, all the baby supplies and a diaper bag. I picked out the furniture myself."

"It looks great." Open shelves over the changing table were stacked with everything a baby might need. The walls were dark blue.

"I love the teddy bears and the tree," she said of the wall mural behind the crib. One bear floated midway up the wall on a couple of heart-shaped pale blue balloons. Three others climbed the tree.

"Harper did that, the mural and the detail stuff. Hailey painted the walls blue. Then the two of them put the furniture where they thought it should go." He gazed at her steadily. "They mentioned you had them over for coffee."

"Yeah. It was great to see them. We had a nice little chat." *About you and me and why we're not getting married. But you don't need to know that, so please don't ask.*

He didn't. He was all about the baby as he circled the room, whispering things in Riley's ear, stopping by the easy chair next to the window and glancing up at Karin. "RG and me, we need to try out this chair."

"Go for it." She leaned in the doorway and folded her arms across her middle.

He sat down. "Check this out." He leaned back and the easy chair became a recliner. "Pretty sweet, huh?"

"Perfect." And it was. *He* was. Totally devoted to his surprise son. It brought her joy to see them together—joy and a bittersweet ache in her chest that Bud had never really been able or willing or whatever to show that kind of steady, doting love to Ben. At least with Coco, Bud had been more affectionate—when he was around.

"What?" Liam was watching her.

She waved the question away with a shrug.

He glanced down at the baby again. For a few minutes, they were quiet. Liam held Riley as Karin leaned in the doorway enjoying the sight of them, the feeling of peace that seemed to fill the blue room.

"He's sound asleep," Liam whispered as he rose. "I want to put him in his crib." It was all fixed up, with cute blue-and-white bedding, including soft bumpers to cushion and protect a newborn. The blue teddy bear was propped in a corner.

"Good idea," she whispered back.

He put the baby down and tucked the blanket around him, bending closer for another kiss.

Rising to his height again, he came to her. She pulled away from the doorway to face him.

And then he was taking her by the upper arms, his big hands so warm and gentle. He caught her gaze and held it, that beautiful smile flirting with the corners of his full mouth.

She just knew he would kiss her and that she would let him.

But he didn't. "Come on," he said. "You know you want that raspberry tea. I haven't taken the baby monitor out of the box yet, but I think we'll hear him if we just leave the door open."

Liam had one of those electric kettles. It heated the water in no time.

As she waited for the tea to steep, he pulled a Boundary Bay IPA from the fridge and popped the cap. "So, what's up?" His strong throat rippled as he took a long drink.

"I thought we should kind of get moving on our parenting plan."

With a slow smile, he shook his head. "Always with the plans."

They stood facing each other on the same side of the counter. She had a strong urge to whirl around, dart over to the table and pull out a chair, put some distance between them. If he came and sat down, too, the table would serve as a barrier to keep her from giving in to the longing inside her.

She felt he was always asking a certain question—he asked it with his eyes and his body language, with his very attentiveness. It was partly *will you marry me?* But it was more, too. He was asking for kisses. And slow, sweet caresses. He was asking for more nights like the ones last winter.

And maybe asking was too weak a word. Maybe he was more…anticipating. Waiting for the moment, the *right* moment to make his move.

What were they talking about?

Parenting plan. Right. "Structure is a good thing." Dear Lord. Could she sound any prissier?

He set his beer on the granite countertop and took a step closer. That brought him right up in her face. She should run for the table—or maybe right on out the door.

But she didn't want to run.

She wanted those kisses his eyes kept promising, wanted to just stand here and suck in the warm, delicious, manly scent of him, to admire the fullness of his lips and the chiseled perfection of his jaw, to drown in the baby blue perfection of those eyes.

"We really don't need a parenting plan, Karin."

"Uh." Her mind felt thick and slow. Warm molasses ran through her veins. "Yes, we do."

"RG is eleven days old. At this point, I just need to

be here whenever you want backup or a break. That's my job and we can't put that on a schedule. Not right now. Except when there's something at Bravo Trucking I have to handle ASAP, I'm yours. And RG's. Push comes to shove, you and our son are the priority and my business will just have to get in line."

What he said made perfect sense—not to mention making her feel looked-after, taken-care-of. It would be so very easy to give in, let him have his way about everything.

To let herself fall.

So easy, to love him, to give her heart and soul to him.

Easy and scary and not in her plans. Because it was better, safer, not to start counting on him. Not to let herself give her trust to him and take the chance that eventually he would let her down.

Her poor heart had had enough of that. She just couldn't go through that kind of hurt and disappointment again.

Good men got right behind the idea of stepping up and making a lifetime commitment when a woman needed them. But sometimes, in the long-term execution of that commitment, they started feeling trapped by the very thing they'd sworn they wanted.

Uh-uh. Not going there again.

Liam moved that extra inch closer. She could feel the warmth of him now, smell his clean, manly scent.

Really, he was much too close. She drew in a breath and her breasts met his chest. Her whole body tingled.

She ought to just step back. But she didn't.

He lifted a hand, slowly, the way a person does around a skittish animal, ready to back right off if she gave him the slightest indication she wouldn't welcome his touch.

She could not for the life of her give him that hint. The delicious anticipation was simply too great.

She thought of all the things a woman considers when she's just had a baby and a man looks at her as though he intends to kiss her.

If she ended up with her clothes off, how bad would she look to him? Her belly was too soft and her breasts were blue-veined and swollen, cradled in a nursing bra. Her panties? Plain cotton and not brand-new. How long had it been since she'd washed her hair?

And what did any of that matter?

There was no way she was getting naked with him tonight. She wouldn't get the go-ahead to have sex for weeks yet—not that there weren't a lot of other things short of the main event they could do if they wanted to.

Oh, why was she thinking about sex right now?

Why was she thinking about sex at all?

She wasn't having sex with Liam. Not tonight, not ever. He was her partner in parenting Riley and the last thing they needed was to muck up that important relationship with something as volatile as sex.

"You're blushing." He leaned close and whispered the words into her ear. His breath was so warm, tickling her earlobe and brushing the curve of her cheek. "You smell like heaven, Karin, always did. Now there's a baby lotion and a fresh-baked cookies sort of smell, too." He actually sniffed at her.

"Cookies? Excuse me?"

"Sorry. I smell what I smell and it smells really good." His lips were right there. She felt them, skimming, soft and warm, against her cheek. He nipped at her, gently, like she was an actual cookie and he wanted a taste.

The light pressure of his teeth on her skin made her gasp.

His hand touched her hair, those long fingers gently combing through it, easing out the tangled spots. He used to do that, stroke her hair, when they were in bed together. "I always loved your hair. Since way back when we were kids."

"You didn't." Her voice sounded so odd to her, husky and low.

"Yeah. It's dark as coffee, and shiny, with red glints in sunlight and a blue-black sheen to it by lamplight. And it's always kind of wild, falling every which way. Back when we were kids, I always wanted to stick my fingers in it, to pull on it and bury my face in it."

"I would've punched you out if you'd tried that."

"I kind of thought you might, so I kept my greedy paws to myself—and then in high school, those two dates we had?"

"Don't remind me."

"I wanted more with you, even then."

"Coulda fooled me."

"But we were barely eighteen, much too young to go being exclusive."

She laughed, a husky giggle of a sound that she quickly stifled. "I can't believe I'm standing here whispering with you, and giggling, too, like some brainless fool. I keep telling myself to step back, step away from you."

He nuzzled her cheek again. "How's that working out for you, Karin?"

"It's not."

"We've got a thing. You know we do."

"Riley is not a thing."

"Karin," he chided. "I'm not talking about RG."

"You *should* be talking about Riley. *We* should be concentrating on Riley."

His hand left her hair. He trailed a finger down the side of her throat, stirring up a naughty string of hot little shivers as he went. And then he put that finger under her chin to get her to look at him. His eyes burned into hers, the blue color deeper than usual.

"I've missed you," he said, "since you dumped me last March."

"I didn't dump you. How could I dump you? We weren't together."

"Yeah, we were. From that first night, I wasn't with anyone but you. How about you?"

"No. But you know what I mean. It wasn't serious. We weren't even dating."

"Karin."

"What?"

"Shut up." He stole a quick, perfect kiss. Her lips burned at the brief contact. She yearned, she really did. Every molecule in her body hungered for more.

And he knew it, too.

He knew it and he gave her exactly what she couldn't stop herself from wanting. Lowering his amazing mouth, he settled it more firmly over hers.

Chapter Five

Liam took care to kiss her slowly, with restraint and yet with promise. He knew she was right on the brink of breaking.

And she could break either way—in surrender. Or in flight.

He wanted her surrender, at least as much as he could get of surrender in a kiss.

"I'm not having sex with you," she said breathlessly against his mouth.

"I know." He'd read the damn books, after all.

Framing her boyish, beautiful face between his hands, he broke the kiss to gaze down at her. He'd always loved the way she looked, with those eyes that were blue and then green and then blue again, seeming to change colors in changing light. He admired those high cheekbones, that pointed little chin. And those plump, perfect lips that invited his kiss.

"It's just a kiss," he reminded her.

"Liam," she whispered. He heard longing in that whisper and he swooped in again to give her exactly what she longed for, going deeper this time, urging her to open, to let him in.

She resisted at first, but then, with a tiny groan, she gave it up. His tongue slipped between her softly parted lips and he tasted her fully as he let his hands wander a little, out along her slim shoulders, down her back.

Good. She felt so very good. She was making him ache, making him hurt in the best possible way.

He pulled her closer, pressing his hardness against her, cupping a hand at the back of her head to hold her in place so he could kiss her even more deeply. She was heaven in his arms and he had missed holding her, missed the fire between them, the way they bickered and nipped at each other.

It was really fun, with Karin. She was the girl he'd known forever, and yet the girl who kept changing. He'd lost her in high school because he'd told her right out that he didn't intend to be anyone's boyfriend. Then she'd married Bud Killigan, who was a couple of years older, a guy Liam hardly knew. And then last March, he'd lost her again, lost her before he even got a chance to persuade her she should spend more time with him.

He wouldn't lose her this time. Now they had RG and that made it necessary that they be together. One way or another, he would convince her she belonged with him.

Sometimes he got impatient. It was his nature to be so. But mostly, it didn't matter to him how long it took her to finally realize he was the one for her. Getting there definitely was half the fun.

With a sigh, she pulled away.

"Get back here," he commanded and dipped close to claim her lips again.

She only slid her hands up between them and pressed them flat to his chest, exerting undeniable pressure, the kind a man had no right to ignore. "I have to go, Liam." She gazed up at him, those blue-green eyes so serious. Her soft lips were red and swollen and he was on fire to taste them again.

That wasn't going to happen tonight, though. Reluctantly, he released her.

She stared up at him, looking earnest and adorable and turned on and embarrassed. "I shouldn't have kissed you."

He dared to put a finger against those perfect, swollen lips. "I'm glad you did."

"But we—"

"Karin."

She blew out a hard breath. "What?"

"It was a great kiss. Let it be." He pushed her mug and saucer toward her along the counter.

"Fine." She took the tea bag out of the mug, plopped it on the saucer and took a sip.

He heard a reedy cry from the baby's room.

She heard it, too, and set down the mug. "Time to go."

Could he get her to stay if he tried? Probably not. He'd pushed her enough for one night.

A few minutes later, in the baby's room at the main house, Karin nursed Riley and thought about Liam.

She really shouldn't have kissed him, but she couldn't quite bring herself to regret that she had. That kiss had been amazing. She refused to feel bad about it.

She just needed to make sure it didn't happen again.

That wouldn't be easy. Liam was proving to be a lot more persistent than she'd ever imagined.

Since the day he learned that she was having his baby, he'd gone right to work insinuating himself into every corner of her life. Her brother, her daughter and her dad had definitely fallen under the influence of Liam Bravo's charms.

Sten was all for the guy, lecturing Karin to treat him right, renting him the damn cottage without consulting her. Coco had what amounted to a kiddie crush on the man.

And since the day after Karin and Riley came home from the hospital, Otto and Liam had developed their very own private tradition: morning coffee, the two of them. Her dad would head over there at the crack of dawn. He'd stay for an hour or so and get back to the main house in time for breakfast.

When it wasn't raining, he and Liam would sit out on the mist-shrouded deck of the cottage together. Most mornings, Karin could hear them faintly, talking and laughing, like they were best buds or something.

Ben was the only one who held the line against Liam. Her older son was always polite around any grown-up. But he hadn't really warmed to Liam. He was civil around the baby's father and not much more.

Ben's reserve didn't stop Liam, though. He was always asking about Ben's latest science project and listening with rapt attention when he finally got Ben to open up a little about it. Twice already, he'd picked up Ben and a couple of teammates from soccer practice when Otto was stuck late at the Boatworks.

Okay, yeah. The more she thought it over, the more she came to the simple conclusion that Liam Bravo was amazing. He was amazing and she had a crush on him just like her daughter did.

But really, how long would he be living next door? When would he realize he missed his easy, independent single lifestyle?

Karin just needed to keep herself from counting on him too much. That way, when he finally agreed on a parenting plan and went back to his own life, she wouldn't be brokenhearted, wouldn't miss him too much.

She just needed to watch herself, not let herself start squabbling with him. Squabbling with Liam was far too much fun. And kisses? No more of those. And she really had to avoid any more trips down memory lane. They had far too much history and it made her feel way too fond of him to reminisce with him about stuff that had happened way back when.

No kisses. No reminiscing. No banter.

"I can do that," she said out loud to no one in particular—strongly enough to give Riley a scare. He popped off her breast and blinked up at her, startled.

"Oh, honey, it's okay..." Laughing softly, she guided him back to her nipple. "You've got a good dad and your mama loves you," she whispered to her baby son. "It's all going to work out just beautifully, you'll see."

As a rule, on Halloween, Karin or her dad would take the kids trick-or-treating along the streets above Sweetheart Cove. This year, Ben had declared himself old enough to take Coco without adult supervision and Karin had agreed to that.

But this year, it was raining. Steadily, in buckets. Coco whined all day and Ben looked grim and unhappy.

Around four, Liam showed up at the sliding door that opened onto the deck. Her dad let him in.

"Riley's sleeping," she said to Liam, when the two men joined her in the kitchen area where she was standing at the open fridge trying to decide what to whip up for dinner.

"No problem," Liam replied. "I'm not here to see the baby."

"We need to talk to you." Her dad shot a quick glance around the living area. "Are Coco and Ben still in their rooms?"

"Umm-hmm. I believe Coco is actively sulking because the rain very likely will mess up her Halloween. Ben's not happy about that either. He's focusing his frustration on working out issues with his latest science project, I think."

"As long as they're not in earshot, good." Her dad kept his voice low, just between the three of them. "We need to talk about tonight."

"There's a kids' Halloween party at The Valentine Bay Theater," Liam said. "There'll be games and some skits and a really simple haunted house—nothing too gory. And bags of treats for everyone."

Karin shut the fridge door and turned to face the men. "Right. I saw a flyer somewhere about that."

"It's a Hailey and Harper production, essentially," Liam explained. "Eight bucks a head to get in."

Otto said, "Liam and I were talking about it over coffee this morning, that it might be an option if the rain didn't stop. The kids could wear their costumes and do something a little different this year. Liam and I will take them and you can have the evening to yourself."

"We figured you might not want to take the baby out on a rainy night," added Liam. "And just as another option, if you'd prefer, I can watch RG and you can go with your dad and the kids."

She'd yet to get out her breast pump and she didn't really feel like dealing with that at the moment, anyway. Not to mention, Riley wasn't even two weeks old. She wasn't ready to be away from him for that long.

Liam read her so easily. "Too soon, huh?"

She nodded, though a Halloween party really would cheer the kids up. And to steal a couple of hours for herself?

Talk about a new mom's dream-come-true. "I have to admit, the idea of me and Riley and the second season of *Killing Eve*, that's pretty tempting."

"We thought so." Her dad seemed pleased.

"So we're on?" asked Liam.

She hesitated. Liam made it way too easy for her to say yes to him and his plans.

And come on. What in the world was wrong with that, when his plans inevitably involved ways to help her make life better for herself and her family?

"Thank you," she said to both of them. "I think it's a great idea."

Liam stayed for dinner—it only seemed right to feed the guy, what with him giving up his evening to take her kids out for Halloween.

They set off, the four of them, at a little before six, Coco dressed as Jewel the Dalmatian and Ben, in a light blue jacket and bow tie, as Bill Nye, the Science Guy.

Once they were gone, Karin grabbed a bottle of ginger beer and sat on the sofa. Sipping slowly, she listened to the steady drumming of the rain on the roof and thought that never in the history of women had there been such a perfect moment. Everybody gone except her baby, who was sleeping.

After she finished her pretend beer, she spent an hour on the phone catching up with Prim and Naomi. Then she made popcorn and watched three episodes of *Killing Eve*, only getting up to pee and to feed and change Riley when he cried.

It was after ten when the Science Guy, Jewel the Dalmatian and the two men arrived home. Of course, they'd stopped for ice cream after all the excitement of Harper and Hailey's Halloween extravaganza. Even Ben was jazzed up, sucking on a Starburst from his bag of treats and raving about the cool ways Liam's sisters had used dry ice to make fog.

"Mom. It was sick. That fog, it not only overflowed from the witch's cauldron. They had it pouring out of the mouth of a giant carved pumpkin and rising from the base of a gnarly 'hanging' tree."

Coco was so happy, she pranced in a circle. Her doggy ears bounced as she pawed the air, fake-growling when her grandpa suggested it was time to call it a night.

Otto insisted, though. "Kiss your mom good night and say thank you to Liam."

Ben and Coco dutifully pecked Karin on the cheek and offered up a duet of thank-yous to Liam. Then Otto herded both of them off down the hall to put on their pj's and brush their teeth.

That left Liam on the sofa with Riley in his arms and Karin standing by an easy chair trying to decide whether to sit down or start hinting that it was time for him to go.

He looked up from their son with a lazy, lopsided grin. "Don't worry. I won't stay long."

She couldn't stop herself. She grinned right back at

him and then said sincerely, "Thank you. You turned a big disappointment into a memorable event."

"For you. Anything." He said it quietly, kind of tenderly and yet teasingly, too, so that she could tell herself he was only kidding around.

She almost opened her mouth to remind him—teasingly, of course—that they were coparents, not a couple.

But why even say it, jokingly, or otherwise? He hadn't done anything to imply there was more than coparenting going on between them. Not really.

And he looked so relaxed and happy. He'd made her kids happy, too, and given her a precious evening all to herself. How could she keep her walls of emotional safety in place when he wouldn't stop being so damn wonderful?

He got up. "Walk me out?" Still holding the baby, he headed for the entry hall.

She followed along, far too content to be going wherever Liam led her. He turned and passed her the baby when they got to the door.

When she had Riley, though, Liam didn't step back. Uh-uh. He leaned even closer.

And she reminded herself to step back. But she didn't. Anticipation flaring inside her, she stayed right where she was.

Their lips met. Her heart lurched and then kicked into a deeper, hotter rhythm. She sighed against his parted lips.

"Thanksgiving," he said as he broke the tender contact.

Puzzled, and a little annoyed at how much she'd wanted that kiss to last longer, she frowned up at him over their sleeping baby. "Um. What about it?"

"We always have it at Daniel's."

Where was he going with this? "Okay…?"

That mouth she loved kissing way too much curled in a slow, ovulation-inducing smile. "This is an invitation, Karin. I want you and the kids and your dad to join me and the rest of the Bravos for our family Thanksgiving. Rumor has it that Sten and Madison just might be showing up, too."

"Do Daniel and Keely know you're inviting the whole Killigan-Larson crew?"

He did that thing, a lopsided grin coupled with a sexy glint in his sky blue eyes. "Say yes, and they will."

"That just doesn't seem right."

"What do you mean it's not right?" He had that look now, the patient one he gave her whenever she threatened to go off the rails over something he was trying to convince her to do.

"It doesn't seem right for you to just invite all of us without at least warning your brother and his wife first."

"It's a Bravo family thing. The more the better. We love a large group and our Thanksgivings and Christmases just keep getting bigger."

"But think about it. Now, counting Madison, there are nine of you again." A brother, Finn, had vanished years ago. The Bravos still had investigators looking for him.

"Karin." Liam spoke softly, gently, as though she were a not-too-bright child. "I know how many siblings I have."

"Of course you do, but I don't think you realize how many people you could potentially be talking about."

"Sure, I do."

"No. Liam, it could be a *lot* of people."

"Didn't I just say I know that and that it won't be a problem?"

"Think about it. Daniel, Matt, Aislinn and Madison are married, so you have to count their spouses."

"So?"

"So some of those spouses will probably have people *they* want to bring. And let's not forget your great-aunt Daffodil and great-uncle Percy. And Daniel's got three kids."

"Why are you telling me all this stuff I already know? Just FYI, Karin, it's *my* family."

She reminded herself not to raise her voice. She would wake the baby. "Well, I know that," she whispered.

"And guess what? Connor and Aly Santangelo got back together."

That gave her pause. The two had been married and then divorced years ago. "Seriously?"

He nodded. "They're in New York, but they hope to be back for the holidays. They remarried in Manhattan, a courthouse wedding a week and a half ago—the day after Riley was born, as a matter of fact."

"Which only further proves my point. Aly's got that big family of her own here in town. Will *they* all be coming? Liam, do you hear what I'm saying? Maybe there isn't room for four extra guests and a baby."

"It's Daniel's house, the family house. There's *always* room. And who all is coming is not your problem. All you have to say is yes. Just tell me you would love to come and bring the kids. I've already talked to your dad. He's all for it."

"You talked to my dad about it without even checking with me?" She spoke too loudly. Riley squirmed in her arms and let out a cry. She lifted him to her shoulder and rubbed his little back. "Shh," she whispered to him, "it's okay, Mommy's sorry she scared you." She rocked him side-to-side a little and he seemed to settle.

"Karin." Liam reached out.

"Don't." She stepped back to keep him from touching her. She wasn't sure why, exactly, she was so upset about this invitation. It just felt like…a big step. A step she wasn't in any way ready to take. A step she kept telling herself she would never take. "See, Liam. You have your family traditions and we have ours. So, doesn't it just make more sense for you to go ahead and go to your brother's the way you always do for Thanksgiving and we'll just have our family dinner here the way *we* always do."

"No." A muscle twitched in his square jaw. "That makes no sense to me at all. I asked you to come to Daniel's because *that's* what makes sense to me. I want you there, Karin. I want our baby there and your dad and Ben and Coco, too. And Madison and Sten, if they can make it up from LA. I want us all together. That's what Thanksgiving is, all the people you care about the most, together, if at all possible. And it *is* possible, completely possible, if you'll just say yes."

Riley started fussing again. She rubbed his little back, pressed her lips to his warm, silky forehead and said to Liam, "You're being purposely thickheaded."

"*You're* being pointlessly negative and obstinate."

"No, I'm just—"

"Enough." His voice was carefully bland. "Think about it, okay? Let me know what you decide." He pulled open the door and went through, shutting it behind him before she could say another word.

Chapter Six

A week went by during which Karin and Liam hardly spoke.

Early most mornings, she heard him laughing with her father out on the deck at the cottage. More than once, she saw him jogging along the sand in a hoodie and track pants, his shoulders so broad, his hips so lean and tight, his long strides carrying him quickly along the shoreline toward the rocks and shallow caves way down the beach. It caused an ache inside her just to watch him, to take in the sheer perfection of him.

Every evening when he returned from Bravo Trucking, he came to the house to visit his son. She would hand the baby over and walk away.

From the kitchen area or down the hall in her room or in the baby's room, she could hear him joking around with Coco and talking to Ben. He would give the baby to her dad when he was ready to leave.

One time, he was still in the great room with Riley in his arms when she wandered back out from her room to check on them. Her dad was nowhere in sight and the kids must've been in their rooms.

"Here's your mama," he said to his son and handed him over. "See you tomorrow, Karin." And he left her standing there by the slider. Turning toward the glass, she stared out at the dark sky. A moment later, she heard the front door open and then close.

Every time she saw Liam, she expected him to ask her if she'd made up her mind about Thanksgiving. She was *waiting* for him to ask, actually. And when he did, she would reply, *Thank you, but no*. She would say that she really had given his invitation serious thought and she appreciated it very much. However, thinking it over hadn't changed her answer; he should go to his family for Thanksgiving and she and her family would have their usual holiday dinner right here at Sweetheart Cove.

But the days went by and Liam didn't ask her, which made her feel edgy and uncomfortable inside her own skin. After all, she knew very well that he didn't *need* to ask again. The ball was in her court. She only had to give him her answer—and that was something she felt ridiculously reluctant to do until he brought it up.

Stalling much? Oh, yes, she was.

On Friday evening, Karin had Riley in the baby sling and had just finished cleaning up the kitchen after dinner when Liam tapped on the slider. She went over and let him in.

He glanced past her shoulder. "Otto okay?" Her dad was conked out, snoring in his favorite chair in front of the TV.

"Just tired. He had a long day rush-retrofitting a fishing boat. As usual, the owner wants the boat back in the water yesterday—sooner if possible."

Liam looked strangely wistful. "The kids?"

"Coco's got a birthday party sleepover. Ben's at a friend's, home at eight."

He came inside, bringing the scent of leather, moist night air and a hint of diesel fuel. "Kind of quiet without them."

"Except for the snoring and the WWE reruns, you mean." She shut the slider, extricated the baby from the sling and handed him over. "Here you go."

He got Riley settled on one arm and then held out a check.

She took it and saw it was made out to her. "Five hundred dollars? What for?"

"To help out with Riley. Since he's mostly with you at this point, I figure five hundred a month, for now. You need more?"

"Of course not." She had a terrible, hollow feeling in her belly as she realized he must be leaving, moving out of the cottage. Just as she'd expected, he was missing his big house and his no-strings lifestyle, so he was going to throw her some monthly child support and go back to his own life.

He spotted the cloth diaper she'd left on the back of a chair and grabbed it, laying it on one broad shoulder and lifting Riley against his chest. "Okay, Karin. Tell me what's the matter."

"Nothing," she lied.

"Then how come your face is red and your mouth's all pinched up?"

"I don't know what you're talking about."

"You're pissed off."

"No, I'm not." She folded her arms across her middle, realized how defensive the posture must look and made herself drop her hands to her sides. "So. When are you leaving?"

He whispered something to the baby and then frowned down at her. "Leaving?"

"Uh, well, I assume you're going back to your own place?"

"No. I live at the cottage now." He studied her, still frowning. "What gave you the idea I was moving out?"

She held up the check. "Well, I mean. I thought..." What *had* she thought? Now, she just felt foolish. "I don't know. I thought you were, um..."

"Paying you off because I won't be around?"

When he put it that way, it sounded awful—even though that was exactly what she'd thought. She waved the check again. "If you're next door, there's no need for this right now, is there?"

"What's my being next door got to do with paying my share of my son's living expenses?"

Nothing, she realized, and felt even more foolish.

He stroked the baby's head with his big hand. "I get it. The Larson-Killigan family is doing just fine. You're not hurting for cash and all the bills are getting paid."

"You'd best believe it."

"So open an account for him. Get going on his college fund. It's RG's money so save it for when he needs it."

Karin cast an uncomfortable glance at her snoring father. "Let's go talk in Riley's room."

"Sure." He followed her across the great room and down the hall.

She ushered him into the baby's room ahead of her. "Well," she said, after shutting the door. "I just thought we would get a parenting plan—you know, a legal, binding agreement. Whatever support arrangement we would make would happen then."

"Why go to court if we can come to an agreement without dragging the state of Oregon into it?"

It was a valid question. Damn it. "I don't know, I…" She blew out a hard breath and busted herself. "Okay, I'm sorry. I jumped to the conclusion that there was no need to start writing me checks unless you were moving out."

He seemed to relax, a ghost of a smile pulling at the edges of his too-tempting mouth. "Apology accepted—and I'm staying right here at the Cove. Get used to it."

The room was too small and he was too big and solid and masculine, standing there holding their baby in his strong arms, not quite smiling as he gazed down at her.

"Okay, then," she said, her voice aggressively cheerful, totally fake. "I'll leave you with Riley and, um, I'm right down the hall if you need me."

"That's good to know." He said it too softly, but with a slight edge of roughness that played a sexy, hungry tune on every nerve ending she had.

She pulled open the door and got out of there, fast.

That following Monday Karin went back to work on a part-time basis. Her plan was to go in for a few hours a day and take Riley with her.

But then when Liam showed up at the door Monday night and she mentioned that she was trying to catch up at the Boatworks, he offered to help out. "I can take Riley for you, at least a couple of times a week," he said.

"But what about Bravo Trucking?"

"It's great being the boss. I can pretty much set my own hours."

There was so much to catch up on. She could get a

lot more done without the baby there to interrupt her. "You sure?"

"Yeah. We should try it. See how it goes. How 'bout Wednesday, nine to noon, to start?"

It was too good an offer to pass up. "All right, then. You're on."

Two days later, she dropped Riley off at the cottage. Liam had everything he needed right there, all the baby paraphernalia a newborn could ever require. All she had to provide was enough pumped breast milk to keep Riley fed until noon.

She passed Liam the baby and set the bottles on the counter. "The milk can be out of the fridge for four hours. If you put it in the fridge, you want to bring it just to body temperature by running warm water over the bottle or letting it sit in warm water."

He kissed Riley's plump cheek and gave her a smug grin. "I've read all the books, Karin."

She bopped her forehead with the heel of her hand. "That's right. You're an expert."

"Yes, I am. Don't you worry. RG and me, we got it all figured out."

When she returned at noon, Liam handed her the sleeping baby.

"How was he?" she whispered.

"Perfect. I can take him Friday, same time?"

"You're on. Thank you." She started to turn for the stairs.

"Karin." Something in his voice sent a lovely shiver racing down her spine. She stopped and met his eyes again. "You don't have to thank me. I hope you know that."

She cradled Riley closer. It was cold out that day. "I, um, well, I appreciate all you do to help out."

"It's my job," he said and she knew he was going to say more. Stuff she probably didn't want to hear. Maybe he was finally going to ask her for her decision on Thanksgiving…

But then he only gave a slight shake of his golden head. "Go on back to the other house. It's cold out."

Relief and guilt swirling through her in equal measure, she turned and hurried down the stairs.

That Saturday night after the kids were in bed, Karin curled up in her room with a fast-paced thriller on her e-reader.

Her dad appeared and tapped on her open door. "Got a minute?"

"Sure." She set the device aside.

Otto just stood there in the doorway, looking at her.

"Dad. What?"

He stuck his hands in the pockets of his ancient Carhartt work pants. He wore a plain white T-shirt and she found herself staring at his arms. They were strong arms from a lifetime of hard work, strong and scarred, freckled and dusted with reddish hair now gone mostly gray. Otto Larson was a good man, a man who had dedicated his life to taking care of his family.

"I'm just gonna say it, Kary. You need to give Liam Thanksgiving. He wants it, a lot. He's gotten himself all invested in this one simple thing, for our family and his family to celebrate Thanksgiving together."

"Dad—"

"I'm not finished. Liam's been nothing but here for you in every way that you'll let him be. Even if you can't give him all that he wants from you, you can say yes to Thanksgiving, you know you can."

"All that he wants from me? What does that even mean?"

Her father looked smug. "You really want to go there?"

She didn't. No way. "He sent *you* after me?" It came out sour and accusing. Because it was.

"No. He asked me what I thought of the idea and I said I was all for it. That was more than two weeks ago. He said he would ask you and then he didn't say anything more about it for days. So *I* asked *him* where we were on that. He said you were *thinking it over*. How long you planning on thinking about it before you actually give the poor man an answer?"

Her dad rarely annoyed her. But right now, he was definitely rattling her cage. "Liam Bravo is a long way from a 'poor man.'"

"Well, I for one feel sorry for the guy when it comes to you—and no. I'm not saying you should give him more than you're willing to give him. I'm saying it's Thanksgiving. And I know that *I'm* thankful for a man who is turning out to be a real dad to little Riley and who has knocked himself out to help you any way he can and been stepping right up for your other two children, too, showing an interest in who they are and what they're up to, driving them to and from wherever they need to go, even coming up with the perfect alternative when Halloween got rained out."

Everything her dad was saying?

True.

She pulled at a thread on the comforter. "You're right," she muttered reluctantly. "He's a terrific guy."

"So show him you appreciate all he's done. Say yes, we would love to go to Daniel Bravo's house for Thanksgiving."

When he put it like that, how could she say no? "Okay."

"What's that? Speak up."

"Fine, Dad. I'll accept Liam's invitation to Thanksgiving with the Bravos."

"Great. How 'bout doing that right now? All three kids are in bed and the lights are on over at the cottage."

Liam heard the tap on the slider and glanced that way. It was Karin, in flannel pajamas printed with penguins, a pair of Uggs and old Portland State hoodie with the hood pulled up over her hair.

"Got a minute?" she asked when he let her in.

He stared down at her upturned face, at that smart little mouth he couldn't wait to kiss again. "What do you need?"

She pushed the hood off her hair. "That Thanksgiving invitation still on the table?"

He felt a punch to his chest. The good kind, like his heart was reminding him that it was still beating. He could see her answer right there in those beautiful eyes. "You're saying yes?"

She nodded up at him, eyes bright and full of light, her face scrubbed clean of makeup, her dark hair a nimbus of shiny, wild curls. "We would love to come. All of us. You really think Daniel and Keely will be able to handle the crowd?"

"No problem."

"Well, okay, then. I'll, um, let you go..."

He caught her arm. "Just a second."

"Hmm?"

"This." He wrapped his other arm around her and swooped down to claim her lips.

She didn't resist.

On the contrary, she slid those pretty, slim, hard-working hands of hers up his chest and hooked them around his neck. "I didn't come here to kiss you," she said, as she kissed him.

He pulled her even closer. "Sometimes good things happen when you least expect them."

She laughed, her breath sweet with a hint of minty toothpaste, her body soft and warm in his arms.

He'd spent a lot of his life avoiding giving his heart. It was all due, he'd told himself, to the tragedies in his family when he was a kid—the disappearance of a brother, the sudden death of both parents. Loving people hurt so bad when you lost them and he loved too many people already. It was too late for him with his brothers and sisters, with Great-Uncle Percy and Great-Aunt Daffodil. He loved them before he learned the sad lesson that love ended up meaning loss that ripped you up inside.

But at least, his younger self had concluded, he could avoid the awful emotional danger of loving a woman.

His younger self hadn't known squat.

It took the birth of RG to show him the big picture. Karin had always been the one for him. All these years, he'd thought he'd dodged the love bullet. Wrong. He'd just been waiting for the right time to admit the truth to himself: Karin Larson Killigan owned his heart.

Sadly, Karin now seemed as determined as he used to be not to go there. He had a bad feeling that for her, the right time to give her heart to anyone was never.

She would probably mess him over royally. He'd get just what he'd always feared out of this deal: disappointment, hurt and the kind of loss that ripped a man's guts out.

He'd get everything he'd always been afraid of.

And he didn't even care. He wanted her and their baby. He wanted serious Ben, bubbly little Coco and stalwart, big-hearted Otto, too. He wanted to make a family with all of them, his deepest fears be damned.

If only he could find the way to get her to say yes to him.

"Liam." She sighed, her soft lips parting. He tasted her, nice and deep and slow.

Until she pulled back and her eyes fluttered open.

He touched her sweet, pointy chin, guided a wild curl behind the curve of her ear. *I want to marry you, Karin.* It sounded really good inside his head.

He almost went ahead and said it.

But he had a crappy feeling that laying another proposal on her right now would just ruin a great moment.

She'd given him Thanksgiving. He'd kissed her and she'd kissed him back.

For now, he would call it a win and not push his luck.

As it turned out, Sten and Madison couldn't make it home for Thanksgiving. Connor Bravo and his wife Aly didn't come either. They were still in New York, where Aly was training her successor at the advertising firm where she'd worked for the past seven years.

But even with two siblings and their spouses unavailable, Daniel and Keely's big house on Rhinehart Hill overflowed with family on Thanksgiving Day. The rest of the Bravo siblings came, including Matt with his wife, Sabra, and Aislinn with her husband, Jaxon, and also the housekeeper and foreman from Wild River Ranch where they lived. Keely's mom, Ingrid, and Keely's aunt, Gretchen, had arrived at the crack of dawn to help with cooking and general holiday prep. The food looked amazing. They had turkey, a gorgeous ham and a beautiful prime rib. And more sides than Karin could count.

Harper and Hailey, the family event planners, had set up ongoing games of turkey bowling and pin the feather on the turkey for anyone who wanted to play. They had a big pumpkin-shaped jar full of candy corn and made everyone guess how many candy kernels were inside for a possible prize of…a big bag of candy corn.

Daniel's twins, Frannie and Jake, were three now, happy kids who talked nonstop. Keely's baby, Marie, born the previous January, was already learning to walk. Marie staggered around on her fat little legs, constantly falling and dragging herself upright to try again. She was also a big talker, though her endless chatter made sense only to her.

Coco found Marie enchanting and spent a good portion of the afternoon holding the baby's fat little hand, helping her in her shaky efforts to stay on her feet. The attention delighted Marie to no end. She beamed up at Coco like she'd found a new best friend.

Ben took an interest in the twins. He bundled them up in their winter coats and took them out to the backyard for a long walk around the garden paths. The Bravo family basset hound, Maisey Fae, loped along in their wake.

Everyone made a big deal over Riley. Grace Bravo, the youngest of Liam's siblings, offered Karin her bedroom off the kitchen for a private place to nurse. Gracie suggested that Riley could have her bed if he dropped off to sleep—which he did, about a half hour or so before the big meal. Keely gave Karin a baby monitor to use and she surrounded Riley with pillows and left him to nap.

When they sat down to eat, Great-Uncle Percy and

Great-Aunt Daffy each gave a toast. Percy raised his glass to long life. Daffy, to true love. Aunt Gretchen said grace.

Karin, seated next to Liam at one of the two long pushed-together tables, felt his big, warm hand brush hers under the table as Gretchen recited her sweet prayer of thanks.

It was good, Karin thought, to catch up with the Bravos again. She'd put up a lot of resistance to coming here today. And now she found herself grateful that her dad had convinced her she needed to say yes to Liam's invitation.

As amens echoed around the packed table, she gave the man her hand, even opening her fingers a little, lacing them with his at his urging.

He leaned close. "I'm glad you're here."

She met those beautiful eyes and almost wished…

Well, better not even to let herself complete that thought. "Me, too," she replied. "I'm glad you invited us."

He gave her a smile that made the tall white candles in the middle of the table seem to burn even brighter. "So, you're having a good time?"

"I am. Very much so."

A teasing gleam made his eyes look even bluer. "Clearly, you should say yes to me more often."

Should she?

Doubtful. Coparents needed to respect each other's space. However, Liam Bravo was turning out to be a whole lot more than she'd ever bargained for. He was not only hot and tempting, but so persuasively persistent, as well. He was good to her kids and friends with her dad and thoroughly determined to do right by his child. She would be lying if she tried to tell herself she didn't find him extraordinarily attractive on a whole lot of levels.

He leaned a fraction closer. "What is that secretive smile you're giving me?"

"Just thinking that you're a really good dad." And he *was* a good dad, so she'd only told him the truth—only not all of the truth.

He laughed. "Do you give that look to all the good dads?"

And she went ahead and answered honestly. "Only you, Liam."

His thumb slipped in between their joined hands. He stroked her palm. It felt so good, so wonderfully thrilling and deliciously naughty.

And she was probably losing her mind a little what with all this…thankfulness she was feeling. Losing her mind and getting crazy ideas.

Ideas like how maybe she ought to be more open to him, to this attraction she felt for him.

Okay, yeah. She knew very well it would be better, smarter, not to mix their mutual parenting responsibilities with physical intimacy.

However, they were really good together in that way. They had chemistry, an excess of it. She'd always been drawn to him, since way back in high school. And the nights they'd shared at the first of the year still fueled her fantasies all these months and months later.

And now he lived right next door.

With every day that passed in which he was funny and kind and thoughtful, helpful and gentle and patient and so understanding—not to mention superhot—well, it just got harder and harder to remember that keeping a certain distance between them was key. It got harder and harder not to wonder why they shouldn't enjoy themselves a little.

As long as they both went into it with their eyes open, as long as they agreed that it didn't have to go anywhere, that they could be together just for now and just for fun. That if it didn't work out in the long run, they would act like adults, reestablish the boundaries and go on as Riley's parents who weren't together but wanted the best for their son.

Didn't divorced people do that all the time?

Really, if they kept it just between the two of them, didn't let the kids or her dad know, so that no one got unrealistic expectations of how things might turn out…

Well, she couldn't stop asking herself, what could it hurt?

Chapter Seven

The Larson-Killigan family had a tradition.

On the Saturday after Thanksgiving, they all went out together and chopped down their Christmas tree. They brought it home and stood it up in the picture window in the great room. From the attic, they hauled down box after box, each one packed full of Christmas decorations collected over the past three generations.

Then they all worked together decorating the tree, decking the fireplace mantel with boughs and twinkly lights and setting up the crèche that had belonged to Karin's mother's mother.

That morning, Liam appeared on the back deck just as Karin, Otto and the kids were sitting down to breakfast before heading to Oja's Christmas Tree Farm.

Karin glanced up and saw him standing there. She knew what was going on without having to ask, but she turned to her dad, anyway. "Looks like someone invited Liam."

"That's good!" enthused Coco. She bounced from her seat and darted over to the door, the black towel she wore for a cape flopping in her wake.

Otto swallowed a bite of pancake. "He has that Supercrew F-150. The console in front turns into a seat, so there's room in the cab for all of us and the long bed is perfect for hauling the tree home."

"Good thinking," Karin said wryly.

Coco, all in black to match her "cape," shoved the slider wide and threw out her arms to the sides. "Hi, Liam! I'm Raven. I have instant healing for me and for others. I travel to different dimensions. I teleport and *astro projet—*"

"She means 'astral project,'" Ben corrected.

Coco turned and glared at him. "You interrupted me. That's rude."

"Sorry," said Ben and crunched a bite of bacon. "But you might as well get it right."

Coco sighed, the sigh of all sisters put-upon by older brothers. "Now I can't 'member the rest—but come in, Liam. Have some pancakes. We got blueberry syrup and plenty of bacon."

Karin, who found she was not the least annoyed that her dad had invited Liam without consulting her, started to rise. "I'll get you a—"

"Don't get up." He was smiling at her, the smile she somehow felt was only for her. "I know where the plates and coffee mugs are."

"Well, all right." They shared a long look full of humor and promise and banked heat, one of those looks she decided she didn't need to think too deeply about. Not now, not on tree-decorating day.

It was good, what she felt for him. She might as well enjoy that goodness, whatever might or might not happen next.

Bottom line, she was getting used to having Liam in her day-to-day life. He wasn't going away and she could either accept the situation gracefully or grump around like a shrew trying to protect herself from some possible future heartache.

And yeah. Overthinking. She needed to cut that out, too.

Liam poured himself some coffee and carried his full mug and a place setting to the empty chair across from her. Karin pushed the platter of pancakes his way and he took four. Otto passed him the bacon.

Coco announced, "Here's the butter and the blueberry syrup for you, Liam."

"Thanks." He captured Karin's gaze again. Little zings of fizzy excitement went zipping all through her. "RG?"

"He went back to sleep after I fed him." She tipped her head at the baby monitor perched on the counter. "So far, not a peep."

"Eat up, folks," said Otto. "The tree farm opens at ten."

For once, the weather cooperated. It was cold out, but clear. They bundled up in winter gear and piled into Liam's big pickup. Otto and Ben sat in front with Liam. Karin sat in the middle in back, Riley in his car seat on one side and Coco in hers on the other.

At the farm, they wandered up and down the rows of trees, finally settling on a nine-foot noble fir with gorgeous, thick branches in majestic even tiers.

Back at the Cove, they took a break for hot chocolate

with miniature marshmallows. Then Karin cued up her holiday playlist. To the holiday stylings of Bette Midler and Michael Bublé, Weezer and NSync, they brought the tree in and stood it up in the tree stand. After that, they trooped up and down the stairs until every box of tinsel, lights and decorations was stacked in the great room, ready to roll.

Once they had the lights on the tree, they stopped for soup and sandwiches.

Karin was having a ball. She loved getting out all the old decorations, remembering who had made or bought or gifted the family each one, and when. They took turns holding Riley when he wasn't napping. Karin got out her phone and snapped lots of pictures. Liam did, too.

It was great, the perfect family activity, all of them working together to kick off another year of Christmas memories, the house all warm and cozy, full of holiday tunes and the smell of evergreen. Karin missed having Sten there, but Liam fit right in. Everything was perfect.

Or it was until they got around to setting up the crèche and Liam suggested, "The baby Jesus in the manger should be right in the middle, under the star."

And Ben piped up in his coolest, most dismissive Little Professor voice, "We like it a little to the side. And I don't think you even really need to be here, Liam. We've been doing this for years without you and we don't need you now."

Poor Liam, standing there with Riley on one arm and the manger with its glued-in hay bedding in his opposite hand, didn't seem to know what to say.

Otto stepped in. "Liam's here because I invited him," he said in a careful tone.

Ben chewed his lower lip. He looked miserable. Had he been this way all day?

Karin couldn't believe she hadn't noticed till now that her serious, levelheaded older son wasn't his usual agreeable self. She asked gently, "What's going on, Ben?"

He stuck his hands in the pockets of his tan jeans and hunched his thin shoulders. "Well, I just mean, we do Christmas with the family and he's not our family. He's not my dad or Coco's dad. He's just the baby's dad."

Apparently, that was too much for Coco. "Benjamin Killigan, you are not being nice."

Ben scowled at her, defiant at first. But then his face kind of crumpled. "Okay." He set down the star that fit into the steepled roof of the stable and turned to Liam. "I'm sorry. I shouldn't have said that stuff."

"Ben." Liam tried to reassure him. "It's all right."

"No, it's not. It's not all right. It's not all right at all." And he darted around Otto's easy chair and took off down the hall. They heard his bedroom door slam shut.

For a moment, no one spoke. There was just Bette Midler singing "Have a Yule that's cool…"

Liam glanced down at the baby asleep in his arms, and then back up at Karin. "Maybe I should go."

"No, you shouldn't." She held his gaze. "Please stay."

Her dad backed her up. "Yeah. Don't go. Your leaving won't solve anything."

For once, Coco had nothing to add. She stood by the sofa, blue eyes big and sad, glancing from one grown-up to the other as though hoping one of them would do what grown-ups are supposed to do and make it all better.

Karin suggested, "Why don't you guys go ahead and put the crèche together? I'll talk to Ben."

* * *

When Karin tapped on her older son's door, he didn't answer. She counted slowly to thirty before trying, "Ben?"

He responded then. "It's open."

She turned the knob and pushed the door inward. Ben sat on his bed hunched over his laptop, looking absolutely miserable and completely not-Ben. Her brilliant oldest child usually took things in stride and never lost his cool.

Karin asked, "May I come in?" She got a shrug for an answer and decided to consider it a yes. When she sat down beside him, the screen of the laptop showed he'd brought up his favorite video game, but hadn't started playing it.

He shut the laptop and set it aside. "What?"

She wrapped an arm around him. He stiffened at first, but then gave in and sagged against her. She dared to drop a kiss on the crown of his head. "I'm not sure where to start. Maybe if you told me what's bothering you?"

He tipped his head back. Their eyes met, but only for a moment. Then he looked down again. "I don't know, really," he muttered in the general direction of the floor. "I miss Uncle Sten. And now there's the baby. It's not Liam's fault, I know that. He's nice, but…" He made a frustrated sound in his throat. "Look. Everything's just different, okay? Everything's *not* the same." He looked up and their eyes met again. She smoothed his hair. It was one fussy, motherly caress too many. "Mom. Don't." He scooted out from under her arm.

Her heart ached as she let him go. Somehow, she managed to let several seconds of silence elapse before trying again. "Uncle Sten won't be gone forever."

He shot her a look of pure annoyance. "Two years. At least. Until Madison gets through making those movies she already signed up to make." Sten and Madison would settle right here in the Cove once Madison had honored her outstanding contracts. She said she was giving up acting, that she wanted a different kind of life—a family with Sten, a home in Valentine Bay.

"In the meantime, though," Karin reminded her unhappy son, "they'll be back whenever they can—including over Christmas. They both seem pretty sure they'll make it home during the holidays."

"Mom. I know that. And I just told you. It's not the same that they come back to visit. Like they're *guests* or something."

"I'm sorry, honey. It's just…the way life is. Stuff changes, you know? People move away. But the happy news is that, in Uncle Sten and Aunt Madison's case, they eventually will come back."

"I *know*, Mom. And I get that you want to make me feel better, but can you please quit telling me stuff I already know?"

"I'm just trying to find out exactly what has you upset, that's all. You mentioned the baby…"

He lifted one shoulder in a sort of half-hearted shrug, but that was all she got.

She suggested, "So the baby's just more stuff changing and that makes you feel unhappy?"

"Mom?"

"Hmm?"

"Can we just…not be doing this right now? Can I just go back out there and say sorry again to Liam and we can fix up the manger with the baby Jesus in the middle and just have a nice time finishing up the decorations?"

"Of course we can. But I do want you to know that

I'm here and ready to listen whenever you want to talk some more about this."

He dropped his head back and groaned at the ceiling. "Mom." He must have stretched that word into at least three syllables. "I *know*. Can we go back out now, please?"

She ought to just leave it at that. But she couldn't stop herself from taking one more stab at making things right for him. "I love you, Ben. I always have and I always will. Having another baby in the family can't change how much I love you or how much Uncle Sten loves you or your grandpa, either. We all love you so much. That's the one thing that is never going to change."

"I know, Mom." He said it kindly that time, with only a hint of exasperation. "I love you, too."

They returned to the great room, where Ben went straight to Liam. "I really am sorry for what I said."

"Apology accepted," Liam answered in that easy way he had. "And you know, I think you're right about baby Jesus. A little to the side is better than directly under the star."

At ten that night, Liam was in the office he'd set up at the cottage. With RG to consider, he wasn't spending as much time at Bravo Trucking as he used to. Having a baby meant rearranging priorities and being more flexible.

He could get a lot done from home, he'd discovered, working at night when RG was with Karin. He liked to watch the fuel situation closely, change his buying strategy whenever better options presented themselves. And he kept on top of the shippers and the brokers he used. Trucking was a cash flow intensive business. If people started paying late, he needed to know and either stop dealing with them or make sure they started paying timely again.

The doorbell rang just as he was thinking he would call it a night.

What do you know? It was Karin—in blue pajamas dotted with snowflakes this time and a green hoodie. Same Uggs as before.

"Is it too late?" she asked.

"For you?" He couldn't stop himself from grinning. "Never."

She held up her phone. "My dad will call if Riley wakes up."

"You should have just brought him over."

"No." She raked the hoodie off her head, revealing all those untamed curls he loved. "It's always best to let sleeping babies lie."

Liam stepped back and ushered her in. "You want a drink or something?" he offered as he shut the door.

She shook her head. And then she took a step forward.

And then, without him having to do anything but open his arms, she was flush against him, all sweet warmth and perfect softness. She surged up. Her mouth met his and clung.

God. She tasted good. He could kiss her forever. No woman had ever felt as right as she did in his arms.

She dropped back to her heels, breaking the kiss, but letting him hold her. "I've been telling myself that we should…" The words petered out. She frowned up at him, her cheeks pink, her breath coming fast. "I don't know how to say this."

"Sure you do." He bent and brushed a kiss between her eyebrows. "Take your time."

"Could we maybe sit down?" She seemed nervous. It

was cute. Like they were back in high school again and she wasn't quite sure how to act with a guy.

He took her hand and led her toward the main room. In the sitting area, he turned on the gas fire and pulled her over to sit beside him on the couch. She set her phone on the coffee table. "Okay. It's like this. I was thinking that maybe you and I could kind of see where this thing might go between us."

Satisfaction filled him. At last they were getting somewhere. He couldn't resist pressing the point a little. "So you're finally admitting that we had a thing—that we *are* a thing?"

She groaned and covered her face with her hands. "Okay. Let's not get caught up in the *thing* controversy again."

"Just admit it's there, between you and me, and I'll let it go."

She dropped her hands, squared her shoulders and drew in a slow breath. "Then yes, okay? It's definitely *there*, between us."

"It never went away."

She pursed up those way-too-kissable lips. "Is this you letting it go?"

He touched her hair—and she didn't duck away. Taking total advantage of this perfect moment in which she was finally saying at least part of what he wanted to hear, he guided a wild curl behind the shell of her ear. "So maybe I want to rub it in a little. Sue me."

She poked him in the side with an elbow. "You're just asking for it, mister."

"You bet I am."

She laughed. And then she sighed. Her cheeks were bright pink. He found her irresistible like this, all shy and kind of awkward. "I was, um, thinking, hoping that we could just have it be between you and me, not say anything to the kids or my dad."

He didn't want to be her secret. He'd *never* wanted to be that. And he especially didn't want to be her secret anymore. But he also didn't want to blow this chance with her. "*Yet*, you mean. Not say anything to anyone *yet*."

"Yes, Liam. I mean, you know, see where it goes."

That didn't sound so bad—scratch that. It sounded damn good. For now, anyway. "Agreed." He took her by the shoulders and pulled her close.

She let him, even tucked her dark head under his chin. They sat quietly, staring into the fire. He stroked her hair some more, kissed the crown of her head and breathed in the citrusy scent of her shampoo. She shifted and let out a sigh.

"What?"

"Nothing." The way she said it, he knew there was definitely something.

"You worried about Ben?"

She didn't answer immediately, but when she did, she told the truth. "Yeah, a little. I think he feels kind of left out. Coco's such a charmer. Her heart is wide open. She's never had a problem demanding what she needs. Ben's the serious one and sometimes he kind of fades into the background. Now there's another boy in the family. Ben's no longer the only son."

Liam stroked a hand down her arm. It felt so good, just to sit here, the two of them, touching. Talking. "And then there's the baby's dad who isn't *his* dad, a guy who moved in next door and is always butting in on all the family events."

"Ben loved the Halloween party," she reminded him.

"And he seemed to have a great time at Daniel's on Thanksgiving."

"But then I kind of pushed my luck with baby Jesus, huh?"

She chuckled, the sound both sweet and rueful. "Ben does think you're a good guy, though. He's said so more than once." She tipped her head back and met his eyes. Hers were sea-blue in the firelight, and troubled. "The truth is, Ben didn't really have a great relationship with Bud—I don't mean Bud was abusive or anything. He was a good man, but kind of hard to talk to. He was gone a lot, working. And when he came home, he was distant and distracted. There were money problems. Plus, Bud hardly knew his own dad. His parents got divorced when he was only two and Bud stayed with his mom, and then she died when he was just nineteen. He didn't seem to know where to start trying to be a dad himself. He was better with Coco, but with Ben he just kind of wasn't *there*."

It was a lot, what she was telling him. More than she'd ever said about her husband before. Liam knew he had no right to resent the guy, but he did. For causing Karin pain and making her wary of trying again—because no matter how she tried to be fair to her husband's memory, it was pretty damn clear that Ben, Sr. had not been around as much as he should have.

In a weird, twisted and unacceptably selfish way, Liam resented that Karin had married the other guy in the first place. If she'd only waited until he got his head out of his own ass, he would have had a lot easier time convincing her she belonged with him.

But then, if she'd waited, there would've been no Ben and no Coco. And the more he got to know Karin's kids, the less he could picture a world without them in it.

She pulled away from him and sat up. "I guess that was way more information than you ever needed."

"Get back here." He caught her arm, but gentled his hold—and his attitude. "Please?"

"I did love Bud." She met his gaze, defiant. "But it was young love, you know?"

He didn't, not really. Releasing her arm, he trailed his fingers over the worn, soft fabric of her sleeve until he captured her hand. "The kind you grow out of?" He turned her hand over and bent close to kiss the heart of it.

"The kind that isn't strong enough to weather the rough patches."

He tugged on her fingers until she swayed toward him again. Gathering her in, he tipped up her chin and took her mouth. She opened for him and he sank into the kiss, drawing it out, making it last.

When he finally lifted his head, he eased both hands under her hair, lacing his fingers at the nape of her neck, tipping her face up to him with slow strokes of his thumbs. "I want to ask Ben if he'll come with me to Bravo Trucking. I was thinking tomorrow, just him and me, a drive up to Warrenton in the afternoon."

"You're looking for my permission?"

"I am, yeah."

"What if he turns you down?"

"That's okay. I'm not gonna pressure him. If he says no, I'll say it's an open invitation. If he changes his mind, he just needs to let me know and we'll make it happen."

She dipped her chin in a nod. "It's all right with me—but be prepared for Coco to want to come, too."

"I was more thinking a one-on-one with Ben."

"I get it. Just giving you a heads-up."

He didn't want Coco feeling left out. "I'll take her, too. Just her and me, another time."

"That actually might pacify her. But are you sure you want to be driving my kids back and forth to Warrenton to take the Bravo Trucking tour?"

"I'm sure." He kissed her again. Because she tasted so good and she'd admitted she wanted him. It wasn't enough, what she was offering, to be together, but only in secret. Not nearly enough.

But it was a start.

And from now on, he needed to have his hands and his mouth on her every chance he got.

That kiss led to another. And another after that. He actually had her hoodie unzipped before she called a halt.

"I need to get back." She zipped up again. "Morning comes early when you've got three kids."

"Damn," he said with a smile. "For a minute there, I thought I was about to get lucky."

"You are." She leaned close and caught his earlobe between her teeth. At his groan, she laughed. "Just not tonight."

He asked only half-teasingly, "Do you have your doctor's approval to fool around with me?"

"I will. My checkup's on Monday." She bunched up his shirt in her fist and yanked him close for another smoking kiss. "And this time we're using two forms of birth control."

"I've got the condoms."

"Great. And after Riley was born, I got an implant before I left the hospital."

"Taking no chances, huh?"

"That's right." She kissed him again, but pulled away much too soon. "You'd better come over for breakfast.

You can talk to Ben then. I'll help you out with Coco, say I need her at home to get going on the Christmas baking."

"Works for me." He yanked her close again and covered her mouth with his. For a moment, she gave in and let him hold her.

But only a moment. "I mean it." She grabbed her phone. "I need to go home."

Reluctantly, he followed her to the door.

The next morning, as usual, Otto came by the cottage for coffee.

Liam mentioned that he hoped to take Ben up to Warrenton that day to show him around Bravo Trucking.

"Kissing up to my grandson, huh?"

"You'd better believe it."

"You'll make Coco jealous."

"Coco will get an invite of her own."

Otto set his mug down on the table and stared out the slider. It was raining pretty hard, the sound a steady drumming on the roof and the deck. "Is that what Karin needed to talk to you about last night—you taking the kids to Warrenton?"

Liam shook his head. "The tour of Bravo Trucking was my idea."

Otto gave him a long, considering look. "So what *did* my daughter want to talk to you about last night?"

Liam got up, got the coffeepot and refilled their mugs. "Lots of things," he replied, mindful of his promise to Karin that they'd keep their new togetherness just between the two of them for now. "We've got a kid. There's all kinds of stuff we need to deal with, day to day."

Otto Larson was nobody's fool. His mouth curved in a secret smile. "You're saying you'll need to spend time, just the two of you, on a regular basis to discuss RG's care, is that what you're telling me?"

"Pretty much."

Otto stared out the window some more. Dawn was slowly breaking, revealing a gray, overcast sky. "She had a rough time, with Bud—and don't get me wrong. Bud wasn't a bad guy. Just too young, wanting to do the right thing and yet not quite up to the job. You'd better be good to her."

"I'm trying, Otto."

"I know, son. I like that about you."

At breakfast, Liam made his move. "I need to head to Bravo Trucking today for a couple of hours. Ben, would you like to ride along with me?"

Ben looked up from his scrambled eggs. His eyes were wary. "What for?"

"Thought you might get a kick out of a tour of the place." He sent a quick smile in Karin's direction, but didn't let his gaze linger. She looked way too damn pretty in a flannel shirt with her hair escaping every which way from the messy bun she'd put it in. "I already cleared it with your mom."

Karin confirmed that. "Fine with me if you want to go."

"Could be fun." Liam kept his tone offhand. "Check out a diesel engine, maybe go for a ride in a semitruck."

Those serious brown eyes flashed with interest, but Ben played it cool. "Okay, I'll go."

"Good. We'll leave in an hour or so, maybe grab a burger on the way back?"

"Sure. I'll be ready."

Coco had somehow managed to restrain herself till then. But she was not the kind of girl to let a good time pass her by. "'Scuse me, Liam? *I* like trucks. Can I please go with you guys?"

"Not today, honey." Karin eased in gracefully with her interference play. "I really need your help with the Christmas cookies."

"But what about Ben? He always helps, too. We should all help because helping is good."

"I kind of want to see that engine," Ben ruefully confessed.

Karin suggested, "I'm also going to need help next weekend with the fudge and divinity and candy cane bark."

Liam trotted out his perfect solution. "How 'bout this? Ben and I will go this week. Coco, I'll take you with me next week. You can each see the trucks and help your mom with the candy and cookies, too."

"All right!" Coco agreed, beaming. "I like making cookies and I like trucks, too!"

The baby monitor on the counter came to life with a questioning cry. The table quieted. They all knew the drill by then—it was always possible that RG would fuss for a minute and then go back to sleep.

Not this time, though. His cries grew more insistent.

Liam glanced at Karin, who was already looking at him. "Please do," she said with a grin and a wave of her hand.

He pushed back his chair and headed for the baby's room.

The rain had let up by the time Liam and Ben got on the road to Bravo Trucking. It was a little awkward, with just the two of them. They hadn't spent much time alone together up till then and Ben's outburst the day before kind of hung in the cab between them.

Liam cued up a playlist on low, just to have a little noise in the background. He asked about soccer. Ben's team, the Valentine Bay Velociraptors, had just wrapped up their fall season. The boy answered Liam's questions as briefly as possible. The subject of soccer died a quick death.

Next, Liam tried science. Ben said he was working on a special project, studying the temperate rain forest of the Pacific Northwest, which stretched from California to British Columbia and was the largest temperate rain forest on the planet. The science conversation fared better than sports, lasting a good ten minutes.

After that, Liam let the playlist make the noise for a while. It wasn't too bad.

Ben really perked up when they got to Bravo Trucking. He happily trotted along beside Liam, who took him through the corporate office, the fuel island and the shop. Even on a Sunday, Liam had a couple of things he needed to deal with in his office, but the few truckers hanging around the driver's lounge were happy to keep Ben busy, telling him stories of the road, answering his every question.

Liam took him out to get an up close and personal look at that diesel engine as promised, and to get a quick rundown on the different types of trailers—from dry vans, to refrigerated trailers, to flatbeds, step deck trailers and lowboy trailers used to haul freight. And for the big finish, Liam took him for a ride in a Kenworth W900B, the kind he used to drive when he first started out hauling timber for Valentine Logging.

It was way past noon when they headed for home. Ben had more questions about the trucking business and the conversation flowed naturally, Liam thought. Halfway there, he pulled the pickup in at a little roadside diner. It was nothing fancy, just burgers, fries and milkshakes. There was a small, fake Christmas tree by the door strung with tinsel garland, lights and shiny balls. The sound system played Christmas tunes.

They got a booth in the back corner and a waitress brought their food. Liam was trying to come up with a good way to maybe get Ben talking about the baby Jesus incident the day before. But he had nothing, really. Every time he came up with a possible opener, he cringed before he could get the words out.

So what, exactly, was on your mind yesterday when you ran for your room?

Maybe not.

Or *Do you resent having me around, Ben? Can we talk about that?*

Yeah. No. Maybe something less direct: *How's it working out for you, having a new baby brother in the house?*

Ugh. Somehow every conversation starter he considered sounded like lame psychobabble in his head. He had no clue where to begin.

And Ben was suddenly way too quiet again. They stuffed fries in their mouths and sucked down their milkshakes, avoiding eye contact as much as possible.

Then Ben surprised him.

The kid ate a giant bite of his burger and stared directly across the booth at Liam as he chewed and swallowed. "I kind of want to ask you something," he said when his mouth was finally empty. "It's got nothing to do with trucks."

Liam resisted a sudden urge to squirm in his seat. "Go for it."

Ben dropped his half-eaten burger to his plate and slurped up more milkshake, setting the tall plastic glass down with a definite clunk. "Well, Liam. I mean, you're always so nice. It makes me nervous. What's up with you?"

Chapter Eight

Liam had to hand it to the kid. "Way to go, Ben. We might end up having a real conversation, after all." Ben frowned at him. Liam ate a french fry. "Define 'nice.'"

"Hmm." Ben took a moment for another giant bite of his burger. Then he said, "You're just too great about everything. You never get mad and so far, you're always there when my mom needs you. You think Riley is the best thing ever, even when he's pooping his diaper and screaming. And you never seem to get annoyed at Coco—I mean, I love my sister but sometimes when she won't stop talking it's like..." He put his hands to either side of his head and made an exploding sound. "And what about you and Grandpa?"

"I like your grandpa."

"Exactly. You and Grandpa are like best friends all of a sudden. You get along with everybody. It's like you actually believe there's a Santa Claus—big news,

Liam. There isn't. Santa is physically impossible and as an adult, you should know that."

"Ben."

"What?"

"I do know there's no Santa Claus. I've known for years and years."

"I didn't say that I think you *believe* in Santa Claus, I said you *act* like you do."

"Point taken. I just felt the need to clarify."

"Liam. Are you messing with me?"

He busted to it. "Yeah. Maybe a little."

"I thought so. And it's okay—but that reminds me. Coco still believes in Santa, so you better not ruin it for her."

"Coco will never hear the truth about Santa from me. I promise you that."

Ben pointed a french fry at him. "Make sure you keep that promise."

"I will—what else makes you nervous about me?"

Ben devoured that fry and two more. "You're always around."

"You sound kind of pissed about that."

"Not pissed, not exactly."

"Then what?" Liam asked. Ben just looked at him, frowning. Liam let the wordless moment stretch out as Bing Crosby warbled "Do You Hear What I Hear?" from the speaker in the corner above their booth.

Ben shook his head. "I don't know. But I'm not pissed at you, okay?"

"Got it. So, you say I'm always around..."

"Because you are."

Liam shrugged and reminded him, "Your grandpa is always around."

Ben gave him that look, the one that said, *grown-ups are so dense*. "Well, yeah. Grandpa lives with us."

"And I live next door. Your brother is my child. It's a good thing, the right thing, for me to be around a lot. Plus, I *like* being around a lot."

Ben stared at him long and hard. "Do you really?"

"Yeah. I do. Really."

"Well, my dad was hardly ever around." Ben said that too softly, his gaze shifting downward. He said to his plate, "I hardly even knew him. And I don't think he liked me very much."

Pay dirt.

And now Liam was scared to death he would blow it. But he'd signed on for this, so he waded in anyway. "I would bet Bravo Trucking that your dad did love you, Ben."

Ben shot him a sharp glance, then went back to examining the puddle of ketchup on his plate. "You're just saying that because that's what you're supposed to say about a kid's dad."

"Uh-uh. You're the kind of kid any dad would be proud of. You're smart and you put other people first, which believe me, *I* didn't when I was your age. You look after your sister and your mom and your grandpa and RG, too. I've only known you for six weeks and I love you already."

Ben snort-laughed. "Right." But at least he looked up and met Liam's eyes.

"It's true, Ben. I really do love you. A lot." Liam realized how much he meant those words as he said them. He also felt so damn sorry for Bud Killigan. For Bud, it was too late to show his own son anything ever again—and Ben was watching him across the table, brown eyes steady.

Liam forged ahead. "It's also true that I didn't know your dad, but I do know that sometimes grown-ups can get so wrapped up in their own problems that they don't realize they're not giving the right signals to the ones they love."

"Signals?"

"Yeah. I mean, sometimes people fail to show how much they love the ones who matter to them, they get lost in the things that are bothering them. When that happens, they can miss their chance to show their love to the ones who mean the most to them. I would bet that's what happened with your dad."

Ben got that look. Like he was deconstructing his latest science project. "You mean that my dad's dead and how he really felt is not provable, so why not just tell myself he loved me?"

"I meant what I said, Ben. Your father loved you. Maybe he didn't do the best job of showing it, but that doesn't mean the love wasn't there."

"But it's not *provable.*" Ben tapped a fist on the table for emphasis.

"So what? It's a hell of a lot more likely that he did than he didn't—and come on, what did I just say? Who *doesn't* love you? Everybody I know loves you."

Ben's mouth twitched, as though he was trying not to grin. "You're exaggerating."

"Nope. Truth. That's all you'll ever hear from me."

Ben grabbed his milkshake and sucked down the rest of it in silence—until the end, the part kids always loved most. Noisily, he sucked air. "I'm done." He set down the red plastic glass. "Thanks for the lunch."

"You're welcome."

"We should probably get back on the road."

Liam debated whether he should try to keep the man-to-man moment going. But he didn't want to mess with whatever progress he'd made.

He grabbed the check. "All right then. Let's go."

Things were quiet in the pickup as they headed home. Liam didn't fill the silence with music this time. A little quiet never hurt. And maybe Ben would have more to say.

They were five miles from Sweetheart Cove, when Ben asked, "So you're staying, then? You're not going away?"

"I'm staying." His own voice sounded so sure and he wondered, was he promising more than he could deliver?

No. However it worked out with him and Karin, he meant to be there—and not only for RG. "There's nowhere else I would rather be than with you and your mom and RG and Coco."

"And Grandpa." Ben said it more as a reminder than a question.

"And with your grandpa, too."

Karin rang Liam's doorbell at nine that night.

He opened the door and then just stood there, grinning at her. "God, you're good-lookin'." She wore yoga pants and a giant Welcome to Valentine Bay sweatshirt, her hair in a bun, same as that morning, untamed curls escaping every which way. "No other woman could ever compare."

She put one foot behind her and executed an actual curtsy. "And as you can see, I got dressed up real fancy."

"I've always been a big fan of the natural look."

"Oh, I'll just bet you have." She held up her phone.

"No telling how long I'll be here. Riley was kind of fussy today."

"You'd better get in here, then." He took her arm, pulled her inside with him, shut the door and reeled her in close. She melted against him. For several perfect minutes, there was just her mouth and his mouth, the feel of her body pressing close to his, the glide of her eager hands up over his chest and around his neck.

Too soon, she broke away and grabbed his hand. "Come on. We need to talk." And she led him into the main room, turned on the fire, pushed him down on the sofa and sat on his lap.

There was more kissing. On his lap like that, she was rubbing him right where it mattered most. He considered all the things that would be okay for him to do to her without her doctor's approval. There were a lot, now that he thought about it, and all of them tempted him.

But then she pulled away again and slid off his lap to sit next to him. She leaned her head on his shoulder. "So. How'd it go today with Ben?"

"Great. He got a tour of the yard, hung out in the driver's lounge. We went for a ride in one of the trucks. I think he had a good time."

"You, um, get a chance to talk to him?"

He balked. Suddenly it seemed wrong to tell her what her son had said over burgers and fries. "We talked, yeah."

"And?"

He rubbed the back of his neck, stalling. "It turned out to be kind of a man-to-man thing."

"That's good, right?"

"What I'm trying to say is I'm not sure I should betray his confidence, you know?"

She got that look women get, a little angry, a lot superior. "One, he's nine years old. Two, I am his mother. Three, that I am his mother means I need to know what's bothering him. And four, did he ask you not to tell me what he said to you?"

"No, he didn't. It's just..." He sought the right words. They didn't come, so he settled on, "Karin, some things a kid doesn't want to tell his mother."

"He's *nine*," she insisted, those beautiful eyes pleading now. "Just tell me this much. Did he mention his dad?"

Her begging eyes did him in. Screw the bro code. He couldn't keep stonewalling her. "Yeah. Ben said he didn't think his dad liked him."

"That's not true." Frantic color flooded her cheeks.

"Hey." He put up both hands in complete surrender. "I believe you. We argued over it. I tried to get him to see that his dad could love him and not be any good at showing it."

Her pretty mouth trembled. "Do you think you convinced him?"

"Not a clue. But he didn't seem upset, honestly. Just kind of puzzled at the weirdness of adults."

"Yeah. He's like that. My little professor..." Her eyes were fond and dreamy—but then she glanced at Liam and demanded, "What else did he say?"

"He wanted to know if I was going to stick around. I told him that I wasn't going anywhere."

She gave him a slow nod, but her eyes spoke of doubts. "It's better not to make him that kind of a promise."

He disagreed. "It's a promise I intend to keep."

"Liam. You never know how things will turn out. People think they want one thing and then, as time goes by, they realize they want something else altogether."

"I know what I want. And I told Ben the truth. I live here and I'm not leaving."

She bit the corner of her lip. "Look. I think you just need to know something. When I married Bud, I was pregnant with Ben." She stared at him, apprehensive, as if she expected him to be surprised.

He wasn't. Not in the least. "I kind of figured as much. People do that, you know?"

She scoffed. "Get pregnant accidentally or get married because they're pregnant?"

"Both."

"Well, we *were* in love, Bud and me."

"Yeah. You told me that last night."

"Bud swore he was all in—with me, with the baby. He made a lot of promises. I was young and hopeful and crazy about him. I just knew we were going to be happy together forever and ever. I said yes. We got married…" Her voice faded off. She stared into the middle distance, her eyes far away.

And then she said, "It was mostly downhill from there. Before Ben was even born, Bud had turned angry. Distant. I think he came to realize that what he really loved was life on a boat. He wanted his freedom. I just wanted it to work with us. I wanted it so much.

"For a while after Ben was born, Bud seemed…better, I guess. He even said that he wanted another baby. Looking back, I think he was trying to get behind being a husband and a dad. At the time, I was just ecstatic. I thought we were going to be all right. So we had Coco. And things were okay, for a while. But it didn't last. Finally, on that final night he was home before he died, we had a big fight. He said he wanted a divorce and I said that was just fine with me. I meant it, too. I knew we were done, that what I'd believed was lasting love just…wasn't. We never should have gotten married in the first place. A week later, the salmon troller he was on sank in the Bering Sea."

Liam reached out to her slowly. She'd always seemed so strong to him. Not now, though. Right now, she was fragile as glass. "I'm sorry. So sorry, Karin. For Bud. And for you."

She flinched when he touched her cheek. But then, with a shuddery little sigh, she sagged against him. "I hate that he died. I hate that he didn't have time to… I don't know. Get to know his kids? Figure things out? Find a little happiness, a life that really worked for him."

"Yeah." He pressed his cheek to her hair and wished he had something helpful to say. "People shouldn't be allowed to die until they're at least eighty and they've worked through all their crap and made peace with their loved ones."

She tipped her head up and looked at him, her eyes wet with unshed tears. "Exactly. There oughta be a law."

On the table, her phone lit up and vibrated.

She pulled free of Liam's hold and grabbed it. "Hey, Dad." Liam heard Otto's voice faintly on the other end. "He's probably just hungry. I'll be right there." She hung up. "Gotta go."

Liam wasn't ready for her to leave yet. She needed time, after the tough things she'd said to him. Time for him to hold her and kiss her some more, time for him to ease her fears, to reassure her that things with Ben really were going to be all right. He wished he could just go over to the main house with her, help her with the baby, sleep in the same bed with her.

But already she was pulling her shell of self-reliance back around her. She'd learned all the wrong lessons from her troubled marriage and her husband's sudden death.

Liam considered himself an upbeat guy. He looked on the bright side as much as possible.

But when it came to Karin, sometimes he wondered if he would ever really break through.

Ten minutes later, Karin sat in the comfy chair in Riley's room with her feet up on the fat ottoman and Riley at her breast. She rubbed his velvety cheek with a finger and whispered, "I love you, Riley George. I love you so much..."

She let her head fall back against the cushion and closed her eyes.

Raw. She felt raw and too open, after the things she'd told Liam tonight. It had seemed best, to explain it all, give him the whole truth about poor Bud. He needed to understand why she wasn't willing to give in and give the two of them a real shot.

Why getting serious with him was out of the question.

Liam was such a good guy and surprisingly persistent.

But she needed to keep a realistic perspective on their situation. No way was she letting herself get in too deep with him. He kept saying he wasn't ever leaving, that he wanted to be with her and her family. She was sure he meant it.

But just because he meant it now didn't mean he wouldn't change his mind someday.

She simply couldn't take that risk. Giving herself to him and then losing him, having him look at her the way Bud used to, like he wondered how he'd got himself into this mess—well, that could break her. And she couldn't afford to be broken. She had a family to think about.

After tonight, she was definitely reevaluating her brilliant plan to climb into bed with him again.

Uh-uh. He would be far too easy to fall in love with. Having a secret sexual relationship with him was just begging for trouble.

No. The sex thing couldn't happen. She needed to make it clear to him she'd changed her mind about that.

Liam got up early Monday morning and drove to Portland for some meetings at the office there. He didn't get back to the Cove until seven that night.

After a shower and some takeout he'd picked up from his favorite Italian place in town, he called Karin. She didn't pick up. He debated just heading over there, saying hi to Otto and the kids and getting her promise that she would be over as soon as she got everyone settled for the night.

But their thing was a secret thing. He wasn't supposed to do anything that might clue the family in to what was going on between them.

So he left a message. "I miss you. Come over as soon as you get the kids to bed?"

And then he went to his home office and dealt with email and messages, feeling antsy, distracted and so damn eager to have her with him again.

Finally, at a quarter after nine, the doorbell rang. He raced to the front hall and yanked the door wide, planning to sweep her up in his arms and kiss her hard and long.

The tortured look on her face stopped him cold. "What?"

"I'm sorry," she said. "But I never should have suggested that you and I get something going again."

He gaped at her. "Wait. No. What are you talking about?"

"I'm talking about you and me. Liam, you know it's a bad idea."

"I don't know any such thing."

"Well, you *should* know. Because it *is* a bad idea." She wore a sweater over jeans and a knit shirt. But it was cold out, with a brisk wind. She was shivering, her arms wrapped around her middle, her hair wilder than ever, the wind catching it and blowing the dark curls along her cheek, across her forehead.

"You're freezing." He stepped back and gestured toward the main room. "Just come in. I'll turn on the fire, fix you some of that tea you like. We'll talk this out."

"No."

"Karin—"

"I really can't. I don't know what I was thinking when I suggested we should start in with each other again."

"Look. You're freaking out. It's okay. We can talk about it—just talk, that's all."

"No, Liam. Talking won't change anything."

"You're shivering." He reached for her.

She stepped back before he could touch her. "No. Really. I just wanted to tell you, to let you know where we are on this. We need to focus on Riley, not end up in bed together. Having sex again, you and me, it's not a smart idea and it's not going to happen."

Five minutes ago, he couldn't wait to see her face. Now he just wanted to put his fist through a wall. He had a thousand reasons why she was all wrong about this. He wanted to start spouting them, frantically, one after the other, until he'd changed her mind.

But where was that gonna go? Nowhere. He could tell by the tilt of her head and the set of her mouth that she wasn't going to give him an inch.

So be it. If she didn't want to be with him, screw it. He was done with this noise.

"Well, okay then," he said. "I can take Riley for a few hours Wednesday and Friday, in the morning, same as last week."

"Liam, please don't be—"

"You've made your point, okay? No need to pound it into the ground."

He watched her throat move as she swallowed. A dark curl caught on her lip. She swiped it away. "All right."

"Wednesday. Nine in the morning. I can do eight, if that's better."

"No. Nine is great. Thanks."

"Don't thank me. He's my kid. Good night, Karin." He shut the door.

Chapter Nine

Karin went home hating herself a little, and yet certain she'd done the best thing for her, for Liam, for Riley. And for Ben and Coco, too. None of them needed Karin and Liam to get into something together and then have it all go to hell. For kids, especially, consistency mattered. Romantic drama between the adults they counted on could scar them for life.

Tuesday morning, Otto went over to the cottage first thing, as usual. When he came back, he didn't say a word about what was or wasn't going on with her and Liam. But he had that look. Like Karin had kicked a puppy or something.

She felt like such a complete jerk.

And it only got worse.

Early that afternoon, she was sitting in the little breakroom at the Boatworks eating a tuna sandwich with Riley snoozing in his carrier on the chair beside her. He made a small sound in his sleep, sort of a cross between a sigh and a gurgle. She glanced down at him.

And she realized that he looked just like Liam—a baby Liam with fat cheeks and no hair. Riley was going to break a lot of hearts, no doubt about it.

Something happened in her chest, like a pinch and a burn. She ached. For Liam. She wanted…

To talk to Liam. To tell him that their baby looked just like him. She wanted to whisper with him, to laugh with him. She wanted to sit next to him in front of the fire.

She wanted so many things, none of which she was ever going to get. Loving a man entailed risk. And after Bud, she was definitely risk averse.

Plus, Liam was sick and tired of her crap. She didn't blame him, she truly didn't. He probably wouldn't want anything to do with her now, not even if she begged him on hands and knees.

And her dad was still giving her dirty looks.

That night, once all three kids were in bed, she went and stood by her dad's recliner and demanded, "Did Liam say something to you about me?"

He muted the TV and then pointed the remote at her. "Liam didn't say a word to me about you. Not one word."

"Then why do you keep looking at me like you're pissed off at me?"

"Because something's bothering Liam and something is way off with you. My guess is, you two are having problems. And I know Liam well enough now to be reasonably certain he'd do just about anything for you. And that means *he's* not the one at fault."

"First of all, we aren't together, Liam and me. How can we have problems?"

"That's a question you need to answer for yourself."

"And second, you're *my* dad. You're supposed to be on *my* side, and yet you jump right to blaming me."

He grunted. "It's not blame, not really. It's more that I'm frustrated with you."

"Oh, really?"

"Yeah, Kary. Really."

"I'll bet you're not *frustrated* with Liam, now are you?"

Her dad heaved a weary sigh. "I'm so proud of you, Kary. I always have been, and even more so in the last few years. It was awful, what happened with Bud. But you've never been one to whine about how rough you have it. You work hard at the Boatworks. You're an amazing mother and you've created a good life for the kids and for yourself, too."

"Thanks," she said flatly.

"It's only the truth."

"And I know you, Dad. I know what you're doing here. Just hit me with the rest of it."

"All right." He swiped a scarred hand back through his thinning hair and leveled his faded blue eyes on her. "Truthfully, Kary, when you know you've messed up and you don't want to admit it, you're a brat, pure and simple." He pointed the remote at the TV and the sound came back on.

She just stood there, glaring at the side of his head, waiting for him at least to glance her way again. He didn't. "I take it I'm dismissed?"

"I love you, Kary," he muttered, still not looking at her. "I love you and you need to work things out with Liam and that's all I have to say on the subject." He stared at the rerun of *Two and a Half Men* as though he hadn't already seen it ten times before.

Karin fumed. She longed to go full-out drama queen

on him right then. But what good would that do—except to prove him right?

Head high and mouth shut, she whirled for her room, where she closed the door, sat on the bed and called Naomi. "My dad's pissed at me and I really can't blame him," she confessed.

"Hold on," said her lifelong friend. "I need quiet for this." A minute later, Karin heard a door shut on Naomi's end. "There. Silence. Such a rare and beautiful thing."

"Naomi, I messed everything up."

"Let me guess. This is about your hot baby daddy, right?"

"Don't call him that. He's so much more than that—and I hate that you know me so well."

"No, you don't, you love it. What happened?"

"Riley looks just like him."

"Kary. Kids do have a tendency to look like their parents."

Whipping a tissue out of the box on the night table, Karin swiped at her suddenly leaking eyes. "My dad called me a brat and I think he might be right."

"Oh, baby. Pretend that I'm hugging you and tell me everything."

That took several minutes and three more tissues.

"So then," said Naomi. "You want to be with Liam, but you're *afraid* to be with Liam."

"Yeah. Completely. On both counts. I want another chance but I still don't want to rush anything. I still want it to be just between him and me, at least for a while, because I have no idea what I'm doing and what if it all goes to hell? That wouldn't be good for anyone, especially my children—oh, and what does it matter what I want, anyway? I've screwed everything up with him six ways to Sunday. He'd be crazy to give me another chance. *I* don't even like me very much right now."

"Well, *I* love you."

Karin fell back across the bed and sniffled at the ceiling. "I love you, too. You're the best, Naomi."

"And what are you going to do now?"

"Try again, anyway?" Karin answered with a little moan.

"That's the way you do it—except minus the question mark. You need to be owning that stuff."

"I'm going to try again, anyway. Period."

"Yeah! Go get him, tiger."

Easier said than done.

Wednesday, she put on her best jeans and a red sweater and took ten whole minutes fiddling with her hair and putting on blusher, lip gloss and mascara before she took Riley to Liam's for the morning.

The extra effort got her nowhere.

Liam hardly even looked at her. "Hey, RG." He reached for Riley.

She handed him over, along with an insulated pack full of bottles of frozen pumped milk.

"Great," he said, and hooked the bag over his big shoulder.

She'd planned to ask him for another chance, she really had. But her throat locked up and the words wouldn't come.

"Noon?" he asked, stroking Riley's back, his blue gaze locked on his son.

"Uh, yeah. Noon is good."

"All right then." And he stepped back and shut the door.

It was the same at noon. She rang the bell and Liam

answered with Riley all ready to go. He passed her the baby, confirmed the time she would be dropping him off on Friday—and shut the door.

That night, Prim called. Naomi had told her everything and Prim wanted to know how she was doing. Karin explained her complete failure to get Liam to so much as look directly at her. "Let alone give me a chance to try to reach out."

Prim gave her a pep talk and she hung up sure she would do better on Friday.

Didn't happen. The baby handoff was faster, if possible, than it had been on Wednesday. She found herself standing alone on the step, minus the baby, staring at his shut door. At noon, he passed her Riley—and closed the door. Again.

Her dad got home at two that day to hang the outdoor lights on the porch, the back deck and down the outside stair railings, front and back. An hour later, Karin was straightening up the great room when she glanced out the slider and saw her dad and Liam hanging the lights together.

At four, when the kids got home from school, the men were over at the cottage putting up outdoor lights there, too. She knew because Coco and Ben had stopped over there before showing up at the main house to beg Karin to be allowed to go help.

"We already asked Grandpa and Liam," pleaded Coco.

"It's okay with them if it's okay with you," said Ben.

Karin gave her permission. The two ran out the slider and didn't come back.

By quarter of six, she had dinner all ready. The outside lights looked great. Karin turned on the tree lights and the star in the crèche and the lights on the mantel, too. She bundled Riley up and took him with her to see how the work was going.

They'd finished hanging the lights on the cottage, too. The big, multicolored bulbs lined the eaves, the railings and the stairs, so cheery and festive, pushing back the cold, foggy night. Feeling unsure and way too nervous, she mounted the steps to the deck.

They were all there, inside, in the living area, decorating a tree that stood near the wide picture window. For a long, bittersweet moment, she hung back in the shadows, cradling her baby close, just watching. They already had the lights on. Liam stood on a ladder holding a big, lighted star. He slipped it over the top branch, took a moment to prop it up nice and straight and climbed back down. The kids and her dad were busy hanging ornaments. Nobody had spotted her out there in the darkness, not with every light on inside.

Really, she didn't want to interrupt them. They seemed to be having such a great time. Dinner could wait.

She started to turn—and then stopped herself.

Even if Liam had decided she wasn't worth the trouble relationship-wise, they still had a baby to raise. He got along with her family and he really didn't seem to be going anywhere.

Sneaking around out in the dark, avoiding him, was no way to behave.

Riley made a tender little cooing sound in her ear as she marched to the slider and knocked on it.

"It's Mommy!" Coco's gleeful cry was clear even through the glass. She hung the ornament in her hand and ran to shove the slider wide. "Come in! We are decorating Liam's tree."

"I see that. It's looking good." She cast an admiring

glance at the tree—and her gaze collided with Liam's. Collided and held.

She pasted on a smile. "Just wanted to see if anyone was hungry?"

"We're *starving*," moaned Coco.

Karin was still staring at Liam as he stared right back at her. She suggested, "Why don't you all come on back to the house, have a quick dinner and then you can finish Liam's tree?"

"Good idea," said Otto. He turned for the pile of coats tossed on one of the chairs and handed the top one to Ben. Coco ran over there and grabbed hers.

Liam didn't move.

"I hope you'll come, too." Karin's stomach was all twisted in knots. Riley, picking up her anxiety, had begun to squirm in her arms. "Please."

Liam didn't smile. But his mouth got…softer. And his eyes got deeper somehow. "How could I say no?"

Dinner lasted maybe twenty minutes, max. They shoveled down the stew she'd made and everybody pitched in to make short work of cleaning up.

They were all pulling on their coats again as Karin finished wiping the kitchen counters.

"You coming?" asked Liam. She glanced up from the sponge in her hand as he pulled on his jacket. His eyes were ocean blue, beckoning her down to drowning. "Please." He said it so softly. Just for her.

And she felt…hope, like a bright pulse of sheer happiness, lighting her up inside.

"Yeah," she said. "I'll grab some cookies and the baby and be right over."

Three hours later, Liam's tree was fully decorated. They all agreed that it looked fantastic. Karin plated the cookies she and Coco had baked and Liam made hot chocolate—with marshmallows—after which he produced a deck of cards and challenged them all to a game of slapjack.

They played for an hour or so. By then, both kids were yawning.

Otto said, "Come on, you two. Time to go home and get ready for bed."

Coco whined, "Not yet…"

Ben tried bargaining. "Just one more game."

Karin shook her head. "Your grandpa's right. It's getting late."

The kids gave it up and grabbed their coats.

Trying for offhand and not really succeeding, Karin said, "I was thinking I would just hang around here with Liam until Riley wakes up." She'd fed him an hour ago and put him in his crib there at the cottage.

"Great idea." Liam gave her a look that sent a sweet shiver up the backs of her knees.

Her dad tried really hard not to smirk. "Come on, Ben. Coco. Kiss your mom good night and let's go."

As soon as her dad and the kids were gone, Karin sat on the sofa and tried to figure out what to say first. Liam, who'd carried the last of the empty cocoa mugs over to the sink, returned and sat beside her.

She felt the cushion shift, but couldn't quite bring herself to look directly at him. Not yet. The great room was suddenly very quiet. Because, sheesh. Where to even begin?

She stared at the tree and considered remarking on the beauty of it. But they'd pretty much covered that subject before the kids left.

Cautiously, she turned her head toward the man beside her.

He was looking right at her, a knowing grin tugging at the corners of that mouth she might actually get to kiss again, after all—maybe even tonight. “You got something to say to me?”

The butterflies in her stomach went wild, bouncing around in there, fluttering madly. “So much for my dad not figuring out what’s going on between us.”

“Not much gets by your dad. I like that about Otto.” He continued to gaze at her, his eyes low and lazy, like a big, golden timber wolf contemplating his next easy meal. “And did you just admit that there *is* something going on between us, after all?”

She wished he would just grab her and kiss her and they could skip the part where she confessed her own stark terror of this dangerous magic that sizzled between them. “I freaked out, okay? I freaked out and then when you said I was freaking out, I lied and denied it. I’m sorry, Liam. I’m such a coward. I don’t want to get hurt again. I don’t want my children hurt again. I want to protect myself. But I want to be with you, too. I want it so much.”

“Hey.” He said it gently and her heart just melted. “I understand. It’s okay. And Karin, I would never hurt you.”

“I know you wouldn’t, not on purpose. And you’ve been amazing, you really have, with me, with my kids and my dad. And our son is so lucky to have you, Liam. A lucky, lucky little boy.”

He reached for her then, slowly, giving her plenty of opportunity to duck away. She didn’t. He framed her face between his hands. “I’m not going to hurt you, Karin. I mean that. I just want to be with you.”

“Me, too. I do want to be with you.” Gladness pulsed through her, simply to feel his touch again. “But I still…" Her chest felt so tight, bursting with emotions that terrified her at the same time as they filled her with hope and yearning. "Just you and me, huh? Nobody else has to know until we see how it goes."

He shook his head. "Didn't you just say that your dad's already on to us?"

"He'll leave it alone if we make it clear we want it that way."

"Fair enough. Not a word to anyone, Otto included."

"Not even in the morning when he comes over here under cover of darkness and you two drink coffee and talk about…whatever you talk about."

"Manly things."

"Oh, I'll just bet."

"I won't talk about you with him, Karin, not even then. Not until you're ready."

"Thank you," she whispered. He smelled so good, of soap and evergreen and the wind off the ocean at night.

Slowly, he brushed his lips across her mouth, back and forth, setting off sparks, making her ache in the best kind of way. The light caress sent a hot pulse of desire straight to her core.

He eased his fingers back into her hair, combing them through it. "I'm so glad you're here. I hope RG sleeps for hours." He fisted her hair, pulling it a little the way he'd said he'd always wanted to do back when they were kids.

She teased, "Good luck with Riley sleeping for hours…"

"You're right." Liam caught her lower lip between his teeth and bit down with a growl. "We need to get moving here. He could wake up at any time." Slowly, cradling her face in his hands, pulling her with him, kissing her all the way, he stood. Once they were both upright, he pulled her even closer.

They shared another kiss. A deep one that went on forever, until her whole body quivered in eagerness and a pleading groan rose in her throat.

"Time for bed." He took her by the waist and flung her over his shoulder, like a fireman saving her from a burning building.

She would have cried out in mock protest, but the last thing she wanted to do was take a chance of waking the baby, so she settled for playfully kicking and pounding his broad back as he carried her off down the hall.

In the master bedroom, he shut the door, took her to the king-size bed and let her down to the rug—but he didn't let her go. He ran both hands down her arms and then back up over her shoulders. His touch felt so right. He cradled her face again and kissed her some more.

When he lifted his head that time, she gave the room a quick once-over. "The bedroom looks great." It was in grays and tans, with black-and-white prints on the walls.

"Thanks. Let's get naked."

She laughed. "Eager, much?"

"How did you guess?" He plucked at the sleeve of her sweater. "This is in my way."

She grinned up at him. "I got my checkup."

"Yeah?" Oh, those eyes of his. He could make her come with just a look.

"I officially have the all clear to do naughty things with you." She sounded breathless. He made her that way.

"Good." He took the sweater by the hem. "Arms up." She obeyed his command and he swept it up and away.

She frowned at him. "Wait a minute. You shut the door. We won't be able to hear—"

"Yeah, we will—stay right there." He went to the dresser and grabbed the baby monitor she hadn't noticed until then. "I have two receivers, one for out in the living area and this one." He flipped it on. The small screen showed the crib and Riley asleep in it. "Infrared, so I can see him even when the light's off. Cool, huh?" He set it on the nightstand.

"Very cool—but do you have condoms?"

He pulled open the drawer and took out a chain of them, dropping them next to the monitor. "Any more questions?" He didn't wait for her answer, but instantly commanded, "Take off the jeans."

He hooked his fingers into her waistband. She moaned just at the feel of his fingers pressing her belly as he undid the button right below her navel.

"Need some help?" She toed off her Uggs, ripped her fly wide and wiggled the jeans down over her hips.

"God. Karin." He looked at her like she was the most beautiful woman in the world, a look that sent pleasure zipping all through her, a look that banished any leftover nerves about how unsexy her poufy belly and plain white nursing bra must be. He whipped off his thermal shirt. "Finally."

He had one of those universal gyms down in a corner of the garage and he ran on the beach just about every day. Keeping fit really paid off. He was so beautiful, everything sculpted and hard, with that wonderful trail of golden hair leading down to the happy place. And she was so glad—to be here with him, the two of them. Alone in his bedroom.

If they got right on it, they might even manage to have actual sex before Riley woke up.

"Hurry," she begged.

They quickly got rid of the rest of their clothes and

he took her by the shoulders and pulled her down across the bed on top of him.

She laughed as she kissed him, bracing her knees to either side of him, rubbing herself shamelessly against his hard belly, reaching back to wrap her fingers around his thick, hard length.

He groaned when she did that, his hands stroking down her back, grabbing the twin globes of her bottom, holding on tight. He felt so good, so solid and strong. The manly scent of him tempted her, promising all the pleasures she remembered so well. She'd missed this, the two of them, naked, together. Missed it so much.

She wanted him all over her, covering every inch of her. "I want you on top of me."

"Done." He rolled them, taking the top position. She wrapped herself around him like a vine.

He kept on kissing her, a kiss so hot it could burn the house down, a kiss that went on forever, his tongue claiming her mouth, his body covering hers.

This. Right now. With him. It just didn't get any better.

He scattered more kisses, across her cheek, down the side of her throat, stopping to nip at her collarbone, sucking her skin against his teeth. She'd have marks there in the morning.

But so what? She had turtlenecks. And every kiss thrilled her. It all felt just perfect. Exactly right.

"I missed you," she cried. It was a confession, one she couldn't hold back.

He caught her face in his hands again. "I'm here. Here to stay."

"Oh, Liam." Better not to talk about it. Better just to grab this moment and squeeze every drop of joy from it.

His palmed her breasts. She moaned at the pleasurable ache. “Fuller,” he said, his voice rich with approval.

She winced. “I’m leaking.”

He pulled back enough to grin down at her. “Shut up. You’re beautiful.” And he took her mouth yet again, spearing his tongue in, sweeping along the edges of her teeth, drinking her down.

When he broke that kiss, it was only to press his lips to her chin, her neck, the hollow of her throat. He dropped a chain of kisses between her breasts. Moving lower, he kissed her belly and the soft points of her hip bones.

And then, easing her thighs over his shoulders and settling between them, he kissed her in the most intimate way. He made her crazy with his lips and little nips of his teeth, with his talented tongue, while his clever fingers played her so perfectly.

It felt so good. She tossed her head against the pillow, whispering his name, moaning it out loud more than once, threading her fingers in his hair, pulling him closer, urging him on.

He eased her legs wider, kissed her more deeply, continuing to stroke her with those skilled strong fingers of his, driving her toward the peak until she gave it up to him, gave herself over completely.

She cried his name as she came.

Had she passed out from sheer ecstasy?

It was just possible.

He moved away. She forced her heavy eyes open and saw he was up on his knees between her wide-open thighs, rolling on one of the condoms.

She reached for him. “Liam. Come here.”

He didn’t have to be told twice. With care, he lowered

himself to her, gathering her into him, taking her mouth again. She tasted her own musky arousal on his lips.

And she was lost again in the glory of it, kissing him hungrily, reaching down between them, taking him—carefully, so as not to rip the condom—in her hand, guiding him to her.

He surged in hard. She rose up to meet him with a deep, needful groan, lifting her legs and wrapping them good and tight around his lean waist.

After that, he took over, hard and fast at first, so that she could only hold on and let it happen, let him sweep her away into a world of pure, perfect sensation. But then he slowed. He rocked her in a steady, thrilling glide, going deep and then pulling back—only to return to her, over and over again, stoking the heat within her, fanning the fire.

She hit the crest so suddenly, chanting his name, pulling him closer, tighter, as another finish rocked her.

There was a lull. She closed her eyes with a sigh.

But then he started moving again and it felt so good, so right. Her body responded instantly. Another fulfillment spun into being from the embers of the last.

Liam stayed with her, whispering encouragements, urging her to take what she needed from him. Sweet bolts of pleasure unfurled within her, spreading out from her core, flowing down her arms, along her legs, bringing hot shivers to the backs of her knees and the soles of her feet. Until every part of her had been swept up, spun around, carried away into complete satisfaction.

And then it was his turn. He thrust in hard and so deep—and stilled. She felt his finish claiming him. Wrapping her arms around him, she cradled him close as his climax rolled through him.

There was stillness. She shut her eyes and sank into the lovely, floating feeling of ease. Of peace.

A few minutes later, he got up to take care of the condom. Returning with a cool, wet cloth, he gently bathed her breasts and down her belly. It felt wonderful, that cloth, cooling and soothing, too.

Her eyes were so heavy. She hadn't realized how tired she was. He left her again. She shook herself awake and started to get up.

But then he was there. He came down to the bed with her and pulled the covers over them, gathering her into him.

"I should get Riley, go home." She kissed the side of his throat.

"Not yet." His lips brushed her ear.

She rested her head on his shoulder, listened to his heart beat deep and steady. So soothing, that sound. "If I don't go, I may never move from this spot."

He stroked her hair, smoothing it away from her cheek. "Stay. Just for a minute or two…"

When she opened her eyes, her baby was crying. She tried to push back the covers.

But the hard, warm arms wrapped around her held her even tighter. He nuzzled a kiss in her hair. "I'll get him, bring him to you."

"I have to go, Liam. What time is it, anyway?"

"A little after one…"

She pushed at his chest. "Gotta go."

He kissed the tip of her nose. "He's going to be hungry. You can feed him. And then you can go."

She looked up to meet his eyes. His white teeth flashed with his grin. "Well, go on, then," she said. "Go get him."

He kissed her nose a second time, slid out from under the covers and turned on the lamp. She squinted against the sudden light and brought up a hand to shield her eyes.

"We'll be right back." Stark naked, he headed for the door.

She shoved the covers away and lowered her bare feet to the rug. Shivering a little, she darted around, snatching up her clothes from the floor, from the chair and from the foot of the bed.

Riley kept crying—in stereo—on the monitor and from the room next-door. "Whoa, buddy." She heard Liam groan. "That's quite a load." She paused after pulling on her sweater to watch the monitor as he carried the yowling infant away from the crib and out of sight.

But she could hear him clearly as he continued to murmur reassurances and promises that everything was going to be fine. Riley wasn't going for it. Every time she thought he might settle down a little, he'd suck in a big breath and start bawling again.

Once she'd thrown on her clothes, she crossed the hall and stood in the doorway of the baby's room. "Thanks for taking on the hazardous waste."

He turned to her with the still-crying Riley cradled against his broad, bare chest. "Hey. It's in the job description."

She held out her arms. "My turn." He passed her the squirming baby and she carried him to the easy chair in the corner. Once she was settled, she put Riley to her breast.

A hearty eater, he latched right on.

She glanced up at the naked man standing over her. "Hear that?"

"Silence," he replied with a nod. "It really is golden."

Showing no inclination to go put some clothes on, he studied her face, his gaze moving from her eyes to her lips and back to her eyes again. "I want to lock you in this house and never let you go."

Did she feel a little thrill at that hungry look he wore, at the low roughness of his voice? Absolutely.

But she gave him an easy shrug. "I think they call that kidnapping. It's frowned upon by law enforcement. And people who get kidnapped don't like it much, either."

"Buzzkill," he whispered tenderly. "Next you'll be saying I should go get dressed."

"Never." She gave him a slow once-over. "You look so good naked."

He braced a hand on the back of the chair and bent close for a quick, hard kiss. "I'll leave you alone." He laid his palm gently on Riley's head, cradling it, encompassing it—but just for a moment. And then he turned for the door.

She smiled as she watched him walk away. Not only did he look amazing, he was funny and good to her. And every time he kissed her, she wanted to hold on tight and never, ever let go.

But that would be rushing things, that would be getting all caught up in big emotions, making life-changing decisions without using her head.

Forever was a long, long time. If she ever headed down that road again, she would be 100 percent certain she'd taken the right turn.

Chapter Ten

Otto came to the cottage that morning, as usual, before dawn. Liam turned on the tree lights and the fire. They sat on the hearth with their full mugs of coffee.

"Karin didn't come in until almost two this morning," Otto remarked in a tone so offhand as to be almost humorous.

"What? You stayed awake waiting for her to come home?"

"The habits of a lifetime, my boy. They never die."

Liam sipped his coffee. "I got orders not to talk to you about what is or isn't going on between Karin and me."

"What she doesn't know won't hurt her."

Liam scoffed. "Easy for you to say. You're her dad. She trusts you absolutely. I'm the interloper."

"Just ask her to marry you. It can't be that complicated."

"Otto. You have no idea."

"I'm on your side. So's Coco. And Sten. Madison, too. I think you've even turned Ben around."

He perked up at that. "Ben? Really?"

"Really."

That felt damn good, to think he and Ben were on the right track now. "And Madison, too, huh? Well, she is my sister. She *should* be on my side—even if we hardly know each other." Liam had only talked to the newfound Bravo briefly, at a couple of family dinners back in the spring when she first came to town to meet the family. "It's not right, that I hardly know my own sister."

Otto raised his mug in a quick salute. "You'll get your chance, soon as she and Sten move home to stay."

"You really think she's giving up her career? I read somewhere that she makes millions a year."

"They say money isn't everything."

"They say a lot of things."

"That's right. Because they're true—and yeah. I think Madison is going to finish out those final projects she couldn't get out of and settle right here on Sweetheart Cove, have a few babies, make a good life with Sten. Just like you and Karin need to do."

Liam stared straight ahead. "Not talking to you about Karin."

"Come over for breakfast, why don't you?"

"For a guy who's supposed to leave it alone, you're damn persistent—and no. Even I'm not *that* pushy."

"Karin said to ask you."

"Stop yanking my chain."

"I'm not. She was up with RG when I headed over here. She said, 'Tell Liam we're having waffles and he's welcome to join us…'"

Liam got up, grabbed his phone from where he'd left it on the coffee table and texted Karin. Your dad says I'm invited for breakfast. He glanced back at Otto. "You want more coffee?"

"Yeah."

Karin answered as he was passing the tree to get the pot from the kitchen. What? You didn't believe him?

Should I?

Liam, please join us for breakfast. Today. Tomorrow. Any morning the mood strikes.

Damn. This was progress. It was going to work out for them. She would get past her fear that he would do her the way Bud had. She was learning to trust again.

He just had to curb his impatience, take it one step at a time.

I'll be there.

She sent back a thumbs-up. He stared at that simple emoji and felt like he'd just won the lottery. Or maybe free soloed up El Capitan and lived to tell about it.

"Told you," said Otto with a self-satisfied smirk. "Now bring that pot over here. I need my caffeine."

At breakfast, he behaved himself. Mostly. Now and then, he would catch himself staring too long at Karin, but he didn't think he was all that obvious.

That night, she came over with Riley as soon as the kids were in bed. She'd nursed him at the other house and when she put him in his crib at the cottage, he didn't even make a peep.

They had a couple of hours, the two of them, in bed. It was so good with her. He got now why some guys never looked at another woman.

Why would he want to look at someone else when he could spend every free moment staring at Karin, talking to Karin, laughing with her, kissing her, having great sex with her?

Sunday morning, he went to breakfast at the main house again. Karin gave him that certain smile, the one that was only for him. After they ate, he helped Coco with cleanup.

She was Batgirl today, rattling off her special powers, leaning in close to ask with completely adorable and uncharacteristic shyness, "Are you still taking me to see the trucks today, Liam?"

"You still want to go?"

"Yes, please!"

"Can you be ready at nine?"

"Yes, I can!"

Karin took him aside to remind him that Coco was only seven and tended to trust everyone she met. She needed closer supervision than nine-year-old, super mature, overly cautious Ben.

"I hear you," he promised. "I won't let her out of my sight."

Coco wore her black tights and yellow rain boots for the trip, but Karin insisted that she switch out her towel cape for a coat and a warm wool hat. The red hat had a border of snowflakes and a big, white pom-pom that bounced all the way to Bravo Trucking. Coco pretty much talked nonstop.

She charmed everyone in the driver's lounge. Liam hung out with her there for half an hour or so, took her for a quick tour of the offices and the fuel island and then out to have a look at the engine of one of the trucks.

He showed her how to pop the hood latches and then how easily the giant hood opened with a tug on the front. When he launched into his spiel about how the engine worked, she stared up at him as though transfixed by his every word.

"Questions?" he asked once he'd given her a quick rundown.

"Um, no." Those blue eyes were so serious. "But I would really like to go for a ride in this truck, Liam."

"Now?"

Her pom-pom bobbed and her smile bloomed wide. "Yes, now, please!" She looked up at him like he'd grabbed her a handful of stars. "I'm glad you're our baby's daddy, Liam."

All of a sudden, he felt kind of choked up. "Me, too."

"I think you should get married to Mommy and we can all live happily ever after like in *The Wild Swans* and *Frozen* and *Beauty and the Beast*."

Me, too! But that time he didn't say it out loud. A guy had to be careful about the promises he made. Especially to children.

Coco had her head tipped to the side now. She stared up at him, frowning a little. "Maybe you should just think about it?"

"I will—now, how 'bout that ride?"

Liam boosted her up into the cab and took the wheel.

They circled the terminal and she pointed out the buildings she'd visited. When they got back where they'd started, she wasn't ready to quit, so he drove her across the Youngs Bay Bridge and into Astoria. They rumbled along Marine Drive, circling back using Commercial.

On the way home to Valentine Bay, they stopped at the same diner he and Ben had eaten at the week before. Coco wanted the works, a burger, chocolate milkshake and fries. She only managed to eat about half of all that before she wiped her mouth with her napkin and gave him one of those looks she was an absolute master at—one of those I'm-the-cutest-little-girl-in-the-universe looks.

"It was really good, Liam, but I'm *really* full. My eyes are bigger than my tummy. That's what Grandpa always says. But Mommy says we have to practice not wasting food."

"We'll take it to go."

"The milkshake will melt."

Was he getting played? It was starting to seem like a definite possibility. "Hmm. Looks like you already ate most of the milkshake."

"It's my favorite." She grinned so wide, he could see the gap on the bottom where she'd lost two baby teeth. The white rims of her grown-up teeth had just begun to show. "I like chocolate milkshakes more than french fries and a *lot* more than a hamburger."

Liam leaned in and lowered his voice to secret-sharing level. "What are you telling me that you're not telling me?"

She giggled. "You're funny, Liam."

"Did you do something you shouldn't have done?"

"Not exac'ly."

"So then, what's going on?"

Her little shoulders sagged. "Well, Mommy usually says if they don't have a mini-burger and a small-size fries, I should just skip the fries. And the milkshake was kind of big, too. I was afraid to ask for a mini-shake because maybe they don't have those and even if they do, I would rather have a big one."

Wouldn't we all? "So you broke the rules about wasting food, is that what you're telling me?"

Those eyes were enormous in that little pixie face with that perfect pointed chin just like her mom's. "Umm-hmm."

How big of a deal was this, really? He had no idea. It was all way above his pay grade, parenting-wise. "I'm not about to make you take the leftovers home."

She brightened. "You're not?"

"I'll just tell your mom that I didn't know the rules and I let you order too much food."

"Liam," she chided. "That's not gonna work with my mom."

"Why not?"

"'Cause my mom knows that *I* know the rules and I'm s'posed to follow them—and you know what? I'll just take the leftovers home."

He kept his expression carefully neutral though a grin was trying really hard to stretch the edges of his mouth. "You sure?"

"Umm-hmm. It's okay if I order too much food as long as I eat the leftovers later."

"Problem solved, then?"

"Yeah, 'cept I have to eat the leftovers."

"Life is full of choices."

She wrinkled her little nose at him. "That's exac'ly what Mommy says."

That night, Karin came over again. She'd left RG sleeping at the other house. Her dad would call when he needed her. "Sorry. I probably won't be staying all that long."

"I'll take you however I can get you." He caught her hand, pulled her into his arms and walked her backward down the hall to the bedroom, kissing her all the way. They made love fast and hard, with no preamble, rolling around on the bed, holding on to each other good and tight. It was great.

And then, when Otto didn't call, they started again, this time making it last, indulging in deep, lazy kisses and slow, sweet caresses. After that second time, they talked.

"Coco can wrap the average adult around her pinkie finger," Karin said. She was lying on her back, the covers pulled up over those breasts he loved to kiss, curling a lock of her hair around one of her fingers. "But you nailed the leftovers issue. Well done."

Feeling contented, happy with the world and everything in it, he scooted a little closer to her side of the bed, braced up on an elbow and just let himself enjoy looking at her, breathing in the sweet scent of her that was a little bit musky from all the fun they'd been having. "I wouldn't say I nailed anything. I just let her talk herself into doing the right thing."

"You're good with kids." She gave him a teasing little smile. "You're going to make some lucky woman the perfect husband."

And just like that, in the space of a few seconds, all his easy contentment vanished. "What the hell is that supposed to mean, Karin?"

"Whoa." She rolled to her side and faced him fully. "What'd I say?"

"You want to see me with another woman?"

"Liam, come on. Of course not." She brushed his shoulder with a tentative hand. He had to consciously hold himself still in order not to jerk away from her. "It was just a figure of speech."

Impatience rose inside him, making his skin feel too tight and his pulse throb like an infected wound. "Sometimes I think you don't take me seriously."

"That's not true." She ran her palm down the outside of his arm, petting him. Soothing him.

It worked. To a degree.

But she'd reopened this can of worms and damned if he was just going to shove the lid back on and pretend nothing had happened. "I don't want *some* woman, Karin. I want *you*."

She put a finger to his lips. "Liam, come on, don't..."

Gently, he guided her hand away from his mouth. "Marry me."

She just looked at him. Her eyes were a thousand years old.

He said it again. "Marry me."

"Because of Riley," she whispered bleakly.

"Yeah. Because of our son. What's wrong with that? Because of Riley and because I want you and I don't want to be with anyone but you. And because of Coco and Ben. Hell, because of Otto. We can make a good life. We can make it all work."

"Don't." She touched his mouth again. "Please."

"Because I lov—"

"No." She glared at him. "Uh-uh. Don't say it. I really and truly do not want to hear it."

He sat up and swung his legs over the edge of the bed—at which point he realized he was staying right here. Because there was nowhere he wanted to be but with her. Even when he was mad at her, he didn't want to walk away from her.

And she had it right. He shouldn't have started in

with this, shouldn't have let himself lose it over some offhand remark of hers.

Behind him, the bed shifted as she rose to her knees.

She touched him. He felt her tentative hand on his shoulder. "Liam." He felt…everything. Her touch, her body behind him, so smooth and soft; her breath caressing the back of his neck. "Liam, I'm sorry. That was a crappy thing I said. I want you, too. I do. I would be so jealous if you went out and found someone else. You're important to me. So much so that it scares me."

"There's nothing for you to be scared of. I'm not Bud. I've had my time to be free, to keep things casual and easy, to answer to no one but myself. I know what I want now and I want to be with you. I want to answer to you, Karin, and to be responsible for you. I want to be the one they have to call if you're in need."

"And I want to be with *you.* So much. But I'm not just jumping into something permanent. I'm never doing that again. I'm not ready to go making promises about forever. I just need to take it one day at a time. And I do love this—you and me, together. Like this. I love how you are with me. And with Riley. With my family. It's only that sometimes it kind of feels like it's too good to be true, you know?"

He shook his head and a humorless chuckle escaped him. "Do you hear yourself? You like everything about me. You just don't believe I'm for real."

"Look, I've got issues, I know it. I'm not blind to myself, to who I am. I'm not the easiest woman to be with. I'm not trusting. I've got…defenses. And I guess I'm always half expecting you to figure out that I'm a pain in the ass and this thing with us just doesn't work for you."

Her hand was still on his shoulder. He reached up and laid his over it, sliding his thumb in under her fingers to rub the soft heart of her palm. "I'm going nowhere. How am I going to convince you of that?"

"Liam…" It was barely a whisper. She moved in closer behind him, pulling her hand out from under his, but not to retreat. To get closer. She pressed her soft breasts against him, wrapped her arms around his belly and rested her cheek on his shoulder. "Liam."

All he had to do was turn his head. Her sweet mouth was right there. She smelled of citrus and rain and baby lotion. She smelled like all the best things, everything he'd ever wanted all wrapped up in one contrary, difficult, big-eyed, wild-haired woman.

I love you, Karin.

No, he didn't say it. She didn't want to hear it. But he thought it, thought it over and over, as he kissed her.

I love you.

He turned and curved his body over her, carrying her down to the bed again, sweeping his hands along her arms, into the silky curve of her waist, down over her smooth thighs, parting her, touching her, so slick and wet, already primed for him.

I love you.

She reached down between them and curled her hand around him, taking command of him. He groaned his pleasure into their kiss as she stroked him, tightly, forcefully. A little bit roughly.

Just the way he liked it.

He reached out, grabbed a condom from the nightstand, managed to get the thing unwrapped. She helped him, taking it from him, rolling it down over his aching length.

I love you.

The words were there, in his head, pulsing with the beat of his heart as he sank into her. As she wrapped herself around him, pulling him tightly to her, so good. So right.

I love you.

As he moved within her, rocking her slowly, taking her higher and higher.

I love you.

As she came apart, chanting his name.

Chapter Eleven

After the night she wouldn't let him say the *L* word, Liam tried to keep his focus on the good things.

Like how Karin couldn't stay away from him. She appeared at his door five or six nights out of seven and she stayed for an hour or two, at least—sometimes much longer.

But she always returned home before the kids woke up. And she continued to insist that they keep their relationship just between the two of them. He hated her restrictions, like she was keeping him in his place, not letting him get too close.

Most Sundays, he went to dinner at Daniel's. It was a Bravo family tradition. He'd tried several times to get her to come with him, to bring the kids and Otto, too. She always had some reason why it just wouldn't work. He asked her again the second Friday in December. Riley was asleep in the crib at the cottage and they were sitting by the fire in the main room.

She sipped the last of her raspberry tea and answered regretfully, "Thanks, but I don't think so, Liam."

"Just one time," he coaxed. "This Sunday."

"Your brother and his wife do not need a bunch of extra people descending on them."

"Yeah, Karin. They do. Especially if it's you and the kids and Otto. You were there at Thanksgiving. They loved having you. You're welcome there anytime."

She set her empty mug down, leaned in and kissed him. "Thanks, but no."

"Then how about Christmas? Come to Daniel's for dinner Christmas Day."

"Liam…"

He pulled her close and kissed the tip of her nose. "Don't answer now. Think about."

"I just don't…"

He covered her lips with his before she could dish out another denial. She seemed only too happy for the distraction. He gathered her closer and deepened the kiss. Then, pulling her up with him, he led her down the hall to his bedroom. As he dragged her down on the bed with him, he reminded himself that he was focusing on the positive, looking for the good things in what he had with her.

Kissing her. Holding her. Having her in his bed…

These were very good things.

And the sex was by no means all of the goodness.

He loved the way she trusted him with Coco and Ben—and seemed to count on him, too. She didn't hesitate to ask him to ferry them around or keep an eye on them when Otto was at the Boatworks and she needed to run over to the store. Who knew he'd ever be the kind of guy who couldn't wait to drive the kids to play dates and sleepovers, to take Coco to her Hip-Hoppin' Dance Class and Ben to Science Club?

The next week, he even managed to get himself an invite to the Valentine Bay Elementary School Christmas show wherein Coco played a singing, dancing snowflake and Ben wore a beard, a yellow robe and a crown as one of the Three Wise Men. Liam was so proud of them, he was first on his feet to lead the standing ovation when they all came out and took their bows.

Every morning, he showed up at the main house with Otto for breakfast. And every morning, Karin smiled at him like she was glad to see him. He kept waiting for the day when she'd move in close, maybe offer her sweet mouth for a quick kiss, the day when she'd say something soft and low and welcoming, just between the two of them.

But the mornings went by, one by one, and a more intimate breakfast greeting didn't happen. He told himself that it *would* happen. Someday very soon. He just needed to stay positive. She would get over her fear of giving her heart to him.

They would be together. *Really* together. Live in the same house, sleep in the same bed—and not just for a few stolen hours, either. Uh-uh. Same bed.

All. Night. Long.

Negativity crept in, though. Sometimes he couldn't help thinking that all he'd ever had of Karin Killigan were stolen moments. From last Christmas to now, she fit him in when she could manage it—and yeah, she fit him in just about every night as of now. That was progress, definitely.

But she wouldn't simply let it be known that she was with him.

Even if she wouldn't marry him, she could let him be *more*. More than her baby daddy. More than her co-parent. More than the helpful guy next door. More than the man who made her cry out his name two or three times a night.

Be patient, he kept telling himself.

And he tried, he really did. But his patience was fraying. No matter how often he reminded himself that he and Karin really hadn't been together all that long and that he needed to chill, back off, let her find her way to him in her own time, he couldn't help feeling frustrated.

He'd finally figured out what he wanted out of life and he didn't want to waste a moment going forward. But he was stuck at the threshold of his own happiness, waiting for Karin to open the damn door and let him in.

The kids had the usual two-week holiday break from school. It started the Friday before Christmas.

Karin needed to wrangle them childcare for when she had to be at the Boatworks. They didn't want to spend their Christmas vacation at a winter break camp and they didn't want to hang around the office at the Boatworks with her, either. Usually, her dad and Sten helped her out. But Sten was in LA. And Otto had a couple of big refitting jobs. He couldn't look after them as much as he usually did.

Liam said he would stay home and watch them a couple of days a week, but she turned him down. He already took Riley every Wednesday and Friday till noon. And he had a business—a busy, successful, demanding one. He needed to spend his workdays running it. He couldn't be hanging around her house looking after the kids.

She had a couple of trusted sitters she'd always used, but both of them were well into their teens now. One had a job flipping burgers and the other was spending her Christmas break at her dad's house in Telluride.

She was kind of at her wit's end with the situation and gearing up to tell Ben and Coco that they were going to have to go to day camp.

And then, Sten and Madison came home.

Sten called on Saturday morning during breakfast to say that Madison had two weeks off from filming the science fiction epic she'd been working on since May. They'd chartered a private jet and would be arriving at Valentine Bay Executive Airport at noon.

At a quarter of one, they showed up at the house in a Lincoln Navigator with Madison's bodyguards, Sergei and Dirk. Everyone was home, including Liam, who'd driven up to Bravo Trucking for a couple of hours that morning, but returned in time to be there to greet the newlyweds.

When Madison emerged from the back seat, her streaky blond hair piled up in a sloppy bun, wearing old jeans and a giant sweater that hung off one shoulder, Coco shouted, "Madison! Merry Christmas!" and ran straight for her. Madison opened her arms and the two of them hugged it out like the best buddies they'd become back in March when the movie star first came to Sweetheart Cove.

Ben went right to Sten for a slightly more restrained greeting. And then there were hugs all around.

Karin grabbed her brother and whispered mock desperately, "Thank God you're here. I need a kidsitter."

He laughed. "Little sister, whatever you need for the next two weeks, you're gonna get it."

* * *

They got the car unloaded and Sten, Madison and the bodyguards settled upstairs in Sten's half of the house. That day, they all mostly just hung out in the downstairs great room around the tree, catching up, taking turns holding Riley and playing board games. Karin kept the Christmas tunes playing in the background. She also cooked a big dinner and they all sat down to eat together.

Once the kids were in bed, Otto headed down to Sten's workshop under the house. He had a few Christmas projects he was working on. Liam invited Madison and Sten over to the cottage for a drink.

"You, too, Karin." He turned those baby blues on her and gave her one of those smiles that melted her midsection. "Bring RG. You can put him to bed over there."

She almost said no, because she didn't want her brother or Madison figuring out how close she and Liam had become—which was a ridiculous excuse, and she knew it. There really was some sense in not letting her kids start to see her and Liam as a couple until they were certain their relationship would last. But Madison and Sten would be fine no matter what happened in the end between Karin and her baby's father.

Karin put on her coat and bundled up the baby and they all five went next door. One of the bodyguards trailed after them to the cottage but didn't follow them inside.

It was nice, really. Riley went right to sleep in his crib. Liam got everyone something to drink and they sat around the fire. It had started snowing, a light snow, one that wouldn't stick on the ground, but they could see it drifting down beyond the windows, lit by the Christmas lights strung in the eaves and along the deck railing, the white flakes spinning in the cold wind.

Madison was all about getting to know Liam better. "It's another of the many crappy things about being switched at birth," she said. "I feel like I have twenty-seven years to make up for. Liam, we should have grown up together. I should know all your quirks and irritating habits and be constantly ragging on you about them." She snuggled up against Sten, who sat beside her on the sofa. "We should be like Sten and Karin."

"Yeah." Sten gave a wry chuckle. "Karin always knows what's best for me. It's really annoying."

No way Karin could let that remark pass. "I'm very wise, actually. I give excellent advice."

"Oh, really?" Liam had taken the seat beside her in front of the fire. She found herself wishing he would put his arm around her—at the same time as she told herself she appreciated his restraint.

Yeah. No doubt about it. She was kind of a mess over him, longing for it to be the real thing with him and simultaneously terrified that it would all blow up in her face—and what were they talking about?

Right. Her willingness to give her big brother advice. "You'd better believe I've given Sten advice. I've made it my mission to set him straight whenever he needs it."

Sten groaned. "Yeah. Whether I want to be set straight or not."

Karin admitted, "Now and then it's just possible that I've been a tiny bit in your face."

"A *tiny bit*?"

"Come on, Sten. Don't give me attitude. You know I was right about you two." Karin raised her ginger beer in a salute to Madison.

Madison asked eagerly, "What did you say to him?"

"Sorry. I can't give you specifics. It was a private conversation between a thickheaded brother and his brilliant, emotionally sensitive and extremely perceptive sister. Let's just say he was scared to take a chance on what he had with you and I helped him to see that he was all wrong."

Now Madison was grinning at Sten. "You *were* scared." She kissed his cheek.

"But I got over it."

"Oh, yes you did." Her voice was soft and she leaned into him. "And magnificently, too."

"Magnificent. That's me, all right." Sten kissed her.

Karin glanced away from the private moment between her brother and his wife—and into Liam's waiting eyes. At least he didn't get on her for her own reluctance to take a chance on love.

Not right then, anyway.

Later, after Sten and Madison had gone back to the other house, Liam locked the door, turned off the lights and led her down the hall to his room.

"I was afraid you'd run right out the door after them," he teased as he took her red sweater by the hem and pulled it off over her head.

She kissed his beard-scruffy, sculpted jaw. "The baby's still sleeping and I want to be here with you—and my brother and Madison are grown-ups. They can think what they want about me and you." She got to work unbuttoning his flannel shirt.

He interrupted her busy fingers long enough to get rid of her bra. Then he tipped up her chin and kissed her, the sweetest kind of kiss, slow and teasing, as she continued to work her way from one button to the next down the front of his shirt.

She slipped the shirt off his fine, broad shoulders. It dropped to the rug.

He asked, "So you challenged your brother to take a chance on love, huh?"

She was just about to kiss him, but defensiveness curled through her as she met his eyes. "Really, it was a completely different situation with Madison and Sten."

Liam dipped his head and whispered in her ear. "Different than what?"

"You know very well what."

He pulled back enough to look at her again. "You mean, different than you and me."

"That's right."

He traced the line of her jaw with a slow pass of his index finger, making her shiver a little, causing that lovely, hollowed-out feeling low in her belly. And he asked, "Specifically, how are Madison and Sten different from you and me?"

"They were both single, no kids involved. It was simpler for them. Less baggage, you know?"

"Kids or not, everybody's got baggage, Karin."

"You're not hearing me."

"Yes, I am." His fingers eased under the fall of her hair and he cupped the back of her neck, rubbing it a little, easing tension she hadn't even realized was there. "When I took Coco to Bravo Trucking, she said you and I should get married and we'd all live happily ever after like in a Disney movie. And as you already know, Ben only wanted me to promise I wasn't going to go away. RG is just a baby, but I have a really strong feeling he's not going to mind if his parents end up married to each other. So I would say the baggage we're talking about isn't really to do with the kids, is it?"

"Of course it's to do with the kids. They're the top

priority—and about Coco saying we ought to get married. How did you answer her?"

He pulled her closer and pressed his lips to the center of her forehead. "Before I could figure out a good answer, she changed her mind and suggested that I just think about it. I said I would. We left it at that."

"Why didn't you tell me this sooner?"

He tipped up her chin so she had to look at him. "Please don't freeze up on me."

"I'm not, I just…" She had no idea what to say next and ended up murmuring weakly, "They're my kids. I don't want them hurt."

"I would never hurt them." He said it sincerely.

And she believed him. "I know." *Not on purpose, anyway.* "And you're right. I do have baggage. Way too much of it."

"You could…let me help you carry it." He gazed down at her so steadily.

She wanted to grab on to him—grab on tight and never let him go.

Because he was so good to her and to her children. Because who did she think she was kidding?

Her heart was already his. And she didn't want to think about that, about how it would all work out in the end, about where they were going and if they would ever actually get there. She just wanted to hold him close and feel his heartbeat next to hers and pretend there was no tomorrow.

Hold him close and lose herself in the glory of right now.

She undid another button. "Liam?"

"Hmm?"

"Kiss me. Now."

His lips touched hers and she slid her hands up to

link behind his neck. All her worries flew away. It was just Liam and Karin, holding on tight, keeping each other warm on a cold winter's night.

"Come with us for Sunday dinner at Daniel's," Madison said the next morning at breakfast. "Let's have the whole family together."

"Yeah." Sten put in his two cents. "Please come."

Coco literally bounced in her chair. "I know I'm not s'posed to interrupt when the grown-ups are deciding things, but just in case you want to know what I think, I think yes! We should go!"

Ben was nodding. "I think so, too," he solemnly intoned.

"I *like* the Bravos," Coco proclaimed. "And I bet they have a big Christmas tree."

Karin slid a glance at Liam. He was looking down, but she knew he was barely hiding a grin. "So Liam. What do you think?"

He glanced up at last and she took the full force of his sky blue gaze. "I'll say it again. I want you all to come to Sunday dinner at Daniel's."

How could she keep saying no when he looked at her that way?

She couldn't. And she didn't.

That afternoon, she packed up plenty of cookies and Christmas candy and the leftover ham from the night before and off they went to the Bravo house on Rhinehart Hill. They took two cars, Liam's F-150 and the Navigator, with one of the bodyguards behind the wheel.

Once they got there, Karin wondered why she'd ever said no. Everyone really did seem happy to see them. She'd always enjoyed hanging out with Liam's sisters, and the giant Christmas tree in the family room was a beautiful sight to behold.

She got to touch base with Connor and Aly Bravo, who'd just returned from New York, where Aly had finished up at her longtime job there, sublet her apartment—and married Connor for the second time.

Aly asked to hold Riley. She sighed when Karin laid him in her arms. "He is just perfect." Connor's bride glanced up with a glowing smile. "Connor and I are expecting in May."

"Wow. Congratulations."

"What can I say? It was unexpected, but we aren't complaining. We both always wanted kids."

Aly had five brothers, one of whom had been born just a couple of months ago. Of her older brothers, two were married with children and Dante, the oldest, was divorced with twin daughters. Aly said that she and Connor would be spending Christmas Day at her parents' house and Christmas Eve right here on Rinehart Hill with the Bravos.

"It's good to be home." Aly smiled dreamily down at Riley. "I love New York. But for me, there's nothing like Christmas in Valentine Bay."

A little later, Keely, Daniel's wife, pulled Karin aside and invited her and the kids and her dad for Christmas dinner. "I'm sure Liam's already asked you, but I just wanted you to know how much we'd all love it if you guys would join us for Christmas Day, too."

Karin shocked the hell out of herself and almost said yes on the spot. After all, Sten and Madison would be coming here to the Bravo house, as would Liam. She and her dad and the kids might as well come, too. But her reluctance to get swept up in too much togetherness with Liam and his family won out. She thanked Keely and promised to talk to Liam about it.

It was after nine when Karin glanced over and saw that Coco had fallen asleep on the floor in front of the tree.

She leaned close to Liam and whispered, "Time to go."

Leaving Sten and Madison and the bodyguards behind, Karin, Liam, Otto and the kids headed for home.

Once they got everyone into the house, Otto said, "Give me that baby."

Karin didn't argue. She passed him the baby carrier in which Riley slept, his chin on his chest, drooling a little.

Her dad said, "I'll put the kids to bed. There's milk in the fridge if RG here gets hungry. You two have a nice night."

"So much for not letting anybody know we're together," she grumbled to Liam several minutes later. They were already in his bedroom, under the covers, cuddled up close.

"You're the one who's all tied in knots over that," he reminded her.

She used her fingers to comb his hair back off his forehead. "I'm…getting used to it."

He ducked close, pressed his mouth to her neck—and blew a raspberry against the side of her throat. When she laughed and wriggled away, he said, "Good. Because I really am going nowhere—as I've said so many times I've lost count."

She cuddled in close again. "Keely invited us all to Christmas dinner."

He slid an arm under her shoulders and drew her closer still. "And you said…?"

"That I would talk to you about it."

"And…?"

Really, why hold out against having Christmas at Daniel and Keely's house? Her family loved going over there. And so did she. "Sure. Let's spend the afternoon at Daniel's."

He tipped up her chin and stared into her eyes. "Tell me I'm not dreaming. Tell me you just said yes to Christmas dinner with the Bravos."

"Yes, I said yes."

He kissed the tip of her nose. "That wasn't so hard, now was it?"

She laughed. "You are impossible."

"But in the best kind of way, right?"

"Oh, absolutely." She settled her head on his shoulder. "I do like this, Liam. You and me, how it's all kind of working out."

"We're making progress, together." He breathed the words into her hair.

"Umm-hmm." Held safe in his arms, she shut her eyes and let herself relax completely. It really was getting easier, day by day, to put the past behind her, to start letting herself imagine a future with Liam.

Yes, at first it had seemed far too similar to the situation she'd gotten herself into with Bud—a baby on the way and a man just trying to step up and do right. But Liam really did seem to like being a family man. And he really did seem to care for her. Not to mention, she was so completely in love with him.

In love with Liam.

Just thinking those words sent a warning shiver through her, no matter that she'd grown increasingly sure they were true.

It wasn't something she felt entirely ready to deal

with yet. And she certainly wouldn't be saying I love you out loud to him.

Not yet. Not until…

Who knew? She didn't. But it was going to take some time yet, before she would be willing to declare her love to Liam. Right now, she couldn't even let *him* say the words.

Right now, what she felt for him was for her to know and no one else to find out. She needed more time to become absolutely certain that what they had together really was as strong and enduring as she had started to let herself hope it might be.

Liam drove down to his Portland offices early the next day for a couple of meetings. He was finished before noon and decided to make a detour into downtown, do a little Christmas shopping at an upscale mall called Pioneer Place.

He picked up a few things for Coco and Ben on the first level and then rode the escalator up to the second. If he remembered correctly, there was a certain jewelry story up there.

Tiffany & Co.

He spotted it right away and a feeling of satisfaction spread through him as he thought of Karin. They were getting it together, him and Karin. They had a happy, healthy baby boy and every day he felt more a part of the Larson-Killigan family.

Her kids and her dad trusted him. And Sten had been on his side from the first, not even hesitating to lease him the cottage all those weeks and weeks ago, when he was a brand-new dad, desperate for a closer connection to his son and to the frustrating, unforgettable woman who was so determined not to let him get near.

Maybe it was a little early to go browsing engagement rings.

But hey, how often did he get anywhere near Tiffany & Co.? Pretty much never.

What could it hurt just to look?

Someday soon, he'd be needing the right ring. And when that happened, it would damn well be the best.

Inside the store, there were fancy wreaths on the walls, a tree all decked out with Tiffany-blue lights and white satin bows. Christmas music played, turned down tastefully low, like a hum of holiday cheer in the background. He was greeted by the guard at the door and by a couple of salespeople. A pretty woman with pale blond hair asked if there was something or someone in particular he was shopping for.

He shook his head. "Just looking."

"Ah. Take your time. Let me know if there's anything I can do to help."

He thanked her and browsed the big, gleaming cases of engagement and wedding rings, each one more sparkly and beautiful than the one before it.

It was a little overwhelming—until he saw *the* ring. It was simple and perfect, with a gorgeous square diamond glittering so brightly on a platinum band.

The blonde stepped near again. In a soft, pleasant voice, she began talking about responsible sourcing, about the four C's of diamonds—carat, cut, color and clarity.

He looked up and grinned at her. "I want that one, and the platinum band with the diamonds for the wedding ring..."

* * *

Liam left Tiffany & Co. feeling equal parts exhilarated and stunned. He'd just bought a matched pair of sparklers that cost more than his truck.

And he'd honestly only gone in there to look.

But hey. When he finally did get down on one knee and offer his ring to Karin along with his heart and all his worldly possessions, she was going to love that ring.

And if the impossible happened and the perfect ring wasn't right for her, the nice saleswoman had assured him that he could bring Karin in to choose something else.

So it was nothing to get freaky over. He'd wanted the best for Karin and he'd gotten the best.

And for now, he had a plan: do nothing. Not for a while. He would put the perfect rings away, enjoy the rest of the holiday season and wait for the right moment, no matter how long it took to get there.

Karin was skittish about love, about marriage. He knew that. He *got* that. He honestly did. He understood her fears and her doubts. The catastrophe of her first marriage still haunted her. And she needed a whole lot of time to learn to trust that he was all in with her the way Bud had never really been.

His phone buzzed with a text just as he reached the parking garage a block from the mall. It was Karin.

Pork chops tonight. 6 o'clock. Interested?

He wore a giant grin as he paused on the sidewalk to answer. I'll be there.

Dinner was great. RG was up, so Liam ate with the baby on his lap. Sten and Madison joined them. Afterward, Coco dragged Liam into her room and whipped out a pink plastic pitcher, her Christmas gift for Karin.

"Isn't it beautiful, Liam? Won't Mommy just love it?"

He agreed that it was one fine-looking pitcher and Karin would be so happy to have it. Next, he checked in with Ben to see how he was doing on his latest project for Science Club.

Around eight, he returned to the cottage and headed straight for the wall safe in the bedroom closet to check out his Tiffany purchase. A part of him still didn't quite believe he'd just gone out and done it—bought Karin a ring.

But he had. And it was freaking gorgeous.

He'd just stuck the tiny black velvet box into the blue Tiffany box and then back into the safe and returned to the main room when she showed up at the slider.

He shoved open the door and she came straight into his arms like there was no place on earth she would rather be. "Dad shooed me out again. He promised to look after RG and make sure Ben and Coco get to bed on time."

"Otto's my hero."

"Mine, too." She sighed and tipped up her mouth in an invitation to a kiss. It was an invitation he accepted with enthusiasm.

Damn, she was beautiful. She just seemed to glow with happiness, so easy and comfortable with him, with the world, with the life they were making, day by day, the two of them—even if she hadn't quite gotten to where she would admit that out loud.

They hung out in the main room for a while, enjoying the fire, discussing Christmas Eve, which they would share at the other house with the kids and Otto, Sten and Madison. Christmas morning, he would cook breakfast for everyone here at the cottage. Then they would return to the main house to open presents.

And then, as she'd miraculously agreed the night before, they would head up to Rhinehart Hill for Christmas dinner with his family.

Life didn't get any better than this.

He scooped her up in his arms and headed down the hall to his bedroom, where he made love to her slowly, his mind and heart overflowing with words of love.

Words that he really didn't intend to try to say out loud again. Not yet.

But she was moving beneath him, sighing his name, those blue-green eyes shining as she gazed up at him through the dark, thick fringe of her eyelashes. All that coffee-brown hair was spread out on the pillow, tangled and wild. He wanted to capture the moment, never let it go.

And then she said it, so soft and low he might not have heard it if he hadn't been staring directly down at her beautiful face. "I love you so much, Liam. I love you. I do."

And it was like a dam breaking inside him, the words spilling out of him, the ones she'd never let him say before. "I love you, Karin. You're everything to me…"

Afterward, she seemed kind of quiet, but she tucked herself in nice and close to him. Idly, she traced the shape of his ear, brushed her fingers along his jaw, combed them up into his hair.

He pressed a kiss to the curve of her shoulder and she made a soft little sound in her throat. It sounded like approval. Affection.

Love.

And he just couldn't do it. Couldn't wait another day,

another hour, another minute to ask her, to promise her everything, to give her the ring he'd chosen for her.

He kissed her shoulder again and breathed in the incomparable scent of her skin. "Do not move from this spot."

She let out a throaty little moan. "No worries. I don't think I *can* move. I just might be in an after-sex coma."

He chuckled. "Try to stay conscious. I'll be right back." He slid out from under the covers and turned for the closet.

"Liam, what—?"

"Just wait. You'll see." He pulled open the closet door, switched on the light and shoved a row of shirts to the side. Four quick pokes at the keypad and he had the safe open. The blue box was waiting. He took out the black velvet box inside and returned with it to the bed.

She was sitting up by then, clutching the sheet to her chest. "What are you up to?"

He dropped to a knee, held out the tiny box and flipped the lid back.

She stared down at the ring, eyes big as sand dollars. "Liam."

"Marry me, Karin."

She just kept staring, clutching the sheet even tighter. "I, um, that's the most gorgeous ring I've ever seen."

"Say yes."

She winced—she actually winced at him. "Liam. I'm so sorry. I can't do that. You know I can't. Not right now."

Chapter Twelve

Karin sincerely hated herself at that moment.

Liam stared up at her from where he knelt on the rug, a frown creasing his brow. He flipped the box shut, fisted his hand around it and let his arm drop to his side. "You said you love me."

"I know. And I do, but…" Really, what was he supposed to think? "I'm sorry," she babbled. "I shouldn't have said it. I didn't mean to say it."

He rose and set the magnificent ring in its velvet box on the nightstand. And then he just stood there by the bed, so tall and strong, wearing nothing but a somber expression, his eyes full of shadows and sadness now. "You didn't mean to say you love me?"

"No! I… Well, of course, I…" She stopped, forced herself to take a slow breath, and tried again. "I do love you, even though I tried really hard not to."

He almost smiled, but then his fine mouth flattened out again. "No kidding."

"I fell for you, Liam. I've fallen. I'm just gone on you. I wasn't going to tell you, though. Not until I was ready to, um, move on to the next step. But it's been so good between us lately. And tonight was so perfect and beautiful and true. I got carried away, I guess. The words just slipped out. I'm so sorry."

One golden-brown eyebrow inched upward. "Sorry that you love me?"

Could she *be* more confusing? "Please. No. That's not what I mean." She reached out and took his hand. He didn't exactly give it to her, but he let her have it, he didn't jerk away. "Come back to bed."

He stared at her so strangely, like she'd hurt him so bad, broken something inside him. "Karin. Are you gonna talk to me about this? Tell me, honestly, why you keep refusing to take a chance on us?"

"Please..." She tugged on his hand. "Come here."

He gave in and got back under the covers with her. They propped their pillows against the headboard and sat up, side by side. "Okay," he said. "Talk."

She put her fingers to her temples and rubbed to ease the tension that caused a dull throbbing behind her eyes. "I just have to be sure that we can really make it work before there are rings and promises of forever. I have to be 100 percent certain. I can't take a chance that I'll mess up again. It's just not fair to the kids—or to you, really. Some things, you can't come back from, Liam."

"You have to know that you're never going to get the certainty you say you need. When you love another person, you're always taking a risk. There are no guarantees."

What could she say to that? She knew he was right.

He held her gaze. "So, Karin. Take a chance. On me. On us."

A frustrated cry escaped her. "But horrible things can happen. You have no idea."

"Yeah, I do. When he was only eight years old, my brother disappeared in Siberia, vanished without a trace never to be seen or heard from again. Two years later, my mom and dad died in a Thailand tsunami. Believe me, I know about horrible things."

Shame made her cheeks burn. "Oh, my God. You're right. Of course, you know exactly what I'm talking about. And I am so sorry—about Finn, about your dad and mom. Could I *be* any more insensitive?" She covered her face with her hands.

"Hey. Look at me."

She dropped her hands and made herself face him. "Yeah?"

"Bad shit happens. To everyone. And for you, that means Bud, right? You're trying to tell me that you're not really over his death, that he's always going to be a barrier between us?"

"Not in the way that you think. It's not like I'm in love with his memory or anything. Liam, what haunts me is that I rushed into marriage with him and it all went to hell. Everybody got hurt—my children included. I wish I could make you see."

He regarded her so steadily. "I think I do see. I don't like it. I think you're punishing yourself for something that really isn't your fault. But I get it. I do." He looked so exhausted, suddenly.

And seriously, who would have guessed that sexy, charming, commitment-phobic Liam Bravo would grow up to be such an amazing man?

She reached out a tentative hand and combed his hair

back with her fingers. He didn't duck away. She tried to take heart from that. "You look worn-out—worn-out from dealing with me."

He caught her hand, opened her fingers and kissed the center of her palm. His lips were so warm, his breath a caress in itself. "Let's try to get some sleep, okay?"

"Yeah. Okay."

They settled down into the bed. He turned off the light and then pulled her in close. She cuddled against him, grateful for his arms around her.

And all too aware that she was the one holding them back.

Karin opened her eyes to daylight.

Morning?

It was morning already? She slid her hand across the bottom sheet.

Empty.

Liam had left the bed.

"No!" She popped straight up to a sitting position, her heart going a mile a minute.

The kids would already be up by now. Up and wondering where Mom had gotten off to.

And her dad…

She'd never asked him outright to keep her nighttime visits with Liam a secret. What if he took her staying here till morning as a signal that she and Liam were outing their relationship? What if he just told her son and her daughter that she was over here? What if he sent Coco to summon them to breakfast?

Uh-uh. No way. The kids were not supposed to know about her and Liam. They weren't supposed to get their hopes up, to start counting on him to be there, be a real father to them, as the years went by.

Because no matter how sure Liam seemed now—getting down on one knee, whipping out the most beautiful ring she'd ever seen, telling her he loved her and asking her to marry him…

He could so easily change his mind, move back to his big house in Astoria, come by Sweetheart Cove only to pick up and drop off his son.

Coco and Ben would be devastated.

No. That couldn't happen. Her kids were innocent. They didn't deserve that kind of pain. They'd already suffered enough in their short lives.

"Liam…?" She heard water running.

The door to the master bath stood open.

The shower.

He was taking a shower.

How could he have just left the bed without waking her up? How could he be so thoughtless?

He knew she should have been back at the other house long before now.

Furious, literally shaking with frustration, she jumped from the bed and started grabbing her wrinkled clothes, yanking them on as fast as she got hold of them.

The water shut off. By then, she'd dropped to the bed again to put on her ankle boots. Liam emerged from the bathroom, a towel around his lean hips, a tender smile on his lips. He looked so manly, lean and tall, like every woman's perfect fantasy man, his hard biceps flexing as he rubbed his wet hair with a second towel.

And for some reason, his tender smile, that easy way about him, it all just made her madder than ever.

She tugged on the second boot and jumped up to face him. "What is the matter with you?"

He stopped drying his hair. Endless seconds elapsed

before he said quietly, "Nothing. Nothing's the matter with me."

"Why didn't you wake me?"

He tossed the towel on a chair. "You looked tired, so I let you sleep."

She wanted to start shrieking at him, to grab him and shake him until he realized how careless he'd been. "You knew I needed to get back. The kids will be up now. What am I going to say to them?"

"Karin. You don't have to *say* anything to them. They won't be damaged for life just because you spent the night over here." He spoke to her so gently, carefully, like she was a crazy person throwing a fit.

And maybe she kind of was. Somewhere in the back of her mind she knew she was behaving very badly. "You are so irresponsible," she accused, though he wasn't. He was wonderful, always there when she needed him, always patient and thoughtful and ready to help.

She was totally overreacting, her heart aching from his beautiful proposal she couldn't allow herself to accept. She knew, absolutely, that one way or another, she was going to lose him. She just didn't know when it was going to happen.

She wished he would just get it over with and leave her, already.

"Liam, I can't do this. I'm so sorry, but we have to stop this. I want you to please go see your lawyer. I want you to decide what kind of parenting plan works for you. Then we can come to an agreement on custody and all that. We need to move on. We need to settle this once and for all."

He just stood there in his towel, looking handsome and bleak, staring at her.

* * *

For Liam, it happened right then, as they stared at each other across a distance of maybe ten feet that suddenly yawned wide as the Grand Canyon. He realized he'd reached his breaking point with her.

He couldn't take anymore. It just wasn't going to work with her. He'd knocked himself out trying to show her how much he loved her and wanted a life with her. But she just would not believe him.

At some point, a guy had to salvage the last of his pride, take the diamond ring back to Tiffany & Co. and get on with his own damn life.

"Fair enough," he said, his own voice dead, flat in his ears. "I'll talk to my lawyer."

She had the nerve to look stricken. Like *he'd* just hurt *her*. "Good," she said, the word breaking a little in the middle. "Talk to your lawyer—and you'll move back to your own house?"

That, he wouldn't do. "I want time with my son and living here is the best way for me to get that. And truthfully, I promised Ben I wouldn't leave. I'm living in this cottage for as long as Sten is willing to keep cashing my checks. If you don't want to be with me, well, that's up to you. But I live here now, Karin. And I'm not going anywhere."

Chapter Thirteen

Karin walked out.

She grabbed her coat from the peg by the front door and went back to the other house. What else could she do? She'd pretty much wrecked everything. Better to just get the hell out.

At the main house, they were all gathered around the breakfast table—the kids, her dad, Sten and Madison. She walked in and they all turned and looked at her.

"Where's Liam?" Ben asked.

She waved a hand, trying to look casual and easy and probably blowing that all to hell. "Oh, he'll be over in a minute, I'm sure." Her gaze collided with Sten's and she *knew* that *he* knew something was terribly wrong. She blinked and looked away—but not far enough to escape the concerned frown on her dad's face.

Right then, the baby monitor on the counter erupted with fussy cries. She had never in her life felt so relieved to hear her baby crying. "I'll, um, just go take care of him..." And she fled for the sanctuary of Riley's room.

After she'd fed and changed the baby and pulled herself together a little, Karin returned to the kitchen. The adults had dispersed, which suited her just fine. Coco and Ben were clearing off the table.

"There's eggs and bacon left for you," said Ben.

"Great. Thanks." She put Riley in his bouncy seat and sat down to eat in spite of the fact that she had zero appetite.

Coco stepped close. She wrapped her arms around Karin's neck, rested her head on Karin's shoulder and said wistfully, "I love you, Mommy."

Kids. They always sensed when things were off with the grown-ups. Karin patted the small hands clasped around her neck. "Love you, too. So much."

Coco pulled away, but then took the seat next to Karin's. "Sten and Madison and Dirk and Sergei are taking us to the ranch where Aislinn lives today." Aislinn was the Bravo sister born to Lloyd and Paula Delaney, the one who'd been switched with Madison the day they were born. Madison was slowly getting to know all her newfound brothers and sisters, but she and Aislinn had hit it off from the first. The two shared a special bond. "We're going to have lunch there," Coco added. "Madison says Aislinn has rabbits that live on her porch and we get to pet them."

"That's great." Karin sincerely hoped she sounded at least a little enthusiastic.

"Liam never came," Ben said too quietly from over by the sink.

Karin turned in her chair to meet her son's serious eyes. "I'm sure he'll be over later." Truthfully, she kind of wished that Liam wouldn't be over at all, though it was both wrong and ridiculous for her to wish such a thing. His son lived here. He was friends with her father. He had actual relationships with her older children.

He'd said it repeatedly himself. He was not going anywhere.

Well, except for as far away from her as he could get. She'd made sure of that.

Liam spent most of the day at the Warrenton terminal. Around five when he packed it in, he was tempted to take a little detour on the way home to the cottage. There were bars on Beach Street calling his name.

But he intended to be at Karin's for breakfast the next morning, whether she wanted him there or not. No way he was showing up at her table with a hangover.

Uh-uh. He needed a clear head tomorrow. He would see the kids and reach an understanding with their mother that nothing had changed in terms of RG. He would have his son from nine to noon Wednesdays and Fridays, as per their prior agreement. And she would damn well reach out to him if she needed someone to watch the baby any other time.

At the cottage, he had a beer and nuked himself some frozen lasagna. Once he'd shoved down the food, he considered calling Deke Pasternak and making an appointment to talk about custody and a damn parenting plan. He'd told Karin he would.

But later for that. Right now, RG needed him nearby and available. He was both. Problem solved.

Just as he began considering the big question of whether or not to have a second beer, he heard footsteps out on the deck. For about a half a second, his heart bounced toward his throat and hope exploded in his chest.

But it wasn't Karin.

It was Ben, sweet, serious Ben. The kid looked apprehensive and that had Liam pissed off at Karin all over again.

He got up and pushed open the slider. "Come on in."

The wind was blowing, the sky thick with dark clouds, the waves out beyond the beach tossing and foaming. Ben hunched into his down jacket, like a turtle seeking the safety of his shell. "I can't stay very long."

Liam stepped out of the way. "Get in here. It's cold out there." The boy crossed the threshold and Liam shut the glass door. "Want some hot chocolate or something?"

"No, thanks." Ben shoved his hands even deeper into his jacket pockets. "So. You and Mom are fighting?"

Liam saw it all in those serious brown eyes. Ben had lost his father. Now he anticipated losing Liam, too—and right now, the boy was waiting for Liam to say something, to somehow ease his fears. Too bad Liam had nothing all that encouraging to say. "Your mom and I are having some problems, yes."

"What problems?"

"Ben, I can't go into detail about it, but things aren't good between your mom and me right now."

Ben's face started to crumple—but he kept it together, straightening his narrow shoulders, hiking up his chin. "So, you're moving out?"

That, he could answer more emphatically. "Nope. I'll be here. I live here."

"What about breakfast tomorrow?"

"I'll be there."

"Yeah?"

"You have my word on it."

"What about Christmas? You still cooking breakfast for us Christmas morning?"

"That is my plan." If Karin thought differently, well, they would have to discuss it. She would actually have to *talk* to him. That could be good, right?

Or maybe not.

Ben wasn't finished. "And will you be there Christmas Eve and are we all going up to the Bravo house for Christmas dinner?"

In spite of how craptacular he felt at that moment, Liam almost smiled. "How come you didn't ask your mom all these questions?"

Ben gulped. "I kind of had a feeling I would get better answers from you."

Liam wanted to grab the kid and hug him, but he had a suspicion that any sudden moves on his part wouldn't be welcome right now. Ben needed reassurance that the ground was solid under his feet, that the people he'd come to count on and trust wouldn't abandon him, no matter what weird stuff happened between the grownups. "I'm not sure about all our specific plans. What I am sure about is that I'm going to be here, just like I said I would. No matter what happens, that's not going to change."

"Not ever?"

"Not for a long while, anyway. You've got my number." Ben had his own phone. They'd exchanged numbers back in October, the first time Liam drove him to soccer practice. "Anytime you need to talk to me, you just call, text or show up at my door."

Ben yanked his right hand from his pocket and stuck it out. Liam shook it.

The hug happened after all when Ben kind of swayed toward him and Liam put his free arm around him.

Ben quickly stepped back. "Okay, then. I just needed to know. See you for breakfast." He turned and shoved the slider wide, stepped through and closed it. With a last, solemn nod at Liam through the glass, he took off across the deck.

"What's going on with you and Liam?" Otto asked Karin that night when the kids were in bed and Sten and Madison had gone upstairs.

"I don't want to talk about it, Dad. I really don't."

"That man's in love with you. And you're in love with him. Whatever it is, you need to work it out with him."

"Stay out of it, Dad."

He narrowed his eyes at her and put on his stern voice. "Fix it."

She knew with absolute certainty that she was about to burst into tears. "Please, Dad…"

His hard expression melted as he reached out his big hands and clasped her shoulders. "Aw, honey."

She sagged against him and whispered, "I messed up. I messed up bad."

He patted her back. "Now, now. You'll work it out, I know you will."

"I don't think so, Dad. I was terrible to him. He's not going to forgive me and I can't say I blame him."

"Love forgives all. Just give it time…"

An hour later, when she couldn't sleep, she put on thermal pants and a heavy sweater, her shearling boots, a winter jacket, mittens and a beanie, grabbed Riley's monitor and went out to sit on the deck. She wasn't the least surprised when Sten, as bundled up as she was, came out the door behind her and took the empty chair at her side.

All the wise advice she'd given him back in April

when he screwed things up with Madison seemed to hover in the cold night air between them, taunting her.

"Colder than a polar bear's nose," he said mildly. "At least the wind's died down a little."

She wrapped her arms a little tighter around herself. "Don't start in on me, Sten. Please?"

He gave a wry chuckle. "Talk of the weather really bugs the crap out of you, huh?"

She huffed out a breath. "Okay, fine. Just say it."

"Not sure where to start. I don't know what's wrong between you and Liam, not really."

She tugged her beanie more firmly down over her ears. "I jumped all over him for no reason at all."

"Oh, come on. There had to be a reason."

"Yeah, well, not an *acceptable* reason. He asked me to marry him and that scared me to death—and let me be clear. I did worse than jump all over him. I told him we were done and he should move back to Astoria and come up with a parenting plan."

He made a thoughtful sound. "You're in love with the guy, right?"

She stared out at the restless gray ocean beyond the wide stretch of sand and found it surprisingly easy to tell her brother the truth. "I am, yeah. I am very much in love with Liam Bravo."

"I used to think you would never marry anyone again, that Bud was your true, forever love, lost tragically at sea, but you'd learned to be happy with the kids, on your own."

She groaned. "So romantic."

"Yeah, well. I never did want to think there might be big issues between you and Bud."

"There were. I never should have married him. He

wasn't ready. I wasn't ready. The love we had was… not that strong."

"This love you have with Liam, is it *that* strong?"

She didn't even have to think about it. "Yeah—but what if I'm wrong? So far, I've kept him at a distance by making him promise that what we have would stay just between the two of us. When he asked me to marry him last night, I turned him down. Then I drummed up a fake reason to break it off between us. I love my children, and you and Dad. But my track record at loving a man? We should face it. It's not good."

"Someone very wise once told me that I shouldn't let getting my heart broken by the wrong person keep me from giving the right person a fighting chance. Take your own advice. Give the *right* man a chance."

"How did I know you were going to say that?"

He grinned. "Super painful, isn't it? When your own words come back to bite you in the ass…"

The next morning, Liam showed up for breakfast. Coco ran and hugged him. Everyone else played it cool and subdued.

Karin ached all over just to see him sitting there at the table with Riley asleep in a sling strapped to the front of him.

So close.

But no longer *hers*.

The plans for Christmas Eve and Christmas Day were brought up and reconfirmed. Karin didn't make a peep when that happened. Liam didn't have to be hers to be part of the family. He was Madison's brother and Riley's dad. And even if he wasn't *hers*, Coco and Ben had definitely come to think of him as *theirs*.

When he got up to go, he still had Riley hooked to

the front of him. "So, Karin, how about if I just take RG with me now? You can pick him up at noon, or whatever. Just take your time."

"Um, that would be great." She smiled at him. It was more of a grimace, really. But hey, at least she tried. She filled an insulated pack with bottles of breast milk to replenish the stash at his place and sent him on his way.

And then, somehow, she got through her morning and showed up at Liam's door at noon on the nose. He had Riley all ready to go. The handoff took maybe a minute. She tried not to look directly at Liam. She had this feeling that if she actually met his eyes, she would drop to her knees and start pleading with him to give her one more chance.

In a way, dropping to her knees kind of seemed like a viable approach to this huge problem she'd created. But she was so afraid he'd turn her down, that he'd realized he'd been all wrong to want to build a life with her. He would say no.

And she would have to know for certain it was over. She just couldn't face that. Not yet.

Liam planned to go up to the Warrenton terminal as soon as Karin came for RG. But the sight of her just kind of broke him. She was trying so hard to be civil, even kind. He'd expected her to give him dirty looks when he showed up for breakfast, to put up a fight about what to do for Christmas, to insist that really, the plans they'd made earlier needed to change.

Those things didn't happen. She nodded when the rest of them agreed that the Christmas schedule would stay the same. And then, at noon, when she came to pick up RG, he'd been sure she would start in about the damn parenting plan.

Nope. She thanked him, forced a smile, took the baby and left.

If she'd only been a jerk to him, he would have found it at least a little easier to hold on to his anger with her. Instead, he missed her, *ached* for her, wished he could find a way to heal the breach between them.

Not thirty-six hours after he'd lost her, he was already trying to figure out how to find his way back to her.

Yesterday, he'd had some vague idea that he'd head down to Portland today after Karin came for RG, that he would check in at his offices there and take the ring back to Tiffany & Co.

But now he realized that what he really needed was someone he could trust to talk to.

He thought of Otto first. He really did trust Karin's dad and the man was older, much wiser and good at heart, with that understanding way about him.

But Otto was Karin's dad. And dragging Otto into this, putting him in a position where he might feel he had to take sides…

Uh-uh. That wouldn't be right.

Liam called Daniel. It turned out his oldest brother was spending the day before Christmas Eve at home with his family.

At a little after one, Liam was sitting on the sofa in Daniel's study at the house on Rinehart Hill.

"Scotch?" asked his older brother as he poured two fingers for himself. Daniel inevitably brought out the good Scotch for man-to-man talks.

"Thanks, but no."

"So, what's going on?" Daniel carried his drink over to the chair across from Liam.

And Liam laid it on him. "I'm in love with Karin—

completely. It's deep, Daniel, what I feel for her. And it's real. I bought a ring and then night-before-last I asked her to marry me. She said she loves me, too, but she put the brakes on, turned me down." He recounted in detail the story of the fight and the breakup that had occurred early yesterday morning.

When he finally fell silent, Daniel said, "And then you realized you were wrong and you don't love her after all?"

Suddenly, Liam wished he'd taken that drink. "What the hell, Daniel? No. Uh-uh. I do love her. She's everything to me."

Daniel sipped his Scotch. "You still want to marry her, then?"

"You bet your ass I do. I just, well, what did I do wrong and how can I make it right?"

"Judging by what you've just told me, you didn't do anything wrong."

"I didn't…? Daniel, if I didn't do anything wrong, then there is no way for me to make it right."

"Not by yourself. At some point, she's going to need to meet you halfway."

"I don't know. It's really hard for her. She had a bad experience with Bud Killigan."

"Not your fault. But you said that *she* said she loves you, right?"

"She did, yeah."

"So stay steady. Don't let her fear scare you away."

Easier said than done. "You know how I am. I get enthusiastic. And that makes me impatient. I *knew* I should've waited. I *planned* to wait until she was more sure of me, of *us*. But then she said she loved me and I completely lost my head. I grabbed the ring and got down on my knees."

"That's okay. You got a right to be you, man."

"I just don't know how you do it, Daniel. How you've done it for all these years, the way you've put up with all of us, *been there* for all of us, even with all the crap we've laid on you, all the challenges we've thrown at you."

Daniel gave a slow, pensive shake of his head. "I've made some giant mistakes along the way."

"Maybe, but you hung in. You always found a way to make it right. No matter how bad things got, you kept stepping up."

Daniel set down his drink and leaned forward in his chair. "And that—what you just said. That's how you do it. That's how you make it work. You have to be there when you're needed—you have to be there just *in case* you're needed. And don't even try to kid yourself, you will always wonder if you're doing it right, if you're messing something up that's going to make it harder for someone you love down the line. No matter what, though, you do the best you can. And sometimes you screw it up. And then you scramble to try to make it right again. But you can never get it right if you don't keep putting yourself out there in the first place."

Bolstered by his big brother's advice, Liam decided that he would reach out to Karin again.

This time though, he would be reasonable and careful. He would make it crystal clear to her that he didn't want to push her, he just wanted to be with her—yeah, he wanted to marry her. He wanted her for today and tomorrow and the rest of their lives.

But if one day at a time was the only way she could do it, one day at a time was just fine with him.

And if she still needed to keep what they had together a secret from Ben and Coco, he would respect her wishes and make certain she got back to the main house every morning before dawn.

At first, he was thinking he couldn't wait. That he needed to try to make things right with her immediately.

But that was just his impatient nature taking over again.

He ordered himself to slow down, to think it through more carefully. It was the day before Christmas Eve. He didn't want to mess up the fragile peace between them. Coco and Ben were counting on their Christmas plans. He couldn't take the chance that Karin would not only turn him down, but decide she just wasn't comfortable having breakfast at the cottage Christmas morning or going to Daniel's for Christmas Day.

No. He needed to wait at least until the day after Christmas to try to make things right with her.

Instead of heading back to the Cove and pounding on her door or blowing up her phone with calls and texts, he went into downtown Valentine Bay.

He loved his hometown at Christmas. All the shop windows had Christmas displays and the streetlamps were wrapped in garland and hung with lighted wreathes. He dropped some bills into a couple of Salvation Army pots and did some last-minute Christmas shopping, more gifts for Ben and Coco, Otto and Sten and his nieces and nephew.

At some point, he started thinking about all the families who couldn't afford piles of presents under their trees. So he bought even more toys and made a quick run by Safeway and Walgreens to help fill the Toys for Tots donation boxes. Before he went home, he stopped at a diner he liked for a quick dinner.

Back at the cottage by seven, he turned on the Christmas lights inside and out, cued up the holiday tunes and spent a couple of hours wrapping the gifts he'd found on his impromptu shopping spree.

It was snowing at nine fifteen when he stuck a bow on the last package and got up to put it under the tree. He heard footsteps on the deck and glanced up to see Karin standing on the far side of the sliding door.

For a moment, he almost didn't believe his own eyes.

But then she raised a hand and gave him a sheepish wave.

Real. She was real.

His blood racing through his veins and his breath all tangled and hot in his chest, he went to let her in.

Chapter Fourteen

Snowflakes glittered in her hair and her cheeks were pink from the cold. She gave him a beautiful, wobbly little smile. "Dad's got Riley. I was hoping we could talk." The look in her eyes? It promised him everything.

He wanted to grab her, wrap her up tight in his arms and never, ever let go.

But then he reminded himself that she'd only said she wanted to talk. The thing *not* to do right now was make wild assumptions.

"Yes," he said. "I would love to talk."

"So then, may I come in?"

Feeling foolish for keeping her standing out in the cold, he stepped clear of the doorway. "Please."

She entered the kitchen and he shut and locked the slider.

"Here. Give me your coat." He moved behind her.

She let him slip it off her shoulders. He laid it over the back of a kitchen chair. "Tea? Hot chocolate?"

"No. I just want to talk."

He ushered her over to the fire. They sat on the hearth side by side.

"You're busy," she said nervously, gesturing at the coffee table, where he'd left the rolls of bright wrapping paper and the big bag of ready-made bows.

"Nope. I'm all done." He turned and stared directly at her then—like a gift in itself, just looking at her. "I have wrapped the last present." And damn it, he couldn't wait another second to touch her. He reached for her hand.

And she gave it, her slim fingers sliding between his, weaving them together.

It was everything he'd ever wanted, her hand in his. He was so glad he'd waited, given her time to come back to him when she was ready—and was he jumping the gun again? Assuming more than she was offering?

"Talk to me," he said.

Her eyes were dark with shadows. "If I talk about the past…is that okay?"

"Anything, Karin. Everything. I want to understand. I want to be the one you come to—for the good things. And for the tough things, too."

"I, um…" She hesitated. He made himself be quiet, made himself simply wait as she blew out a slow breath and tried again. "I didn't love Bud—I mean, I didn't love him enough. Not the way a woman needs to love a man she builds a life with. I married him because he said he loved *me*, because I was pregnant and worried about the future. Saying yes to him seemed like the answer to a bunch of questions I didn't even really know how to ask. It was not the best choice. It was, in the end, a pretty bad choice, to marry Bud. And when he died, I swear I felt like I had killed him."

He couldn't let that stand. "No. What happened to him wasn't your fault."

She leaned her head on his shoulder. "You're right. I know that I didn't *really* kill him. But for a long time, I blamed myself for his death."

"But not anymore?"

"No. Bud really was like those songs you hear and those books you read about sailors. He was married to the sea. He loved the life on a fishing boat. And he died doing what he loved. I can't say I take comfort from that, exactly, but it is what it is and at least I'm no longer telling myself it was all my fault. I've made a lot of progress with that."

He kind of wanted to scold her for ever having blamed herself. But this was *her* story she was sharing. He had no right to tell her how to feel about her part in it.

She lifted her head from his shoulder and grinned at him. "Look at you. So restrained."

"I'm trying." He pressed their joined hands to his heart. "Go on."

She drew in a slow breath. "So, I got over blaming myself for Bud's death. However, I have remained absolutely determined never to make the same mistake I made with Bud. I have sworn to myself that I will never again marry a man for the wrong reason." She gazed directly into his eyes. "But what is the wrong reason? *That's* what I didn't really understand—not until the last couple of days. Not until I felt I had lost you. Only since then have I started to see that the wrong reason wasn't about the baby I was going to have. It had nothing to do with being pregnant. It was about the love. I didn't love Bud enough. And for that reason and that reason alone, I had no right to marry him." Her eyes gleamed so bright. A tear escaped and slid down her cheek.

"Don't cry, sweetheart." Liam leaned in and kissed the wetness away. "I love you. I want you. I want a life with you. I love you way more than enough."

She touched his cheek with her free hand, a quick brush of a touch, too quickly gone. "When I put off telling you I was having your baby, it was because I knew you were a stand-up guy, and I was dreading that you might ask me to marry you for the same reason Bud had, because you felt obligated."

His laugh sounded pained to his own ears. "Okay, yeah. In the beginning, that day I spotted you at Safeway and the truth came out, I honestly didn't know my ass from up. I was only trying really hard to do the right thing."

She sniffled a little, smiling at him through her tears. "And I knew that."

"But doing the right thing isn't the reason I want to marry you now. Not anymore. Everything's changed now. Now I've figured out what I had no damn clue about for way too long. Not back in high school. Not last winter, in those amazing nights you gave me before you broke it off. And not that day in October when I finally found out I was going to be a dad."

She searched his face. "What? Tell me."

"I've figured out why I could never really get you out of my mind. I understand now why I was pissed off when I heard you'd married Bud, why, through all the years since high school, I've always felt this pinch in my chest whenever I thought of you. It's because you're the one. The one for me. I do love you, Karin. I will always love you. More than I'm ever going to know how to say."

Karin just stared at him.

He squeezed her hand. "What did I do?"

"Liam, you said exactly what I needed to hear."

"But are you okay?"

She drew a slow, shaky breath. "Never better. And I mean that sincerely."

Holding hands was not enough. He pulled her into his arms. She lifted her beautiful face to him.

And he kissed her, deep and slow and infinitely sweet.

"I love you, Liam Bravo," she said when he lifted his head. "So much. Way more than enough to last through the hard times. I love you enough to be with you forever."

"So then, it's good that I didn't take the ring back?"

"Yes." She kissed him again, hard and quick. "Yes, to everything. To that amazing, perfect ring you chose for me. To the future. To our wedding. To me staying right here with you all night long and then the two of us going to the other house together for breakfast tomorrow, where we will break the big news to the family that we're getting married."

Maybe his mouth was hanging open. A little. "You mean that?"

"I do. Every word."

He pressed his lips to the velvety skin at her temple. "Well, all right then. Count me in." He claimed her mouth again, a kiss that melted into another kiss and another after that.

A while later, they turned off the fire and switched off the lights. He led her down the hall to his room.

"I should probably be patient," he said, "but I'm going for it anyway. I don't want to wait. I want to get married right away. If that doesn't work for you, just say so right now."

"Yes."

He blinked down at her. "Yes, you agree to getting married right away?"

Her grin was slow and full of equal parts joy and mischief. "Maybe at New Year's?"

He couldn't stop himself. He pushed his luck some more. "Matt and Sabra got married last New Year's. It was just the family and close friends, at Daniel's house."

She didn't balk, didn't even ask for time to think it over. "I would love that."

It was stacking up to be the best Christmas ever. "We can discuss the idea with Keely and Daniel on Christmas Day."

"Totally works for me."

Had he ever been this happy? He couldn't remember when. "Wait right here?"

"Yes."

He was back with her in under thirty seconds. She gave him her hand and he slipped on the ring he'd chosen for her. It fit perfectly. The saleswoman at Tiffany & Co. had helped him guesstimate the size.

"I love it," she said and reached up to frame his face in her two soft hands. "I love *you*."

"I love you, Karin Killigan. And I will be loving you every single day for the rest of our lives."

"We did it all backward," she whispered. "This shouldn't be possible. But somehow, it's all come out absolutely right."

They were married on New Year's Day at the house on Rhinehart Hill. A trucker friend of Liam's who also happened to be an ordained minister officiated. Karin had no bridesmaids and Liam skipped the groomsmen.

The bride and groom stood up together in a room full of family and friends, with Ben on Liam's side and Coco next to Karin. Riley George slept through the brief ceremony, held close in his father's loving arms.

They settled in together at the main house on Sweetheart Cove. Sten sold Liam the cottage for a bargain price and Liam had the cottage rebuilt to accommodate a growing family. By the time Sten and a very pregnant Madison returned to Valentine Bay to make their home in the main house, the cottage was ready for Liam, Karin, the kids and Otto.

A year later, Karin gave birth to another boy. They named him Aiden at Coco's request.

* * * * *

COMING SOON!

We really hope you enjoyed reading this book. If you're looking for more romance, be sure to head to the shops when new books are available on

Thursday 12th December

To see which titles are coming soon, please visit

millsandboon.co.uk/nextmonth

MILLS & BOON

Coming next month

CRAZY ABOUT HER IMPOSSIBLE BOSS
Ally Blake

There was no way he wasn't fully aware she stood behind him. The man's ability to read a room was legendary. He noticed changes in temperature, pulse, breathing, tone of voice the way other people noticed being kicked in the shin.

Yet still Lucinda took a selfish moment to drink him in before making herself officially known.

For Angus Wolfe's profile was a study in staggering male beauty.

The man was all chiselled angles. Sharp jaw close shaven. Hair darkly curling and a mite overlong. Reading glasses he refused to admit he needed to wear did nothing to soften the impact of the most formidable pair of dark hazel eyes that had ever been seen.

Even the tendons in his neck were a sight to behold.

Then he shifted. Slowly. Like a big cat stretching in the sun. The lines of his charcoal suit moved with him, cut as they were to make the most of his…everything. Each one cost more than she'd spent on her car. She knew. She paid his bills.

Then she spotted his socks. Peeking out from the top of his custom-made dress shoes she saw the merest hint of a wolf motif. She'd given him those socks for Christmas.

Her heart gave a little flutter, releasing a gossamer

thread of lust that wafted from throat to belly to places less mentionable.

She squished the thing. Fast.

Angus Wolfe might be able to read a room, but if anyone dared claim that Lucinda Starling - his long-time Executive Assistant, his right-hand woman, his not-so-secret weapon – was a teeny tiny little bit in love with him, he'd have laughed till he split a kidney.

Either she kept her cards closer to her chest than she realised, or he had a blind spot when it came to her. The fact that he had no clue was a gift. And she planned to keep it that way…

Continue reading
CRAZY ABOUT HER IMPOSSIBLE BOSS
Ally Blake

Available next month
www.millsandboon.co.uk